PROJECT
ANAN

BOOK 1 OF THE
ENERGY EXCHANGE

LIONEL LAZARUS

First published in 2015
Available as eBook on Amazon

This novel is entirely a work of fiction. Any resemblance to actual persons, living or dead, is entirely coincidental.

ISBN-13: 978-1516804160
ISBN-10: 1516804163
Book cover design by The Scarlett Rugers Design Agency
www.scarlettrugers.com

Author Website; www.lionellazarus.com

Email; lionel@lionellazarus.com

To the People and City of Christchurch.

TABLE OF CONTENTS

PROLOGUE

IN THE DEPTHS OF EMPTY SPACE THAT SEPARATED GALAXIES, the ethereal minds of ten powerful entities confronted each other. The One, lord of their kind, looked warily across at the others. 'Our fading energy supply has changed everything. Blue energy was once ours to use for our life force. Now it is a commodity, traded for fuel and power. It is running out — that must stop. Soon there will not be enough to sustain our energy masses. We will cease to exist.'

They remained silent and then, The Sixth spoke; 'that is your fault. You allowed that to happen. You allowed the mortals to use it. I control what's left of the blue energy supply and the worlds that produce it.'

'What are you trying to say?' The One asked.

The Sixth pulsed with clear blue light. 'Must I say it again — I control what energy is left. It is time for change and I have support.'

'For eons we always shared our energy.'

'Energy is power. I will not share that. I challenge you to become The One.'

The others remained silent. They had never seen such contempt for The One — it was a new departure for their kind.

'They are silent, you have no support left. There is not enough blue for all of us. Those who have no blue are facing extinction. We waste precious energy with this meeting,' The Sixth said, as he retreated back to his home galaxy.

'I will not allow a small group of Overlords exclusive control of our energy. Those of you who are with him, tell him that,' The One said, as he and his companion, The Eight, withdrew to their home in the Anan galaxy.

'That did not go well,' The Eight said.

'No, it did not. I have never seen such evil in our kind before. I should have taken his energy mass before he developed into this.'

'Well you never did, and we are where we are. My reserves of blue are dwindling, but I do have a plan. You remember that planet I visited so long ago?'

'Which one, there were so many?'

'The one where the population was given enhanced intelligence.'

'I thought you expunged them.'

'No, my Lord, you said I was to leave them.'

'Yes, you are right. I am getting old. I remember now. You told me what was done. That old biped meddled in matters beyond him,' The One said, as a faint pulse of blue light emitted from his energy mass. 'You will transplant them?'

'Yes, it will be difficult. I need a grav ship, and help from the House of Aknar.'

'I will arrange that. But remember, the purebreeds' abilities are limited. I am not sure if you will succeed, but you must try. You know our survival depends on it.'

'Yes, my Lord, I do.'

At the end of the trading period a troubled Haret, the chief energy trader, left the Exchange and made his way home. *I have never seen it this grim*, he thought, *there is hardly any blue energy available.* The orders were not being filled; they were backing up and then getting cancelled. He couldn't understand it, *only the Overlords could authorise this.* Ships were screaming for blue. Everybody was switching to grav, but nobody was talking about it. The price of grav had increased to a record high. There was plenty of it available, along with fusion, but it was much slower and unsuited for long intergalactic runs. There were dark days to come, he realised, as he thought of the axiom that formed the basis of their trading logic: "all usable forms of energy are finite".

When he needed to think, he took the long way home, around the back of the Exchange. He liked to sit at the rear viewing platform looking out over the vast Intergalactic Space Docks, where the trading ships came and went. As he sat alone and contemplated the dilemma he noticed one of the old ships, "the derelicts" they were called, moored in the old and least accessible part of the space structure, cautiously moving out from its berth. He watched as it stopped and started and finally made its way out of the Intergalactic Docks and off into space. *Probably going to the breakers yard*, he thought, as he got up and continued on his way home.

FIRST CONTACT

CHAPTER ONE

The small shuttle, invisible to Earth based-sensor systems, navigated slowly through space and entered Earth's atmosphere above the southern hemisphere. Over the South Island of New Zealand it descended to three thousand kilometres above Christchurch, the Garden City, where it slowed to allow the three occupants to view the final landing coordinates.

'It's clear, you should easily blend in with the population when we land,' the pilot said to the other two occupants.

The ship continued down to the landing site as the outer hull shimmered with holographic projections, the chameleon effect making it completely invisible. It settled down amongst the trees in South Hagley Park on a site chosen to give the most cover for a clandestine landing close to the Central Business District.

At nine o'clock in the morning, the local population was mostly at work and the park was relatively empty. To anyone looking, they would see two tall people step out of what appeared to be fresh air, into a small clearing in the trees. Both were dressed to match the "smart casual" office attire of the location and wore hats, light jackets and full-length pants, with dark wraparound sun glasses, shoes that matched their khaki-coloured attire and a small pack on their backs. At a quick glance they blended into their surroundings. Closer inspection would show how unearthly their clothes really were. Concerned at how nondescript they would appear on their short walk — and the protection they needed from the strong ultraviolet light —

they had spent a great deal of time on their mother ship in the design and manufacture of these garments.

Until now, their ability to move on foot in the outside Earth environment had not been tested. Walking away from their ship, they turned around and stood looking in its direction as it silently took off. Feeling the rush of the air it displaced as it took flight above them, they heard the reassuring words of their pilot in their communication devices.

'As we planned, I will park above the city and watch over your movements. If you need an immediate pick up, I'll be there.'

Taking a deep breath, they looked at their surroundings. The air in New Zealand was considered some of the best on the planet with relatively little pollution. They did not realise that the cacophony of sounds and the loud, continual "creek, creek, creek" noises from the cicada, a cricket-like insect, would have such an effect on their hearing. Both adjusted to this change and soon, over the loud noise from the insects, were able to distinguish and tune into the new and different sounds around them. With the sunglasses, their sight quickly adapted to the bright New Zealand sunlight and they found the landscape more beautiful than what they had previously seen on their ship's view screens.

The taller of the two, taking deep breaths, looked at his companion; 'are you all right?' he asked.

'I am a little disorientated, but we anticipated that. I did not realise that the air would be so clear. It is a welcome change from the stale air on the ship.'

'Yes, it is. Let's go, our bodies will adjust as we walk. We cannot be late for the meeting,' he said as they started to walk away from the landing site.

They walked diagonally out of the trees onto a pathway that stretched along the park boundary at Riccarton Avenue. The short walk was pleasant, through the trees, and they could see the large building of Christchurch Hospital across the road. Other than on the ship's view screens, this was their first sight of an Earth building. They wondered at its alien appearance, and how different it was to the buildings on their own home world.

The two strangers walked out of the park at the busy junction of Riccarton and Hagley Avenues. Normally, on arriving at a new planet they would not interact with the inhabitants or their infrastructure. There were transport devices on the mother ship to get around and to communicate with the local population. Their use here today was not an option. It would compromise the covert nature of this initial visit. From their arrival in Earth space they had found it hard to believe some of the daily practices of the inhabitants. Crossing a road was one: the interaction between moving vehicles and pedestrians was antipathy to them. And so it had come to this, crossing a road. The fate of their people and their leader's survival depended on the success of this mission. Failure was not an option.

'Let's get on with this. It's simple; we cross on a green light.'

'We stop here. This is not what I imagined it to be,' said the taller one. He looked at his companion and placed his hand on her shoulder. 'Look, we did not see those strange objects or the people on the roadway when we watched from space. We cannot afford to have you injured or, worse, killed. If one of us ends up in the hospital across the road, do you realise what hysteria that would create?'

'You are right. It is very different. They appear to be working on the roadway. What do we do?' asked his companion. 'We can't go back; we need to make this meeting.'

They watched as the orange-clad road works crew continued with their site set up, installing the orange cones and traffic diversions at the busy junction.

One of the workers suddenly turned to the two strange characters. 'Do you guys want to cross?' he asked, never to realise these were the first human words spoken to them.

Taken by surprise by the human's question, the tall one maintained his composure and smiled back at the worker. 'Yes, thank you,' he said, as he watched the worker walk out onto the road and stop the traffic for them. 'Let's go,' he said to his companion and as he held her arm they walked across the busy Hagley Avenue, in front of the traffic stopped by the friendly human.

Ignoring the other humans congregated at the junction, they continued on. The tall one noticed some were in uniform with badges hanging around their necks. 'They must work in the hospital,' he whispered to his companion as they arrived at the junction of Tuam and Antigua. 'Now we must use the traffic lights.'

'Yes, it is easy, we follow the other humans as the lights change,' whispered his companion.

They both had to concentrate hard to continue walking despite wanting to stop and enjoy the new sights, sounds and smells. However, the importance of the meeting and their personal exposure was motive enough to keep going.

It was as they had anticipated; once they were walking, nobody noticed or bothered them. Walking east on Tuam and crossing the roads with more confidence they soon arrived at their destination. It was a plain building that easily blended into the surrounding commercial area.

'Finally, we are here,' said the Leader. The nine hundred metre walk took them just over ten minutes. It was the hardest part of their long journey to Earth. They had travelled six earth months through space from their home galaxy and spent one month cloaked in orbit, surveying the planet. To the side of the door an intercom was located alongside a name plate, which read, 'Katherine Phillips Human Resources Consultancy, First Floor'.

On Monday 16th February 2026, Katherine Phillips's fiftieth birthday, she came in early to prepare for the arrival of her prospective new clients. She really didn't need the work, but after their initial email she was intrigued. What had the email said? she mused. "A chance to get involved in a ground-breaking new project which could change people's lives forever." This was normal company new-speak, probably a drug manufacturer or IT company re-locating to Christchurch. Funny though, she thought, there were no rumours doing the rounds as to who it might be. Maybe they had kept the wraps on this one and it was still at the concept stage. The people she would meet today were supposed to be the directors, and wanted to keep a high level of security regarding this meeting and the project. The rest of the email was couched in secrecy with no mention as to what the "project" actually was or who she was to meet. Even the advert they asked her to run for prospective project management personnel gave no hint as to who they were. But it was the final personal message that had piqued her attention: "Katherine, we have watched you for some time and really believe you are the only person for our project. Please grant us this meeting. It would mean so much to us." That was so out of character for a multinational, so personal and the "watched you for some time" part; that was strange. Anyway, she wanted to keep busy, and this new client, who had agreed a generous fee, would do just that for her.

The tall one pushed the button on the intercom. A bright cheerful female voice responded.

'Come on up, Kath is expecting you,' said the voice, and then a buzzer sounded. They both looked with surprise at the door.

'What do we do now? How does it open? We didn't plan this,' said the tall one. Nothing happened. They waited until the female voice returned again with more precise directions.

'Come on up, push the door when the buzzer sounds, please.'

The tall one pushed the door and they both entered the lobby. 'It starts now,' he said, turning to look at his companion. 'This will not be easy. Meeting aliens like this. They will be surprised.'

'We have no choice, come on; it's up the stairs. I am keen to meet them.'

Continuing with the final part of their journey, they arrived at the reception area, where they were faced with the source of the voice sitting behind a glass desk. This was it, the first steps in their vital project. The tall one nodded and smiled at her.

'Hi, I'm Janet,' said the receptionist. She looked at the two people before her. Something wasn't quite right. She couldn't wait to get into Kath's office. 'You're both very welcome. Kath is expecting you, and will be with you in a minute. Do you want anything? Water or tea? Take a seat, yes, yes right there. I'll be right back.' Smiling and waving at the visitors, she directed them to sit on the chairs in the waiting area. She then fled into Kath's office, closing the door behind her.

'Kath, those two guys you are expecting are outside and, boy, they are the weirdest people I have ever seen.'

'What do you mean, Janet?'

'Well, at a glance, their clothes look like the usual smart casual stuff, but up close they look really weird. I don't know where they would have got that stuff. They still have their hats and glasses on and their skin is white. As soon as I met them, I got this funny feeling and then, well, there's a strange smell.'

'What type of smell?'

'Well,' she said, pausing as she tried to think how to describe it. 'It's not a bad BO smell, but nothing like I've smelt before. Maybe like really stale perfume.'

'Wow, Janet, our new clients are smelly, badly dressed and weird. According to the email they sent, they're supposed to represent a multinational relocating to Christchurch. But, with the multinationals, nothing surprises me anymore. I'll come out and meet them.'

Waiting in reception, the two aliens noticed the attractive female was about thirty years old. She seemed polite and cheerful and had directed them to sit down. However, they both sensed her immediate and deep fear of them and her desire to get away as quickly as possible.

So much for first contact, this wasn't going well. Usually they would deal with the leader of a species and only then after much time and communication, and, best of all, they always had an army behind them. Times were now different. It was a sad day for their once-powerful species, thought the tall one as he sat down.

'Let's see what happens next. We still haven't met the consultant,' said his companion. They could hear the conversation going on in the adjoining office between Kath and Janet through the thin partition. 'Earth structures do not take account of our enhanced senses,' she said as she turned to smile at the tall one.

'Gentlemen, welcome to Christchurch. Please, come in,' Kath said, as she led the visitors into her office and directed them to sit at a large round table. 'Good to meet you, did you have a good journey? After all those emails it's lovely to finally meet someone associated with your company. You know, put faces to the people. I'm Kath. You have met my assistant, Janet Cooper.' Kath reached out to shake hands with the visitors.

'Hello, I'm Theia Aknar. Please call me Theia. This is my associate, Arie Machai. You may call him Mack,' she said in a soft feminine voice as she reached out, taking Kath's hand in her own.

Shit, thought Kath, *Janet was right. This is weird and, I've just called their boss a man.* Kath looked more closely at the two visitors. They were both tall and wore the same clothes. Theia was slender with feminine lines, was quite good-looking and radiated an air of authority. Mack, on the other hand, was definitely male in his appearance and taller than Theia.

'Theia, Mack good to meet you both. Did you have a good journey, did you come far?' asked Kath, now probing for information.

'Thank you, Kath; it was a long and arduous journey. And yes, we are delighted, finally, to be in your office in Christchurch,' Theia said.

'What made you choose us and Christchurch, Theia?'

'We spent a lot of time choosing with whom and where we would like to launch our new operation. Kath, I am pleased to say this city, with your expertise, was our logical choice. You have all the qualities we were looking for.' Theia paused, as she looked at the pictures of Kath's previous projects on the wall. 'You worked in human resources in the multinational sector. As the human resources lead, you managed the hiring of people for some very large projects. You have many contacts in New Zealand and your brother Alan is a financial controller. We need those skills for our project. As for Christchurch, we saw some of the rebuild on our way here. The city is the planet's newest, and also one of the safest. The secure nature of its location is a real attraction to us,' Theia said, omitting one of the other reasons for choosing New Zealand.

'Wow, thank you, that's a real compliment. What can we do for you?'

Theia paused and took a small device out of her bag, asking Kath to close the window blinds; she placed it on the table and turned it on. It projected a large holographic image of their mother ship, the *Hela* in space, above the meeting table.

'Kath, this is where we came from today. It was a long journey, but, believe me, the last nine hundred metres by foot across your beautiful city was the hardest for us. Please listen and trust us. I know you will think what I say is quite unbelievable. However, what you see is really an image of our mother ship, the *Hela*, in orbit around Earth. We come from a galaxy many light years' distance from Earth. Our species and our Overlord have been here in the past. For Mack and I, this is our first contact with your species and we are, as you would say, humbled by it. We need your help in advancing a major project our Overlord has embarked on. In doing this, we believe it will mutually advance both our species; and, most importantly, adequately recompense you for your efforts,' Theia said as she stopped and looked at Kath. After a silence, Kath slowly smiled and then burst out laughing.

'Oh well done, well done,' she said, when she finally stopped laughing. 'I just couldn't figure it out. You guys are my fiftieth birthday surprise. What a surprise. I bet it was my brother Alan who arranged this. You guys are really good. Are you the actors from the horror show, the new attraction outside town? The clothes, the makeup, your stage presence; wow, it's fantastic, and hey, what on earth is the weird smell? You even got one of the new gadgets the tech companies are developing. Janet, come in here and get Alan here as well.'

Hearing the commotion and Kath's outburst, Janet, purposely staying out of the office, shouted for Alan. *This is definitely not a birthday stunt*, she thought. She and Alan had arranged something completely different and it wasn't here at the office.

Surprised at the reaction, Mack spoke to the human for the first time. 'We mean you no harm. Please believe us; we do need your help.' His voice was distinctively male and conveyed authority in his tone. He looked across at Theia, who was as bemused as he. They had both expected deep fear and perhaps someone running from the building.

Kath, still smiling at the perceived prank, looked at Alan. 'Did you set this up?'

'Nothing to do with me,' he replied, looking warily at the two visitors. He had heard Theia's speech from his adjoining office. 'Who set you up to this caper? Was it one of our local competitors? I don't find it funny, it's time wasting, upsetting and downright rude. Leave now or I'll call the police.'

'Believe us, please,' Theia said, as she placed her hand on a blue pendant hanging around her neck. The room slowly filled with a light that started to emit from the pendant. It immediately silenced Alan and Kath. They felt a soft numbness when the blue light touched them and, strangely, both were filled with a warm and safe feeling. 'This is the light from our blue energy. It is the building block of our universe and comes from the energy that feeds our Overlords and the worlds we inhabit. Please do not fear us.' As she took her hand from the pendant the light faded. All four stood and looked at each other.

Trying to put them at ease, Mack smiled at them all, 'let's sit down and start again.'

'Yes,' Theia said, and trying to convince them continued, 'I am Theia Aknar, Empress of the planet Anan. This is General Arie Machai, the leader of my Protective Guard, also from the planet Anan. It is a cloudy planet six of your months' travel from here. We had a long journey in an old ship, and, as I said, the walk from the landing site was the hardest of all.'

'Why did you walk; if you are who you say you are, don't you have transporters?' Kath asked, now sitting with head between her hands looking intently at the visitors.

'That's a fair question, Kath. We normally have our own ground transportation and an army, but this time it is different. It is the first time we had to make first contact in this clandestine manner.'

'So why did you do it like this?'

'If we didn't have to do it like this we wouldn't, but we do. So we are here now, we are real, we are not from the horror show, we are not wearing makeup, we are from a galaxy many light years away from here. And believe me, we wouldn't be here if we didn't have to be. As for the smell, we synthesised a formula of an earth perfume on our ship, which we obviously got wrong. Yes, I agree it smells foul.'

'Theia, it still doesn't make sense. Look, I can see you are getting annoyed. Before we go any further, we should stop. You will agree that, to us, it sounds so farfetched. Can we take this a step at a time? We accept you are both potential clients, who have travelled far to meet us. We will listen, but first, we offered refreshments when you arrived. We should have it now.'

'Yes, Kath, I am tired, thirsty and I smell, so I would really like to try some hot tea and cold water.' This was a defining moment in the project; *if these humans are not up to it, I've failed*, thought Theia.

Shortly afterward Janet and Kath came in with trays of tea, water and fresh muffins. Mack noticed the cakes. *Carbohydrate, sugar and fat*, he thought, primitive but welcome after their ordeal. As she set the refreshments down on the table, Kath restarted the awkward conversation.

'Theia, Mack, I still don't know what to believe. You must understand this is very strange. To get our head around the concept that we have aliens as clients in our office is a major issue, and that one is an empress and one a general is even more difficult to understand. I mean, why not land outside the United Nations or the Parliament in Wellington?'

'I will explain that—,' Mack started.

'No, no, don't explain yet,' Kath replied, now relaxing into the role of entertaining aliens. 'It's normal on Earth when we greet people to offer refreshments, food and drink, and when we meet our Royal Family we would bow or curtsey. I'm not going that far but I must apologise again for laughing at you, Theia. Let's eat; I've been looking forward to these blueberry muffins all morning. They go straight to my waist, but hey, who cares? You might both eat us before the day is out,' she said, smiling at her own joke.

'No, Kath, we don't eat humans,' Theia said, smiling at the humour that had now entered the much lighter conversation. She tasted the tea and muffins. 'This is welcome. Normally Mack cuts off the head of those who laugh without permission in my presence, but, considering the circumstances, I will excuse you today. Also you must get used to the fact that my subjects prostrate themselves on the ground in front of me and I walk across them when we first meet—.'

'Really, you must be joking now,' Alan said, interrupting the conversation.

'She is,' Mack said. 'She read this in your old Earth texts and couldn't wait to use it today. Can we remove some of our outer garments before we get, as you say here, down to business? We would like to be more comfortable.'

Theia and Mack first took off their dark glasses, then the hats and then their light outer coats. For the first time their eyes, heads and necks were revealed. Theia had deep blue eyes, her ears were similar, but smaller to those of humans, and she had no hair on her head. She had a small nose, and her skin was smooth and white like porcelain. The simple blue pendant, that glowed with a gentle light, hung around her slender neck. Her features were distinctively female and similar to an Earth woman. Mack's eyes were deep green, his ears were similar to Theia's and he also had no hair. But the similarity ended there as his features were distinctly male. He had white skin, quite wrinkled, and his nose looked like it had been broken once. His neck was thick and muscular. With the coats off, the difference in body type was now apparent. Mack was quite muscular while Theia was slender and feminine. They were both strikingly tall and attractive. Overall their bodies were similar in build to that of a human. The garments, simple pants and shirts worn beneath the coats, were of the same unusual material as the coats and matched the "smart and casual" fashion.

Janet, re-entering the office to clear the table, didn't know where to look when confronted with the two exposed alien beings. 'Before you start your meeting, there are some mundane housekeeping issues we need to discuss.

First, my phones and internet don't work. I guess they were disabled. I need them back. Second, do you want lunch? I heard the aliens don't eat humans, so best we order in.' Theia and Mack smiled at her forthright manner. 'Finally, considering the sensitive nature of our guests, we should organise transport for them away from here in the evening. I suggest we rent something appropriate to take them out of the city. How does that all sound?'

Mack stood up. 'Great. I'll help Janet take care of that,' he said.

He and Janet left the office. In the reception area Mack deactivated the block he had secretly placed on the phone and internet connections. Without directly looking at him Janet watched him work; strangely, she felt safe with him and was not repulsed by his presence anymore. She couldn't understand that.

'It takes some time to adjust,' he said, as if reading her mind.

'To what?'

'Us,' he said. 'If you have not interacted with any alien species before, your own body may reject a "first contact". It is your fear and flight mechanism protecting you from the unknown.'

He was standing closer to Janet now. She finally lifted up her head and forced her eyes to fully look at his strange features. Looking into his green eyes she felt a strong sense of power and strength emitting from him; however, it was tempered with a deep feeling that he would not harm her.

'Don't underestimate yourself, Janet Cooper,' he said, 'you have much to offer our project.'

'What do you mean? I'm just the receptionist.'

'On the contrary, you are the organiser, you do all the work. You will turn out to be our main administrator and planner, you'll see. Also, you need to know, if the Empress doesn't like the food, I have to kill the server.'

'You have a sense of humour,' replied Janet, smiling at him.

'Yes, although different species, we share many similar traits. We both get these from the same Overlord, The Eight. Don't forget that. It's what links us,' Mack said and mysteriously added, 'you will learn who your friends and enemies are in space.'

As he returned to the office Janet wondered what that last part meant.

▼

Mack re-joined the meeting. He nodded to Theia, conveying all was OK and she was safe. 'Right,' he said gently. 'I need to answer your first question, Kath – why we didn't land at Parliament or the UN? Can you imagine the geopolitical wrangling if we first approached the UN?'

'But, if you are who you say you are, it is where you should have gone first.'

No, we couldn't. Look at Earth's political organisation, nobody can agree with anybody. Their first thought would be which country would get its hands on our technology to outdo or attack another. The EU, a smaller organisation, can't even agree on the price of basic commodities like bread and milk. They have stifled the workforce with unnecessary regulations and then approved trade with countries that use slave labour. It would be a political nightmare, and we would not get our project started. Unfortunately, Earth politicians serve only their own interests and that of advancing their own power. One part of the population is starving while another is suffering from obesity. It's shameful. We cannot do business with them.'

'That's a pretty hard way of looking at our planet's institutions,' Kath said.

'Yes, unfortunately, it is. Now, why did we not approach your own government?' Mack paused, shook his head and then continued. 'We couldn't at this stage. Can you imagine trying to keep this secret here without the proper contacts? Do we knock on the prime minister's door in Wellington and ask for an audience? That won't work. We would be running down the road chased by the news media. I don't relish that, running away from the cameras.' He paused as Kath and Alan digested this, smiling and nodding at his analogy.

'Yes. When you put it like that, it makes real sense,' Alan said.

'We realised the only way this would work, was to keep the Project secret. It will be a major undertaking, but keeping it from the public, the media and the general world's knowledge is a real priority. We do realise that, at some point, we will need to make clandestine approaches to both the New Zealand and Australian Governments. That is something we hoped you would also help with.'

'Wow,' Kath said. 'OK, tell us more about the project. I'm intrigued now.'

Theia and Mack smiled at Kath's reaction and started to explain their long story. And so the Project began at ten forty-five a.m. in a nondescript office of a human resources consultant in Christchurch in New Zealand. The

Overlord, listening above in the mother ship, breathed a sigh of relief. *There is hope*, he thought.

THE PROJECT TEAM

CHAPTER TWO

MILAN, ITALY 15TH FEBRUARY 2026

L ooking out of the hotel window in Milan, he watched as the grey light of dawn started to intrude on the night sky. Robert Leslie couldn't sleep; he was a long way from where he had been born, forty-two years ago, in the north east of Scotland. Finally, tired of the view, he sat down in a chair and took out his laptop. As he sat, he watched June sleep deeply in the luxurious big bed. Her long blonde hair was tossed across the pillow. She was beautiful, the night with her had been good, but it just wouldn't work, he thought. *It's not her, it's me.* The scars were too deep after the event everyone was now calling the Wave.

His eyes glazed over as he remembered parts of his previous life. It was five years since he met his wife in that notorious night club close to the harbour in Aberdeen. Considered as one of the oil capital's finest, the eclectic establishment always bubbled with the enthusiasm of the crowd looking for a good night out. She was in there with her mates, up from Edinburgh on a hen party. He was there with his crew on their last night ashore. He met her at the bar as she was trying to order drinks for the hens. Their attraction was mutual. He helped her in the pushing and shoving at the bar with her drinks and, although he left early, he made sure he had her phone number.

His crew stayed on until the bitter end. As with most of the patrons, they were rapidly transforming into a hedonistic group all intent on using their charms to entice the opposite sex into a sexual liaison. No one was very particular about the age or attributes of the person they might end up with. This place had fostered many legends within the oil field crews. As the last dance played, the noise and furore of the crowd increased. Their desires were not impaired by the effects of the copious amounts of alcohol consumed. Indeed, the alcohol just fuelled the process that was sparked by the primordial desire within the human species to procreate. Some would consider the patrons of the club to be coarse or crude in their pursuit of a good night out. However, they were only following their natural desires, similar to those that attracted Robert to his lady. It is considered throughout humanity to be "nature taking its course". However, unknown to modern day scientists and psychologists, at the dawn of modern man's evolution, nature was actually altered.

FIRST TOUCHING OF EARTH, 67,975 BCE

'We have never had this chance before,' said the Anan geneticist to The Eight as they looked down from their ship in Earth orbit at the planet. 'The volcanic eruption has shrunk the human population to below ten thousand. The ash blocked out the sun for years, and inhibited all growth,' he said, as he changed the view on the screen. Pointing to a complex graph he continued. 'Overlord, the humans are at a population bottleneck. Such a chance to manipulate their DNA during this first touching will never come again. If we don't do this now they will die off within a few hundred years.'

'What do you propose?' asked the young Overlord.

'They have low birth rates; their drive to procreate is impaired by the near extinction event. Like other species, they only mate once a year. I suggest we remove the humans' limitation of the yearly mating season and enhance their natural procreation drive.'

'Have you calculated the future population size and the consequence of making such a radical change?'

'Yes, they will stay within the normal population expansion we see on other worlds. Overlord, we are starting from a small number. I believe their expansion will not reach one billion for maybe another seventy thousand years. We can monitor this and make adjustments, if needed.'

'Old man, I must remind you, we are only here for a short time to prospect for blue. This solar system is a long way from our home galaxy. We cannot expend energy on "monitoring" as you suggest.'

'I understand that, Overlord, but you can't waste this opportunity,' he said as he knelt before The Eight to plead his case. 'Believe me, if you allow me to make the changes, it will serve you well into the future.'

'Is that it? Breeding improvements, is that enough?'

'No, we should give them more. Give them free will and enhance their intelligence slightly above what we normally impart. It will give you a clever working population,' replied the geneticist as he looked at The Eight's shimmering blue energy mass.

'I will ask The One. It is a big change to their evolution, beyond what we planned. You know I have responsibilities to the planet as well. I cannot allow our meddling to endanger it.'

The geneticist left the Overlord's chamber and returned to his laboratory. *He has to approve this*, he thought. It is the only hope for both Earth's human and Anan's purebreed survival. Secretly, he had examined the DNA and population characteristics of the Anan purebreeds. His discovery didn't bode well for his own people. They would face sickness and procreation problems in the future as their DNA started to break down and eventually, they would die off. A prospect he could not allow to happen. The changes he planned to make in the humans would help future Anan geneticists repair their own purebreed DNA. If he could achieve that adjustment, both species would be linked across time and the intergalactic space that separated their worlds.

'Old man, I talked to The One. When offered another race of intelligent workers he gave his approval. But he wants you to install a marker in their DNA. Over time, they may cross-breed with other unintelligent biped species. We will need a method to locate those with the gene enhancement when we return in the future.'

'Yes, Overlord. I can do that. When I am finished, future Anan visitors will be able to locate the predominance of this DNA change in the humans.'

'Leave the details of what you do and the marker code in the ship's database.'

As the great ship left orbit, the old geneticist smiled to himself as he watched the planet recede in the distance. He had done it, changing the human race forever.

EDINBURGH 2023

Robert met her again two weeks later in Edinburgh after his trip offshore. From then on they were inseparable. Two years after they first met they were happily married, living on the coast of East Lothian with little Flora. It was the best time of his life. Like all daughters, Flora had her daddy wrapped around her little finger. He couldn't believe how lucky he was to have them both. She was six months old when their house was engulfed by the Wave. The last time he saw them alive was when he left for the rig. He was flying in from the North Sea after two weeks offshore when the Wave hit. Nothing could prepare them for the carnage they witnessed when they reached land. There was nowhere for the helicopter to land in Aberdeen and eventually they made it to the highlands in the nearby Grampian Mountains where an emergency landing base was established. He spent the next year working with the disaster recovery teams but, so large was the scale of the catastrophe, it was an immensely depressing and feeble effort.

THE WAVE OCTOBER 2023

There were many predictions, forecasts and graphic computer simulations of what would happen when or if the volcanic ridge called the *Cumbre Vieja* on the island of Palma erupted. Simulations based on a massive eruption all predicted a giant tsunami of biblical proportions, one that would engulf the eastern seaboard of the United States and the western seaboard of Africa and Europe, and become a major population extinction event. However, none of the predictions factored in the effects of climate change or the ever-increasing intensity of the North Atlantic storms.

When it happened, it followed a massive deluge from a super storm. As it moved slowly northwards, the October storm dumped millions of tons of water onto the small island of La Palma, loosening the rocks of the *Cumbre Vieja*. Climate change had spawned a series of new names for the storms that raged across the planet. Super-storms, weather-bombs, mega typhoons and mega hurricanes, were some of the catchy headlines that splashed across the globe, announcing the arrival of another Earth-shattering weather event.

Satellite pictures of the massive storm that raged in the North Atlantic, that fateful October of 2023, showed it to be the biggest ever recorded. Its gigantic girth blotted out the whole Northern Atlantic. The energy it contained was unprecedented. The storm propelled a massive surge of energy to form its own rogue waves. This epic storm surge, on its own, was capable of unleashing huge destruction when it made landfall.

When the mountain exploded, the collapse of the now drenched and weakened ridge containing billions of tons of rubble heralded the birth of the mega-tsunami. As this mega-tsunami radiated out from the island into the energetic turmoil created by the storm, the Wave was born. It swelled its own mass and height from the energy it absorbed from the swirling tempest. As it travelled out at great speed across the ocean, the Wave defied the natural order governing its energy depletion. Fuelled and pushed by energy from the great storm, the Wave grew in height and mass until it finally made landfall. The destruction it caused to the eastern seaboard of the United States, Canada and to Europe was more than ever predicted. Whole population centres were wiped out, with an approximate death toll of over one hundred million people. Some of the countries in Europe's western islands and lowlands were completely destroyed.

Following its destruction, the Wave caused major change to global order. The post-Wave world was very different. The demise of the United Kingdom and the loss of North American and European cities weakened the "Western Alliance". World order changed, with the rise of the Dragon and the Bear, who quickly forced their own political agendas ahead of any help or reconstruction efforts. The Russian Bear re-took old Soviet era territories and renamed itself the Great Northern Union. The People's Republic of China lost no opportunity to stamp its authority on the world as the most powerful nation on Earth.

It was left to Australia, and New Zealand, with the help of Canada, to marshal what was left of the United Kingdom forces and, from this, formed the new "Combined Forces". The United States of America retreated into isolation. Its government, hijacked by religious fundamentalists who used the biblical destruction to further their own isolation policies, closed its borders. The already failing European Community retreated into further non-functioning bureaucracy. It was a very different world for those who survived the Wave that they were left with.

MILAN, ITALY 15TH FEBRUARY 2026

With the demise of the post-Wave North Sea oil industry, energy prices soared. Every recoverable source had to be exploited. Robert's expertise as a rig superintendent was in demand. He returned to work for an Italian oil company, working in a politically changed Poland on a shale gas recovery project, or fracking as it was commonly known. He thought it would be a better option to help get over the shock and ordeal of losing his family, home and country. He immersed himself in the hard work in that tough environment. "More cost effective" and "we need to do more with less" were the buzzwords and the company speak for cheap and nasty equipment and no more pay rises for harder work over longer hours. He took to the challenge, had a firm style, led by example and expected attention to detail.

He met June, the petroleum engineer, in Poland. She always had the answers to his questions and no problem was too great to solve. Coming from the south of England, she had also lost her family and, like him, was trying to get over the trauma by immersing herself in work. They grew close and enjoyed each other's friendship. Eventually, she asked him to accompany her to Milan to try the pampering of a four star hotel in the centre of the city. It would be a welcome break from the sparse camp in the gas field in Poland. Now, however, as he looked at her lying asleep in the bed, he thought it was a mistake. Instead of moving on together as a couple, he believed he had just lost a good friend.

His thoughts turned to the web advertisement he had replied to before leaving Poland. It was posted by Kath in Christchurch before the arrival of her clients. Replies were sent to her and her client's email, which unknown to her, was a computer on the *Hela*.

Checking his email, he noticed he had a reply to his application with an attachment. The email thanked him for the CV and asked if he could complete and return the attached digital form. Opening the attachment he could see it was a questionnaire with instructions on how it should be filled out. The applicant was advised that once started they could not start again or go back and change previous answers. It was more like an examination, he thought, rather than a questionnaire.

After some examples, he was off, quickly answering the questions. He could see it was designed to determine the personality type and intelligence of the applicant. However, there were some bizarre questions with colours and moving shapes; more like shapes from a computer generated game. Unknown to Robert the computer on the *Hela* scanned the return, ranked and grouped all the personnel based on their score and answers. The results contained an indication of the predominance of the gene enhancement introduced by the geneticist some seventy thousand years ago. The program he had left in his ship's database was transferred over time to the *Hela*. It manifested itself to the candidates as the colours and moving shapes Robert found mystifying. Those with the intelligence to answer the questions did so automatically. Those without the intelligence, failed that important part of the questionnaire.

He finished and pressed send. Hearing a rustle of the bed, he looked up right into June's eyes. He wondered how long she had been watching him.

The quiet tap, tap, tap of the keys on the laptop had disturbed her. She was initially surprised to see Robert sitting in the chair with a towel wrapped around him working on his laptop. But then, if he felt like me, she thought, it was understandable. It was an easy and enjoyable night. They'd had dinner in a restaurant near the Duomo and walked back to the hotel. The sex was good, their first time together, but that was all it was. She was surprised at the empty feeling afterwards. No emotion, no closeness, just emptiness inside.

'Morning,' she said to him. 'You hungry?' She was unsure how to break into the delicate topic she knew would have to be discussed.

'Yes,' he said. He had lost his harsh north-east brogue and now spoke with a much softer Scottish accent, easier for others to understand. 'We need to talk first,' he continued softly. He was always blunt and to the point.

'Look, I'm sorry. I don't know what to say, but I thought this would work.'

'I'm sorry, too,' he said.

'It was good, Robert, but I expected more.'

'Emotion, closeness, that sort of thing.'

'Robert, there was none. I still feel empty; are we scarred forever by that horrid event?'

'I really don't know. I'm the man, remember? We don't do very well with these issues,' he replied, looking at her with real concern. 'I don't know what else to say, other than I really don't want to lose a good friend.'

'No. That's not going to happen,' she replied, with a little more optimism.

They left it at that and went for breakfast. As it was Sunday they decided to spend the day sightseeing in Milan. During the day Robert explained to her that he was going to hand in his notice the next day. It was time to move on.

Monday 16th February 2026, some twelve hours after the Empress and the General landed, Robert Leslie handed in his notice to their shocked manager who, with no hesitation, offered his job to June.

LYON, FRANCE 16TH FEBRUARY 2026

Niamh Sullivan joined this prestigious European project six months after its pompous start. Working for the A&M Construction Group as one of the lead mechanical engineers, she thought the job would prove to be her payback. All the long hours of studying for her honours degree and masters, and the hard work on construction projects had brought her here.

Superseding previous failed collaborations, it was supposed to be Europe's first operational fusion reactor. It was a disaster from the start, with setbacks and disagreements hampering any possible progress, and was years behind its planned development. To add to the shambles, the Wave event had sucked all available European resources, forcing the project into temporary suspension.

Niamh had lost her family and country after the Wave event. Now, at thirty-four, she was faced with losing this job as well. *Its future is grim*, she thought, sitting at her desk and sipping hot coffee. The writing was on the wall. She was retained through the suspension period to work with the designers and the construction teams that remained. However, the meetings were increasingly becoming acrimonious. The designers were mostly theorists and academics. *They just couldn't see the practical side of what needed to be done*, she thought.

She had built the fusion reactor in her mind and knew what would work; however, they just would not listen to her. She knew it was time to go, before they used the project suspension as an excuse to get rid of the "argumentative construction engineer". She knew that was just what the designers considered her to be: argumentative and obstructive. To make matters worse — she wasn't getting paid — with no resolution to that problem in sight.

She looked at the advert on her computer screen and decided it was time to try something different. She had no ties here in France and her family was now gone. She had her CV attached to the email and pressed send. Within five minutes she received the reply with the questionnaire. As with the other replies, the *Hela* computers were now busy analysing the incoming data.

SYDNEY, AUSTRALIA 18TH FEBRUARY 2026

In a quiet bar in downtown Sydney, Thomas Parker was sitting alone. It was oppressively hot outside and the air-conditioning and cool beer were welcome. He had left his offices with disgust. The security business he had tried to start was failing. No matter how hard he tried, it just would not turn a profit. He was great in the field but unable to handle the mundane day-to-day tasks required to operate a business. Paying the rent and tax, managing the accounting and complying with the regulations overseeing the security business was not something he enjoyed. Running covert ops, recognising and neutralising threats, intelligence gathering and protection details; the actual hands-on action was what he excelled at. And he missed it now.

He was a long way from his roots in east London. His family had a military background and, like them, he started his career in the Royal Marines. He quickly moved up through the ranks and his family were so proud of him. He never told them what he did, but they could see from his scars and marks that he was always at the centre of where it was all happening. He maintained an active career, always occupied in the thick of every skirmish. By the time the Wave destroyed his family and country, he had reached the rank of commander in a branch of the secret service that remained obscure and veiled from the public eye. At the time of the event, he was supervising a mission in Eastern Europe. When command was finally taken on by the Australians, he was offered a discharge with a pension which he readily took.

His initial thoughts of making lots of money in the private sector were sadly wrong and misplaced. At thirty-eight, he knew he needed a radical change; he answered the advert and completed the questionnaire before leaving the office. Like Robert and Niamh he got a positive response in the dialogue box. He needed a new direction and hoped something good would come out of this.

HONG KONG 19TH FEBRUARY 2026

Kath's advert drew the attention of many others looking for a change and a better life. What was normal and anticipated was the attention it attracted from others in the recruitment business. What was not welcome was the attention it attracted from some agencies in the business of industrial espionage. The knowledge of who was setting up where, and what industries were developing new projects or building new factories, was key information. It could be used by competitors, by investors or others following the global markets. Industrial espionage was big business.

The advert caught the attention of three such specialist firms. It was the prospect of an unknown new project which caught their eye as they applied for the jobs. When the strange questionnaire bounced back from the *Hela*, they were salivating at the mouth with excitement, all convinced they were on to something big. Two of the firms tried to crack the code of the questionnaire. They were quickly identified by the *Hela* computer, blocked and flagged to the general.

However, one well-resourced firm specialising in undercover industrial intelligence took a less invasive approach. Not knowing what they were getting into, they quietly fielded three separate candidates from different locations. The two who failed the questionnaire were told immediately. One succeeded in passing, and at the end of the questionnaire, received the same positive dialogue box that Robert, Niamh and Thomas had. In a cheap and insignificant office in the back streets of Hong Kong, the industrial spy was elated to have passed. He informed his contact at the agency and patiently waited for "someone to get in touch".

THE OVERLORDS

CHAPTER THREE

I t is time, thought The Eight. Looking at his meagre store of blue he realised this would be the last time he could communicate directly with The One until he physically returned to their home galaxy. Concentrating his mind and energy, he projected his consciousness through the vast expanse of intergalactic space. They arrived simultaneously, at a pre-agreed time and location.

'My Lord, it is pleasing to communicate with you over such a distance,' The Eight said, as their consciousness mingled in the vastness of space.

'Yes, I agree. Have you made progress?' The One asked.

'We arrived and made first contact on our forgotten planet the inhabitants call Earth.'

'I am impatient to know what is happening. What news do you have? The journey, how did it go?'

'We had a slow start from the Energy Exchange, the purebreeds found it hard to adapt to the ship. The journey in the old grav ship pushed their abilities to the maximum. They were unable to solve the day-to-day ship-based problems. Despite the technical problems, the journey was uneventful. We did not encounter any external threats and I did not see any evidence of dangers that may compromise our outward journey to the new planet.'

'So, the Anan purebreeds fail us again. Their lack of imagination and initiative must have tested them on the journey. Unless they radically change and heal their aging sickness, their time is up. How did you get on with the ship?'

'My Lord, as you are aware, I am always forthright with my opinion. I do not couch my views in the flowery language of those more politically minded than me. It is that trait that has left me as The Eight while you advanced to The One.'

'I know that; get on with it. The ship — how is it?'

'I must thank you for giving me one of the most unremarkable vessels in our fleet. It is nothing short of a rust bucket. That we have trusted our survival to this is unthinkable.'

'Stop complaining. It was the only grav vessel that has the size and capacity for your project; and, it was the only remaining operational Earth System transport vessel at the Intergalactic Docks.'

'I am not complaining, my Lord. I am only stating the facts. I remember using the *Hela* before. Its use of gravity energy is economical, and if needed, can function without any blue. I limit my use of blue to monitoring the ship's flight and my own life needs.'

'You see, there are some positives.'

'Yes, my Lord, there are. But there are many technical issues with the controls and propulsion that need engineering repair. The purebreed crew just can't use the tools to fix it. They have not fully explored the ship and openly display fear at some of the unmapped dark spaces. There are vast areas on the ship that are not yet surveyed.'

'What plans have you for the ship?'

'We will repair it on Earth, we plan for a full refit.'

'I have so many questions. Will the ship be able to transport your colony; we have so much invested in this, can the humans repair it?'

'Have no fear, my Lord, it will do the job. Once we have finished the refit, it will be well able to transport the intended loads. And I am pleased to say there are skills we can utilise within the human population.'

'Our planet — how is it? From what I remember, you said it was one of our best; a lush green gem teaming with diverse life.'

'The level of degradation the planet has suffered under the human occupation was an unwelcome surprise. During the passage of the last two hundred and twenty-five years, the population has exploded in an uncontrolled fashion and well beyond the planet's capability to sustain it. The human population is now at eight billion.'

'That should not have happened. I am also surprised. Well, we got that wrong. It is not the first time. Do not upset yourself — there are bigger mistakes out there.'

'Yes, my Lord. The level of uncontrolled expansion had major effects on the other life forms and, more importantly, on the whole environment. The planet is now in its twilight years, eons before its time. This major difficulty has prompted a change in how we manage first contact with the humans. The normal methods of establishing communications with the rulers, of whom there are many, will not work and we are employing a more surreptitious approach.'

'That is wise. It will be traumatic for the humans when they learn the truth about their origins.'

'No, they won't be happy when they learn their ancestors are back.'

'This is interesting, for a change, so much new information. If you could see my energy mass it would be pulsing blue. Get on with it — tell me more — how did they develop?' The One asked.

'When I returned to extract blue in that quadrant over three thousand years ago, the population was approximately seven million. Not an unreasonable figure and within our calculations. During this period we completed the second touching, enhancing the population's knowledge and introducing our basic tenets and morals.'

'I know that. Tell me something new.'

'My Lord, I am only trying to put everything in context. As you know, we stayed five hundred years during our second visit. However, after we left, the populations developed into fractured communities. Those diverse communities looked to advance their own needs, their individual beliefs and to gain power over one another.

'I had seen evidence of this before we left, but believed they would eventually develop their intelligence and overcome their community diversities. I was wrong. As we have learned on other worlds, free will must be earned over time and the level of intelligence supervised closely by an Overlord. I know this was an out of the way system and it did not merit a presence once we extracted all the blue, however, although unintended at the time, I should not have left the population unsupervised,' The Eight said.

'Well, you did and you had no option. It was so far from our own galaxy. I could not justify energy usage for such unproductive visits.'

'The different communities developed into diverse civilisations. They have established religious beliefs which are, in some places, extreme. Since we left, wars have been pursued time and time again in the name of religion. But I cannot attribute all war to religion; that would be naive. The usual divisions of greed, power, control of energy, commodities and land grabbing is, in reality, behind all of these wars. After reaching an industrial age, the planet was embroiled in two great world wars. Two primitive atomic bombs were dropped to end the second war.'

'That's amazing – they split the atom in so short a time. No other species we have touched have achieved such advancement on their own. Such good news. There is hope. You were right coming here. They could change everything. Preventing any leakage of our technology to the humans is now more important than we ever believed. I know you will manage this. And the nuclear armaments, you plan to disarm them?' The One asked.

'Yes, I do. We cannot countenance such weapons in the hands of unsupervised bipeds.'

'You might want to think about that. We may need them ourselves. What else have they done?' The One asked.

'The biggest threat to all species on the planet is climate change, propagated by industrial development and the burning of fossil fuels. They have burnt a significant portion of the planet's liquid and gas fossil fuel energy resources; unfortunately, all within a period of one hundred and seventy-six years.'

'No, not possible! How did they do that?'

'They developed a vehicle called a car for personal travel. The vast majority of these vehicles are powered by an internal combustion engine that uses fossil fuels. Extensive climate change is now clearly visible; I believe it is irreversible and will shortly cause the demise of this civilisation. Frequently, large storms circle the planet, causing ever-increasing destruction. Water levels in the planet's oceans are rising due to the melting of ice at the polar caps. A recent minor extinction event caused the death of over one hundred million people. I forecast that more of these events will occur in the near future.'

'The planet starts to heal itself. We haven't seen that in a long time. And their economy — I suspect it is not Utopian from what you have told me so far.'

'No, my Lord, it is not. There is a big difference in the distribution of energy, food, wealth, shelter and commodities. Some of the population is wealthy way beyond the dreams of others and have excessively more wealth than they will ever need. Some die in poverty and hunger. Others are bred as consumers to maintain the failed economies their governments pursue. The divisions in social order, ability to feed the population, the economic chaos that currently exists and the fractured political divisions are also factors feeding the demise of the human species.'

'You paint a poor picture of the future for the planet and humans. Do you have any good news?'

'Yes, my Lord, I do. On a more positive note, the planet survey discovered the assets we left behind are secure. The *Hela* database contains the asset plans, some of the inventory and access codes we need. I am pleased our assumptions to base the project on this were correct. We will land the *Hela* at her home port for its refit.'

'That is good news. What are you doing now?'

'We are currently maintaining a position in an outer orbit around the planet. Secret meetings are taking place on the planet; we are engaging an agent and are in the process of employing a working population to advance the project to the next stage.'

'An agent, what type of agent?'

'She specialises in human employment. The humans are physically similar to the Anan purebreeds and the initial meeting went well. As a new species, they have done well, my Lord. They are inventive and always look to advance. Sixty-three years after their first powered flight they landed a man on their moon. I cannot predict the future, but I see this as a positive outcome and, as we hoped, we will make good use of their abilities.'

'As The Eight, and my loyal friend, once again, you deliver. Is there anything else?'

'My Lord, what do we do about the planet? The option is open to us to protect it from further damage by the human population. I refer to a population cull, something we have not done for eons and that only you can approve. I believe there is no gain from this and we should let nature take its course. Their own wars and our planet's defensive mechanism will perform the cull.'

'I agree. A cull is a waste of blue. If it works out as you hope, we will have plenty of use for the humans in the future. However, if there is unauthorised leakage of our technology to them, our hand is forced. I will authorise a cull, or if necessary, extinction. The humans are too intelligent to use our technology without proper supervision. It was a good plan to return here, I believe there is hope for us, my friend.'

'My Lord — what news of The Sixth?'

'I discovered his two supporters, The Seventh and The Ninth. Together, they form an evil troika. The Sixth blusters and flashes and continues to control the supply of blue. He gets stronger, and I fear soon I will not be able to resist him. You have given me hope with your project. The humans may present us with some moral contradictions; however, such dilemmas are nothing compared to our own extinction.'

'I will do my best, my Lord.'

'Go now. Keep future communications short. So far the others know nothing, and we need to keep it that way. I will leave it to you. You know what must be done, take whatever action you need. I suspect we may lose contact and you must be prepared for the worst.'

'Goodbye, my Lord,' The Eight said as he let his consciousness return to his energy mass back on the *Hela*.

CHAPTER FOUR

CHRISTCHURCH 16ᵀᴴ FEBRUARY 2026

'Stop, stop, that's enough information,' Kath said. She was now leaning back in her chair, looking bedraggled from the efforts of the day. Her hair was in a mess and her makeup smudged. She was finding it hard to take in all that Theia and Mack were telling them. They had been at it all day. It was now past three o'clock and she felt they were getting nowhere. Looking at the other four around the table, Theia, Mack, Alan and Janet, who had joined them after a quick lunch, she realized they were all exhausted from the intensity of this first meeting. The body language said it all. They were all slouched in the chairs with their heads sagging; it was amazing to see the same traits in the purebreeds as the humans. Yes, they were showing signs of fatigue.

'Let's just recap on the main points you have given us so we can at least understand what you are asking us to do for you,' Kath said.

'That would be sensible,' Mack agreed. He was beginning to tire of the historical narrative and explanations. 'We do need to move on.'

'As I see it,' Kath started, 'you are from a distant planet called Anan and it took you about six months to travel here. The boss, or Overlord as you refer to him, is an intelligent entity that lives on pure energy. The blue energy you showed us earlier. From the way you explained the Overlords, you don't know how long they have been around, but you believe it is since the dawn of time. Yes?' Theia and Mack nodded and Kath continued: 'There is a problem with the supply of blue that threatens the existence of the Overlords and your own civilization. No, don't tell me the problem; we don't need to know that. Your Overlord, The Eight you call him, knows of a system of planets in a far distant galaxy a long way from Anan and Earth where there is an untouched supply of blue energy. A new energy source that will supply your worlds well into the future. You believe you can get there in about six months from Earth in your ship, the *Hela*. You need a colony to populate a planet, that has similar characteristics to Earth, in that system. It is on this planet that the extraction of blue will start. You expect the colonists to do your bidding in extracting the blue so you can ship it back to the Overlords and,' her voice was rising now, 'you want me to hire two thousand five hundred of Earth's best people to join that colony. Right?'

'Yes,' Theia said. She did not like where this was going.

'Ah hell! That's slavery. How do you expect me to agree to that? How do you expect us to gather two and a half thousand people into your ship for a six month journey? Do we pressgang them and march them up the gangplank? And what's in it for the colonists? It's a one-way trip since you really don't know what's on the planet, do you? Why did you bring this to me?'

Theia looked crestfallen. She was now slouched in the chair with her head hanging down. She really did not think they would see it this way. However, unknown to her, Mack always suspected this would be a hard sell. He had been expecting this reaction and it was a good indication of Kath's morals. Smiling at Kath, he replied.

'It's those very questions you are asking, that questioning attitude and your morals, that's why we come to you. If we cannot convince you, we won't be able to get the buy-in from the colonists,' he said.

'So, convince me,' Kath asked, looking negatively at Mack.

'It's a symbiotic relationship,' started Mack. 'I am sorry to say that Earth's population is too large for the planet to sustain it. You have a good life here in Christchurch; however, those in other parts of the planet do not. Your own country and Australia is under increasing pressure of immigration from those displaced by the Wave event and from the large population in what you call the Middle and Far East.' Mack paused for this to sink in and then continued. 'The future prognosis for Earth's population is grim. We can provide an alternative to those who are displaced or looking for a major change. It is not slavery.'

'However you look at it, Mack, it is a one way trip for the colonists. They will always be indentured to you.'

'They will be rewarded for their efforts, Kath. The first two thousand five hundred will have property rights on the planet and be regarded as the founders of a new civilisation. Some will form their own trading houses and become prosperous in their own right. Others may remain in our employment and continue extracting blue on the other nearby worlds.'

'And what of the competition, Mack, surely there will be other life on this new world?'

'There are no intelligent life forms on this planet or within the system, so the colonists will not be faced with the problems of re-colonising an occupied land as happened in Earth's history.'

'Mack, I still see it as a form of bondage,' Kath said, her face pale and wrinkled as Mack tried to placate her worries.

'Kath, believe me, they will not be slaves; they will be paid handsomely for their efforts. It is a chance for a new start for some. We do not come with whips or chains, as your slavers did in the past. It is an employment contract and yes, I agree, it is a one-way trip and there are perils that may be unforeseen now. I agree we do not know everything that is on the planet now; it was last visited some time ago. However, importantly, we have not introduced intelligent life there, it is an available planet for human colonisation, and we will need more than the initial two thousand five hundred. We are offering mankind an option for survival on another world, and yes, we will benefit from that,' Mack finished with real conviction.

The room was quiet now. They'd all sat up in their chairs during Mack's speech, as he made his point well. Janet was the first to speak.

'You know, Kath,' she started quietly, 'that makes sense. Look at all the new immigrants arriving from what was the UK and Ireland now. They have nothing; they lost everything: families, houses, money and even their own country. It's terrible for them.'

'OK, so we target those miserable people as our prospective colonists?' Kath asked, in a sharp voice. 'Convince me of the ethics of that.'

'I agree with Janet and Mack,' Alan said, now happy to join in the conversation. 'We cannot walk away from this. It is too big for us to say "No". I know Theia and Mack will go elsewhere with their offer if we turn them down. You have obviously done this on other worlds, yes?'

'Yes,' said Theia. 'One of my functions as Empress is as a designer of civilisations. As we said, our kind was here before. We have done the same with other worlds. The cycle of life starts with the Overlord touching a population with intelligence, or as we are now suggesting, transplanting a population to another galaxy. It is how things progress. As Mack said, it is a symbiotic relationship between the populations and the Overlords. And yes, if you don't agree, we will go elsewhere. But I really don't want to do that,' she said, looking at Kath and smiling at her. 'I think we have said enough, you need to consider this. I suggest we break for about ten minutes. OK?'

'Agreed,' Kath said, clapping her hands together and smiling back at Theia.

Kath sat down on her own in the reception area, sipping warm coffee. Janet was right, she thought. She had taken a quick look at the CVs that had come in so far. Most were from those who were displaced by the Wave event. All were single and had lost families and their country. What right had Kath to deny someone a fresh start? She knew that Theia and Mack would just move onto another agency if she refused, they had a second plan in place. Regardless of what she said the project would go ahead. The question really was; did she want to be a part of it?

The others watched Kath sitting alone. They quietly sipped their warm drinks and then filed back into the office. Kath followed them in. Before they all could sit down Kath spoke, her voice quivering as she delivered her decision.

'Janet, Alan, you're both right. We're in,' she said to Theia and Mack. Surprising Kath, Theia threw her arms around her and hugged her tightly. As they withdrew Kath looked into Theia's eyes and saw the deep feelings beneath the hug.

'Thank you,' Theia said, her voice choked with emotion.

'Well, that's the first time I've been hugged by an empress,' said Kath, dissolving all the tension in the room.

Taking their seats around the table again Alan was the first to speak. 'The first order of business is money. Before we even start the planning process, how are you going to fund your operation on Earth?'

'As a start, we estimated we need about a billion dollars to fund the Earth operation,' Theia said. 'More will be needed, and, depending on how the refit of the *Hela*, goes it could be a five billion total spend. Today we don't have any earth currency. Until the funding issue is resolved we are depending on you totally for support.'

'Those are reasonable numbers. What do you have that we can use?' Alan asked, now in his element as the financier.

Mack lifted his bag off the floor. Setting it on his lap he took out three large pouches. One was noticeably heavy and larger than the other two. All eyes were on the pouches as he emptied them on the table. Out spilled plain unstamped gold bars, uncut diamonds and a selection of emeralds, rubies, and sapphires. It was late in the day and they were all getting tired and irritable.

Alan rubbed his eyes and looked at the offering on the table. 'Is that all you have?'

'We have a lot more on the ship,' Mack replied. 'They are a by-product of the blue energy extraction process.'

'And how is that supposed to work?' Alan asked. 'If we introduce that amount of precious metals and gems into the market at once it will drop the price. We will not be able to remain anonymous, and it's not nearly enough. Surely you have more than that to offer?'

'Yes, we do, and you are right, we didn't expect to use all of the precious metal and stones. I intended to use what you see, with the careful introduction of more from the ship, as seed capital for investment funds,' said Mack, pausing and looking at Alan.

'OK, I'm listening with interest.'

'Our computers can predict the price changes in your financial markets,' Mack said. 'We suggest you slowly sell the precious metals and stones to generate cash and open broker investment accounts with the funds. We can link the accounts to our computers. They will provide the investment details, the buy and sell orders you need.'

'Mack, that's positively brilliant, provided what you say about your computers is right.'

'Yes, it is,' said Mack, smiling now. 'We will run tests with you on the broker accounts to prove the system works. We can provide you with a technician to help with the investments. You will need to plan the logistics of selling the metals and stones. But yes, it will work,' he said as he passed the bags of stones and metals to Alan.

'Right,' Kath said. 'The rental SUV is here. We need a change and it is getting late. I want to be out of town before the traffic gets busy.'

Theia enjoyed the journey out of the city in the comfortable SUV. The tinted windows preserved their anonymity from the outside world. She was impressed by the diversity of the buildings, the gardens and the surrounding vegetation. It was quite different from her home world on Anan.

Some forty minutes after departing the city they arrived at Kath's house, which was located on the outskirts of Christchurch's northern suburbs. Theia and Mack were fascinated by the building. The large house was located at the end of a driveway well back from the main road. The property, on approximately one acre, was enclosed by tall poplar trees which added to the shelter and seclusion of the place.

'Your house is beautiful.'

'Thanks,' replied Kath, smiling back at Theia. 'I knew I would have an alien empress around for my birthday, so I just had it remodelled and decorated.'

On entering the house, Kath was taken aback by an abundance of balloons and streamers announcing her age. She couldn't believe that the tables were set with food and drink and the place set up for a party. She turned and smiled at Alan and Janet, who were watching her reaction with pleasure.

'Happy birthday, sister,' Alan said, smiling back at her. 'This is your birthday surprise; you can thank Janet for organising it. We had the caterers set this up today, but I completely forgot about it after these surprise visitors showed up. There will be guests arriving at about eight. Theia, Mack, you are very welcome to stay, but I suspect the crowd will quickly see through your disguise.'

The two aliens stood at the door, watching the proceedings unfold. *No matter how much we study a population, we never get to see all the individual cultural differences that define each civilisation's personal attributes*, wondered Theia. She realised they had just witnessed a rare and personal moment in Kath's life. She watched Janet and Alan taking pictures of Kath's reaction on their personal communication devices. Both were careful not to capture

Theia or Mack in the pictures. Theia looked at Mack. He knew what she was thinking and nodded in agreement.

'Can you set the picture device to capture us all together?' Theia asked Alan.

'Yes, I can,' he replied, 'but are you sure about that?'

'I know today is an important day for Kath. It is also an important day for both our species. It is our first contact. We always record that for posterity with pictures of both species together. Usually it is with the leaders and full of pomp and ceremony.' Theia paused. 'And, of course, I trust you all now. I know you respect our secrecy and will not release it on the World Wide Web.'

Alan set up the photographs. Theia Aknar, Empress of the Planet Anan and General Arie Machai of her Protective Guard were positioned on each side of Kath. Janet was beside Mack and Alan, after setting the timer, stood beside Theia. They were grouped in front of the kitchen island with the fiftieth balloons and streamers in the background.

After the pictures were taken, Theia called a halt to their work for the day. 'Our ship is waiting for us here,' she said. 'You need time to yourself, and we need to get back to the *Hela*. Come and see our ship, it has landed behind the house. It is cloaked but you will still notice it is there.'

Sure enough, when they walked to the back of the house, they could see a slight depression in the lawn. They could also hear a humming noise and there was a gentle shimmering in the air in front of them. Theia and Mack said their goodbyes and stepped into the ship. To Kath, Janet and Alan it looked like they just disappeared. It dispelled any remaining thought that this could possibly be a hoax. There was a rush of air as the ship took off and then the humming noise was gone.

THE HELA 23RD FEBRUARY 2026

'You have made progress with the finances, General,' said The Eight as he floated across his chamber.

'Yes, Overlord, It is going as we planned. Our computer technician is working on Earth with Alan.'

'How is that going?'

'They both found it strange working together at first. However, once they got down to business they got on well together. The similarity between us, Anan purebreed, and the humans is easing the integration.'

'There are differences, General, but yes, you are both a linked species. What is he doing there?'

'He is installing the Anan computer in the basement of their building, the first part of our funding plan.'

'You have a self-destruct.'

'Yes, Overlord. The humans will not be able to tamper with it.'

'How long will it take to get the Project Anan financial structures in place?'

'Anan Corporation and our other companies will be open for business within a week, Overlord.'

'A week, so short a time. How is that possible, General?'

'It's the money, Overlord. Everybody is bending over backwards to help. The humans are falling over themselves to get a slice of the action. Worst of all are the human bankers. They have strict money laundering rules, which are easy to circumnavigate. They call it "greasing the wheels of commerce." Such a polite term, Overlord.'

'Bribery and corruption. We come so far across the universe and nothing changes.'

'That should not be a surprise, Overlord. The humans are just like us. We will use it to our advantage,' he said as he watched The Eight pulse with faint blue light. 'There is no cause for concern. This will work. There will be more than enough resources to fund the project.'

'But I am concerned, General. We lost control of the planet when we left.'

'We will regain it Overlord. I will not let you down, we will slowly claw it back.'

CHRISTCHURCH 25TH FEBRUARY 2026

Alan watched the *Hela*'s computer technician working on the "black box," the Anan investment computer, he was installing in Kath's basement. He was much smaller and paler than Mack and quite thin with long fingers and large enquiring eyes. Small sores on his face made him look like a sick patient from a hospital and that had surprised Alan the most.

He had set up his financial team across the street from Kath's office. The Anan computer would provide them with the investment information, the vital buy and sell signals they needed, to generate the funds. His team would not interact with Kath's "off world group", now hosted in her office. They would have no knowledge of the "alien" nature of the project. To them, it would be corporate structures, banking and investments.

With the help of his new team and some carefully chosen third party professional services agencies, Anan Corporation Ltd, and Mack Investments were incorporated in New Zealand. The offshore companies, Anan Holdings Pte Ltd and Aknar Investments Pte Ltd were incorporated in Singapore. As Mack had planned, the seed capital to launch Project Anan came easily from the sale of the gold and gems in New Zealand and Singapore.

To add authenticity to the illusion, Alan quietly dispersed a rumour about a multinational and a new mining development in the Australian desert. In addition to the financial benefits, the rumour paved the way for the next stage of the project. The story gained traction on social media and within the various chat feeds and boards that the industry analysts and self-proclaimed financial gurus frequented. It gained a life of its own and pretty soon he was reading about it in the online news, and watching it on the financial news channels.

Finishing off his work, the technician delivered a list of instructions on the inner workings of the system, pointing out different settings and techniques on the screen beside him. 'And finally, I have programmed a failure rate into the system. If there are no unsuccessful or failed trades within a specific period, the box will give a false signal. As you are aware, if we are too successful, we will draw the attention of the brokers,' he said.

'Good,' Alan said. 'We have also identified this as a problem and intend to use multiple brokers and diversify the trades over the different exchanges.'

'Yes, that will work. Now, I need a favour from you,' said the technician, looking at Alan out of his big round eyes.

'What can I do for you?'

'You can see I am sick,' started the technician. 'The time I have spent on the ship is nearing eight of your months and it is making me worse. I find my time on your planet beneficial to relieving my condition,' he said as he gently stroked one of the sores on his face.

'And what is it you want?' Alan asked, keeping his distance from the technician.

'You and Kath have what is called a "bach." I believe it is a holiday home, yes?'

'We do,' replied Alan, now understanding what was wanted. 'And yes, you and the crew of the *Hela* are very welcome to use it. It's out of the way and you will not be noticed easily. We can make arrangements for food and all that you may need to make your stay comfortable.'

'Thank you,' said the technician as he smiled for the first time.

Alan wondered what the sickness was. The poor wretch looked absolutely miserable from the time he started working on Earth. Alan noticed that there were times when he had fallen asleep in the garden of Kath's house while waiting for the shuttle back to the ship and that when he awoke he looked fresh and more alive. 'Demard. Is that your name?' asked Alan as he sat down beside the Anan technician.

'Yes, it is.'

'Demard, forgive me if I appear too forward, but what is the sickness you have?'

'It is the Anan sickness; a curse on our purebreed kind and we are dying from it.'

'Is there no cure?'

'No. It takes its course, ravages us and finally we expire; an early painful death. You are shocked, Alan. I can see it in your face. We are born with it. It developed in our people over the last forty thousand years. Our DNA is slowly breaking down. Don't worry, it's not contagious. Come; help me carry my tools up. Your offer of help is enough,' Demard said as he placed his bony hand on Alan's shoulder and started to get up from his chair. As he followed him up the stairs of the basement, carrying the Anan's tools, Alan watched silently as Demard struggled with the steps. *How long will he last*? wondered Alan.

To Alan's delight the "black box" worked like a charm. To ensure their trust and loyalty his team was rewarded with generous salaries. The corporate accounts soon began to fill with funds and the aliens' ability to conduct business on earth was now becoming a reality. *Power comes with money*, Alan thought, as he plotted the potential profits the system could generate. He quickly realised the long term outcome could have serious consequences for Earth's major banks and industries. If unchecked, their alien corporations could become the largest on the planet. If the aliens wanted to control the planet, they would not have to conquer it, they could just buy it up. As he looked over the financial projection he realised the Anan black box in the office basement was a powerful financial weapon.

THE HELA 27TH FEBRUARY 2026

Scrolling down through the data on the bridge view screen, The *Hela* captain, Brizo Sema, quickly digested the information. He pointed to the view screen; 'we can do this, Siba, look, the flight description and location is all there.'

Siba started to read the old texts; "In the ocean off the south-east coast of the main continent in the southern hemisphere locate two large islands. They are easily visible and are the largest of the islands in this region of the southern ocean. The base is located in a deep sea inlet of a mountainous region in the south-western end of the longer south island—." She stopped there and turned to face the captain. 'Bri, you are not reading it right. Mountains, the base is in the mountains,' she said, as she continued to scroll down through the data.

'We will find it, Siba, it will be easy.'

'And what about this, Bri, you missed this,' she said, pointing to the end of the text. 'The area is wet and misty with snow in the winter months and can be subject to high winds creating navigation difficulty. It should only be approached with a grade one pilot and navigator.'

'It's the summer there now. It's our best chance. The weather will be settled, you will see.'

'And the rest. Did you not look at my flight qualifications when I came on board? I am a grade two shuttle pilot, and as for you, Bri I doubt you're a grade one navigator. It's madness.'

'Let's talk to the General and the Pilot. It won't hurt. We do need to find that base.'

'The Pilot will agree with me, you will see. If we go it will not end well.'

'General, Siba is right. It will be difficult to find in the mountains,' said the Pilot as he looked over the maps of the region.

'Pilot, we do need to find that re-supply base. The old texts say there was some blue left there. We need that blue.'

'There are so many variables in the fight plan. I should go.'

'No, I need you here for the Christchurch shuttle. Can you work out a flight plan with the two? You can include hold points and weather checks.'

The Pilot looked at the two young purebreeds, he could trust one but the other — this was difficult. 'I could do that, General, but—'

'Yes…Brizo, if I approve this, you follow the Pilot's flight plan to the letter. Is that clear?'

'Yes, General.'

'It is an exploratory flight only. I do not expect you to gain entry to the base. Get close up pictures of the area. See what we will need to get in. And, Brizo, do not compromise our security. Stay away from the humans.'

'Yes, General, thank you,' Bri said, nodding in agreement with Mack.

NEW ZEALAND SOUTH ISLAND 28TH FEBRUARY 2026

'What you suggest deviates from the Pilot's flight plan, Bri,' Siba said as she looked at Bri's navigation plot.

'There's no need to follow it, look, there's the lake they referenced in the text,' he said as he recalled the old text onto the shuttle view screen. "It is north-west of a prominent and easily visible long inland lake." 'Look. I can see the lake, Siba, we just fly north-west from the top of the lake, and there's the mountains where the base is.'

Siba pointed to the dark clouds working their way across the Tasman Sea. 'And what about that, the weather front, Bri?'

'It's still over the sea. We'll be long gone before it arrives. You worry too much, just fly straight down to the lake, keep the cloak on, they won't see us.'

Following Bri's flight plan Siba brought the shuttle down over the middle of Lake Wakatipu.

The A320 Airbus lifted off from Queenstown Airport with one hundred and seventy souls on board. Oblivious to the impending danger, the cockpit crew followed their fight plan, out over the lake, steadily gaining height to clear the surrounding mountains.

'Bri, there's a human town… Where did that come from?' she shouted as a huge silver object flew straight towards the shuttle. Wrestling with the controls, Siba accelerated the grav drives to their maximum and managed to turn the shuttle away from the approaching plane. However, its increased speed sent it careering above the lake towards the side of a mountain just above the town.

'Stop it, you'll crash, you'll crash,' Bri screamed as he hung on to his seat, his eyes bulging from the effects of the acceleration.

'I need full power to the grav dampers,' Siba shouted above the noise of the vibration and the air screaming across the shuttle's hull.

She waited, it seemed an age, and as she watched, Bri slowly reached out to the grav dampers and dialled up maximum. Wrenching back hard on the engine controls, she reversed the grav drives. The shuttle shuddered with the reverse thrust coming to an abrupt stop, fifty metres out from the mountain side. The two purebreeds slumped back in their seats and looked out of the cockpit window at the strange and colourful moving structure that had appeared in front of the shuttle.

'It looks like a transport device,' Bri said, as they watched a procession of gondolas full of humans silently work their way up and down the cables strung along the side of the mountain above the town.

'Bri, your navigation stinks. You should have seen the airport and the plane. We need to get out of here, plot a course over to the base,' she said. As Siba slowly turned the shuttle away from the human settlement she looked across at Bri. The young captain was shaking as he tried to bring up a navigation projection. *He's no good to me now*, she thought as she flew west and then north above the lake. When they reached the end of the lake she stopped. From what she remembered from the maps, she believed they should be well away from the large human settlements. She watched Bri take a long draught from a silver flask he had beside him.

'What's that stuff?'

'Salt and sugar drink. It helps me concentrate.'

'Give it here, Bri, can I have a taste?'

'No. You should have brought your own.'

'Bri, that's not—.'

'Not what? What are you saying, Siba?' he said as he grabbed his blue pendant again. 'There,' he said as a navigation projection appeared above the shuttle's control console. 'There's your course to the base. Look, the mountain is just where I said it would be. It's directly north-west of here. Get on with it, we should be there soon.'

'All right, can you look out further, I want to see where that weather front is?'

'Sorry, Siba, that's as far as I can see, but it should still be out over the sea.' Thirty minutes later they arrived over the mountains beside Milford Sound. 'There's the mountain. The base is inside. You see I was right.'

'And there's the weather front, you see the old texts were right. We need to get pictures of this. I'll fly along the mountain. We will get what we need from the shuttle.'

'No, Siba, I'll go out in the grav platform and find the entrance.'

'You'll do no such thing. Look, the clouds are spilling over the mountain top. The front is here. We have minutes left before we must go. Soon I won't be able to see,' she said as she started to fly past the cliffs of the mountain, the shuttle's cameras capturing the valuable data. Bri ignored her, climbing out of the cockpit and down into the shuttle's cabin. Starting up the grav platform, he opened the shuttle door.

'That is enough, Bri, you are not going out there on that. I can barely hold the shuttle in position. You will be smashed to pieces.'

'You forget, I'm the captain, I give the orders.'

'Oh please, Bri — spare me that — we all know how you got that position,' she said as she closed the shuttle's door and flew away from the mountainside.

'That's enough, Siba. You're disobeying my orders, I'll have you—'

'You'll have me what… Do you think the General will throw me out of an airlock for following the Pilots flight plan? I think not. Stow that grav platform and get up here and navigate back to the ship now. Bri, I'm flying blind. I need that projection now,' she shouted as she did her best to hold the shuttle in position in the buffeting winds and clouds that were quickly enveloping them. 'Where's the navigation projection?' she asked as Bri sat back into the cockpit beside her.

'I… I can't get one. It won't work, Siba,' he said as his hands shook and the sweat ran down his face.

Siba grabbed Bri's blue pendant and focused her mind. As the fear-charged adrenalin rushed through her body she projected their location above her console. With one hand on the shuttle controls and the other on Bri's pendant she slowly manoeuvred the shuttle clear of the mountains and climbed up into space. Dividing her mind in two, she was able to focus on the two tasks. It was something Siba had never done before and, she hoped, she would never have to do again.

THE HELA, 28TH FEBRUARY 2026

'Well, Siba, how did it go?' the Pilot asked as he put his bony hands on the girl's shoulders.

'I pulled him out of the excrement again.'

'Yes, I knew you would.'

'How hard will it be, to get in there?'

'You were right, Uncle, we will need the humans.'

'Tell me the whole story.'

'You won't tell the General, will you?'

'No, Siba, the Captain can tell him what he wants.'

PROJECT ANAN

CHAPTER FIVE

Thomas Parker spent most of the day doing what he did best, covert surveillance. Two weeks had passed since he completed the job application and strange questionnaire. He received two calls over the intervening period. The first was an informal online interview with the human resources manager, Katherine, and the second from her assistant Janet, inviting him over to Christchurch for an interview with their clients. They booked the flight from Sydney and accommodation arrangements for him which, unknown to them, he immediately changed. He arrived two days earlier than expected, and for those days checked into a small hotel around the corner from the one they booked. He always investigated any potential client or contact before meeting them. He needed to know their business and make sure that the meeting was not a trap. He had made enemies in the past, and some had long memories. It would not do to unknowingly cross their path.

Today was the day they had scheduled him to arrive, so he checked into the large new hotel in the Central Business District where they had a reservation for him. As he sat in the lobby with a laptop on the table, he easily passed as any anonymous businessman working hard on the daily corporate grind. While watching who was coming and going, he reflected on what he had found so far, and those findings troubled him. He couldn't identify the client's core business or who they were. He usually found this out using one of the computer "programs" he had collected in his past life in the intelligence game. Except for the human resource agency, there was nothing.

Yes, there was chat, innuendo and rumour about a new mining project in Australia, but it was just rumour. He noticed some peculiar behaviour that puzzled him while watching Katherine's house and office. The strangest of all was the "disappearing duo", as he called them. They disappeared in the evening into a small structure like a garage outside the house and appeared in the morning from it. They did not stay in the house, he was sure of that.

As yet, none of this posed a direct threat to him. However, of real concern was the other team in the intelligence game he encountered. Their presence surprised him. They were clumsy and easy to spot. He suspected they were from the industrial intelligence world and he found they were only watching Kath's office. To his surprise, their boss walked into the hotel. Tom listened as he spoke to the receptionist. 'You have a reservation for me, it's made by Janet Cooper,' he said in a South African accent. *So I have competition*, thought Tom.

The others were easy to spot. The big Scotsman checked in earlier. Tom suspected he had lost everything in the Wave. He arrived dressed in a new kilt, another one in a suit bag marked with the Auckland kilt maker's name and address, and a small kit bag. He was probably interviewing for the project manager's job. He watched Niamh check in that morning. *Dishevelled*, thought Tom, probably just arrived from Europe and again with a small bag. The threadbare nature of her clothing didn't help her appearance. Her long red hair was tangled and untidy and her pale freckled face looked exhausted. She was average height and very slim. He had watched her leave a short time ago. *Shopping trip*, he thought, *clothes for the interview tomorrow*. Sure enough, she was back soon after with two meagre bags marked with the logo of the large department store around the corner. *Blimey*, thought Tom, *she didn't get much, must be flat broke*. He wondered what position she was here for.

He identified one other. She was a tall, broad and muscular woman with an Australian accent. *A project manager,* thought Tom, *the Jock's competition*.

CHRISTCHURCH, 4TH MARCH 2026

Next morning, before the interviews started, Tom went for a walk to scope out the area immediately around the offices. Hidden from sight, he quickly identified the South African sitting in a parked car across the street, taking pictures of all entering the office. It was an ungainly approach, thought Tom. The car had tinted windows, but the man was sitting in the driver's side with the offside window down. Tom could see Katherine, Janet and the two tall people, his "disappearing duo", entering the office straight from an SUV. Thirty minutes later, he watched as the Scotsman walked confidently into the building. He looked formidable in the kilt. *The Aussie lady doesn't have a chance*, thought Tom.

Robert bounded up the stairs to the first floor and entered reception. He had been delighted to get the two calls and had easily agreed to come out to New Zealand for this interview. The stop in Auckland had reinvigorated him. He loved the city by the sea and its beautiful waterfront. Robert, from a proud family with noble roots, had grown up in Peterhead, beside the North Sea. He was not born with a silver spoon in his mouth and had worked on fishing boats until he was old enough to go offshore and work on the rigs. It was a tough life, but he had loved every minute of it. Today he hoped for a real change in his life and was looking forward to this interview.

Kath and Janet were waiting to meet him as he entered the reception area. They were both left speechless by his appearance and presence. *Why did it have to be a fiftieth birthday*, thought Kath? *Oh, to be thirty again*. And then, to make matters worse, he spoke in a soft and polite Scottish accent. It made them both weak at the knees.

'Good morning, ladies. I'm Robert Leslie. I'm here for the interview,' he said, smiling at them both. There was a short silence as Kath and Janet composed themselves. 'Am I in the right place?' he asked, concerned by their silence.

'Yes, yes,' Kath said as she reached out to shake his hand and continued, 'welcome to Christchurch.'

After the usual polite pleasantries about flight, journey and the hotel, Kath led Robert to the interview room, which was set up to the rear of the building away from reception. The room was carefully arranged with Theia and Mack behind a one-way view screen. Kath and Alan were at a desk together with the candidates sitting across from them. She directed Robert to sit and introduced him to Alan.

Using her blue pendant, Theia started to gently probe Robert's mind looking for any signs of deception. The pendant, a blue diamond recovered from a crystal node containing blue energy, enhanced the mental capabilities of the wearer. It worked like a power source, enabling the person to project their mind into the physical world or into the thoughts of others. Those purebreeds, endowed with the rare gift, served as space navigators, mapping out space and projecting a navigational plot above their work stations. Theia was endowed with a powerful form of this gift. However, as their species aged, fewer and fewer purebreeds were capable of such feats, and some found the potency of their ability impaired.

For a brief moment, Robert could sense something touching his mind and noticed a soft blue light emitting from one side of the screen. It was like a flash and then it was gone. *Strange*, he thought, as Kath started the interview. She asked all the usual questions, and he maintained a confident and cheerful attitude throughout. After forty minutes, Janet came back and he was shown to reception. When Robert left the room Kath turned to Theia and Mack.

'Well, what do you think?' she asked.

'Perfect for the project manager role,' said Theia. She had already told Mack what she had seen in Robert. She believed they could trust him with their lives and that he would protect his colonists until his dying breath. 'Rare qualities, and with the exception of you, cousin, ones I have not seen for a long time,' she had told Mack, placing her hand gently on his.

'He is impressive, his whole package, the clothes, his impeccable appearance, the stature and confidence. I agree with Theia and want him for the PM,' Mack said.

'From the human resource perspective, he has all the management experience you would want. Strong industrial background, good leadership skills and I got a great report from his previous employer. We won't do any better,' said Kath.

'Agreed, arrange for him to join our meeting on the *Hela* tomorrow,' said Mack.

Just over an hour later, Tom watched a smiling Robert leave. *Good on him*, thought Tom. He watched as the South African extracted himself from his car, straightened up his clothes and started off towards the office. Decision time, and Tom did not hesitate. He quickly called the office, Janet answered the phone.

'I need to talk to Katherine Phillips immediately, please, it's Thomas Parker,' he said in a tone that he knew would convey real urgency.

'Hold on, she's right here.' Gesturing urgently to Kath to come over, Janet handed her the phone.

'Hi, this is Kath,' Tom heard on his phone. He started his reply in a clear authoritative voice. 'Kath, it's Thomas Parker. Listen carefully and please do not display any surprise in your manner, and don't mention my name in the conversation. The man coming up to you now is not what he appears to be. He was watching your offices and I believe he has a surveillance team in the area. Do you understand?'

'I think so,' replied Kath and, hearing the candidate coming into reception, turned away from the door.

'Is he there now?'

'Yes, what do you suggest?' she asked.

'Are you safe, are you OK with this?'

'Yes, there doesn't seem to be an immediate issue,' Kath said. She had now turned around and was smiling at the South African gentleman.

'I'm here and will be outside. I doubt if you will need me. He is there to infiltrate and gain information. You understand that?'

'Yes, I do. And thanks, I suspect you will follow this up later. If you're delayed this evening, let me know. Must go now. Bye.' Although scared, she finished the conversation in her sweetest voice.

'Sorry about that,' she said to the candidate. 'I'm Katherine Phillips. You're Charl Jacobs?' she asked, as he nodded and smiled. 'Welcome to Christchurch, Charl.' Kath stretched out her hand to shake his and smiled at him. They both shook hands and engaged in the usual pre-interview small talk, after which Kath led him down to the interview room. *I will have to alert Theia and Mack about this*, she thought, wondering how Thomas had identified that Charl was an industrial spy. Not being so naive, she also wondered if it could be a ploy by Thomas to unseat his rival for security manager. *Anything is possible*, she thought.

As soon as they entered the interview room Charl sensed something behind the screen. Theia and Mack could easily feel the deception he radiated. It was clear to Theia he pursued another agenda; she did not need to look into his mind to see it. His guilty deception triggered their fear of him and it was pure emotion that they projected back to Charl. Charl felt weak, he had this horrible indescribable feeling. It was fear, fear like he had never felt before as he felt nausea and cramps building in his stomach.

'I… I need the toilet,' he gasped to Kath.

Kath looked at him, surprised to see he was sweating and very distressed.

'It's out here,' she said, opening the door and leading him back down the corridor to the men's room at reception. Returning to the interview room, Kath was again surprised to see Theia and Mack looking grey and concerned. *Whatever is going on?* she thought.

'He is dangerous and a threat. You must get rid of him as quickly as possible,' said Mack. 'His sickness was from our emotional rejection of him. It was our fear he felt.'

'Well, that puts a whole new meaning on scaring the crap out of someone,' replied Kath, trying to lighten the event. She told them about Thomas's call and how he had tried to warn them first. 'Thomas will follow him when he leaves here. I guess we will learn more from him later,' said Kath, and then returned to meet Charl in reception. He was still sweating and apologised; he thought it better to defer the interview.

'Must be something I ate,' he said to Kath. She commiserated with him, agreed he should leave, and that she would be in contact with a new interview date. Charl left the building. He was so happy to be out of that mad and horrible place, he thought, as he tried to shake off the residue of his fear.

Charl sat back into his car, and reeling from the fearful experience, he immediately locked the door. Closing his eyes, he tried to relax his still churning stomach. Suddenly an arm locked itself around his throat. *No,* his mind screamed as he tried to pull it off. But his efforts to fight off the assailant behind him were too feeble and he slowly asphyxiated from the vice-like force of the arm on his throat. He couldn't reach his attacker, as the mysterious aggressor pinned him back into the driver's seat. Before he blacked out his thoughts turned to the deep fear he felt during the preceding interview and then it was blackness as he slumped down into his seat.

Tom removed his arm from around Charl's neck. Well prepared, he had the tools of his trade ready. Duct tape for the arms, torso and head, and plastic tie wraps for the legs. Climbing from the back seat into the front passenger seat, he made sure Charl's windpipe was open, with his head taped to the head rest and tilted back. *Good*, he thought, as he heard the deep breaths of the South African, he would come around shortly. Asphyxiating an opponent was a skill – you needed to know how much pressure to apply and for how long. Too long and the brain would die, too much pressure and you crushed the larynx. Tom had got it just right. He was surprised at how quickly Charl had returned from the interview. The foul smell from Charl's breath was also unexpected. *The smell of fear, that's curious*, thought Tom, as he worked. Using the precious time wisely, Tom searched Charl. As expected he found a communication device, and Charl's wallet. It revealed little other than Charl's name. Then, putting on a pair of sterile medical examination gloves, he set Charl up for the interrogation. Finally, he removed the digital memory card from Charl's camera.

When Charl started to come round, he sensed something was very wrong. He couldn't move; he could feel his trousers and underpants were pulled down around his legs and there was something cold, like plastic, under his scrotum and naked thighs. His head was taped back to the seat rest so he couldn't see down to his thighs. He tried to speak and realised his mouth was taped. Then he heard a quiet voice beside him and, looking to his left, could just see his attacker sitting comfortably in the passenger seat.

'Please don't move or struggle, nod slightly if you understand,' said the voice. It was English, polite and with a trace of a London accent, thought Charl, as he nodded his head in the taped restraints.

'I'm going to loosen your head restraints.'

Charl felt the tape around his head loosen. As he looked down to his thighs he nearly choked on what he saw. It took all his self-control to maintain his breathing. The cold plastic was exactly that, plastic sheeting tucked under his naked thighs and scrotum and stretching to the floor of the car. It was there to collect the mess from a very thin steel wire with a small wooden handle that was looped around his scrotum and penis. Beside the garrotte was a wad of bandages to stem the flow of blood that would come, should it ever be used. He looked into the eyes of his attacker. They were brutally cold and there was a violence there he did not want to antagonise. *I'm not paid enough for this*, thought Charl.

Tom smiled; he had seen the deep fear in Charl's eyes. It always worked, it was the attention to detail that made it so convincing. The plastic sheet and the bandages gave the position of the garrotte the final touch, he thought. He didn't want to use it here in Christchurch, the clean-up logistics would be challenging, but if necessary he would.

'Charl, is it?' he asked, and Charl quickly nodded. 'Charl, I must apologise for the theatrics, but I'm in a hurry. So, I'm going to ask you some questions which you will carefully answer. Before that, I will take the tape off your mouth. If you scream or shout, I'll cut your balls off; if you don't answer my questions, yes, you know it now. I'll cut your balls off. Is that clear?' Charl nodded emphatically, his eyes wide with fear.

Once the tape was off his mouth, Charl let it all out. Yes, his real name was Charl Jacobs, he worked for a global private intelligence consultancy, and yes, he was here, intelligence gathering on Kath's operation and her clients. He even detailed the events during the interview and the fear he felt. 'Look, man, there is something terrible in that office.'

'You forgot two important details,' Tom said, ignoring Charl's last remark.

'No, no, I've told you everything.'

'What about your back-up team? And I want to know who your client is,' Tom asked, as he gently fingered the small but menacing garrotte.

Shit, who is this guy, thought Charl, *and how does he know so much?* He really did not think Tom would know about the back-up team. Very easily now, Charl caved in. He told Tom the back-up team's location, which Tom already knew. Most importantly, and what Tom really wanted, was the location, the codes and passwords for their computers and data storage drives. However, it was Charl's client's name, who he worked for, that deep down shocked Tom. He would need time to think about that. His poker face did not reveal he recognised who Charl's client really was.

On his phone Tom took a picture of Charl. He carefully removed the garrotte, and then tucked a coat he found on the back seat around Charl's naked legs and thighs. Locking Charl in the car, he set off for the back-up team's office.

The two Hong Kong hackers did not know what hit them. Unfortunately, as computer nerds, they had no field training and it took Tom just minutes before he overpowered them, quickly tying them to a desk. He showed them the picture of Charl he had just taken in the car. One lost control of his bladder as Tom noticed a wet patch appear at his crotch; both trembling with fear, they pleaded with him not to hurt them. 'We are not paid enough for this,' they both burbled in tears.

After that it was easy. Tom got all their data and more besides. He had come prepared and was able to download everything off their company servers onto a small portable hard drive. He then took out a pen drive from his bag of tricks. Tom wasn't a technology nerd but over the years he had learned some tricks. Using a program on his pen drive and the access codes divulged by Charl and his two agents, he uploaded a virus to the intelligence consultancy's servers.

That will cause them some delays and problems, thought Tom. It would give him time to assess what they had found out. Before he left, Tom wiped their two personal laptops clean and took their memory devices. Satisfied he had as much data as possible and that their operation was now terminated, he released the agents, gave them the car keys and told them where they would find Charl.

Leaving their office, he checked the time; the whole operation had taken forty minutes. *Good*, he thought, but the discovery of Charl's employer still troubled him. Before going back to Kath's office he returned to the hotel. He needed to review the data and freshen up his appearance.

Theia and Mack did not need to see the second candidate, as they both wanted Robert for the PM role, so Kath agreed to interview the Australian in her own office. It was the right thing to do; the woman had travelled over from Sydney and deserved the courtesy of an interview. Also, thought Kath, there were other positions she might be suitable for. It wasn't a good interview. Kath found that the woman had two grown up children and really didn't want to travel outside the southern hemisphere. One in, two out and two to go, thought Kath. Next up was the Irish girl.

Niamh arrived early, and while waiting for Kath to appear for the interview she contemplated her work for the Europeans. She was broke and realised her existence in France was grim. After the Wave, her salary, previously paid by the Irish Government, stopped. She managed to get some payment from her direct manager, but that was quickly terminated by the European bureaucrats. 'No payment authorisation,' they said. It was a hard time existing on promises. This interview meant so much to her and, she hoped, it would be a life-changing opportunity.

When she entered the interview room, Niamh noticed the screen and the pulse of blue light. She briefly flinched at the strange feeling of intrusion, as Theia probed her mind, but it quickly passed. Although she did sense there was something different in the room, she felt calm and relaxed throughout the interview. It went very well and Theia and Mack told Kath to arrange for Niamh to join the meeting on the *Hela* tomorrow. Scoring highly on the questionnaire, Niamh was the only acceptable candidate for engineering manager. Theia and Mack were delighted with her. Her intelligence was way beyond anything they had seen so far on Earth.

After a quick shower in his hotel room, Tom sifted through the data he had recovered on his laptop. Fortunately for Kath, Charl and his surveillance team had less than Tom on her operation in Christchurch. The only surveillance was at the office, there were some details from phone conversations, but they revealed little about the client's business, or who they were. They were just setting up, thought Tom, and were banking on Charl infiltrating the operation for the real information. The data he downloaded from the intelligence consultancy servers was a different matter. Quickly skimming through the files, Tom realised it was real gold. There was information detailing money transfers, bribes, illicit deals, technology transfer and industrial espionage operations. It was the video and picture files that Tom thought would cause the most upset. He could see the names of famous politicians, bankers and industrialists heading the files. *Dirt*, thought Tom, *and dirt worth killing for.* The data would serve him well in the future. He turned his thoughts to Charl's client. He would have to tell Kath about him and the danger he posed to her and her client's operation. They needed his services and they needed them quickly.

Tom's interview was rescheduled for mid-afternoon. Theia left to return to the *Hela*, leaving security solely in Mack's domain. She would leave it to The Eight to probe Thomas's mind; she knew he had killed people and had no appetite to see that darkness. As Mack wanted to talk to Tom, the room was rearranged with him seated beside Alan and Kath and a light shining behind him. Janet had worked magic with makeup, and, with the light shining behind him, she easily disguised his alien features.

At precisely three p.m. Tom entered reception. After the preliminary introductions, Kath led him to the interview room. Now seated, Tom noticed the room was not as Charl had described, there was another person at the table. *The client*, thought Tom, and as he looked at Mack, he could not make out his features or where he was from. With the light behind him, the clothes and garb didn't reveal anything. He wasn't Middle Eastern or African, possibly from the Far East, thought Tom, totally mystified by Mack's appearance.

Kath started with the introductions. 'Gentlemen, this is Thomas Parker; he said you can call him Tom. Tom, this is my brother Alan, our financial controller, and our esteemed client, Mack.'

They all looked at each other intently, with Mack and Tom in particular sizing each other up. Mack was surprised, he couldn't get anything from Tom. *Amazing self-control*, he thought. Oh well, the man had proved his worth earlier in the day.

'I'm not sure I should thank you for what you did today, Tom; after all, you were also watching the place,' Mack said.

'No offence, but I always check out my potential employers and clients first.'

'No offence taken and, yes, that is understandable. Thank you for what you did.'

Tom paused, and then decided to take the bull by the horns. 'No, don't thank me. I've now stirred up the hornet's nest. You are all in danger,' he started, quite seriously. 'I am sorry to have to tell you this, but Charl's client is Chang Jin, a spy master with the People's Republic of China. Our paths have crossed in the past and I have found him to be particularly ruthless,' Tom said, putting emphasis on the word ruthless. The colour was slowly draining from Kath's and Alan's faces as Tom continued. 'He's usually concerned with military intelligence, so I don't know what you have done to attract his attention. I suspect this was one of many low grade industrial espionage operations he runs. Its discovery and the exposure of Charl will undoubtedly attract his attention.'

Kath and Alan were now visibly distressed. Their faces were white and they were both slumped in their chairs. Mack, however, was smiling at Tom.

'You have done well, Tom. We anticipated there would be major security issues and yes, the Chinese were one of our big concerns. Did you find out how much they know or suspect of our operation?' That broke the ice, with Tom recounting the events of the day and what he had found. He did redact some of the details; they wouldn't want to know it all, he thought.

'I have a financial team in an office around the corner,' Alan interrupted. 'Do you know if they discovered it?'

'No, and well done, I didn't see it either. Are there separate communications, phone and internet?'

'Yes, it is a separate business, we set it up that way.'

'Good,' Tom replied as he looked directly at Alan, 'but it is a matter of time before they will link the two.'

Things were going too well, thought Kath. They had made real progress over the past two weeks and there were no surprises until this morning. They had even organised shore leave for the *Hela* crew. There were two baches available and Kath had a guest apartment in her own house. Janet, who was now working exclusively as the project planner with Mack, had a rotation schedule in place. There were always ten of the crew resting on Earth in New Zealand. It was a logistical nightmare to maintain their secrecy without any support, but Janet had arranged it and the crew were ecstatic with the "shore leave". For the first time in her career, Kath lost it in a job interview.

'Ah shit, the baches,' she shouted, looking at Mack as her face wrinkled with fear. 'Your people are there with no protection.'

'What are baches?' Tom asked.

'They're what we call our holiday homes.'

'It will take Chang some time to re-mobilise a new team. New Zealand is a difficult place to operate in. Your location here on the South Island affords some security as it is so remote,' he said as he wondered who they had secreted in the holiday homes.

'That is one of the reasons we chose this place to start up,' Mack said, as he tried to steer the conversation back to Tom's employment, 'but we urgently need a security team and I would like you, Tom, to lead it. Yes, I know you have concerns,' he added, as Tom started to object, 'which I won't answer now. We have arranged a meeting tomorrow with two others who will join our project. We will explain it all then. How does that sound?'

'That's fair enough,' Tom replied.

'Tom, you have a security company and property in Sydney?' Alan asked.

'Yes, I have but it's not doing too well. That's why I'm here.'

'Well, don't do yourself down with that,' Alan said as he smiled at Tom's honesty. 'It's an asset you have and we could use it. We need a staffed office in Sydney, and your company would fit the bill. If you agree to join us, we can buy out your company, or arrange a share swap. Think about that until tomorrow as well, please.'

Tom took his leave and went back to the hotel. Before he left he confirmed with Kath the names of the other two and their arrangements for the morning. It would be a good chance to get to know them and exchange notes, he thought.

CHAPTER SIX

With Tom's prompting they met for dinner that evening and swapped stories. The following morning after a breakfast together, a taxi dropped them at the top of the driveway of Kath's house.

'This is interesting,' Tom said pointing down the driveway, 'we are going inside the building that looks like a garage.'

'How do you know that?' Niamh asked.

As they walked down the drive to meet Kath and Janet, Tom told them both about his disappearing duo.

'Hi. Welcome to my house. Good to see you all,' Kath said 'Janet will take you inside to our changing room. The client will send around a bus shortly to take you to their location. Niamh, you're familiar with "clean-room" clothing? Yes. Maybe you can help the guys?'

'I'm sure the lads won't have a problem, will ye?' Niamh replied, as Robert and Tom nodded in agreement.

The inside of the small building looked similar to the sterile changing rooms typically found in food, pharma or semiconductor factories.

They could see the stainless steel benches, lockers and the "clean-room" clothing hanging neatly on racks. The clothing looked like some of the garb Tom and Robert had seen workers wear in semiconductor or satellite manufacturing factories featured on television. They were simple one-piece light blue suits, with a hood to cover the head and built-in boots.

Holding one of the suits, Niamh turned to look at Janet; 'this clothing is nothing like I've seen anywhere else. It's so different; what's going on, Janet?'

'This is difficult. Can you trust us, please?'

'Yes, I can. But I must know, are my people in any danger?' Robert asked.

'No, Robert, honestly no,' she replied as she started to put on her own clothing.

Ignoring Janet's reply, Robert sat on one of the benches. 'Tom, you were watching the place. What do you think?'

'Janet, I never saw a bus.'

Janet stopped and turned to Tom. He had noticed she looked different this morning, her hair was tied in a bun and she wore loose fitting casual clothing. She had prepared for something different, definitely not a day at the office, he thought. Now, as they questioned her, her demeanour changed. He could see small beads of sweat run down her flushed face and her answers become shorter.

'It's a vehicle then.'

'What kind of vehicle?'

'You'll see when you get inside —'

'Right, lads, come on now, let's go with this. It's just some strange clothing,' Niamh said defusing the tension.

'You seem impatient, lassie, what's the hurry?'

'I'm mad keen to see what happens next. You're both not really helping. Here, this is a giant size, it'll fit you, Robert,' she replied as she laid the suit down next to him. 'Tom, here, take this, it'll fit you. Can we leave the hoods down, Janet?'

'Yes,' she replied, nodding her head as she looked at Niamh; the ghost of a smile appearing across her strained face as she watched Tom and Robert struggle into the strange suits.

'Great. Jeez, would ye hurry up, lads. I've got mine on already. OK, Janet, I'm ready, where's the bus?'

Janet started to open the rollup door at the end of the building. 'It's here. Come on inside, please,' she said as she directed them forward through the opening.

Inside the vehicle, Niamh looked around. The four rows of three seats were fitted with harnesses similar to what an airplane pilot would use. There was a strange looking screen mounted on what appeared to be the forward bulkhead and the windows were blacked out. As soon as they were inside the vehicle, Janet pressed a button and the door closed behind them.

Niamh quickly sat down into one of the seats, 'OK, lads, we know the drill here. Sit down and buckle up. Where are we off to, Janet?'

Tom looked around and placed his hand on the recently closed door. 'Slow down a minute, it's not a bus or any other vehicle I've seen. Those are flight harnesses, Janet.'

'Yes, they are. Look, guys, I'm no good at this. Mack, you met him Tom, asked me to accompany you all in their shuttle—.'

'Shuttle, what kind of shuttle?'

'Tom, would ya leave her alone. I'm dying to see what this is about. Until you both sit down and buckle up we're going nowhere.'

'She's right Tom, what harm is there in humouring our new prospective employer?' Robert said as he sat down and buckled up his harness.

'OK, but I'm not happy about this. It doesn't feel right.'

Once all three were finished, Janet started to check their safety harnesses, ensuring they were tight exactly as Mack had shown her. The stress of the situation and the responsibility now placed on her was showing on her face. Her lips were pursed, and her brow furrowed with wrinkles.

'Aye, that's OK Janet,' said Robert. 'We're fine with this. Don't look so worried. If you need us to adjust anything, just say so.'

'No, it all looks OK. It must be tight for the flight,' she said to them, while pressing another button on a small console beside her. As she started to buckle up her own harness, the view screen came alive. It was Kath who appeared.

'Hi guys, I see you're ready. You're in one of our client's shuttlecraft. It's going to take you to their mother ship, the *Hela*, which is in Earth orbit. I haven't been there before, but as you can see, Janet has. You'll meet them on board. During the flight I need to brief you on the project. Now, last chance, does anyone want to get off? No? OK, the pilot wants to have a quick word with you all first,' said Kath, smiling cheerfully.

A small partition opened up in the forward bulkhead and they could see two figures sitting at a control consol. One turned around.

'Welcome, Earthlings, to my ship. My name is Zaval. I am known as the Pilot. Janet, are you all strapped in?'

'Yes.'

'Good. It's an easy flight to the *Hela*, fifty-five minutes. It is important you stay strapped in. Janet put sick bags in the pockets in front of you, but I don't think you will need them; the grav dampers are working fine on this ship. OK, here we go.' With that, he turned around to face the control console again.

They heard a small hum and then felt movement as the ship took off. The blacked-out windows became transparent and they could see they were rising above Christchurch. Kath came back on the screen.

'Kath, is this a joke? Is it some new theme park ride they're making here?' Robert asked.

'No, it's not a—.'

'Kath, whatever this is, can you stop it? Stop it now please,' Tom said, as he looked out the windows watching the ship rise above Christchurch. Who was it, he wondered, who was trying to get him, and why such an elaborate plot?

Niamh turned to look at them both. 'Lads, would ye just settle down for a minute. Just stop. Look, look at Janet, the receptionist. Calm and smiling, while ye both, big fellas, are shitting yourselves. Are you not curious?'

Resisting the urge to unbuckle his harness and break into the Pilot's cockpit, Tom turned to face her. The colour had drained from his scowling face as he stared straight into Niamh's blue eyes. 'I am curious, Niamh, but I object to being abducted, which is exactly what this is.'

'Don't you look at me out of those cold eyes, Thomas Parker. And as for that chilling voice, you need to lighten up. What have we got to lose? Nothing, absolutely nothing. After all that's happened to the three of us.'

'She's right, Tom,' Robert said, putting a gentle hand on Tom's shoulder. 'I don't know about you two, but whatever this is I want to know more. I have nothing to go back to and from what you two told me last night, ye have nothing either. Go on, Kath.'

'So now you can see the reason for the secrecy. If I told you we were part of an alien project, would you have even answered the advert?' Kath asked.

'I would,' replied Niamh.

'Robert, Tom, what about you guys?' asked Kath.

'No,' Robert said. 'I wouldn't have believed you.'

'Me neither,' Tom said, 'and I still don't believe it.'

OK, I can get that. Relax now and I'll brief you what Project Anan is all about.'

For the next forty-five minutes Kath, with the help of Janet, briefed them on what the project was about. Finally, when they got near the *Hela*, Kath signed off the transmission. They had no doubt about where they were as throughout the journey they could see the change from Earth's atmosphere to space. The small partition opened up in the forward bulkhead again and the strange pilot turned around.

'We're approaching the *Hela*. I'm going to enable a viewer in the windows so you can see her. The general has instructed me to fly you around the ship, but please stay strapped in.'

The long cylinder-shaped *Hela's* colossal size completely dominated the view from the shuttle's windows. Its hull was so long, they couldn't see it all through one window and had to strain and turn to get a full view of its massive length. Three round rings, set at equal distance along its length, interrupted the flat underside of the hull – docking ports, explained the Pilot. The smooth lines of the lower hull section were broken by the main engine drive outlets. On the forward section of the great ship there was a landing deck, where they could see three parked shuttles. The superstructure of the vessel continued upwards from the shuttle deck, where a long curved clear window looked out over the landing deck. It was the only part of the ship with clear see-through bulkheads and formed the bridge, explained the Pilot. The sides of the ship was made up of gold coloured panels giving it the appearance of a great golden, cylinder shaped beast, floating in space.

'How long is it?' asked Niamh, totally engrossed in the spectacle.

'Eight hundred of your metres,' the Pilot answered. 'I will put the specifications on your view screen.'

Niamh was amazed at the size, weight and capacity of the ship. Nothing had prepared her for this.

'How's the engineering manager now?' asked Robert, looking at her with a grin. 'Is your curiosity satisfied?'

'Jeez, give us a break, will ya?' she said as she feasted her eyes on the scene unfolding before them. Looking closely at the *Hela*, she could see a small contrail coming from a bulkhead on the side.

'Hey,' she shouted to the Pilot. 'Can you take us closer to that, there, yes that contrail?' She pointed to the area of the ship she wanted to see.

Surprised at the request, the Pilot obliged. He flew under the ship and they could now see into one of the large docking ports that he had shown them earlier. There was a hatch in the centre and the surrounding structure appeared to be a latch mechanism. As the ship came up close to the small vapour trail, Niamh could see it was coming from a joint between two of the gold panels that formed the hull.

'Is that a leak?'

'It would appear to be,' the Pilot replied.

'Did you know about it?'

'No, we didn't notice it before.'

'I see,' she said, looking at Robert and slowly shaking her head, then putting her hands over her face in anguish.

Robert just smiled, and placed a reassuring hand on her shoulders. 'That's why we're here, lassie, we'll fix it. I can assure you I won't be leading two thousand five hundred colonists to another galaxy unless we are all happy with that ship.'

'Pilot, if I said that was in the starboard aft section of the ship, would you know what I was talking about?' Robert asked.

'Yes, I do, I understand your language and you are right with the location. I have sent video footage of this and the exact panel numbers back to *Hela* control. We need to dock now.' The bulkhead hatch closed and the ship started to turn and head to the landing pad on the forward section of the *Hela*.

'Robert.'

'Yes, Niamh.'

'Could you explain to a farm girl what starboard aft is, please?'

Before Robert could answer, Tom pointed to the back of the shuttle, 'right hand side at the back, it's a nautical term.'

After his long sullen silence Niamh smiled at him. 'Oh, he speaks, finally. What does our doubting Thomas think now?'

As he looked at her, she could see his face still wrinkled with worry. 'Secrecy is a colossal problem, Niamh. I am surprised they are still undiscovered. I'm sorry, but, it's not the job I expected.'

'Will you take it?'

He paused, and she watched his eyes drop away from her curious gaze. 'I'm not sure whether we will be given an option to refuse.'

'What do you mean by that?'

'What he means, Niamh, is that the "undecided" would never get to see the light of day again, if he was in charge of security. Isn't that right, Tom?'

'Yes, something like that, Robert.'

'Jeez, you're a monster. Janet, that won't happen, will it?' Niamh asked, looking at Janet for some semblance of reassurance. But Janet's stony silence added to the foreboding feeling Tom's comments instilled.

The ship set down on its landing pad just below the bridge. The pad formed a lift that lowered it into the *Hela*'s docking bay. It was a simple system with a series of airlocks designed to minimised energy and air wastage. Standing inside the door of the shuttle waiting for it to open, Janet noticed Niamh holding both Robert's and Tom's hands. Their anticipation of what was to come was very evident in their body language. Janet remembered when she stood here with Mack for the first time. He had done the same, held her hand and reassured her it would be OK. It wasn't, and she still found it hard to adjust to what was coming next. Janet took a deep breath as the door opened.

It was the smell. It was so bad it lingered at the back of the throat. When trying to categorise it Janet's nearest analogy was rotten eggs. Mack had said it was the stale air in the ship and there were technical problems with the air conditioning equipment. One of Niamh's first jobs, hoped Janet. Unlike Niamh and Tom, the smell didn't trouble Robert.

'Hydrogen sulphide… aye, Janet,' said Robert, as she nodded in agreement. He was used to the hydrogen sulphide smell from his days on the older oil platforms in the North Sea. 'Nasty stuff, but as long as we can smell it we'll be all right.'

'Why is that, Robert?' Janet asked.

'The lethal concentrations kill the sense of smell. These low doses smell terrible, but won't kill us.'

As they looked out into the shuttle's docking bay, the dark and grimy appearance of the *Hela*'s interior complemented the foul smell of the air it contained. Few of the lights were working and there was a thick film of grime on all the surfaces. They appreciated now why they had the ship garb. It was essentially to protect them from the ship's hostile and dirty environment.

'Welcome to the *Hela*,' said Janet, looking at the three of them. 'The living quarters are not as bad as this. Let's go, I'll take you up to meet our clients.'

'Hold on a minute, why are there no guards or aliens to meet us?' Tom asked as he looked down the empty dark corridor.

'A good question, Mr Parker,' the Pilot answered as he stepped out from the cockpit. For the first time they could see his grimy suit and alien features. He stopped to look at the three Earthlings, rubbed a bony white hand on his white face and continued, 'there are no guards. We didn't take any from Anan. It is only a small crew on this ship. Janet will show you to our living quarters. Don't linger here or on the way. As you smell, the air is not the best.'

'Come on, please, do as he says. I hate this part of the journey and want to get into the living quarters as soon as possible.'

Tom looked at Robert, they both nodded, 'All right, Janet, lead on,' Robert said as he stepped out into the dark corridor.

Janet quickly led them up some stairs, along a corridor and up in a lift to the next deck. The journey took just over five minutes. All the corridors were dark and grubby with only some of the lights working. It was eerie and felt more like a ghost ship than the technological marvel they expected. Robert noticed Janet was following some marking conventions and signs on the bulkheads and in the lifts.

'You're doing well to find your way around this maze,' Robert said to her.

'It's actually easy. The Anan signs and directions are very logical. You will find it easy to learn.'

'Janet did a good job getting them on to the *Hela*,' Theia said.

'Yes, she did. By now they will have no illusions as to the scale of the project. I am concerned with the leak they discovered. I cannot understand how our crews, or indeed I, didn't see that,' Mack replied.

'Don't beat yourself up about it. It can be fixed, but we have to do it before we land. We can't fly the ship into Earth's atmosphere with that. It will break up.'

'Empress, it will be difficult to repair in space and its location is in an unexplored part of the ship.'

'I know. I wonder what else the human engineer will find — we still haven't been able to start the reactor. Our technicians tried again yesterday, they couldn't pull a vacuum on the core chamber.'

'If the humans can't repair it, we are finished,' Mack said, shaking his head. 'We may as well settle down and live on Earth.'

'No, never, we cannot fail. Look, here they are, don't say anything about the reactor today,' she said as their visitors entered through a door into the ships living quarters. 'Welcome to the *Hela*,' Theia said, beaming with a welcoming smile as the four Earthlings approached and stood in front of her.

Janet immediately started the introductions. 'Niamh, Robert, Tom, this is Empress Theia Aknar and General Arie Machai, our clients. You can call them Theia and Mack. Tom, you already met Mack.'

'I believe you all have many questions, and we have much to show you. We should start with introducing you to our Overlord,' Theia said as she looked at them. Their unease was clear, and she could sense their fear and distrust.

Taking the lead, Robert spoke first. 'It's quite a shock. We didn't expect to be working for aliens. Before we go any further can we sit and get to know you both and touch base on the Project?'

'Yes, of course,' Theia said, as she led them all to a nearby room. It was set up with flasks of drinks and the walls were pasted with Janet's planning charts. There were tables and benches to sit on, and it looked much like any project meeting room on Earth.

'Before I start on the project, Robert, Tom, Niamh, your contracts are here, you can take them away, read them and hopefully sign them and then give one copy back to Kath,' she said.

Tom looked warily at the contracts as they were handed across the table. 'And what if we don't sign?'

'You can leave. I will show you to the airlock, it is close by,' Mack said, looking directly at Tom. 'That's what you would do in these circumstances, would you not, Tom?'

'You must be joking. Tell me you're joking,' asked Niamh as her hands trembled. The colour drained from her face as she thought of the others she worked with in France. She had urged them to apply for work on this project as well.

'Yes, Niamh, I am. I apologise for the crude joke, but you must know you will not be harmed. We know you will all join us. We wouldn't have asked you here if we doubted that.'

'So, Mack, how do we manage the undecided and the deserters? They won't all come happy to have tea and cakes in space. If I take the job, how many will I have to kill to keep your secret?'

'Jeez, Tom, you're horrible. I've asked my friends to join this project as well, and here you are talking openly about murder.'

'Niamh, it's the practicality of security. This is something nobody ever envisaged. It is a modern day epiphany and will change the course of Earth's history. I can appreciate your technological interest. But for me it's different.'

Mack raised his hand gently to stop the argument. 'Niamh, Tom is right. For him security will be a nightmare. Killing to keep our secret is the last resort, Tom. Our Overlord has powers that will help with those you call "the undecided and the deserters". He can wipe their memory of us. Not something he does easily - but an option he has. If any of you want out, you can. We will return you to Earth and you will have no memory of what transpired so far. But first we need to get down to business.'

Robert nodded in agreement and pointed to the charts on the wall, 'I see some schedules and dates there. Janet, are those the planning charts? Can we start with that?'

One hour into their meeting, Theia called a halt. 'We need to stop now,' she said reaching for the flasks of drinks.

'Thanks, we would appreciate that,' Robert said, taking the first drink and wondering what it was.

As they relaxed, Niamh was intrigued to know the social order of the purebreeds. She had watched Mack and Theia and could see they were both very close. When they sat down, he was always right beside her. It appeared he was more than her protector. Now and then she would touch his arm reassuringly.

'So, Theia,' Niamh asked, while sipping the sweet hot drink. 'How does social order work in Anan? I mean, you know all about our lives now. So, is there an Emperor?'

'Yes, there is. He is my, what you call, husband, and rules with a Council on Anan.'

'And do you have children?'

'No, unfortunately I do not.'

'Mack, do you have family?' Niamh asked more tactfully now.

'No. Unfortunately, my wife died years ago. It is a sickness that afflicts our species. The Empress is all the family I have now. We are what you call cousins; Theia's father and my mother were brother and sister. We grew up together. I am an Aknar, a member of the royal family, as you would call it here on Earth,' Mack replied.

'I'm sorry to hear that.'

'Thank you, Niamh, it was a long time ago. You three have lost all your family and your countries,' Mack said as he looked intently at them. 'This is a big venture for you, including you, Janet. It's a step into the unknown. You have many changes to face.'

Theia had watched Niamh with interest. The *Hela* computers had chosen her as the most intelligent of all the human applicants. As she watched the red-haired girl cheerfully chat with Mack, she wondered what the Overlord would see in her. 'Talking about changes, they need to meet The Eight,' she said, ending their conversation. 'He will get impatient if we keep him waiting any longer.'

The Eight looked at the group assembled before him. They represented his and their respective species' hope for their survival in the universe. He knew the purebreeds understood that, but he doubted the humans realised how important this project really was. 'Finally, we are all together,' he said as they watched his every move.

'You're just a ball of pure energy,' Niamh said, as he floated around his chamber.

'Yes, I am. What you see is my energy mass,' he said, as they watched the oval translucent entity glow with blue light. They had not known what to expect and before entering his chamber, Theia had given them strict instructions not to approach or touch him. Today, as he existed on a limited supply of blue, The Eight's energy mass was about five foot high and three foot wide at its centre. The blue light increased in its intensity at his core while the colours constantly changed in tone. Occasionally his energy mass pulsed with a soft blue light.

Niamh listened to his voice; it emitted from the air around him and, she thought, it was soft and even. Not the deep booming voice she would have expected from a powerful entity.

'Niamh, my child, come closer to me,' The Eight said, now using a powerful voice that caused Robert and Tom to step back in surprise.

'Wow, you're reading my mind, that's rude,' she replied, as she stepped closer to the entity.

'Does that surprise you?' he asked, his voice returning to the soft and even tone.

'No, not really,' she replied, and she carefully squatted down in front of him.

'You may touch me, do not worry, I will not hurt you.'

Totally captivated by the entity, Niamh gently touched him. She felt a tingling sensation in her hand and then a short blue flash in her brain.

'What was that?' she asked, as she quickly withdrew her hand.

'That, Niamh, was my blue energy. I see you have intelligence, far beyond what you think. You inherited a gene that gives you a powerful ability to navigate through space. It is a skill you will need in the future. The Empress will teach you how to use it.'

Robert, Tom and most of all Niamh were all stunned with this disclosure. They did not notice Theia's smile; she had suspected the path to the purebreeds' survival was through the humans, and now she wondered what magical gene the human girl inherited.

'Rather than bore you with explanations, I want to show you where you came from and the link between both your species. Please sit,' The Eight said.

Theia and Mack directed them to some benches at the side of the room. As they sat down the room started to glow. The Eight had prepared a selection of video clips from the ship's database and from his own memories that showed the first and second touching, some of the assets on Earth and the links between humans and purebreeds. Not all the information was included, but enough to show human origins and the link between the three species in the room now. It was news to Theia; she knew some of the information, but did not realise there was video still available. It would be invaluable in her research to find a cure to the purebreed sickness, and, she knew The Eight would not show it all here today.

When the video clips stopped, the humans and purebreeds looked at each other in silence. It was the gravity of the situation that captivated them. The humans finally realised the fate of the three species would rest on the successful outcome of the project they were embarking on together. It was a pivotal moment in Robert, Tom and Niamh's understanding of the project, and the origin of intelligent life in the universe. It was not the theory that history or science books attempted to outline. It was simpler than that. The Overlords were the source of all intelligent life in the universe and imparted a level of intelligence to the different species they chose to interact with.

'I'm overwhelmed and actually speechless,' Robert said.

'I understand that. Before I returned, I knew such news would shock mankind.'

'Overlord, my biggest fear now, today, from what I can actually see, is the ability of this ship, the *Hela,* to do what we need.'

'Yes, Robert, I agree with that. The ship is your first task; you must approach this one step at a time, for without a space-worthy ship, we are all doomed.'

'Aye, we can do that.' After The Eight's simple response, he was feeling more upbeat now and responded to the challenge. 'We'll open two work fronts. Niamh, can you get the basic repairs to the ship done in space, just enough to get her ready to land?'

'Once I get my head around the technology, I believe I can do that. I'll need a team here on the *Hela.*'

'I'll set up a support team on Earth and we will need to prepare the Australian base for the *Hela*'s refit once she lands,' Robert said as he looked at the projection of the Australian base's location The Eight had left on above his chamber. 'You do know, Mack, that will be a major construction project on its own. It's going to take some time to get that place ready.'

'Yes, we did realise that. We do need to establish contact with the Australian and New Zealand governments for permission to land at our bases,' Mack said, looking at Janet. 'Janet, you and Kath will have to make contact with the New Zealand Prime Minister. He will be Project Anan's first official point of contact on Earth.'

'And how will we keep this secret?' asked Tom who, for the first time in his life, was afraid he would actually fail at his duty.

'With difficulty,' Mack replied, placing his hand on Tom's shoulder. 'Tom, it will eventually leak out, we just need to control it as much as possible and protect our people.'

'It's huge, Mack, countries will go to war to get their hands on your technology.'

'Yes, I know that. Remember you will work for me, Tom, and believe me when I tell you I will help you in whatever way I can. We do have some tricks that will help. We also have an unlimited cash budget, enough for you to put together our own security force.'

'Don't tell him that, he'll be buying tanks next!' Niamh said, shaking her head.

'No, Niamh, too noisy and they are hard to hide; however, I would like to take a few with us when we leave Earth. Yeah, that would be good.' He was smiling now and nodding thoughtfully. He was glad she had mentioned tanks; he knew she was joking, but he needed to plan for their final departure. Weapons were easily available on short notice, but the good stuff, that was hard to get and had a long lead time. He would have that conversation with Mack and Robert.

The Eight was pleased with the noise in the room; it was not what was said but what they were thinking. He could hear Tom's thoughts on the weapons and could see into Tom's dark past, what Theia didn't want to see, and he was delighted with Tom's full commitment. He could see all their commitment. There were no threats of deception which he feared most. *Good. We are at stage two*, he thought. 'OK, you may all go,' he said to the surprise of the Earthlings.

The Eight relaxed after the meeting. He had used more energy than he planned, but was pleased with the outcome. *Another project milestone reached*, he thought. They had a team in place, and, thanks to the Anan technicians' abilities, they were amassing the resources needed on Earth to finance the operation. But it was the girl who pleased him most. She had abilities beyond what he thought humans were capable of. She had the original essence of the intelligence the old geneticist introduced all that time ago. It was not diluted as in the others of her species. For some reason it had resurfaced after all that time in her body. He wondered how many more were like her on Earth, and how long would it take the Empress to figure this out? He knew she intended to work on a cure for her people, and that, he mused, could lead to her discovering his secret.

'That was an abrupt way to end a meeting,' Niamh said.

'That's how the Overlords are. They only meet at crucial times and do not waste their energy on small details. Always remember, if they wish, they can read your mind wherever you are so they can keep track of the important details,' Theia said.

The team had returned to the project meeting room. Everyone wanted to say something after meeting The Eight, so Robert now took the lead.

'All right, all right. We're in. Yes?' said Robert, as he looked at his team. They happily nodded their heads in agreement. 'We need to see as much of the ship as possible and to get as much information as we can before we return. No, Niamh, don't interrupt; you're coming back with us. No, no arguments on that.' He knew she wanted to stay on the *Hela* rather than return to Christchurch with Robert and Tom. As far as he was concerned, that was not happening on their first visit.

'Yes, Robert,' she replied.

'Janet, is that OK with you?' he asked.

'Yes, that's fine. We planned a twenty-four hour visit.'

'I have arranged for some of the crew to show you the parts of the ship that are accessible,' Mack said, 'we should get started now.'

The next twenty hours proved intensive for Niamh, Robert and Tom as they tried to pack as much work as they could into that limited time. They saw the cargo bay that would house the colony; Niamh visited the engine room; and they were all given a tour of the bridge by the *Hela* captain, Brizo. Twenty-four hours after they arrived, the four humans returned in the shuttle to Christchurch. They were physically and emotionally exhausted from the trip and Robert, Niamh and Tom were amazed by what they had seen and learned.

'Well, that puts a whole new take on the saying "you're going to meet your maker". Instead of him living in the customary heaven, he's now in residence on a clapped out old space ship in orbit around the Earth,' Robert said on the journey back. The others laughed at his analogy of The Eight. By the time they returned to Christchurch, it was Friday night, and Robert, Niamh, Tom and Janet went out to celebrate.

Sitting in the lobby of a small hotel on the Kowloon side of Hong Kong, Charl looked across at his Chinese client, Chang Jin. He had no concrete information and this meeting, with his best client, wasn't going very well. His pictures were gone, the data wiped from the laptops and what had been sent also deleted from the servers. How that was done, he didn't know. But when he looked at what information he actually had, there was nothing. He explained to Chang how he felt afraid and terrified in the interview room and that there was something very different that he couldn't understand behind the screen. To make matters worse, there was a counter intelligence team watching him. They had stolen his pictures and attacked his own surveillance team.

'Chang, there was something sinister beyond my understanding and beyond anything I have ever encountered in that office,' Charl said, finishing his explanation of the events in Christchurch.

'Such measly excuses. We paid you lots of money for this and all you give me is something from a stale outdated TV series.' Chang paused, staring at Charl with his cold unblinking eyes. 'How bad is that? What am I supposed to tell my superiors in Beijing? "We have uncovered a sinister plot in Christchurch in New Zealand. We don't know what it is, but there was real evil in the room with our agent". They accuse me of watching too much TV and fire me.'

'I'm sorry, I've nothing else. But that is how it went down.'

'Charl, Charl, can you not see how weak that is? You have failed me in this. Go now, go. Your pathetic explanations disgust me.'

As Charl got up and left, Chang reconsidered all that he had told him. *Look at the facts*, he thought. Previous to this event Charl, and the agency he worked for, had an impeccable record. They had never let him down before. Charl was bested by a superior force, most likely military grade. Who they were and why they were in Christchurch interested Chang. And the Englishman, who was he? It merited further investigation. He would have to carefully consider how they should move ahead. He didn't like putting Chinese agents in New Zealand, but that approach may be necessary now. Chang had also noticed a rumour about a new company exploring for minerals in the Australian desert who were hiring from a base in Christchurch. He wasn't sure how all this tied together but he knew that doubt and rumour must be squeezed to render the facts. It was the squeezing he did best and loved most.

Niamh sat back in the seat on the *Hela* bridge. Returning to the ship yesterday with a small crew, this would be her first space navigation training session with Theia. She listened to Theia's soft voice and as she relaxed, she tried to forget about the air purifiers they had installed today and the work planned for tomorrow. Slowly, as the busy mess of the day's work cleared from her mind, she focused on the blue crystal, concentrating more and more on its centre, and then it happened. Like an electric shock in her brain there was a flash of blue light and she was out of her body looking back at herself.

'Jeez, Theia, I'm looking at myself.'

'Describe what you see.'

'I'm sitting in the chair with my eyes closed, holding the blue crystal you gave me. It's still in the pocket of the navigation console. I'm quite pale. Jeez, I look wrecked.'

'What colour is your hair? Tell me what you see, not what you know.'

'It's red, and it's a mess, hard day at the office type of mess.'

'Good. Concentrate and tell me what I am pointing at.'

'My face.'

'Yes, but what exactly am I pointing at?'

'My cheek, no, it's my freckles? Yes, that's what you're pointing at.'

'Describe the colours, look at them now.'

'My face is pale white, some red on my cheeks and my freckles are a soft shade of brown.'

'Good, watch me and tell me where I go.'

'You're walking behind me, over to the engineering console. Oh! Oh! Theia, I'm scared, I can't feel my body. How do I get back?'

'Take it easy, Niamh. Just relax and focus on the crystal again.'

'It's not working, Theia, I'm so scared, look, my body's trembling, I can see it, but I can't feel it.'

'Let go the crystal, now. Let it go.'

'Jeez, that was terrible, Theia,' she said as her eyes popped open wide with fear. 'I feel sick to my stomach.'

'It's normal when you project your mind out from your body for the first time. It will take some time for your body to adjust to the changes. We need to train every day at this. That's enough for today, Niamh, you have done well, but you need your rest now. I will see you here tomorrow.'

CHAPTER SEVEN

THE HELA 14TH MARCH 2026

'General, after such a long time, today you start to get my assets on Earth back.'

'Yes, Overlord. I know you have waited patiently for this. I meet the New Zealand Prime Minister first.'

'No doubt that will be a surprise for him.'

'Yes, Overlord, Thomas Parker and Katherine have arranged the meeting. He will not have a large security detail. He likes his privacy and quite often travels alone.'

'My base on the southern island was one of my most favoured. It is of strategic importance to our project. It was always intended as a re-supply base. I believe there may be some blue stored there. If so, it should sustain me until we get to the New World. Do whatever is needed to guarantee our access, but remember, it is mine and I want it back.'

'Yes, Overlord,' replied Mack as he bowed to The Eight, and then turned to leave his chamber.

WINERY NORTH OF CHRISTCHURCH 14TH MARCH 2026

'Katherine Phillips, you look great, how long has it been?' he asked.

'Prime Minister, last time we met you were just plain Harold, a Member of Parliament and now look at you,' Kath said, shaking his hand. He had a firm grip and appeared genuine in his greeting towards her today.

'It's good to see you again, Kath. How are you?'

'I'm good, busy at work, which is why I am here. But it is good to see you too, after so many years. Come, let's walk,' she said as she took his arm.

Kath, in agreement with the PM's Diplomatic Protection Services, had arranged the meeting in this winery in one of the many vineyards north of Christchurch. She'd used it in the past for corporate events and knew the owners personally. They continued the small talk as he walked with her to a secluded section of the garden where a table was set with tea and coffee. He noticed it was set for more than two.

'Kath, whatever have you gotten yourself into? I mean your request, national security, the secrecy and the special contact you want me to meet. It's so cloak and dagger,' he said, as they sat down at the table which was conveniently surrounded by hedges and trees.

'Well, Prime Minister, it's better I show you rather than try to explain,' she answered. 'And I think your DPS officer should sit with us as well.'

Kath took out a small device from her handbag and, pressing it gently, said, 'OK, we're ready.'

Tom accompanied Mack on this mission and insisted on surveying the area before they touched down in the shuttle for the meeting. As they watched the PM's car turn off the main road, another car that followed at a distance stopped and two Asian figures disembarked. They looked up and down and quickly realised they would have to stay at the main road.

'As we expected, Chang has his people here,' Tom said. 'They won't make it to our meeting.' The winery was five kilometres from the main road and there was a deep river to cross. It was a spectacular crossing over a narrow gorge spanned by an old steel bridge. The only approach was by road over the bridge or by air.

'Good location, if you are happy we should land,' Mack said.

'Yes, I am. Pilot, you can land beside that table in the garden. Leave the cloaking device on, the ship must stay invisible.'

Kath, the PM and his DPS Officer approached and sat at the table. Tom noticed Kath had them sitting facing the shuttle. Then they heard her signal over their comms system: 'OK, we're ready.'

'Open the door, Pilot,' Mack said.

The PM and his DPS officer, hearing the strange humming noise from the activation of the shuttle door, stood up. When they looked closely in front of them, they could make out a slight shimmering in the air and noticed a small depression in the lawn. To add to their amazement, a doorway was opening in the hazy air. When it opened fully, they could see two figures. Tom stepped out of the ship, leaving Mack in the doorway. He walked straight up to the PM and the DPS officer, stood to attention and saluted.

'Thomas Parker, sir,' he said, addressing the PM. 'May I present General Arie Machai, of the Anan Protective Guard?' He stepped to the side but remained close to the DPS officer.

'Prime Minister, thank you for meeting me,' said Mack as Kath waved at him to approach. They had rehearsed this, wanting to get the initial shock of the meeting over as quick as possible.

'Mack, please come and meet the Prime Minister,' she said. 'We call him Mack, Prime Minister, his name is quite a mouthful.' Mack walked over to the PM, smiled and held out his hand.

Nothing had prepared the PM for what he was seeing now. In front of him stood a tall man, or what appeared to be a man, dressed in a smart dark blue uniform. It had golden buttons and was quite simple in its design. His ears were oval with no earlobes and he had deep green eyes. His skin was very white, he had no hair and his most distinctive feature was his long thick muscular neck. *Not quite human*, was the first thought that entered the PM's head as he took the man's hand in his and shook it, not knowing what to say.

'Gentlemen, please sit, tea, coffee,' said Kath, busying herself pouring the refreshments that had been left out beside the table. 'Don't worry, Prime Minister; they don't eat humans.'

'Kath, what were you thinking of when you set this up?' asked the PM, in a strained and halting voice. 'I mean, if this is what I think it is, do you realise the repercussions?'

Kath stopped what she was doing, and putting the teapot back on the table, she turned to look at the PM. 'Harry, I did not "set this up" I set nothing up, they came to me. They're aliens; yes, aliens from a planet called Anan and, believe me, I've served my country well in all my dealings with them. In the fifteen years you have been in government I haven't bothered you once. Have I?'

'No, Kath you haven't.'

'Not one favour, no, not one. Do you remember?' she asked, dropping her voice. 'It was after our graduation, it was in that flat in Auckland, the whole gang was there—.'

'Kath, really, there's no need for that,' said the PM. He didn't want to recall what happened all that time ago.

Tom silently tapped the DPS officer on the shoulder. 'I think we should put a discreet distance between our masters and let them get on with their delicate negotiations,' he whispered to the officer, who was more than willing to agree. He could see the PM was in no mortal danger and he really didn't need to hear any more as he tactfully withdrew with Tom.

'Prime Minister,' Mack said, not wanting Kath to dig up old dirt. 'We approached Kath because, amongst her other attributes, was her ability to arrange a meeting with you. We knew she was acquainted with you in the past.'

'I see,' the PM replied. 'And what do you want from me?'

'A lot, sir, and we will need the Australian Prime Minister as well.'

'Before I do anything to help you, assure me you pose no danger to our country.'

'My people and our Overlord do not, but others on your planet may pose a danger to you. Do you know Chinese intelligence followed you to the turn off?'

'No, I did not. Officer,' the PM hastily called to his DPS officer.

'Yes, sir, Thomas Parker already informed me of the threat. The local police are dealing with them as we speak.'

'Good,' the PM replied, nodding in approval at the DPS officer's news. 'So, General, we have an hour. Enlighten me as to why you are here.'

With the aid of his holographic projector Mack briefed the PM. Kath left them to it and joined her friends in their house. She returned just over one hour later and was not prepared for the surreal tableau that greeted her. Tom, the DPS Officer and the Anan pilot were sitting at one table playing cards. There were two open bottles of wine on the table and to make matters worse the DPS officer and the pilot were also smoking. They were actually serving the Pilot red wine and cigarettes, she thought. The PM was showing Mack how to open a second bottle of wine while they were engrossed in conversation. As nobody noticed her, she returned to her friend, shaking her head. *Men*, she thought, regardless of the species they were all the same.

'I married her cousin,' the PM said. 'It was after that time in Auckland she was referring to. Strange how things turn out. You married, General?' he asked as he poured more wine.

'No, my wife died of the sickness that curses our species.'

'I'm sorry,' replied the PM, now looking straight at Mack.

'Thank you, I appreciate your concern. It was a long time ago. Time heals, slowly, but it heals.'

The PM paused, took a drink of his wine and finally broached the subject that had flashed through his mind when he first met Mack. 'General, you never told me why you chose New Zealand for first contact.'

'Prime Minister, we have bases in New Zealand and Australia. My ancestors were in New Zealand long before the human species ever arrived. It was our last inhabited outpost before they left this solar system.'

'That is probably your biggest revelation to me today,' the PM said, sitting up with interest.

'My ancestors chose this part of the southern hemisphere for their home as it was sparsely populated when they arrived for the second touching. It was very much out of sight of the main population centres at that time. The *Hela*'s home port is in the Australian desert. The location was in an inhospitable area with a very low population density, as it is today. The New Zealand outpost was chosen as there were no humans here then. It was considered a secure outpost and a re-supply base for future visits.'

'Ha, you'll be asking me for back rent next,' the PM said, as the effects of the wine started to lighten their conversation.

'No, no,' Mack replied, now laughing as well at the bizarre nature of what he was telling this man. 'No, I don't want the rent, I just want the two

Islands back.' They both roared with laughter, disturbing the other three who were engrossed in their card game.

'What is this you are serving me?' Mack asked as they regained their composure.

'It's New Zealand's finest and it wasn't around when your ancestors were last here,' he said as he held up his wine glass. 'And you're not getting the two Islands back. But, of course, whatever help you need, I will gladly facilitate as long as it does not put our population at risk.'

'Thank you, Prime Minister. I appreciate that and we will not harm your people. Do not fear us, our species are linked together,' Mack said, smiling at his new friend. 'Our Overlord will be happy with that.'

'You're both drunk,' said Kath, returning when she heard the loud laughter.

'We're not, and what do you expect when you leave a case of that beautiful red beside the table?' replied the PM.

'Mack, have you drunk a whole bottle of wine? Yes, you have,' she said, picking up the two empties on the table. 'And was anyone watching the Pilot, how much has he drunk? Can you fly that thing, Pilot?'

'No, I'm drunk,' he replied in Anan, and they all looked at him in alarm at the strange sounds he was making. Luckily, with the exception of Mack, they couldn't understand a word he said.

'Just joking, Earthlings, just joking,' he said in English, walking towards the shuttle carrying two unopened bottles of wine with him.

'General, a pleasure meeting you. Get in touch if you need my help accessing your base. I will arrange a meeting with the Australian PM as well.'

'Thank you, Prime Minister, I appreciate that.' They shook hands firmly before they both departed.

CHRISTCHURCH OFFICE 16TH MARCH 2026

'So, farm girl, are you happy working in space?' Robert asked, smiling at Niamh on the view screen.

'Robert, would ya give it a break?' she said, smiling back at him. She could see the office behind him was now mobbed with new people. *The first teams have arrived*, she thought. She could see some of the people she had worked with in France and had recommended for the project. Some had spotted her and waved at her on screen. She waved back and gave them the thumbs up. She needed them here on the *Hela* yesterday.

'So, how's things on the *Hela*?'

'I found a bigger problem.'

'No, no, no, what's bigger than what you found already?'

'I'm sorry, Robert, but it's the reactor, it's shot. I'm sure our employers knew about it, before we arrived.'

'The fusion reactor — is that not the ship's main power source?'

'Yes — that one. The grav drives are working a treat and can give us some power. But to sustain life, and power the ship with the full cargo, we need a reactor.'

'So, what do we do about it?'

'I have a plan — can ya get Tom as well?'

'I never doubted you, lassie,' he said as he went to get Tom.

'Hi, Niamh,' Tom said as he looked at Niamh on the view screen. 'I guess your plan involves some sort of skulduggery if you want me involved.' They had moved into an office with more privacy for this conversation.

'Yes, Tom, I need you to steal some parts from a warehouse in France.' Tom and Robert looked at each other in disbelief.

'Say that again, Niamh?' asked Robert.

'I need parts to repair the reactor. There are some in the *Hela's* home port in Australia, but that's not enough. I can use the parts in France, you know, where I worked before,' she said, smiling.

'So why do we have to steal them, can't we just buy them?' Tom asked.

'Lads, you're dealing with Eurocrats. They won't sell anything out of that place. The parts I need for the reactor are ones I ordered months ago. They were never used. There is also a whole range of unused equipment that I can use on the *Hela* for the repairs to the other systems. It's the most advanced technology available on Earth. And it's sitting in their warehouse, all surplus stock. No one will ever notice if it goes missing.'

'So why can't we just order them ourselves?' asked Tom. 'Why does it have to come from France?'

'What's the lead time on your high tech weapons? Don't tell me, I already know you've been ordering them now from the factories for delivery when we leave,' she said, grinning at him as Robert looked at him in surprise.

'You haven't done that. Have you, Tom?' Robert asked. 'We haven't agreed load limits yet.'

'Well, my technology is the same,' she continued. 'It's all special order and will take months to make. We need to get our hands on that equipment. It's all that's available on Earth. There is no other alternative.'

Mounting a raid on the site of the European fusion reactor project was possible but it would leave their fingerprints all over the operation, thought Tom. There had to be a better way.

'Niamh, what do they do when they want to sell off surplus equipment or scrap? I mean, they are bureaucrats so there must be a written procedure for this?' Tom asked.

'Yeah, there is and it's long and detailed. Before we go any further you need to meet Demard, he's the computer technician that worked with Alan,' she said as she adjusted the camera to bring Demard into view.

'Hi, Demard,' said Tom looking at the small and pale Anan with long thin fingers and large eyes slouched in a seat beside Niamh.

'He's brilliant,' she said. 'He showed me how to access the ship's systems and all the old records and databases. He found the list of parts that are supposed to be in the Australian base. There's not enough there, we do need the stuff in France.'

'Demard, if you got this procedure, could you create the documents necessary for us to buy all the warehouse stock Niamh needs?'

'I believe I could. Have you got a copy there, Niamh?' asked Demard. They all watched as Niamh nodded and started to log on to her previous employer's computer system.

'Do you still have access to their computers?' asked Robert, surprised and suspicious that she could get access so easily to the French system. 'Did you quit your last job, Niamh?'

'No. Sure, they weren't paying me anyway, so why would I need to quit?' she replied, as she worked intently at the computer. 'There it is, have a read of that, Demard.'

Tom and Robert watched Niamh and Demard read the procedure on their screen on the *Hela*. They were looking intently at it, taking some time to decipher its large content.

Tom started to drum his fingers on the desk, finally he lost patience. 'Well, what do you think, Demard?' he asked.

'It was easier to crack the stock exchanges. It requires many different approvals and meetings, but I can create that, and embed it in their own emails and records. No one will notice what I do, but, because of the quantity of documents I must create, it will take about a week.'

'Great, you come down here and we'll get you some help with that,' Tom said. 'OK with you both? Yes, good, it's settled then,' he said as they both nodded in agreement. 'I'll plan how and when we want to collect the equipment. Alan will arrange the money transfer.'

'Lads, before you go there's one more thing ye need to see,' she said, as she placed a round shiny cylinder on her desk. Taking a small box from the floor, she carefully laid out some odd looking tools and a pen on her desk, and then started to open the cylinder. Carefully taking off the lid and placing it on the desk, Niamh took up one of the small tools and stuck it into the cylinder while thin white vapour started to creep out.

'Are you sure you should be doing this, Niamh?' Robert said as he noticed Demard back away cautiously as Niamh continued with her work. She now had a pen in one hand and the tool in the other. Holding the pen up, she touched it with the tool and they noticed a very small blob of jellylike substance stick to the side of the pen.

'There,' she said, as she put the tool down and started to screw on the top of the cylinder. The pen floated horizontally in the air in front of her as Tom and Robert watched, mesmerised by the show. 'Meet grav, it's what powers the ship and the shuttles, it counteracts the effects of gravity,' she said, as she placed her finger behind the pen and then flicked it. Struck by the sudden force of her finger, the pen immediately shot off out of sight of the camera. The surprised Tom and Robert heard a crash, then a shout coming from Demard.

'Oops, I didn't think it would go that far,' she said, turning the camera so they could see her handiwork.

'Now, lassie, ya need to pay attention to what you're doing. That was not funny, not funny at all. You could have hurt yourself or some other poor unfortunate coming into your office,' Robert said in a tone they had not heard before.

He was on his feet now, pacing up and down. Tom had his head in his hands and was trying hard not to laugh at the picture of a large wall panel lying on the floor with the pen embedded into it. Knocked out by the force of the pen's flight, it had crashed down onto the floor just missing Demard. Finally Tom let go and burst out laughing, fuelling Robert's anger. All Niamh could see was the kilt swaying up and down across the screen and when she heard Tom's laughter, she started laughing herself. Things finally settled down after five tumultuous minutes. A shaken Demard also appeared on screen.

'I'm coming up tomorrow with the new teams,' Robert said. 'We need to establish some ground rules before we get hurt or damage the ship. Am I clear?'

'Yes, Robert, perfectly clear,' Niamh replied, as she tried to contain her laughter. It was Tom; every time she looked at him, he had this wicked glint in his eye and he seemed like a boy with a new toy. She knew all he was thinking about was, "How do we weaponize that stuff?"

THE HELA 17TH TO 18TH MARCH 2026

The new hires were assembled at Kath's house. It was a momentous day for all of them. Unlike the others who had made this journey before them, they now knew what the project was about. They all knew either Robert, Niamh or Tom and had the nature of the project explained to them the day before in the Christchurch office. None of them had any idea of what to expect on the *Hela* but they were all committed and looked forward to building a new life away from Earth. The group did find it hard to grasp the reality of their situation; however, Robert's commanding style soon put them at ease. With skills from the oil industry, the military, the mechanical, electrical and construction industries, they represented the best in their fields and were eager to prove themselves.

Today, Tom was sending four of his security team up to the *Hela*. He needed the larger force in New Zealand to provide security to the Christchurch base personnel. They were a welcome addition to Alan's financial team who, by now, were generating millions. The matter of the "baches," the *Hela* crew on shore leave in the holiday homes, complicated his daily routine. It was imperative the purebreeds resting on Earth remained anonymous and undiscovered. As always it concerned Tom his teams may be spread too thin on the ground. He looked forward to the arrival of his next new crew in seven days. The four going to the *Hela* standing before him now, two male and two female, were his best. They were to fulfil a role specifically requested by Theia and Mack. The request had not surprised him and they were pleased when he informed them he already had that protection detail planned.

'You are her personal protection detail,' Tom said. 'Without her, the project will fail, it's that simple.'

'What do we protect her from on the ship?' John asked. He had worked with Tom for some years in the service and was surprised at this apparent babysitting detail.

'From herself to start with,' Tom explained. 'Question everything she does and where she goes, leave nothing to chance. We are starting to explore an alien ship that was laid up thousands of years ago in a dock in some distant galaxy. The aliens don't even know what's on it.' He had their attention now. 'The alien crew are afraid to go into these areas. That's why we are doing it. Not only will you be her protection detail, you will need to make sure the areas are clear of anything hostile before you enter. That's why I chose you. It's a mission you've never undertaken before.'

'Now I'm interested.'

'John, you're the team leader. Nothing happens until you're happy.'

'What's she like?'

'She's like you, John, intelligent, stubborn and the best in her field. Unlike you, they believe she has the ability to map space, something to do with interstellar navigation.'

'Are there any more like her on Earth?'

'We are looking, but so far nothing. That's why she is so important, if we lose her there is no one else we have found on Earth that can replace her. Theia and Mack personally requested she has her own protection detail.'

'That's a tall order, Tom but I won't let you down,' John said as they shook hands before he departed.

'I know you won't, John. Here's the shuttle now, good luck.'

Tom watched the shuttle leave. He thought about the task the departing crews would face. To gain access to the compartment with the leak, they would have to pass through hundreds of metres of darkened corridors. Despite his military background he shuddered as the thought of their task. John and his team were trained field medics; Tom hoped their skills would not be needed.

✗

Shona stood beside Robert just inside the entrance to the vast *Hela* forward cargo hold; she squinted, trying to see deeper into its darkness. 'It's huge.'

'Aye, Shona, it's near the size of four rugby pitches and eighty metres high. You can just make out the curvature of the ship, see over there,' he said pointing into the gloom. 'We're lucky there's air still here.'

'It's no too bad either, Robert, stale but it doesn't smell too bad.'

'Shona, you should have smelt the place when we arrived first. It was worse than those old platforms we worked on. Remember them?'

'I do, Robert, I do. It would be nice if we still had them around today to complain about. Who rigged these up?' she asked, pointing to a simple assembly of hoses, air movers and filters stuck together with grey tape.

'Those are Niamh's quick fix air purifiers. She set them up in the habitable parts of the ship when she came on board first.'

'What are you two jawing about?' interrupted Blair, another one of Robert's old crew, as he stepped into the cargo hold laden with equipment. 'Robert, you're just holding up the work. Where do ya want this stuff? It's a long way down from that shuttle, and it's no getting any lighter.'

'Aye, put it there beside that corridor, Blair.'

'Is that where we're going, Robert? Down that dark hole? There's no lights.'

'There might not be any air either,' Robert said as they gazed into the gloomy corridor that ran lengthways through the *Hela*. Interrupted by airlocks at its main junctions, it formed the *Hela* lower deck access artery, and traversed the full length of the ship.

The fifteen people, who were a mix from Robert's, Niamh's and Tom's teams, laid out the supplies for their impending journey of exploration into the bowels of the *Hela*. It was a journey that would end in the aft compartment where the fatal leak in the ship's hull was.

Blair set the last of the equipment down, sitting on one of the boxes he looked at Robert and Niamh. 'I cannae believe they came across the universe in this rust bucket. Have ya seen the engine room, it's a bloody mess. I'm surprised it still works.'

'That's the mid ship engine room, you were in, Blair,' explained Niamh, 'It's where the fusion reactor and the main grav drives are. The grav drives powered the ship for their journey from Anan. The purebreeds could control them from the bridge. They hardly went into the engine room. You're right, it's a mess,' she said as she took out some blueprints from a large folder. 'Did you know, Robert, there's another engine room in the aft section. It's beside the compartment where the leak is.'

'Another engine room. No. I didn't. Do you know what it is and how it works, Niamh?' Robert asked as he looked at the drawings she laid out.

'I don't. Apparently, some modifications were made to the ship. But whoever made them didn't update any of the records. We just don't know what's there.'

'What?' Robert asked, now leaning over the blueprints, 'they're supposed to be the source of intelligent life and this is what we have to work with? Niamh, you must have missed something, surely they know what's there?'

'No, Robert, they don't, I went through everything with Demard. And The Eight doesn't want to use his energy to survey the ship for us. Also, Mack told me there's supposed to be an armoury here,' she said pointing to an aft section on the plans, 'but he doesn't know what's in it either. He wants us to locate the access point as well.'

'I'm no impressed with them, Niamh. All that important information, how could it be missing? And now the job gets bigger, first it was locate and fix the leak. Now we're exploring half the bloody—.'

'Another fine mess ya got us into, Robert. "Come and work with loads of new technology on a cutting edge ship". That's what you said. We should have known better.'

'Dinnae be so negative, Blair, it's no as bad as the shite we had to put up with in Poland.'

'There was no flesh-eating monsters there.'

'There's none here either, Blair. The Overlord assured us of that.'

'Well, if he's so powerful why doesn't he come down his self and look?'

'He hasn't enough energy, Niamh told you that before. That's enough, Blair. Right, everyone, to business,' Robert said as he shook his head, exasperated by Blair's comments. Composing himself, he looked around at the team. 'Our priority is to get back aft to repair the leak. There's an armoury and an engine room we need to locate as well. Niamh wants to look into the other compartments with these,' he said, pointing to the four small drones sitting on the deck.

Niamh had redesigned some small earth camera drones, augmenting their lift capability by adding grav. Lifting one up, she explained how they would work; 'we only need to see into the compartments. We really don't know what's in them. Would you allow this ship to land on Earth without knowing what's on it?' she asked as they all shook their heads. 'No, I didn't think so. Also, I want to make sure there's nothing loose in the compartments. We don't want it to break up on entry either.'

'Don't get side tracked. Stick to the plan and, above all else, John and his team decide what areas are safe before we go in. There are no exceptions, are we clear?' asked Robert finishing their brief.

'Yes, Robert,' they replied.

'OK, we'll meet here tomorrow at seven. That's it for today. John, Niamh, a quick word before we go.' Feeling apprehensive about the task they were attempting, Robert was pleased with the arrival of the military team. He had discussed their need with Tom, and after meeting them, they had impressed him with their confidence.

'What is on your mind, Robert?' John asked.

'No human has ever done this before. We really don't know what's past the first airlock. Do we, Niamh?'

'No, Robert, but I'm pretty sure it's helium,' she said, explaining that it was used by the purebreeds who first put the ship in storage. Amongst its properties, as a noble gas, was its inability to react easily with other elements and materials. It was the ideal purge gas to preserve the unused areas of the ship.

'If it is, we have portable airlocks, breathing apparatus and protective clothing,' said John. 'Stop worrying, Robert, we'll manage this.'

'Aye, you're right. We'll start at it tomorrow.'

'Theia, how far can I project my mind with this?' Niamh said as she settled into another training session with Theia on the *Hela* Bridge. It was a long day, rigging up everything for their impending journey into the depths of the *Hela*. She looked forward to these sessions with Theia, they were enlightening and different to anything she had ever done before.

'It depends on each individual's ability. I can navigate across galaxies.'

'Could you map the ship and help us with our survey?'

'Yes and no. I did when we left Anan. The plans you downloaded from the computer were generated by me. But I cannot see what your drone cameras see with their lights. I cannot see to that detail in the darkness. With more powerful crystals, there are others who can do that. Watch what I mean,' she said as she put her crystal into the console and brought up a projection of the *Hela*. Niamh watched in amazement as Theia started to map out the corridors and compartments. However the darker they became all she could see was the outline of walls and equipment. 'You see I have limits. You may not. It depends on your ability and the power of the crystal.'

Niamh looked at her own blue diamond, turning it over in her hand. 'How powerful is the one you gave me?'

'It has the same power as mine. Niamh, you must remember this, the crystals are blue diamonds soaked in blue energy. The energy amplifies your mind, your thoughts and your feelings, but you must be careful with the power you use. The more powerful the energy, the more you can do, and it could change you. Do you understand that?'

Niamh paused in thought before she replied. 'No not really, how can I get more energy from this?' she said, holding up her blue diamond.

'You can't. Each crystal has its own limits. It will only do so much for you. But you will grow into it. It will take a while for you to learn how to use all its power. Think of it like a battery, the bigger the battery the more power you have. I use these,' she said, pointing to the two crystals, 'they are enough for what we want to do without changing us.'

'Jeez. How can they change us, Theia?'

'You ask so many questions. Enough. It's training time. I want to see the constellation you call Orion.'

Keen to get started, Niamh placed her crystal into the navigation console, and closing her eyes, she concentrated. Within seconds a projection of the constellation, glowing with the light of the stars, burst out above the navigation station. 'That's Rigel,' she said now with her eyes open, pointing at the brightest star.

'Good, Niamh, how do you feel now?'

'I'm fine, Theia, this looks great. Can I explore the constellation for a while?'

Theia smiled and sat down beside Niamh. 'Yes, of course you can,' she replied as she watched Niamh's curiosity drive her thoughts around the constellation. The projection swirled and changed as Niamh's mind visited the stars and their planetary systems. *She has made amazing progress*, Theia thought as she looked across at Niamh's smiling face engrossed in her celestial navigation.

THE HELA 19TH TO 24TH MARCH 2026

Robert and Niamh continued with the exploration on the lower deck of the *Hela*. Once they confirmed the presence of helium, they pushed on with the work using the portable airlocks and breathing apparatus. Due to the massive volume of helium, purging all the compartments with breathable air would have to wait until they landed the ship. Niamh's camera drones saved them days and days of work. They found they could quickly build up a picture of the ship without physically entering each compartment themselves. The drones did all the hard work.

'That's what Mack told us to look for,' Robert said. He and John were looking at the remote view screen for drone two.

'Is that the Aknar royal crest on that doorway?'

'I believe it is, laddie, I believe it is,' Robert said, his voice rising with enthusiasm. Finally they were making progress, he thought.

'How do we get access?'

'John, apparently we don't,' Robert said as he shook his head,' only a purebreed, from the house of Aknar can activate the locking mechanism.'

'So we get Mack down here and fit him up with breathing apparatus.'

'Not going to happen, Mack said we should just locate the access point. We can get into it on Earth once all the helium is purged.'

'Lads, I have an option that could give them access to their armoury and will make the rest of our work easier,' Niamh said, seated on a box of equipment beside the view screen. 'We're here,' she said, pointing to the ship plans. 'We've a hundred-metre corridor left to explore to get to the leak and the aft engine room and look, it's through another airlock, the last one on the central corridor.'

'OK, so what's your point?' John asked.

'The armoury entrance is two thirds of the way along the main corridor, on our side of the last airlock. We seal all the compartments explored, we found nothing and they all look empty. That leaves three hundred metres of corridor with helium from here to the armoury. I can purge that with a breathable atmosphere within two days. We can move our operations base to get us closer to where we need to be,' she said, now smiling at the two large men in front of her.

'Brilliant,' John said.

'Aye, well done, Niamh,' Robert said, as he nodded his head in agreement. 'I'll get the crews to set up the purge hoses from the shuttle landing bay.'

'I'll order more nitrogen and oxygen, two shuttle loads will be enough,' Niamh said.

'What about the helium?'

'I'm sure we can dilute it into the atmosphere, I'll have us all quacking like ducks,' she said, smiling at them both again.

'No, no, Niamh, the purebreeds won't see the funny side of that,' Robert replied, 'Niamh, you haven't thought this through, have you?'

'Robert, do you think I would do that? Really, I'm surprised at you,' she replied. 'I have a vacuum pump. As we displace the helium with breathable atmosphere we can vent it into space.'

Theia and Mack were not as receptive to the idea of relocating the operations base to the last airlock as Robert would have expected. They wanted to push on with the work.

'Why do you want to do that?' Theia asked.

'It gets us nearer to our objective; we have more usable air in our breathing apparatus when we get to the compartment where the leak is,' Robert replied. 'It simplifies the logistics and makes it easier to get materials up to repair the leak.'

It was a logical explanation. It actually made good sense to do it this way.

'OK, we agree to that.'

'Good, we stop here until after the purge,' he replied. 'You'll see, Theia, it will work easier this way.'

CHAPTER EIGHT

THE HELA 22ND MARCH 2026

Theia was getting nowhere with the Anan doctor on the *Hela*. 'I am not a geneticist, so why do you keep asking me those questions? I don't know. I didn't want to come on this mission,' were the constant negative replies given by the doctor. The long space flight aggravated the effects of the Anan sickness and those affected by it got progressively worse. With the increased pressure on her to treat them, the more belligerent the doctor became. Theia realised the doctor was right about her own skills, she was totally lost with the problems she faced. As she was the only one they could get for this mission, Theia suspected the medics on Anan were secretly glad she was gone. When the medical institution were asked for a geneticist for a secret mission that may have far reaching influences on discovering a cure, they insisted their current research could not be disrupted. They were adamant, and no amount of personal appeals from the House of Aknar would sway the close-minded institution. This was how the mission ended up with this miserable wretch, Doctor Rhea Lupe.

Realising she would not get the answers she needed, Theia trolled the Earth's databases for a suitable candidate. Anybody else who had a basic understanding of genetics would be better than her, thought Theia. Finally she found a candidate. He was a young Englishman working in Switzerland in a biotech firm on the new stem cell treatments that was taking Earth's medical industry by storm. As an accomplished geneticist he had completed some extensive research papers on the source of DNA for his doctoral thesis.

He had noticed some common traits across different and diverse populations and postulated that they may share common ancestry dating back some seventy thousand years. His thesis was based on a volcanic eruption catastrophe theory that significantly reduced Earth's population. *Amazing,* thought Theia, the first touching of humans left a fingerprint for someone who knew what to look for. It was all in his doctoral thesis and that led Theia to him.

Getting him to the *Hela* required a complex web of deception. There were emails inquiring about his thesis and the promise of vital additional information which would help him advance his theory. It was not deception, but the actual truth. He would get all the answers to his questions, thought Theia. With the help of Tom, he would arrive on the *Hela* tomorrow. Theia had one more challenge to overcome and was in the process of resolving it now.

The doctor's response to Theia's announcement to her, in her own med-bay, of the impending arrival of a human was scathing.

'What do you hope to achieve by bringing a primitive human geneticist here? He will have no understanding of our technology. I refuse to work with him. You have no right to do this to me, really, it is beyond reason,' she said to Theia.

Theia was now exasperated by this tedious negativity; with lightning speed she reached out with her right arm and clamped her hand around the long neck of the doctor. As her pendant glowed blue she squeezed the doctor's neck. Her eyes bored into those of the doctor, who finally buckled at the knees. Theia looked into her mind and could see the terror within. She tried to find any source of remorse or hope where she could spare the life of the doctor. It was a long time since she had killed one of her subjects, she hated the lingering feeling it left afterwards. Killing was something she abhorred. It would take her some time to get over it, but, if it was necessary, it was her role as Empress to commit this horrible deed. And then she heard it: the doctor was pleading now for her miserable life, the thoughts now coming from the depth of her terrified mind.

'No, Empress, no. Please have mercy. I will change, I will. You need me to show him how to work with our technology. I will do it. I will,' she pleaded, as tears spilled from her bulging eyes. Theia knew she was right, she still needed her.

'I will watch you. If you do not hold up your end of this bargain, I will kill you,' she replied, letting go of her grip on the doctor's neck as her pendant stopped glowing.

The doctor, now kneeling before Theia, felt the burn marks of the Empress's hand on her neck. It was known as the mark of the Empress and now everyone would know her shame. It would serve Theia well as the rest of the crew would pay more attention to their duties, she thought.

'You will be in the bridge at watch change, and I will address the crew,' Theia said as she left the med-bay. Things needed to change, she realised. The humans had been here for one week and she was amazed at the progress they achieved. Niamh had started with a small crew of five with the air feed system. Within two days, with things she called duct tape, carbon and hepa filters, items she had easily sourced in Christchurch, she had solved the air problem in the accommodation block and the shuttle landing bay. It was a problem the purebreeds had spent six months living with, and the humans had solved it in a week. It was one of the reasons The Eight had come to Earth. The humans would adapt easily to the New World. They would work hard and achieve much more than the purebreeds ever would.

There were other simple attributes the humans displayed that drew her attention to them. Before they started to live or work in a space they spent time cleaning it. At the end of a long shift Niamh, who was an executive member of the team, returned with the same dirty grime of the ship on her as her crew did. She worked side by side with them. When Janet first arrived, Theia was surprised to see her cleaning down the offices before she occupied them. Theia realised how lazy and unproductive she had let the crew become; if they were to survive they needed to step up to the mark.

At watch change, Theia ordered the crew to assemble in the bridge. Two humans working there were told politely to leave. It was an Anan gathering, it was explained. If the crew were surprised at the call, they were now shocked when the doctor entered. Her head drooped down on her long neck with shame; the mark of the Empress was quite clearly visible. The crew had heard about it, but never seen it before in their lifetime. They were horrified that this was done by their Empress.

Once they were assembled, Theia entered and stepped out in front of them. Mack stood to the side and watched silently as she addressed them in their own language. Her voice was deep and showed the anger she felt. It was something they had not heard before.

'It is time to change,' she said to the crew. 'Those of you who want to actively join me in trying to save our species must now step up and engage in our project. Some of you have excelled in this and given your dedication to us. However, the majority have adopted a lazy approach to this project and to what we need to do.'

There were gasps from the crew at the use of the word lazy. Those who were working hard like the pilot and the computer technician were secretly pleased with this. *Finally*, they thought, *we might have a chance.*

Theia continued in a commanding voice, 'If you don't want to change and engage you don't deserve to survive. Look at those who are sick amongst you. There are twenty-five per cent of all purebreeds struck down with this horrible sickness. Are you happy to let them die, are you so conceited that you don't think it is important to help? Those who don't change will be asked to leave and you all know the only way off this ship in space,' she said. Horrified, they all knew she was referring to the airlock.

That did it, thought Mack. Theia had surprised him with the violence of her reaction. He knew how much it hurt her to mark someone like that, but it worked. He would watch the crew closely. If they didn't change, he knew it would be he who would be showing them the way out.

Doctor Alex Barber arrived on the *Hela* the following day. Once he recovered from the surprise of where he was, he was led to the project offices by a purebreed. By chance he met Niamh, who was taking a break with her small crew.

'Did you just arrive?' she asked cheerfully in her lilting Cork accent.

He was surprised to see this Irishwoman and quite taken by her appearance. She was relaxing on a bench with her feet stretched across it and her back propped up against the wall. Her ship garment was pulled down to her waist revealing her lithe female torso covered by a slim T-shirt. To add to the mystique of her appearance, her face and hair were grimy from the work. He gazed at her in wonder as she sipped some unknown drink. She was not what he expected to see on a space ship.

'Yes, I did,' he replied.

'What do you do?' she asked.

'I'm a doctor. What do you do?' he asked.

'A doctor. I thought we had one already,' she replied. 'I'm just a mechanic.'

'Are there many of you here?' he asked. He wondered how many humans were on board.

'No, not nearly enough,' she said, looking at her small crew as they laughed. 'We're off, back to the dirt mine, see you later.' She smiled at him as they all left.

Shortly after meeting Niamh, the purebreed returned and led Alex to the med-bay, where Theia and the Anan doctor were waiting. Theia introduced herself, welcomed him to the *Hela*, and introduced Alex to Doctor Rhea Lupe, the Anan doctor who would be assisting him in his work. Alex made the unfortunate mistake of asking about the other humans he had met on the ship and the Irish girl.

'Doctor, you are here to begin one of the most important projects you have or will ever complete in your lifetime. I made that clear, did I not?'

'Yes,' Alex replied. He did not anticipate the feeling he got from Theia. It surprised him, he thought, it was pure anger.

'Focus all your energies on that. If you touch a hair on the head of the Irish girl you will regret it. She is equally important to our project and is not something you trifle with. Understand?' she asked, looking him straight in the eyes, leaving him with no doubt as to how serious she was.

'Yes, I do. I didn't mean any harm, I'm sorry if I caused offence. Please forgive the indiscretion,' he said, keen to apologise to his new benefactor. She was right, it was a mammoth task he was faced with and he found the whole thing fantastic. Whatever this powerful alien wanted, he would try to deliver.

Rhea, knowing the Empress's single-minded obsession with finding a cure, watched this with some level of understanding. Strange, she thought, she agreed with Theia's abrupt scolding of him, minutes after meeting him. Yes, his comments regarding the other human were inappropriate. From what limited knowledge she had of humans, she believed the males were driven by an insatiable desire to procreate. *Disgusting, how am I supposed to work with him?* she thought.

'Now, where do you propose to start?' Theia asked. 'What do you need?'

Alex looked at the med-bay with some alarm – he was shocked at its appearance. He was apprehensive as to how he could broach the situation with Theia but realised, before he even started work, his professional reputation was at stake.

'Empress, I must apologise, but really I can't work in this place as it is now. It needs—.'

'A deep clean, yes, I must apologise about that,' she said, smiling at him now and pleased with his forthright reply. 'It is some time since it was used. I can arrange some help from my crew.'

'Thank you, but there is no need for that,' Alex replied, gesturing to himself and Rhea, 'we will take care of it. I need some medical supplies, though; they are easily available in Christchurch.'

'If you give me a list, we can have them up in the shuttle first thing tomorrow.'

As the Empress left, Alex looked at Rhea, his Anan counterpart. He could sense her deep feeling of resentment towards him. She was radiating it and he was amazed at how easy it was for him to pick up on her feelings like that.

'I am surprised she asked me to come here. Your technology is far more advanced than ours,' he said, trying to break the ice with her.

'I am not a geneticist, just a normal doctor. You, on the other hand, are.'

He suddenly noticed some bad burns on her neck that were hidden by a scarf. 'What happened to your neck?' he asked, with real concern in his voice.

'It is nothing,' she said, as she tightened the scarf around it, wishing he had not seen the burn. It would take some time to heal and it would leave a lifelong mark.

At first, she found the menial cleaning task degrading, but his enthusiasm was infectious. As she saw the results of their labour and derived satisfaction from it, she began to enjoy working with him. Her days were now busy and filled with purpose. She showed him the facilities and machines they had and what they could do. The depth of his knowledge surprised her, and what he didn't know he quickly researched and made it his business to understand. Rhea was quite startled at how quickly he learnt to operate the Anan medical devices and provided she translated the data to English, he could easily understand it.

Theia supplied them with the video of the first touching the Overlord had shown to the project team. Alex suggested they study the video from the beginning to see if it revealed any clues as to what the old geneticist had done. They worked for three days, reviewing the video footage over and over again. He zoomed in on each sequence to try to reveal what the old geneticist was up to, explaining to Rhea that their first goal was to gain an understanding of the process he had used.

Rhea, while painstakingly reviewing a particular video sequence, realised something wasn't right. Finally, it hit her; there was a gap in the sequence. Something was missing. It was an important finding, she showed it to Alex and he called Theia.

'Empress, it was your doctor who made this important deduction,' he said, as he started to explain what they had found so far. Rhea was astonished by his unexpected disclosure. No purebreed would ever give credit to another for a discovery as important as this.

'Well done, Doctor,' Theia said, now smiling at her. 'I am glad our understanding bore fruit.'

'Look, here it is, there is a gap in the video recording,' Alex explained. 'You see the old geneticist adds that compound, there, from that flask. I believe it is the DNA splice he is preparing. Now look at the next scene, you can see he has the compound mixed in the delivery flask. It's sealed, ready to go. There is an important ingredient that we are not seeing,' he said with delight. He had now a fundamental understanding of what the old geneticist had done and it was confirmed by his original doctorate research.

Their news hit Theia hard. *A secret ingredient,* she thought. There was only one thing the old geneticist would want to keep a secret, and she would as well. *I will take that to my grave,* she thought. As The Eight suspected, she had discovered his secret. She never expected Alex would get so far so soon and wondered if he could develop a cure without knowing what the ingredient was. Alex had paused to allow her to ponder this dilemma. Speaking again now, he interrupted her thoughts.

'From the *Hela* database we know some of the compounds and the DNA source the old geneticist used. Knowing we have a missing ingredient at the final stage before delivery is a vital clue. Whatever was used is still out there in the human DNA,' Alex said, smiling at Theia.

'Good,' she said, surprised at his confident manner. 'Continue with your research. Do you think you could make a cure from what you know and have now?'

'I need blood samples from purebreeds and humans,' he said. 'I will gladly give mine but I need some diverse samples. I can ask the other humans. Once they know I am trying to build a cure for the purebreeds they will no doubt help. You will see.'

And he was right. The following day there was a queue of humans ready to donate blood. They were delighted at a chance to help develop a cure for the Anan sickness. When Theia and her crew saw this they were amazed at the affinity their sister species displayed towards them. The purebreeds quickly followed, donating their blood to help as well.

Alex had anticipated the need to take blood samples, and ordered sampling kits and a small sample fridge from Christchurch. It surprised Rhea that he used such a primitive method, but he was adamant.

'It's not that I don't trust your machines, but I prefer to do it the way I was trained and with methods that I can validate myself,' he explained to her, 'and the humans will be more receptive to this. It is what they understand.'

The progress would have delighted the old geneticist. Although he did not leave the formula for the cure in the *Hela* database he had left a trail that, if followed, would lead any focused geneticist to a cure.

CHAPTER NINE

CHRISTCHURCH 28TH MARCH 2026

Events today would prove decisive for the long term benefit of the three species; Overlord, purebreed and human. The New Zealand Prime Minister, true to his word, organised another discreet rendezvous at the same winery north of Christchurch where he had originally met with Mack. This time the gathering included the Australian and New Zealand Prime Ministers, accompanied by selected people from both their governments. The Empress, Mack and the Project Anan team, Robert, Tom and Niamh, represented The Eight. As the first official meeting of a "First Contact" on Earth between purebreed and human, it included the signing of treaties.

'You have done well to get this far so soon,' The Eight said.

'Thank you, Overlord, I wish you could come with us today,' Theia replied.

'I cannot, I am down to my last reserves of energy, and going to meet the Earth leaders is a waste of blue. I would achieve nothing more than what you can achieve today. Besides, you have the message I recorded.'

'I accept what you say, but disagree with you. Your presence would overwhelm them,' she said.

'Perhaps, but today should not be about overwhelming them. I believe you need to gain their trust.'

'Overlord, your energy. I know I shouldn't ask you this, but as the Protector, I need to know how you are?' Mack asked, looking at his Overlord's dwindling energy mass.

'Always you worry. Yes, I am using my last reserves, but you know my concept of time is different to yours. The improvements the humans have made to the *Hela* have reduced the ship's draw on my energy. I can last quite some time like this. After today, you can make plans to visit our re-supply base in New Zealand. Pass on my salutations to the two leaders you will meet today. I look forward to this alliance.'

'Why are you driving, why didn't we go in the SUV with the team?' Niamh asked.

'I have an early flight on Sunday,' Tom replied. It wasn't quite true as the flight was at midday.

'You're lying,' she said, looking at him intently.

Tom hadn't expected her intensive questions when he planned this trip together to the winery. 'I'm not, I have a flight on Sunday, it's to get your parts from France,' he said as they both got into the car.

'But that's not why you rented the car.'

'All right, I wanted some quiet time with you, some privacy.'

'Why?'

'I want to talk to you…'

'About what? You trying it on with me?'

'No, it's not that.'

She looked out of the window, staring at the grey walls of the hotel car park. She had come down on the shuttle late last night looking forward to this break, away from the confines of the *Hela*. She had hoped for some distraction from her punishing workload, and, although she hadn't spent much time with Tom, she looked forward to seeing him again. 'Jeez, Tom, that's blunt. So you don't find me attractive. That's handy to know.'

'No, I mean yes. Yes I do. Niamh, you look really good today,' he said as he admired her pouting beside him. 'You scrub up well, farm girl,' he said grinning at her.

'Ya don't look so bad either, soldier boy,' she said as she turned to look at him. 'I suppose you have a girl in every port.'

'No, Niamh, I don't. It was never like that.'

'What? Your secret agent jobs?'

'Yeah, I never put down roots and always stayed under the radar. Female company was a complication. There was some, but nothing like you see in the movies,' he said as he drove the car out of the car park. 'What about you? How come you have no one?'

'Career, Tom, I put my heart and soul into it. No time for idle dalliances, that sort of thing. Yeah, like you there were some, but nothing lasted, and then well you know, family's gone and the world went mad.'

'It doesn't go away, does it?'

'The loneliness, no, it doesn't, not having anyone to talk to, just to run things by them, you know the job, life in general, that's hard. I miss my big brother the most, he was my sounding board. And you?'

'My dad, he was the rock of the family, he was in the same regiment as me. He understood how things were when I came home. Never asked anything but was always there for me.' They sat in silence for a short time as he drove out of the Central Business District. 'I got you something. It's in the glove compartment.'

'Jeez, what's this?' she said as she opened the box and looked inside.

'Blue pearls. Do they remind you of anything?'

'Wow, they're the same colour as The Eight's energy mass. Where do they come from, Tom? I've never seen anything like them before,' she said as she put the blue and gold earrings on.

'They're grown here in New Zealand,' he said, smiling, as she kept admiring and touching them while looking in the mirror.

'I like that,' she said, leaning over to kiss him on the cheek. 'Nobody has ever got me anything so beautiful, thank you.'

His heart skipped a beat with her closeness and her sweet smell. 'Really? Well, you're welcome,' he said, getting embarrassed as his face flushed red.

'I'm not ungrateful, and I do love the earrings, but later on I want something else.'

'Oh, and what's that?' he asked, worried at what was coming next.

'You promise you won't laugh?'

'No, I won't,' he replied, really worried now as to how this was going.

'I want my own spaceship, like the *Hela*.'

'Ha, ha, ha.' The more he laughed the more she scowled, and like a little boy it made him worse. Eventually he finally managed to stop.

'You said you wouldn't laugh, you're a real maggot, Thomas Parker, a horrible man, you are, and I thought you might be different.'

'I'm sorry, but it was the surprise. You know, girl, that's the best idea you've ever come up with,' he said with real enthusiasm in his voice. 'It's brilliant. Will they ever let you have one, I wonder?'

'Yeah, I'm not sure how that would go, but actually getting my hands on one would be easy. Demard showed me a list on his computer from a place that has scrap ships and parts for sale. They will even pay you to take some of the stuff away, you know, for recycling.'

'You mean like a "buy and trade" in space?' he asked, and they both laughed at the thought of an intergalactic "buy and trade". As they drove north she poured out her thoughts and aspirations. She was like a fountain of information and he listened to her, truly amazed at her level of understanding of the alien technology. *Yes,* he thought, *this was a good idea to travel on our own*. Her idea was a real way forward. With both of their skills working together they could make it happen. He remembered some of the clauses in their employment contracts with Anan Corporation.

"The first two thousand five hundred colonists will have property rights on the new planet and will be regarded as the founders of a new civilization. The colonists may form their own trading houses and become prosperous in their own right as they earn or amass their own personal resources."

"The Project, Engineering and Security Managers, as shareholders in Anan Corporation, are entitled to-" and so it went on in legalese. There was also the mention of options to purchase more shares in the corporation, and he remembered Alan had included Tom's own company, now the Anan offices and warehouses in Sydney, within the Anan Corporation holdings for a share swap. He had not paid much attention to the contract, but after what Niamh suggested, Tom realised they were shareholders as well with access to huge resources on Earth. He would serve the Overlord and the purebreeds well, now fully realising what the future may hold for the both of them.

Kath was determined to keep it a very informal meeting and, once the government delegation arrived, she made quick introductions. To break the ice, and to dispel any thoughts of a hoax, Mack suggested Niamh show them around the cloaked shuttle, parked on the lawn of the winery. It worked. The delegation were totally mesmerised by the oval shaped shimmering shuttle.

When the beautiful woman in the elegant, figure-hugging, light blue dress started to explain how the ship worked, you could hear a pin drop.

They are paying more attention to her elegant curves and shapes as she bends over and points to the spaceship, thought Tom jealously. He gave dagger looks to the Australian science minister, a physics professor, who was drooling at the mouth while she enchanted him. Tom finally restrained her from climbing into the oily engine room cavity in her beautiful clothes to demonstrate its workings. Abruptly ending the show, he suggested they get down to business.

Kath led the group to two large circular picnic tables in a secluded sunny part of the garden. They didn't notice a grumpy Niamh walking behind them, quietly berating Tom for interrupting her moment of technical rapture.

'It's truly a pleasure to be here with you all,' said Theia, as they all sat informally at the tables. 'Harold, thank you for organising this.' She nodded in appreciation to the New Zealand PM seated across the table from her with Kath by his side.

'You're welcome, Empress. Where do you suggest we begin?' he asked, getting down to business.

'First, I have a message from our Overlord, The Eight, which you need to see,' she said. Mack placed his holographic projector on the table and started to play the short message The Eight had recorded earlier for them.

They were captivated by the technology used in its presentation, The Eight's explanation of the origins of intelligent life on Earth and, finally, his own personal message. 'Prime Ministers, you are both good men, true to your beliefs and the peaceful co-existence with others of your species. I look forward to working with you.' After its dramatic conclusion, Theia waited a moment for its content to be absorbed.

'Now, the Overlords prohibit the transfer of Anan technology to other species without their approval. However, Niamh has something which is Earth-developed that may interest you. Niamh,' said Theia, turning to her, 'sit here and take over, please.' The others looked on, wondering what was coming next as Niamh sat down beside Theia. She was holding a large white bulging folder and a small data drive.

'I know you plan to build a fusion reactor,' she started to explain, nervously looking at the Australian PM. 'I have developed a design that will work with Earth-based technology. I worked on the European fusion project, and, based on their failures I made my own unique changes to the design.' She passed the folder and data drive across the table to the Australians.

'Does it only use Earth technology?' asked the Australian science minister, Charles.

'I fine-tuned the design based on the reactor on the *Hela* which is slightly different. It uses a substance called grav for the containment, which you don't have access to on Earth. But, as you well know, fusion energy recovery is based on how efficient the containment is. You will see from the calculations in the work pack, with an Earth containment system, it will prove to be a lean machine with an ample power yield—.' She stopped as Theia placed her hand gently on her shoulder. Niamh had worked on the design pack during the evenings with Demard on the *Hela*. It was part of an overall redesign of the *Hela*'s reactor they planned for the future.

'Thank you, Niamh,' Theia said, looking at the Australian PM. 'George, if Earth is to survive climate change you have to halt the reliance on fossil fuel, and this will help. It will work, you can check the design calculations yourselves.'

'What about fuel?' asked Charles, now leafing through the folder. 'Your reactor uses Helium-3, yes? We don't have that on Earth, you know that – the Chinese just started mining it on the Moon.' He was disappointed now with her offering.

'We will provide you with enough fuel for four of these reactors for ten years,' said Theia, smiling at them. 'It is approved by The Eight, and will allow you to get started. In the future we can help you with harvesting your own Helium-3 or barter or trade it. Let us say initially it is as rent for access to our own base in your desert and noted in the Treaty.' She looked at George and waited for his reaction.

'Well,' said George, 'you guys are full of surprises. I'm sorry, Empress, but it's a lot to take in.'

'Yes, it is,' Theia said, nodding her head in agreement.

'So, let us say I accepted this, the plans for a working fusion reactor and a fuel deal which will save the Australian tax payer billions of dollars… What does Harold get out of this? I mean, we have twenty-five million people, making fusion a cost effective solution, but Harold, you have only five million, fusion isn't so cost effective for you, is it?' asked George, looking at the New Zealand delegation.

'We get an exclusive trade agreement with the purebreds, Anan Corp and the New Colony,' said Harold, in a matter-of-fact deadpan voice.

'Ah hell,' shouted George. 'You set me up, Harold, an exclusive trade agreement with the biggest players in the universe? When were you going to tell me about that? And to think I was concerned about what you were getting.' He pointed his finger at Harold. The New Zealand delegation were trying hard not to laugh at his outburst while Theia and Mack were completely surprised at this unfolding political rivalry.

'Calm down, George, it's not like that,' said Harold, trying to maintain some sense of diplomacy. Then to the complete surprise of Theia and Mack and their project team, George and Harold burst out laughing. Their relaxed and easy manner infected the others sitting with them, including Theia and Mack. But it didn't continue for long.

'You know, Empress, if that was our biggest problem, we would live happily ever after,' said George, looking at her and speaking with real concern in his voice.

'Yes,' agreed Harold. 'Mack and I touched on this, but go on, George, this is better coming from you.' Theia and Mack realised what was coming next. It was the sad reality of what their arrival had stirred.

'It's the Dragon and the Bear in the north,' said George. 'It's early spring there so the Bear still hibernates, it's always one step behind the Dragon, who is alive and, as you experienced, kicking our door down. Your presence in New Zealand has aggravated the Dragon. When the news of who you are leaks out, as it surely will, the Bear will join the Dragon in a battle for your technology. I believe the presence of your bases in the southern hemisphere will draw both our nations into a war with China and Russia. They will not rest and will not accept a superior force on this Earth. No, they will not. I fear our days are numbered. Admiral, please continue,' requested George, moving aside for the Admiral to sit beside him.

'Empress, General, I am Admiral Cyril White, the Commander of the Combined Forces of Australia, New Zealand and what is left of the United Kingdom. Unfortunately, since your arrival we have seen an increase in activity by the People's Republic of China armed forces and their spy network. I know, General, this is not news to you. But it is of grave concern to us. There is a mobilisation of forces in the South East Asian Theatre directed towards us and we see an increase in their satellite launch sequence. Our intelligence sources hint that they are chasing a ghost signature in space.' He had Mack and Theia's attention now as they sat up in surprise. 'It was news that we discounted and actually laughed at. I put it down to their paranoia. But, as we recently learned, it is your ship, the *Hela,* that emits that ghost signature.' He paused, and the shock and silence around the table was agonising. 'Empress, General, if they come for you, and I believe they surely will, we do not have the power or the forces to help you. Since the Wave event, we are largely on our own. We can call on our good Canadian neighbours, but what help they give is limited. Europe, well, Europe is being European. The United States, a closed state within a fortress, is out of the picture. I have little contact with their military command and cannot count on their help. I'm sorry, but unless you have your own weapons, it's a grim picture,' he finished quietly.

'Admiral, thank you for your candour. I don't have extinction weapons. It is something we are not allowed to have by our Overlords. I never expected you to protect us, never. But we do have some items on the *Hela* that we use to defend ourselves,' said Mack.

Robert looked up at Mack. He was now very interested in what Mack would say next and how this would play out.

'Our main protective element is our Overlord. You have no idea of the force he can wield. We rely on him for our protection,' said Mack, looking directly at the Admiral, and omitting the current weakness of the Overlord from the conversation. It was the leak on the *Hela* that was causing the ghost signature, realised Mack, as he added access to the armoury as one more item to his list of priorities.

The leak was always a priority and, since he talked to the Overlord this morning, access to the New Zealand re-supply base was a looming necessity. He couldn't contemplate the result if the re-supply base was empty of blue. To complicate matters, Tom was to depart for Europe in the morning to complete their "purchase". Mack realised disaster would strike their project if he dropped one of the growing number of balls circling ever faster above his head.

He smiled to them all and continued, 'I understand all of your concerns. We did not come back to Earth to start a war and I accept, as a consequence, that may happen. But remember our Overlord, The Eight, will be fighting in your corner. He has formidable power. Any species using nuclear weapons will incur his wrath.' That was the truth. He had seen what the Overlord was capable of.

'Ladies, gentlemen, I suggest we take a break. Lunch is laid out in the marquee behind us,' said Kath, hearing the rattle of plates coming from the tent behind them. Following the gloomy discussion the group quickly welcomed her suggestion.

Before they settled down to eat, Tom went straight up to Admiral White, saluting him smartly.

'Thomas Parker, good to see you again. I was sorry to hear you left us,' the Admiral said, smiling at Tom.

'Yes, sir, good to see you and congratulations on your promotion. Had it happened earlier I wouldn't have jumped ship so easily.'

'Well, you have. You are an asset to your new masters. And I am glad we are still on the same side,' the Admiral said with mirth in his voice.

'Thank you, sir.'

'Parker, that intelligent woman who showed us the ship, she must be quite unique on Earth.'

'Yes, sir, she is and our project depends on her abilities.'

'You know the Chinese will learn of her and Chang will come for her. I am sorry to tell you, they will not rest until they have her.'

'Yes, sir, I realised that. She has her own protection detail, our best.'

'Yes, I noticed you didn't leave the services on your own,' said the Admiral, who had recognised some of Tom's security team as they smartly saluted their previous boss. 'And, Parker, don't leave it too long, marry her.' He smiled at Tom.

'Is it that obvious, sir?'

'Yes, Parker, it is, you never leave her side. The world has changed; we have all lost so much. When an opportunity like that comes along, seize it,' he said, making a forceful grabbing motion with his hand.

'Yes sir,' was all Tom could say. He knew that, like most others who survived the Wave, the Admiral had lost all his family.

'Does Chang know you're still alive?' the Admiral asked, returning to business.

'I'm not sure. Our paths have crossed and will again. If he doesn't, he soon will,' Tom replied as they entered the marquee. Sitting together over lunch they reminisced over the days gone by and how much the world had changed. The Admiral's words had left Tom with an uneasy feeling in his gut. There was only so much he could do and Chang was resourceful. He was definitely coming. He smiled across at Niamh, seated at another table having lunch with the Australian PM and his wife. His heart skipped a beat as their eyes met and she returned a cheeky smile and a wave to him. He wouldn't lose her, he couldn't, he knew he would give his life to protect her, not for the project but because he was falling in love with her.

After the revelations of the morning discussions Robert found the rest of the day boring. The treaties were signed between the House of Aknar, representing The Eight, and the Australian and New Zealand Prime Ministers.

'Finally we should get access to the two bases,' Robert said as he sat with Tom and Niamh.

'Have you talked to The Eight lately?' Tom asked.

'I see him occasionally,' Niamh replied.

'And?' he prompted.

'And what?' she said.

'The elephant in the room, his energy mass, unless they have magical weapons in that armoury, he's all there is to protect us.'

'Tom, you're getting paranoid about this, they're nae coming tomorrow,' Robert said.

'Believe me when I tell you both, Chang Jin is unstoppable. He is a monster. Niamh, when he learns how important you are he will not rest until he gets you,' Tom said and paused to let his message sink in.

Listening to his chilling voice, Niamh shuddered. The fear was etched in his face and his foreboding news turned her stomach, so soon after the delight of their journey together.

'War is coming and our employers are the catalyst,' Tom said as he reached out and took Niamh's hand. 'Niamh, you need to stay on the ship. Don't come down to Earth without checking with me. Robert,' he said now looking at the big Scotsman, 'they have weapons that can hit the *Hela* in space—.'

'Jeez, Tom, you're full of doom and gloom,' she said squeezing his hand in fright at what he had just revealed.

'It's OK, Niamh, I don't believe they'll use them. They'll want the technology first. But, Robert, you need to seal that leak.'

'Aye, you're right, Tom. I dare say our masters will be flapping now their great golden beast is hanging out in space in the scuddy.'

Niamh looked at him and before she could ask, Tom translated, 'naked, Niamh, that's what he means. It's not as bad as that, Robert, the cloak is still working.'

'Aye, Tom, you're right. We need to fix it, and then get on with trying to get him his blue. I dare say our master will prime us for that job next,' he said as Niamh and Tom nodded in agreement. The three managers of Project Anan continued with their dour discussion. They had hoped for an enjoyable weekend, but now, the foreboding news dampened their spirits.

CHAPTER TEN

LYON FRANCE 30TH MARCH 2026

The small man pored over his computer. 'Philippe, did you see that email?' Maurice asked. 'It was sent late Friday evening. We must have the equipment ready for dispatch this Thursday.' First thing on a Monday morning, this intrusive email had discommoded his leisurely return to work in the warehouse after such a restful weekend.

His boss, sitting at his desk with his feet up sipping coffee, looked across at him. 'No, Maurice, not yet.'

'Who do they think they are, giving orders like that?'

'Who is it from?' Philippe asked.

'Jean Claude, the project director. He wants all the surplus equipment ready for collection this Thursday. This Thursday, is he mad? I can't do it, it's too much, too much.'

'Calm yourself, Maurice, let me see what it says.'

'It's not good enough, Philippe; they give these orders without thinking about me. Yes, nobody thinks about me. Equipment is ordered and not used, it goes out, it comes back and they ask for things they don't order. It's terrible, terrible, I tell you.'

'Now, Maurice, yes, I am reading it and look they are sending in a private contractor to do the work for you.'

'No, they wouldn't do that.'

'Yes, read your email, they are to arrive this morning at eleven o'clock.'

'Typical, nobody tells me anything. It's a disgrace. Well, don't expect me to do the work.'

'No, you don't have to. All you have to do is show them where it is and they do the rest.'

Philippe was not surprised they were to get rid of the surplus equipment. Maurice was right; the warehouse was so full of it, they could hardly move and it just wasn't used. The director must have listened to his complaints, finally, thought Philippe, although he wondered why he had not told him about this earlier.

'Well, that's OK then. It will be good to get rid of that crap. I can't move with it, all they do is order and order and then they don't use anything,' continued Maurice in his complaining monotone voice. But Philippe, engrossed in the review of the long list of equipment to be dispatched, had stopped listening. Sometime later he was aware Maurice was back in the office.

'Philippe, do you think I should go for my coffee break before the contractors come, or wait until they arrive, they might want a break as well?'

'No, Maurice, I think you should go before. If you remember the last time you waited the extra hour, you complained about the texture of the pastries. I believe they were not fresh enough for your palate.'

'Ah yes, I remember, I shall go now,' he said, grateful for the help with this major decision.

Relieved that Maurice was now gone, Philippe continued to prepare the dispatch list for the arrival of the contractors. Very quickly he noticed the equipment was bought and paid for by a Singapore company, Purchase Investments Pte Ltd. They owned it all. No doubt the contractors, when they arrived, would have a list of what was purchased. However, it would be remiss of him not to check what equipment they owned and where it was. He had an inkling that it was not all in the warehouse where it should be.

'You tired, boss?' Bill asked.

'No, slept all the way, business class was great. Gained a day as well,' Tom said.

'We'll be on site for eleven; the others will be waiting just outside for us.'

'You did good to get all that planned in so short a time.'

'It's the money, boss. You know that. When you don't have to ask how much, they fall over backwards to oblige.'

Tom was looking forward to this. Finally, back out in the field with his team away from the office, the security details and meeting Prime Ministers. Demard's work, with the help of two of Kath's office staff, was incredible. He had embedded an illusion within the reactor project that the sale and dispatch of the surplus equipment was a "Team Initiative". Creating a fictitious email account and identity for himself as the team administrator called "Julie" he could easily manage the process. As "a buyer" was available to take everything at the original purchase price of the equipment, the initiative would be cost neutral to the reactor project and generated over eight hundred million euros.

Under Niamh's direction, Demard had marked the emails with a boring header: "Team initiative to maximise efficiencies in procurement and stock control". Nobody read the long emails, the meeting minutes and forms he carefully crafted. As with most large projects, it was suffering from email overload. Where he needed a digital reply or approval, he simply accessed the person's email and sent it on himself.

Tom smiled as he thought through the careful timing and planning of their illusion. However, before they could leave with the equipment, there was one final signature he needed and, to add to its complexity, the project director and his immediate superior could stop the operation with a well-timed call or email.

'We're here,' Bill said, disturbing his thoughts as they pulled up outside the site. 'There's the rest of the team.'

It was a mix of Tom's security team, and six others from a local, heavy lift moving contractor. Tom, introduced as the client's representative, shook hands with the team and after a quick brief they set off for the site security gate, arriving at exactly eleven o'clock.

'Philippe, it's Louis here at the gate. I have your contractors here. Yes, I'll direct them down to you.'

So far so good, Tom thought, as they drove along the road to the warehouse. He could see the car parks for those working on the site stretching out on each side of the road. Niamh had told him there were nearly eighteen hundred workers left on site. *Perfect*, he thought as he looked at the cars, one way in and out, it would serve their purpose well.

'Philippe, good to meet you,' Tom said as he shook his hand. 'I'm Thomas Parker, the Purchase Investments representative.'

'We were surprised at how quickly this happened,' he replied. 'We were not notified about this until today. I'm not sure we will have everything ready for Thursday.'

Expecting this reaction to their sudden appearance, Tom smiled. 'I must apologise about that, but we were dealing with others on the project, you know how this goes sometimes. May I have a quiet word?' he said, gently directing Philippe aside.

'Yes, yes,' he answered as he watched Tom reach into his jacket pocket.

'I must apologise again, Philippe. Perhaps this small token of our appreciation will alleviate the disturbance we will cause,' he said while handing Philippe a thick white envelope, 'but we must meet the Thursday deadline. I'm sure you understand.'

Feeling the crisp notes inside the envelope, Philippe smiled, 'yes, yes, I do and we will do everything we can to help.' *Unless it's all in five euro notes, which would be an insult, it should be nearly three thousand*, he estimated, as he discreetly put it in his pocket. He was wrong with the estimate, he found out to his joy that evening when he counted it out. It was five thousand euros. 'One thing you should know… I started to prepare the dispatch list this morning when I received the email,' he said, now ready for business. 'I don't think all of the equipment you own is in the warehouse, I believe some is on the reactor site.'

Tom frowned. 'Can we check that out?'

'Yes, I will know later today.'

Tom nodded thoughtfully. Niamh was right, with the proper incentive Philippe would prove his worth to them.

At half past three in the afternoon Philippe gave Tom the bad news. 'It is as I suspected, the six cryo pumps are at the reactor site. It was Maurice, he—.'

'Can we go down to get them?' Tom said with an innocent smile. He knew this was going to be a problem.

'No, I will need permission from the director first. I can call him now if you wish?'

'No, don't bother him. We can tackle that in the morning,' Tom said. The last thing he needed was to inform the director they were here. He needed to talk to Niamh. Back in their control vehicle he put the call in up to the *Hela*. As it kept Kiwi time, it would be an early morning call for her. Eventually, Niamh looked back at him on the view screen. 'Thanks for the wake-up call, you horrible man,' she said, as she rubbed the sleep from her eyes and yawned.

'Sorry to wake you. Before I go any further, do you absolutely need the cryo pumps?'

'Yes, absolutely, and all six. What's up with them?'

'They're down at the reactor site.'

'Don't tell me, it was Maurice?'

'Yes.'

'Ah, the indispensable Maurice, the director's nephew,' she said, as the sarcasm seeped into her voice.

'Nepotism is still flourishing after the Wave,' Tom said, smiling at her. 'How do I get them back to the warehouse without asking the director?'

'I could do that. I still have access and, according to the records, I am still employed there. I've been off site for just over a month, so my badge will work. On the project hierarchy, I still own the system and the parts.'

'Where's your swipe badge?'

'Believe it or not, with my work gear on the *Hela*,' she smiled. As an alternative to the ship garb she had taken her work clothes with her, and generally wore them in the *Hela* accommodation. The reactor project swipe badge was jumbled in the bottom of her kit bag with the other souvenirs of her working career. 'But I'm not sure I can get down to you. I believe the Pilot doesn't fly his shuttle in the northern hemisphere.'

'I can guess why.'

'Yep, air traffic.'

'OK, you wake up Mack and Theia and discuss it with them. Meantime, I'll get a night moving crew ready with a crane, forklift, flatbed truck and a low-loader. Will that do?'

'Yep, that'll do it. I'll send an access approval email for your moving team to the security gate. What's the low-loader for?'

'To land the shuttle on. We can cover it with a tarp,' he said, smiling at Niamh as she grinned at his plan.

'Air traffic is much denser over that section of the northern hemisphere,' said the Pilot, pointing to a map of the air routes over Europe on the *Hela* bridge's big view screen. 'It's far greater than what I deal with in the southern hemisphere. Even when we fly to Australia the density will be nothing like Europe. Also, I can't see stealth fighters on military manoeuvres. I'm just not happy about flying with the limited navigation systems I have. We can't use an earth system either, the outgoing signals will be detected,' he said, looking at Theia and Mack.

*Time is moving o*n, thought Niamh. One hour had passed since Tom had called her and if they wanted to do this, she had a three hour window to get down to the site. Starting after eight in the evening would hamper their chances of completing the work by the morning, before the day shift crews arrived and discovered them. Dressed in her reactor project work gear, loose orange overalls with a fluorescent green jacket, she was sitting silently on the *Hela* bridge with Theia, Mack, the *Hela* captain and the Pilot.

'I do not want to compromise the integrity of the holding company, or disrupt Tom's illusion by coercing the director into doing our bidding by force,' Mack said. 'We have eight hundred million euros invested in this. And Niamh, we need the parts, yes?'

'Yes, we do.'

'Pilot, I can launch a small satellite to help you with the navigation. From the *Hela* bridge, with the data from the satellite, we can plot and monitor the flight plans over Europe. Niamh, how are your abilities coming? Empress, what do you think, is she ready?'

'Yes. Niamh, you have made progress. It is a good opportunity to test your navigation abilities before we land the *Hela*,' Theia said.

'What do I do?'

'You will be able to see any other aircraft in your flight envelope.'

'But the military stealth planes, they travel faster than sound, will I see them in time?'

'Yes, you will. The last time we trained, how far into space did you see?'

'The Southern Cross,' she said, as she nodded her head in understanding and smiled back at Theia. 'I get it. Yes, I need to test this before we land the *Hela*. I'm up for it.'

'I guess that's Cork language for I can do it,' said the Pilot, grinning at Niamh.

'Yes, it is. Are you happy with this?' she asked him.

'Yes. With the satellite, the bridge team monitoring the fight plans and your help, we can make it down to Lyon.'

Niamh looked at her watch; *we're running out of time*, she thought. One and a half hours after the meeting on the bridge, their shuttle was in position two hundred and fifty kilometres above Lyon in the thermosphere, still waiting for decent clearance and a flight plan from the *Hela* bridge.

'Time is not an issue,' said the Pilot, interrupting her thoughts. He had noticed her preoccupation with the watch and guessed she was worried they would arrive too late to complete her task before the morning. 'The *Hela* bridge is waiting until after the evening commuter flight rush. Less air traffic after nine o'clock.'

'We may not get the work done tonight.'

'We can stay over. I might get lucky and score with a French woman. I hear they are hot.'

'Pilot, will ya behave yourself, please? And before we start down, how is this going to work?'

'You have your blue diamond in the navigation port, now touch it. Yes, like that.'

'Now what?' she asked, looking at the Pilot as nothing had happened.

'Close your eyes and concentrate on your crystal, just like you did on the *Hela* bridge with the Empress.'

As she concentrated, her mind suddenly opened, revealing the blackness of space beyond. As she focused, the blue diamond projected the picture of space above the console in front of them. The more she concentrated, the more she was able to see out into space in whatever direction she chose.

'Wow, that's awesome, nothing like the training sessions with Theia,' she said quietly, overawed at what she could do.

'We're in business. Can you show me a cone shape of what's below us, please?' the Pilot asked in a soft voice. He knew if she was upset or disturbed in any way, she could lose the projection. He wondered if Theia had warned her how demanding this would be. He doubted if she would get any work done on Earth tonight. 'Yes, that's it. Please don't talk unless you have to,' he said, in the same soft voice he had used previously.

The flight plan shortly arrived on his console and the Pilot started his descent towards Lyon.

'There are three objects approaching from the west. They're coming up fast, look there,' she said, pointing at her projection.

'Yes, I see them. They're not on the *Hela* flight plan. Military stealth planes, I guess. I'll hold until they pass below us.' Her abilities surprised him, she was good, he thought as he looked across at her. He had never seen such talent in a new navigator before. *A change is coming*, he briefly thought, as he flew down to Lyon with Niamh's help.

Tom and Bill heard the faint hum of the engine first and then watched the low-loader settle down under the shuttle's weight as it landed. It was parked beside their control vehicle, in a small disused car park that had served as a holding area for site vehicles during the busy construction period. Outside the site and secluded by trees, it was an ideal location for them to use as a temporary base. The main shuttle access door opened, but no one appeared.

'Where are they?' Tom asked, after they waited for about a minute.

'Earthlings, can you please come and help me?' they heard the Pilot shouting from inside the shuttle.

Quickly climbing into the shuttle and up to the cockpit, Tom was not prepared for the sight that greeted him. Niamh was slumped unconscious over the control console with her hands spread out in front of her as one hand clutched her blue diamond with the Pilot gently trying to revive her.

'What the hell happened?' Tom asked.

'Mental exhaustion from her first spatial navigation. You can lift her out of the shuttle. I will get something that will bring her round.'

Without another word Tom and Bill carried Niamh out from the shuttle and into their control vehicle, where they laid her down on a small bed in its rear. The Pilot, carrying a small flask, quickly followed.

'This will help her recover,' he said.

Tom looked at the flask. 'What are you giving her?'

'It's a magical alien potion that will transform her into a—.'

'Be serious, Pilot, for a minute please be serious? What's that stuff?'

'Sugars and salts, that's all it is, Tom. We have the same metabolism as humans.'

'Look, boss, she's fine, she's starting to come round now,' Bill said.

'Tom, will ya stop fussing. I'm fine, I'm fine, ya big eejit,' said Niamh, in a weak and groggy voice. 'Will that stuff help? Give it here.' She sat up on the bed and took the small flask. Between gulps of the sweet tasting drink she looked at Tom. 'Don't worry — you're not going to get rid of me that easy.'

He watched as the colour started to return to her face. 'Pilot, it seems I owe you an apology.'

'No, Tom, you don't. I am not the easiest to get on with. But know this, you can trust me. Whatever happens between our species I will be truthful in my dealings with you. Now to more important matters, did you bring what I asked?' he said as he looked around.

'Yes, I did, there's some inside the door of the shuttle, and—.'

'What time is it?' Niamh asked in a much stronger voice, now feeling the kick from the energy drink.

'Twenty-two forty,' Bill said. 'If you're up for it, we can have you on site within an hour with the rest of the crew.'

'Yeah, I'm up for it.'

Handing the Pilot a mysterious bag, Tom smiled at her and said, 'Come on, girl; let's go get your pumps.'

Julie, the night security guard, was expecting them and smiled when she recognised Niamh. 'Niamh, haven't seen you for a while. You look great, you been working out?'

'Ah you know, I was away for a couple of weeks, a holiday,' Niamh evasively replied as she signed in Tom and their crew at the security gate.

It took over two hours to find the six pumps. Niamh started at the loading dock of the ground floor of the reactor building, where she expected the pumps to be. However, they were nowhere to be found inside the building.

At two-thirty in the morning, having moved the search to outside, the moving crew supervisor, tuned in to the hapless idiosyncrasies of the construction world, found the pumps in the waste compound. Their location, and the disorganised heap in which they were left, shocked Niamh.

'Are they OK?' Tom asked.

She was on her knees looking for any signs of damage, and finally she replied, 'The packaging looks unbroken. They should be fine. Do you know I ordered those six pumps especially? They're one of a kind. Over three million euros each and twenty million euros for the whole order, and here they are left, with the rubbish.'

'You should order at least six more, you know, for future use,' he suggested, wondering if she fully understood what he was asking.

'Why would I do that?'

'Niamh, you missed the point,' he said, now looking directly into her eyes and holding her by her shoulders. 'You need to order them and anything else on a long lead time before we leave Earth, Alan will happily pay.'

'I never thought of that,' she said, as she realised what he was implying. 'What I said in the car, on Saturday, on our way to the winery. You believed me?'

'Yes, of course I did. Remember what I'm good at: planning, deception, illusion, security. If you want what you asked me for, we need to take every opportunity on the way. It won't fall into our lap.'

By Tuesday morning, before the construction crews started on site, the crew had successfully transported all six pumps back to the warehouse storage area.

'Niamh, this is a surprise,' said Philippe, who had just arrived for work. 'You look great, where have you been?'

'On holiday. I came back late yesterday evening and was roped into finding my pumps,' she joked. 'How are you Philippe, and your wife and kids? You all good?'

'Yes, all good and looking forward to the holidays,' he said. Seeing her here, Philippe realised he wouldn't have to bother the director about recovering the pumps. He had seen them outside on the trailers and wondered who had arranged to recover them. *Mystery solved*, he happily thought.

By midday, Niamh had finished her work with Philippe and confirmed they had all the parts she wanted. It was as she hoped, the best of Earth's technology and all in the one place. Not only had she the cryo pumps for the reactor, but there was a plethora of machinery she could modify to refit the *Hela*. Smiling happily she returned to the control centre vehicle to get some rest before the journey back to the *Hela*.

'Mind yourself exploring the ship,' Tom said, as they stood outside the shuttle before she left. He knew she had a hard week's work ahead of her and that he may not see her for some time.

'Your goons won't let me do anything on my own,' she said.

'You mean John and his team are goons?'

'No, they're great, Tom, really great. Thanks for sending them,' she said, looking into his brown eyes. They embraced and he kissed her gently on the cheek.

'Earthlings, we have to go now,' the Pilot said, intruding into their romantic farewell.

Tom could feel Niamh starting to laugh as they slowly released from their embrace. 'Pilot, did you enjoy the wine and cigarettes I left for you?' he asked.

'Well, the wine was not as good as what you gave me in New Zealand. I found it didn't explode on my palate and it lacked the fruity flavour I prefer.'

'I'm sorry,' Tom said, now smiling 'I didn't realise you were such a wine buff. Did you drink it?'

'Of course he did,' she said, laughing as she held up two of the empty bottles thrown on the ground outside the shuttle.

'Pilot, you really have to learn to recycle, you know? "Save the Planet", that sort of thing?' Tom said, trying to sound serious.

'You're joking now, it's a bit late for that – your planet is doomed. Doomed, I say, you destroyed it,' said the Pilot, now laughing himself as he and Niamh climbed up into the shuttle. She was still laughing as she plugged her blue diamond into the navigation console projecting a picture of the clear night sky above them.

LYON FRANCE 2ND APRIL 2026. HOLY THURSDAY.

"Holy Thursday", the Thursday before the Easter weekend, arrived to the excited workforce at the reactor project site. There was an air of exuberance about the place as the tired workforce planned their long weekend break. They looked forward to the Easter holiday and an early finish, with most planning to be off the site by three or four that day. The chat was all about what they were doing, where they were going and how the holiday would be spent.

'Philippe, I apologise, I forgot to get the director to sign the final release document,' Tom said at twelve-fifty, ten minutes before his trucks were to arrive. 'I don't know what happened; I missed this.'

'Let me see.' Tom handed the documents to him. 'Yes, I see. I will send it over to the director for signing. We'll need to be quick about it, he is not too good after lunch, you know.' Philippe made a gesture with his hand indicating the director liked a drink.

At one o'clock, twenty articulated trucks with the capacity for eight hundred tons of cargo arrived at the site entrance. It was the final act of Tom's carefully planned strategy for the "purchase". He smiled as he heard the noise of their horns and engines as they jostled for pole position on the main road. Their arrival would expedite the issue of the one vital signature he needed for the conclusion of the "purchase".

By one-thirty the news that the gate was blocked with trucks had reached the director's secretary, who was entrusted with getting the all-important signature. The secretary quickly put two and two together and realised if the release document wasn't signed there would be the mother of all traffic jams at three o'clock as eighteen hundred excited workers tried to leave. By one forty-five, he was outside the director's office, waiting for him to return from lunch. At one-fifty Jean Claude Bouteillier, the project director for the European fusion reactor, arrived relaxed outside his office after a splendid lunch complemented by a bottle of burgundy to find his secretary pacing up and down in angst.

'Jean Claude, Jean Claude, you forgot to sign the release documents for the equipment we sold in the warehouse. The trucks are here to collect it now. They are blocking the access road,' the secretary said, in a perplexed tone of voice.

'What equipment, what sale, I know nothing of that?' he said, surprised at the information.

'Yes, yes, you approved it by email, Jean Claude. You received the collection details and dispatch lists the day before yesterday by email,' said his secretary. 'And the payment, a bank transfer for eight hundred million euros is in the project account, I just checked it.' The secretary was furious with Jean Claude for not briefing him about this. *The drunk doesn't trust me,* he thought. *I bet he got a large kick back and doesn't want me to know about it until the last minute.* 'Here is a pen, sign here,' said the secretary, forcefully offering the documents to his boss, leaving him no leeway to refuse.

'Ah yes, I remember now,' Jean Claude said as he signed the documents. That explained the email from his personal bank this morning, he thought. He had wondered who the fifty thousand euro transfer marked, "Thank You" was from. Yes, he remembered, Philippe had mentioned they should sell all the surplus equipment. The scrap was ordered by that girl, the argumentative construction engineer. That they had sold it was the best news he had heard all day. Looking out the window he saw the trucks on the access road.

'Hurry with that, and get those trucks moving. I don't want any back chat from the unions if the road is blocked at quitting time,' he snapped to his secretary. Jean Claude Bouteillier smiled as he closed and locked the door of his office behind him. Taking the phone off the hook and putting his mobile on silent he sat down at his desk. Still smiling, as he thought of the fifty thousand euros stashed in his bank account, he placed his feet on the desk, reclined in his big leather chair and closed his eyes as he happily drifted off into his daily wine-induced siesta.

By five past two, Philippe, with the signed dispatch order from Jean Claude, rang the security gate to approve the truck movements. With military precision, only the vehicles that were needed proceeded to the warehouse. The remaining trucks, there to block the road, immediately returned to Lyon, leaving the road miraculously cleared for the workers' exit. It was all going well and Tom believed his equipment would be loaded and dispatched to Lyon Airport by five o'clock that evening. Nonetheless, he had plans in place to alleviate the one potential dilemma remaining. If it reared its ugly head, it would scupper the whole job.

By the end of the World War II, most mainland European countries had dispensed with their royal families. The demise of the great royal households included the fall from grace of the many hangers-on who benefited from patronage, friendship, nepotism or other nefarious connection to the ruling houses.

By the middle of the twentieth century a new bourgeois class emerged from within the governing framework of the European Community. They quickly replaced the privileged hangers-on of the preceding feudal system. Their gathering momentum steadily advanced, and by the arrival of the twenty-first century, unelected officials, with enormous salaries and pensions ruled the EC. Placements or "jobs for the boys" were gifted through nepotism and political favour by the age old adage of "who knows whom". Fine dining and quaffing expensive wines was the order of the day. To add insult to injury, this perfumed privileged class paid less tax and earned more than the rest of the European peasants, or "the coping classes" as they were now referred to.

Bubbling to the top of this cesspit floated John Claude's boss, the Director General for Science. The man was gifted this position after his illustrious, or as some would maintain, infamous political career in France. It all ended as he fell from grace due to some unjust and unproven allegation of corruption. With his French ministerial pension and the generous salary promised with this EU position he was happy to go quietly into the night of political obscurity. In fact, he was seen dancing out of the Palais Bourbon on his last day at the National Assembly.

Seated in the temporary offices in Strasburg of the European Commission for Science, the Director General was troubled by the call he had just taken. It was from his niece who worked as a designer on the fusion reactor project in Lyon. She was a good girl, he thought; unfortunately, her grades were not so good. He had intervened gently to get her a position on the reactor site. It had paid him dividends as she always kept him in the loop of the goings on there.

'Uncle,' she had said, 'you must put a stop to it; they are moving all our parts out of the warehouse. Everything is going. We will have nothing left to work with. I'm sure it is the drunk. You know I bet he sold it all. Yes, Uncle, he did.'

'I will take care of it, don't worry, I will call them now,' he had told her. *Jean Claude, what are you up to*? he thought now, as he stroked the fabric of his new designer suit. He had purchased it for fifteen hundred euros that weekend in Milan with the new shoes and silk shirt he was wearing, it was on sale and a bargain. His new garments were all "styled" in Italy and made in a sweat shop in the Far East. Looking at his diamond encrusted watch he realised Jean Claude would be indisposed, so he dialled the number of Jean Claude's unlucky secretary.

Bill, sitting in their control vehicle, listened to the call coming in on the surveillance equipment.

'Is Jean Claude there?' the Director General asked.

'Yes Director General, but you know, he is indisposed,' replied the secretary, now standing up at his desk.

'What's going on in the warehouse?'

'We are de-cluttering the excess equipment,' replied the secretary, realising where the Director General got his information. *The interfering bitch*, he thought.

'I was not informed or consulted. Stop this—' and then the line went dead.

The secretary looked at the phone, pressing the hook switch. 'Director General,' he called into the phone and not hearing a reply placed it thankfully back on the cradle.

'Tom, you're up,' Bill said as he stood up from the surveillance equipment after cutting off the Director General's call to Jean Claude's secretary. He watched as Tom entered a number into his phone.

The Director General turned to look at his mobile now ringing on the desk beside him. Who could have his private number? he wondered as he answered the call. 'Hello.'

'Director General, I represent a firm that has legally purchased excess stock from the warehouse in Lyon.'

'I did not approve that. I am trying to stop its dispatch.'

'Well, we have paid the project eight hundred million for the equipment. Before I go any further, are you at your computer?'

'Yes.'

'There is an email with a small attachment for you. Did you get it yet?'

'Yes, it's here now,' the Director General said as he opened the email and the attachment.

Tom waited, first silence, and then he could hear the moaning sounds in the background from the video playing on the Director General's computer. Tom had found it amongst the data he obtained from Charl's employer's servers in Hong Kong. It was taken when the Director General was a Minister in the French Government. Most unflattering, it revealed him naked, in *"une position délicate"* with three naked ladies.

The Director General watched the short video, closing his eyes at the part where he snorted a white powder laid out on the large breast of one of the ladies while the other two attended to his carnal needs. He could feel his heart pound. This was not now as enjoyable as when he first consummated the act. 'What do you want from me?' he asked, as Tom noticed a marked change in his voice.

'Call Jean Claude's secretary back. Thank him for his diligence in moving the reorganisation of the warehouse stock forward, and ensure there are no delays in the dispatch.'

'Is that it?'

'Yes, all we want is what we legally bought with no delays,' Tom said.

'I'll do that now,' he said and abruptly ended the call.

Tom listened with Bill as the call came through to the secretary, it was done. By five o'clock that evening, their "purchase" arrived at Lyon Airport to be loaded on to the six cargo planes. That evening, carrying two hundred thousand kilos of equipment comprising the "purchase", the planes took off for six different destinations. When the last plane departed, Tom sent a simple message to the *Hela*. "Purchase dispatched".

CHAPTER ELEVEN

THE HELA 2ND APRIL 2026

History shows disasters are not caused by a single instantaneous event; they are generally caused by a group of related failures, commonly known as the domino effect. That fatal effect propels the participants into an unstoppable calamity. In most instances, human error is responsible for these failures. Humans are good at making mistakes, not surprisingly purebreeds, the close relatives of the human race, are no different. Purebreeds and humans, put in the perilous environment of the broken down *Hela* to work together, failed to foresee the inevitable calamity that briskly approached. They never imagined the consequences the domino effect could have on them.

Niamh's purge of the helium along the three hundred metre section of the central corridor to the armoury airlock was a success. It gave the crew valuable working space and reclaimed a previously inaccessible section of the *Hela*. When they returned to the *Hela* after their eventful weekend at the winery, priorities dramatically changed. Mack was insufferable. He wanted to beat the door down to get into the armoury. He was impatient, and could not understand delays due to technical problems. To make matters worse, Robert, also impatient, wanted to crack on with the work and pushed his crew to the limit. They had to move their equipment three hundred metres down the darkened corridor and set up at the airlock outside the armoury. To complicate events, Niamh left the team just as they started the work to go to France. With the time difference between the north and south hemispheres, she was gone for over two full days.

To add to the disruption, in an attempt to confuse the Chinese monitoring the ghost signature from the leak, Mack decided to reposition the *Hela*. The purebreeds failed to tell the humans, who were busy moving heavy equipment along the central corridor in the bowels of the *Hela*, about the upcoming change in the ship's orbit. It was the final ingredient in the recipe for the inevitable disaster that approached them all.

'What's that?' screamed a terrified Blair, who had just floated up about one metre off the floor while carrying a large air compressor along the central corridor. Unknown to the humans, the *Hela* bridge crew had activated the main grav drives to "nudge" the ship into a higher orbit. It was the direct cause that began the domino effect in their dreadful disaster. The old and worn grav dampers on the *Hela* took seconds to adjust, but it was enough to cause mayhem for the human work crew as they and the equipment floated up off the corridor floor. They were about one metre off the floor when the grav dampers kicked back in and everything and everyone came crashing back down in a heap. Blair ended up under the compressor he was carrying. As he fell, it landed on his chest, forcing the life-giving air out of his lungs and crushing down on his heart.

'Is everyone OK?' Robert shouted. 'John, you check your security crew, I'll check mine,' as he rushed along the corridor shouting the names of his crew and checking they were all right.

'It's Blair,' Shona shouted above the confusion. 'He's hurt bad, he's here, look,' she said in tears as they approached him.

He was lying on his back with the compressor on top of his chest. Robert and Shona quickly lifted it off him and Robert, seeing the man wasn't breathing, tilted his head back to open his airway. He figured Blair was lying there for about two minutes. Feeling at Blair's neck he couldn't find a pulse. Ignoring the emotion that started to sweep over him, he realised Blair's survival depended on him and his immediate actions; it was life or death.

'Get John, tell him we need the defib and his full medical kit,' he shouted at Shona. 'Go, go now,' he said as she turned and ran down the darkened corridor shouting for John. Looking at the lifeless Blair lying on his back on the corridor floor, Robert remembered a video he had seen over and over again during his oil field training. Playing it in his mind now, he kneeled over Blair, clasped his hands together and, placing the heel of his hand on the centre of Blair's chest, started chest compressions to the beat of a song playing in his mind. The punishing regime of trying to maintain one hundred and twenty compressions a minute was physically and emotionally exhausting, but Robert did not give up. His actions would sustain Blair's life by pumping oxygenated blood to his brain and other vital organs. Although quickly exhausted, Robert continued with the chest compressions as he heard John and his team set up their equipment and the defibrillator beside him.

'Boss, we have it now,' John said, placing his hand gently on Robert's shoulder.

An exhausted Robert quickly withdrew with Shona and the rest of his work team who were now gathered close by. He had worked on and off with Shona and Blair for some years. They were both from the north-east of Scotland and had lost family in the Wave. Amongst the first he asked from the oil field in Poland to join him on the project, they quickly accepted, both hoping for a new life together and the chance of raising a family on a new world. Blair, lying lifeless on a cold floor in the dark and dismal corridor of a spaceship, now depended on John and his team for his very survival.

The clinical sounds of "clear, clear, clear and shocking, shocking, shocking" emitting from John's teams and the defibrillator attached to Blair heightened the emotion and drama of the scene as they worked to revive Blair. Robert had his comforting arms around a distraught Shona who, with her face buried in his chest, was crying uncontrollably. Finally, John looked up and nodded confidently to Robert after the words "pulse detected" came from the machine attached to Blair.

'He's fine, Shona, he's alive lassie, he's alive,' Robert said quietly to Shona. He breathed a welcome sigh of relief, and a buzz of hope emitted from his team around him. Hugging Shona in turn they cried and laughed in a cathartic release of their emotions.

John quickly arranged a stretcher party to carry Blair off to med-bay. Alex and Rhea, advised in advance that there were injured on the way, were ready. They treated Blair for three cracked ribs and some bruising to his chest. They also treated six others who had a mixture of broken bones, cuts and bruises. Miraculously there were no life-threatening injuries and with the use of Anan technology, all the injured would make a quick recovery. A lucky outcome, Alex told Robert, it would have ended quite differently had Robert not intervened so quickly in the treatment of Blair.

The event devastated Robert. 'Mack, I can plan for just about everything we tackle, but this, well, I am disappointed. We failed. We're lucky that young man wasn't killed,' he said as they both inspected the damage in the central corridor.

'You take it too personally. I told you before we sometimes experience a ten per cent population loss in replanting new colonies.'

'And I told you I wouldn't accept that loss rate. I won't accept the deaths of two hundred and fifty people,' he replied. 'It's failure. I expect, and have always expected, attention to detail and excellence from everyone connected to a project I lead. No exceptions, Mack.'

'You will not achieve this, your persistence is annoying. You cannot protect all the colonists, all the time. There will always be a degree of risk.'

'Mack, those are my principles. I will not compromise them, you knew that when you hired me. If you cannot accept that, I will leave,' Robert said, abruptly ending the discussion. Parting company, and both exhausted, they retired for the day.

LYON FRANCE 4TH APRIL 2026

The European reactor project did not escape the attentions of the industrial espionage agents. At the outset, security was a major concern to the project supervisor who constantly bombarded the employees with new meaningless security initiatives. Tom and his team proved how useless they were. The espionage agents considered it a fertile ground for information and were always on the lookout for recruits who would succumb to their temptations. They proved a magnet for Maurice, the director's own nephew, who loved the good life and constantly worshipped at the Temple of Bacchus. Maurice loved easy money for little effort and worked for one of Chang's operations for two years. Most of what he gave to his control was of low value, but, it was the dispatch list and the news about a mysterious buyer for the excess equipment in the warehouse that heightened control's interest. When details of the operation emerged, control quickly flagged it up the line to Chang. An operation like this was unheard of, its masterful precision and timing left no doubt of a military involvement. When Chang got the details, he asked control to arrange a meeting with Maurice.

When control asked him to meet his employer, Maurice puffed up with importance. He was, however, a little taken aback by the location of the rendezvous; instead of the usual plush Lyon office, he entered an old rundown warehouse on the outskirts of Lyon. To add to his surprise, Chang was not what Maurice expected – instead of the Adonis type secret agent he envisioned, he was met by a portly Chinese man of about fifty, similar in height to Maurice's five foot six.

Wearing a creased cheap looking grey suit, Chang, with his arms open, smiled broadly at Maurice. 'Come in, Maurice, thank you for meeting me,' he said as he led Maurice into a small bare room with a desk and two chairs. Maurice did not notice a small bag placed unobtrusively under the desk. Chang the chameleon could change his demeanour as he changed his appearance. Now he was warm and welcoming, putting Maurice at ease, later this would change to the role Chang loved most.

Two hours later a hungry Maurice, who rarely missed a meal, was feeling sorry for himself from trying to answer all of Chang's questions. They were the same ones over and over again. Who was there, what did they look like, how did they do it, how many, where did they come from and what was the equipment for?

'Mr Chang, I am getting tired now. Perhaps we could take a lunch break?' Maurice said, determined to exert his authority.

'Good idea. I be back shortly,' he said, as he got up and left the room, surprising Maurice.

'Prepare him for the next session and he hungry, give him something to eat,' Chang said to his two associates waiting outside.

After a coffee and some food, a relaxed Chang re-entered the interrogation room. A very different scene greeted him. With an apple stuck in his mouth, Maurice was restrained in the chair with grey duct tape. His outstretched hands were taped to the table in front of him. The chair was placed on a plastic sheet and Chang could see the wet stain on Maurice's crotch. Fear, thought Chang happily, as he admired the tools from his bag that his associates laid out in front of Maurice on the table. He slowly fingered them as he looked at Maurice.

'You didn't enjoy your lunch? What's wrong with the apple, not good enough for you?' he said, toying with a petrified Maurice who could only grunt.

After another hour of questions, where Maurice lost four fingernails and had his left thumb amputated by a small guillotine, Chang finally got results. Maurice wasn't deliberately hiding anything, he was unable to remember or recount all the details that had happened. The violent torture, with Chang screaming at him, encouraged him to recount everything, even the details he forgot.

'What girl?' Chang screamed.

'The Irish girl, Niamh, she was there just for part of the operation.'

'You are protecting her,' he shouted, as he slowly tore back another part of Maurice's fingernail.

'No, noo,' screamed Maurice. 'Kill her for all I care, but we thought she was gone. She left the job in February. She was back there for a few hours only with the Englishman, Thomas Parker. Stop, please stop,' he sobbed.

It was the gold Chang needed. From the reactor site database, his hackers quickly located Niamh's picture. Is that her? they asked Maurice, as they put a small screen in front of him displaying her site badge. Yes, he confirmed. The Englishman in charge, what did he look like, when did he arrive? Nobody flies anywhere in the world without appearing on a security database. A trawl of the arrivals to Lyon on Monday morning, thirtieth of March, revealed over twenty candidates fitting Tom's description. Although Chang had seen him first, Maurice soon confirmed his identity. Chang was shocked; he thought his old adversary was dead, killed by the Wave. Chang knew him by many different names and Thomas Parker was not one of them. Although Tom travelled under a different name they were easily able to track back his embarkation point.

Surprise, surprise, thought Chang, *Christchurch, New Zealand*, as he realised Thomas Parker was the Englishman responsible for outing his South African spy Charl and his Hong Kong team. As for Niamh Sullivan, her last hit on a global flight database was her trip to Christchurch at the beginning of March, the same time Charl and his team were deposed. After her arrival in Christchurch, there were no records of her travelling anywhere. How could she get back to France? Where did she go? It looked like she had disappeared off the face of the Earth, thought Chang, mystified as to how the Irish girl could travel halfway round the world, then come back and then disappear again. He had not expected so much from this small French operation. It was bigger than he thought possible.

Chang, leaving Maurice, settled in the adjoining office with his associates, both hackers from the Chinese cyber war division. He called them his data miners.

'So, now we find out where the equipment went to and who bought it,' he told them. They set to work on their laptops and shortly after that, he returned to Maurice.

'Miss me, Maurice?' he asked. But Maurice, slumped near unconscious in the chair covered in blood and vomit, was in no fit state to reply. Disappointed, Chang took out a gun and shot him in the forehead. It was nothing personal, but Maurice had a loose mouth and just couldn't be allowed to live after his interrogation.

Returning to his data miners, as they worked, Chang thought about what he would tell Beijing. They needed to know and soon. It was big. What did Parker want with the most technically advanced equipment available on the planet? he wondered. It could only be used in high end advanced machinery similar to the fusion reactor. Where had the money come from?

After two hours of painstaking review, his data miners came up empty. The equipment was lost in the transhipments, flight plans and over ground transfers. Trying to trace the money back to its source proved fruitless, as it ended in complex financial swaps and bogus broker accounts. Alan, with the help of Demard, had done his job well. It had all disappeared. The lack of the data piqued Chang's suspicions. The disappearing Irish girl, the disappearing equipment and the cold money trail. Find Niamh Sullivan and Thomas Parker and it would all fit into place. He opened his sat phone and called his surprised superior in Beijing. After the long report to his superior, he sat back and thought. Then reaching into his bag, he took another sat phone, leaving the room, he placed the call. 'I have something of interest for you...'

THE HELA, EASTER SUNDAY 5TH APRIL 2026

It took two full days to sort out the bedlam the unannounced move of the *Hela* and the momentary loss of the grav dampers created. Fortunately, the loss of the grav dampers was not a ship-wide event and appeared to be localised to the lower decks of the ship, something that surprised Niamh, who as engineering manager, wanted to take the blame herself. The event created visible rancour between human and purebreed, who both blamed each other. The morale of the twenty-three human crew was now at rock bottom, particularly when they were told they would have to stay on board to recover the lost time over the Easter weekend.

One month into the project, after their first serious accident, Robert recognised their collective failings. They were at a low point in morale, progress and their relationship with the client. It was a bad place to be. The fear of the Chinese had aggravated the situation and forced unplanned change on the project. The humans believed danger would come from the unknown, unseen monsters, sickness or other alien threat. So far, all the dangers were technological and psychological, with this new real and present threat coming from the Chinese on Earth. Robert realised if they were to succeed a change of management and direction was needed.

They needed to thrash out their differences and, looking at the people seated around the table in their small meeting room, Robert would ensure this happened. At his request, Niamh, John, Mack and Robert were joined by the *Hela* captain, Brizo Sema. Up until now, he had for some unknown reason stayed away from the humans and confined himself to the bridge. He was a slim young Anan of about five foot ten, dressed in a light blue uniform, and answered to the nickname of Bri.

'So, Bri, how come no one on the bridge informed us you were changing orbit – after all, you are the captain?' John asked. 'I would have thought it common courtesy to let us know. It's not like it's a small ship. It's a beast and it must take some push to get it going.'

'Are you blaming me for this?'

'No, on the contrary, Captain, I'm not trying to blame anyone. I am merely stating a glaring fact of the matter.'

Robert sat back for a few moments as the recriminations were thrown back and forth between Mack, John, Bri and Niamh, who tried to take the blame herself. Finally, and to the surprise of all, a totally infuriated Robert slammed his hand down on the table with a loud bang. They looked at him in shock; they had never seen him so black or foreboding. He stood up and slowly paced back and forward as he started to speak.

'Listen to ourselves, we're the senior management of this project and we're bickering like children. In case it escaped anyone, we nearly killed

Blair. And I use the term "we" as it was all of our faults,' he said forcefully. 'We have only twenty-three crew to deal with. What will happen when we have two thousand five hundred depending on us for their lives and safety? If we continue like this, they will all surely die.' Robert stopped to look at them, he had their attention now. *Good*, he thought, as he continued.

'Let's look at the accident. Mack, we have these long detailed investigation processes on Earth, I'm sure you have the same?' he said as Mack nodded in agreement. 'I'm not going to waste time with that, what happened the other day was our reaction to fear,' he said as he continued to pace up and down the small room.

'The knowledge and fear that the Chinese were looking for us in space pushed the button that started the event. It was a change to our circumstances. Following that change, Mack, you and I wanted everything done immediately. Prompted by fear of the dragon, our Chinese enemy, we pushed our crews too far. History shows unplanned change causes most disasters. If we can't manage fear, and any change in what we do, we are ruined.' He paused again, stopped his pacing and looked at them.

'Before we go any further — we have to demonstrate to the twenty-three human crew that purebreeds and humans can work together. Look at it from their point of view, their morale is shot. They'll leave the project as soon as they get back to Earth and we'll see them on the internet and the television within a few hours, telling the world they were kidnapped by aliens and made to work in horrible dangerous conditions on their ship. So, ladies and gentlemen, we need a plan to get back on track,' Robert said as he sat back down.

Three hours later work was stopped early and the human crew invited to the bridge. It was an open discussion where purebreeds and humans were introduced to each other, apologies were made and new command and communication structures put in place. Some of the twenty-three would be key supervisors after the next new hires were taken on, and their understanding of what happened was vital. Finally, they were all to be compensated handsomely for missing their weekend off.

The extra pay was a hollow gesture after nearly killing one of the humans, Theia thought as she sat on the bridge after their meeting. But what else could she do to appease their failing morale? She thought about how they had arrived on Earth powerless in the beat-up old *Hela*. Even with the vast financial wealth Alan had generated they were still vulnerable. They had completely underestimated the task now before them. To Theia, the humans' concerns were meaningless. She closed her eyes, as the same thought rattled around in her mind over and over; if they failed in this project, she and her purebreeds would be stranded on Earth forever.

THE HELA, EASTER MONDAY 6TH APRIL 2026

Following the intensive clean-up of the chaos created by the loss of the grav dampers in the lower corridor, Robert and his crew were finally ready to re-start their work. Niamh set up a remote feed from their cameras to the *Hela* bridge view screen so Mack and the purebreed crew could follow their progress and talk to them as well. This simple change brought the two species closer together. With everything ready to enter the armoury, sitting on one of their equipment boxes with Niamh and John, Robert was surprised to see the captain walking along the corridor towards them. He was wearing the same ship working garb as the human crew.

'Bri, are you joining us today?'

'Yes, Robert, I am if you will allow me,' he said 'Niamh, are you ready to open the armoury?'

'Yes, can you, I mean —,' she said, also surprised to see Bri. She had expected Mack. They needed an Aknar, someone from the Anan royal family to activate the locking mechanism.

'Yes, I can open the seal, I am an Aknar,' Bri said, as he placed one hand on a flat plate and keyed a code into a small pad beside it with his other hand.

The crew standing behind them backed away in anticipation of what would happen next. They were disappointed, as the quiet sound of a click announced the release of the lock and a small blue light above the doorway lit up.

'There, it is unlocked. I believe we fit your airlock over it and then activate the opening mechanism?'

'Yes,' Niamh said, surprised, as Bri assisted them in fitting the portable airlock over the armoury door.

Shortly after, Robert opened the door and deployed the camera drone. The armoury was divided into three compartments; the inner, closest to the corridor, was a small chamber filled with various small tools and specialist equipment. It took the camera drone minutes to explore it and once they confirmed all was in order, Robert opened the second door to a larger middle chamber. It took over an hour for the drone to explore this chamber, with Mack asking for a close up of this equipment and that piece over there. They could hear the delight in his voice at what they had found so far.

'Robert, Niamh, can you purge the small inner chamber with breathable air? Mack asked over their comms system. 'It will give us easy access to that equipment. We may need it before we land.'

'Yeah, give us an hour,' she said.

They quickly worked to rig up the purge hoses, and the crew were surprised when Bri again started working alongside them. He was limited in what he could carry, but his contribution was welcome. When the purge finished, they entered the small armoury chamber. Niamh and Robert watched as Bri went from device to device, checking it over while reading from a data pad and talking to Mack on his communicator.

'OK, all done, we need to look into the large port side outer chamber, that's where all the "goodies" are,' he said, turning to address Niamh and Robert.

One hour later, after a survey with the camera drone confirmed the outer chamber was safe, Bri and John, suited up in breathing apparatus went in. With their head cameras on, Robert, Niamh and the bridge team could monitor their progress. Their journey would take them deep into the inhospitable depths of the *Hela*, further than anyone wearing breathing apparatus had gone before. It would be a long and dangerous journey and Robert had two rescue teams ready to go in case of trouble.

Inside the compartment, Bri knew exactly where to go, walking along a gantry that overlooked a large array of cylinder shaped objects mounted in clamps. They were drones, he explained to John, who wondered what they could do. Finally, at the end of the gantry they climbed up a ladder and then along another gantry to arrive outside a small control room.

Entering the darkened room through a disused airlock, Bri went to a control console and located a plate and pad similar to the one on the armoury door. As he placed his hand on the plate and entering a code into the pad, the console activated, bursting into different coloured lights. He sat down at the console, and while talking to Mack on his communicator, tried to enter the activation sequence.

'Have you control now, General?' he asked Mack in Anan.

'No, I haven't, try the second sequence the computer technician devised.'

As Bri continued with the re-sequencing John looked at his watch, half their usable air was gone. Watching Bri work, he realised he would not be finished soon. 'Robert, can you send in two twenty minute escape sets? We're in a control room, just have the team follow the rope line I left,' he said.

'Anything yet, General?' Bri asked.

'No, it's not working. We can't see anything here. Are you sure the console is connected with the *Hela* computer?'

'No, I'm not, that's a good point, I'll check that,' he replied as he started to explore the small command room.

'What are you looking for?' John asked.

'I'm not sure, John. The console has power but doesn't seem to be communicating with the *Hela*. Something's wrong or missing,' he said, as he looked under the console for any tell-tale signs of damage.

Noticing a small door in the wall, John cautiously opened it. 'Bri, look here.'

'What's in there?'

'Looks like the electrical systems,' he said, 'and there are some parts missing. You see that cabinet? It's empty and the wires are just hanging out.'

'Yes, I see, who would do that?' he asked. 'Are you getting this, General?'

'Yes, I am. The computer technician said it looks like the main relays to the *Hela* computer are missing. Captain, please check the console has control of the armoury.' Mack had hoped they could switch control of the armoury and its drones to the *Hela* Bridge. He still hoped they could at least get control of the drones.

Bri worked frantically and slowly the lights started to come on around them. Very soon he had blue lights flashing all over the console. He stopped the start-up sequence as lights started to come on outside in the drone bay. He smiled at John. 'General, we have it, all of it,' he said to Mack in Anan. There was no mistaking the relief in his voice, thought John, as he realised they had minutes of air left and there was still no sign of the crew with the escape packs.

'Robert, where are the escape sets?' he asked as he heard Bri's air alarm sound off. *He is down to his last reserve of air*, realised John, knowing his own would go off soon.

'They should be with you by now,' Robert said.

'Let's go now, Bri. Shut it down, let's go,' he said. If they didn't meet the relief crew on their way out, they would die in here. Powering down the console, Bri followed John out of the control room. They quickly worked their way back the way they came following John's rope.

Ten minutes later, the rescue team with John and Bri wearing the escape sets emerged through the airlock.

'What happened in there?' Robert asked.

'We couldn't get through the outer chamber door, it was locked. Then when the lights went out we heard it unlock and open,' said Kim, one of John's security team who was delivering the spare escape sets.

'My fault again,' Bri said. 'When I powered up the armoury, the default is for doors to be closed and locked. When I shut it down, the relief team were able to open it.'

'Luckily, we met them both at the bottom of the ladder,' Kim said.

'Don't beat yourself up about that,' Robert said, smiling at Bri. 'You happy with that, Mack?'

'Yes, but I wonder where the relays went? Captain, will you please return to the bridge? Robert, Niamh, John, that's a good day's work, thank you.'

'Great, we'll deal with the leak tomorrow, Mack, and I bet I'll find the missing relays,' Niamh said.

'How and where will you find them?' asked Mack, looking at a smiling Niamh on the bridge view screen.

'I'll put one hundred dollars on it, Mack,' she said, with confidence in her voice.

'That's a bet I'll take, and be happy to lose.'

As Bri made his way back to the bridge, he thought how he had enjoyed every minute of the work with the humans. They were polite, and accepted what little help he could give them with gratitude. The physical work was exhilarating and he had learnt more about the ship in one day than in the six months he had spent on the bridge. Since his ill-fated outing with Siba, he had changed the dosage. It had worked and he couldn't believe how alive he felt.

THE HELA, TUESDAY 7TH APRIL 2026

The following morning the same team assembled in the aft section of the *Hela* lower deck corridor outside the airlock. Robert's crew were delighted to see the purebreed captain returning in his ship garb to work with them. They deployed the camera through the airlock set up at the entrance to the starboard aft compartment where the leak was. What it revealed surprised them all. Parts of the bulkhead between the starboard aft compartment and the adjoining engine room were removed. They could see equipment located in the compartment connected through the bulkhead openings to the engine in the adjoining room. But it was the engine that caused the surprise. Niamh had expected something different, another grav drive or fusion reactor, but not this.

'Is that what you call a blue drive?' she asked Bri, who was standing beside her, looking at the small view screen.

'I don't know what that is. I have never seen anything like it before.'

'I am mystified,' Mack said, looking at the picture on the bridge view screen. 'Pilot, you ever seen anything like this before?'

'Long time ago, on an old ship like this, they used a hybrid drive, it used less blue than the modern blue drives. It doesn't go through the fold in space but uses the curve. If you use it with the grav drives it cuts down the grav-powered journey time by nearly half. They used them the last time when blue was scarce.'

'Did you all hear that down there?' Mack said.

'Yes we did,' Niamh said. 'I'll try to get that going for ye as well, Mack, if we can get some blue to fuel it. And look, there's your relays,' she said as the camera drone started to examine the equipment.

'How did you know it was there?'

'I noticed missing equipment in other parts of the ship, taken out just like the relays in the armoury. When we first looked at the drawings of the auxiliary engine room, ye didn't know what was in there. We realised some modifications were made. I just put two and two together. When they made those changes, the parts were robbed from the other systems to get this engine going. Now let's look for the leak,' she said as she manoeuvred the camera drone to the starboard aft exterior bulkhead.

'Look, Mack, do you see that? Whoever made the changes used the ship's bulkhead to support some of the cables running to the new engine. The support's been dislodged, it looks like it has recently broken off.'

Yes, Niamh, I see it. It probably broke from the stress of our long voyage from Anan.'

As Niamh adjusted the camera, they could see a small dent in the exterior bulkhead panel, where the support fell, and a pinhole leak at the base of the small dent.

'Can you repair that?' Mack asked.

'Yes, we can, although it will be difficult in breathing apparatus. The two compartments are too big to purge. But we can do a temporary fix and brace the panel for the stresses exerted during the landing,' she said.

Within two hours the leak was temporarily sealed to stop the vapour trail. To preserve their cloak they also stopped all purging of helium out into space. With the move in orbit, and the leak sealed, the ghost signature the Chinese were tracking would disappear, gaining the project valuable time. With the help of the electricians, Niamh recovered the missing relays and put them back into the armoury where they belonged. By the end of the day Mack had full control of the armoury at the bridge security station, including the launch capability for the drones.

'You look happy, Uncle,' Bri said, sitting next to him on the bridge.

'I am. We have full defence capability, two thousand five hundred drones and the rest of the equipment in the armoury. I am proud of you.' He couldn't believe one so young was capable of so much. 'It wouldn't have happened without your help.'

'You're too kind, Uncle. Good night,' said Bri as he retired for a welcome rest. Back in his cabin he picked up the silver flask and took a small draught from it. Yes, he thought, the dosage was just right.

CHAPTER TWELVE

PROJECT REPORT ONE. EARTH DATE 8TH APRIL 2026. TO THE ONE.

My Lord,

Never before was I faced with such a low reserve of blue. I underestimated the period it could sustain my powers. To reduce my energy consumption, I intend to upload my memory and consciousness to the *Hela* databanks, leaving a small amount behind to protect my energy mass. It is the only acceptable method of fully preserving my life force until the Empress and her team can source more blue. There is risk involved, with disastrous consequences, should I fail.

Our Current Status and Plans:

The humans excel in their output and capability. The survey of the *Hela* is complete with control of the armoury restored. It gives the General defensive capabilities to protect the ship from an aggressive Earth government. The ship survey located a crudely installed hybrid engine. The incompetence of its installation bears the hallmark of The Sixth, who I believe was the last to use this ship. Unknown to us, damage was done to the *Hela* during this installation. Parts were cannibalised from other control systems and the poor workmanship compromised the operation and defensive capabilities of this ship. In contempt for any future user, no records of these crude modifications were left. They have resulted in structural damage to the ship, including a hull breach, which must be repaired before we land. We were incredibly lucky to have made it this far.

Contact is made with the governments of the lands where our assets are located. They are friendly and helpful to our cause. A team leaves shortly to enter our re-supply base. If this is successful you will hear from me again. If you do not hear from me within half an orbit of Anan, you will know our cause is lost. I waste no more energy on this brief report.

Dedicated to your Service.

The Eight.

There, it is sent, that is enough information for him, thought The Eight. *If I return to Anan, I will challenge The Sixth*, he thought, as he commenced his preservation plan.

She awoke suddenly. The deep feeling of loss that enveloped her disturbed her restful slumber. She felt tears streaming down her face as the emotion overwhelmed her. It was so overpoweringly dark and depressing, she couldn't move. And then Theia slowly realised what was missing. The Overlord, The Eight, was gone, she couldn't feel his presence. It was the rush of adrenalin from this great loss that gave her the energy to sit bolt upright and run from her bed to his chamber.

What has happened? she thought, as she looked at his energy mass, encased in the large glass holding chamber he used for rest. She couldn't understand what was going on. The energy mass was there in front of her, but The Eight, his consciousness, his very being, was not. She heard others approaching and pretty soon all the purebreeds on the *Hela* were assembled outside his quarters. The sound of moaning and crying filled the corridor and spilled out into the wider accommodation, waking the sleeping humans.

'What's wrong?' Robert, accompanied by Niamh and John, asked Theia. They had followed the crying sounds which led them to the corridor outside the Overlord's chamber. The purebreeds were now sitting on the floor rocking back and forward as they cried and moaned in unison.

'Oh, Robert. It's The Eight, he is gone, we can't feel his presence,' Theia replied, as the tears streamed down her face.

'Show us,' he said.

Theia led them into the Overlord's chamber. Robert, John and Niamh, not affected by the emotional loss experienced by the purebreeds, started to look slowly around the chamber.

'Well, he looks all there,' Robert said, as he approached The Eight's glass holding chamber. 'So where is his mind? I guess that is the question, right, Theia?'

'When he is near we always feel his presence, but now we don't,' she replied. 'His consciousness is gone; we can't feel him with us. It is over, I'm afraid. We are too late and have failed.'

'I think you're wrong, Theia, we're missing something,' he said.

'Look, look at the view screen,' Niamh said, as she checked the chamber computer. 'He's in the *Hela* databanks, look!'

They all approached the view screen and looked at the strange words continually scrolling across it. *I am here, I am here, I am The Eight.*

What have you done to yourself? typed in Niamh.

Preserved blue energy for my survival, replied The Eight, as the words scrolling across the view screen changed.

Will you come back? Can you come back? typed in Niamh.

When you get more blue, he replied.

'There's blue on this ship,' Robert said.

'No, Robert, there's none, you're mistaken,' Theia said, shaking her head in annoyance at his flippant manner.

'I believe there is,' Niamh said, now realising what Robert was talking about.

'If there's any left, can you recover it?' he asked her.

'Not sure. I don't have the technology for that.'

'What are you both talking about? That's ridiculous, there is no blue on this ship. We would have used it by now if there was,' Theia said.

Robert paused and looked at Theia. She was shaking and her normal white skin was grey. *She's angry and not thinking straight*, he thought. 'The hybrid drive, Theia. There must be residue blue energy in the engine, in the feed pipes and the tanks. But we don't have the technology to recover it.'

Theia looked at them both in stunned silence. Her mouth was open but she just couldn't form the words to reply. She found his reply incredible, and yes, they could be right. The answer to their problem may lie on this very ship, and there was a device Bri had found in the armoury that could possibly recover some blue if it was there in the hybrid. Surprising Robert, Niamh and John, Theia rushed from the room, shouting Mack and Bri's name over and over in Anan.

'We have a device that recovers pure energy,' explained Mack, now in the Overlord's chamber with Bri and Theia. 'We use it for spill clean-up, and for defensive purposes when dealing with other types of energy. There is more than just blue energy out there. I believe we can use it as you described. The engine builders use something similar when cleaning and servicing the blue drives on other ships. But can you get into the engine, the feeds and the tanks?' he asked.

'I believe so,' Niamh said. 'We found maintenance manuals in the hybrid engine compartment, it will have the information. I believe the special tools we need are there as well. So yes, it will be difficult in breathing apparatus, but we need to try.'

'Tell The Eight we are going to the re-supply base today as well,' Robert said, as Niamh typed in their plan on the computer.

'So you plan to get me the dregs from the hybrid drive, who thought of that?' he asked, as his reply scrolled across the screen.

Me and Robert, and beggars can't be choosy!

Ha, ha, ha! came the response on the view screen.

Oh, so you have a sense of humour on your dying bed? she typed back.

Yes, my child, I do, and I'm not gone yet. It will work, all of it. Well done, I never thought of that. Good luck with those endeavours both in the engine room and at the re-supply base.

Robert was now faced with the dilemma of planning work at two locations with unknown consequences. He had intended to go to New Zealand to the unexplored base, where John's expertise was also needed. However, he didn't want to leave Niamh alone to deal with the hybrid. It would be a complicated job that required his support and attention. To aggravate matters, the purebreeds were completely demoralised, and would have difficulty helping the humans. Theia had explained to them what The Eight had done. To some degree, it helped, but they were hurting, some more than others, and it affected their ability to function. The decision was made, John was needed in New Zealand with Bri, and Robert would stay with Niamh on the *Hela*.

MILFORD SOUND 9TH APRIL 2026

'They picked this place as it was in an uninhabited wilderness and easy to find when entering the atmosphere. I read the location description in the *Hela* database,' the Pilot said as they approached Earth's atmosphere.

'What did it say?' John asked, sitting beside Siba and the Pilot in the cockpit of the small shuttle.

'I made a rough English translation, you can read it on the view screen here,' he said, as he brought the short article up on the cockpit screen for John to read.

"The location is uninhabited by bipeds or mammals or other harmful creatures. The base is constructed for a five thousand year lifespan and due to its remote location the area should remain uninhabited by the human population—." The synopsis continued with more detailed flight plans, the base coordinates and the weather warnings Siba had noticed when she read the text before their ill-fated first visit.

The base, inside a mountain behind the deep fiord, had remained hidden and undiscovered for near three thousand years. The choice of its location insured that. The fiord was now an international tourist attraction in an uninhabited wilderness. From the pictures she had taken, Siba had identified the most likely entry point. Its location, in a cliff face high in the mountains behind the fiord, was the reason they needed the humans.

Their first sight of Milford Sound was from their approach into it from the Tasman Sea. As forecasted, the weather did not disappoint, and the small shuttle was buffeted by winds and heavy rain. The Pilot flew slowly into the fiord, giving them a magnificent view of the dramatic beauty that shyly protruded through the clouds and mist. As the shuttle advanced slowly into the fiord the mountains, interleaved with the lush green vegetation, disappeared up into the thick mist and cloud that enveloped the fiord. Long waterfalls swollen by the incessant rainfall fell down the steep sides of the fiord, their spray blowing up in the wind and adding to the dark and beautiful mystique of the place. Through the mist and rain they could see the tourist boats plying back and forward along the fiord. The wet misty weather hampered their view of the surrounding mountains, but did not detract from the beauty or drama of the sights enfolding before them as they advanced slowly into the depths of Milford Sound.

Navigating with a GPS they had purchased in Christchurch, the Pilot skilfully flew the shuttle up the fiord until he located an expansive waterfall cascading down the cliffs on the northern shore of the sound. The cliff above was obscured by a billowing spray generated by the waterfall's voluminous deluge. He stopped in the middle of the sound with the shuttle cockpit facing the waterfall. They looked with awe at the majestic scene before them; the wind, rain, mist and spray all camouflaging their destination into the mountains rising from a hidden hanging valley above the waterfall. The old purebreeds were right, thought John, navigation would be a challenge.

'That's as far as I can go with this primitive GPS system. It could be twelve to fifteen metres out, enough to slam us into a cliff and we need satellite sight all the time. Siba, you need to navigate,' he said in Anan.

Siba turned to face the control console and, placing her blue diamond in the navigation port, closed her eyes. The clarity and depth of the projection of the waterfall and the hanging valley above it surprised John and the Pilot. It was as if Siba was flying herself, and she was, as her mind, amplified by the power of the blue diamond, flew through the hanging valley plotting the cliffs and mountains before her.

'Excellent, Siba, here we go,' the Pilot said and he flew the shuttle up the waterfall through the spray and into the deep valley beyond. Completely enveloped in cloud and rain and guided by Siba's navigation projection, the shuttle continued up the valley to a sheer cliff below an imposing mountain.

'We're here,' the Pilot said, checking coordinates on his console. 'We will have to find the entrance and a landing site above it in this thick cloud and rain. Siba, can you maintain that navigation projection?' he asked.

'Yes, Uncle, I can. Look, the entrance to the base is high up on this cliff,' she said, pointing to the upper reaches of the cliff face on her projection.

Using Siba's navigation projection and the pictures she had previously taken, they eventually found the base's concealed entrance. It was shaped like a cut back chimney and embedded deep into the cliff face. The recess was smooth and stretched down to a sloped step covered with thick vegetation. The wind constantly buffeted the shuttle, preventing it from closely approaching the cliff and the base's small portal door.

'Captain,' shouted the Pilot, 'come up here and take a look at Siba's projection — hold on tight – you see, there, that is where you will have to go with John. Down that cliff. The portal door is concealed behind the vegetation and the access pad will be beside it,' he said pointing at the projection. 'Can you do that?'

'Yes, of course I can,' Bri said as the projection flickered.

Siba felt it, his fear. *He's lying*, she thought, as she watched his smiling reflection in the cockpit window.

'We will rope down from the top. I will set it up, Captain. First I'll need to clean away the vegetation. You will be safe, I haven't dropped anyone yet,' John said.

'Always a first time, human, always a first time,' the Pilot said, grinning at John and Bri. 'Time to go, we can land there,' he said, pointing to a flat area clear of vegetation on top of the mountain. 'I believe that is a protective cap rock put over a docking ring for the *Hela*. It's the right size and directly above the base.'

On the top of the mountain, John's team tied the shuttle down with cables and rock anchors to prevent the wind from moving it. By the close of the evening the small team had set up the winches and ropes for the next day's work on the cliff face.

THE HELA 9TH APRIL 2026

'What do we do with it, Theia?' Robert asked, as they placed an energy tank of blue beside The Eight's energy mass in the glass holding chamber.

'Place it in here,' she said, pointing to a receptacle behind the glass chamber. 'It is how he recharges with blue. It flows into the chamber and he absorbs it.'

Using Mack's pure energy recovery device, Niamh, Robert and two of his rig crew recovered four precious energy tanks of blue from the hybrid drive and fuel tank. It was twelve exhausting hours of intensive work in breathing apparatus. Niamh, ensuring their work would not go to waste, followed the maintenance protocol she found in the engine manual. She was right; all the special tools they needed were stored in a locker in the engine compartment. It "killed two birds with one stone", she explained to Robert.

She was delighted with the condition of the engine and found it was hardly used. Would they ever find out who installed it? she wondered, and why it was never used was another mystery. It was a welcome find, and if they could get enough energy to fuel it, Niamh was determined to make use of it. But now, she was thankful for what they had reclaimed from the engine and hoped it would restore The Eight.

We recovered four energy tanks of blue for you, Niamh typed into the chamber computer to The Eight.

My child, you have done well, was his reply across the view screen.

Is it enough?

Yes, however there is another problem.

What's that?

I can't transfer back without damaging the Hela *databank.*

Did you not think of that before you jumped? You're supposed to be the all-seeing, all-powerful entity. Jeez, what a—. Sorry, Overlord. I know. It's you in there.

You're right, my child; I should have thought this through and should have called you first to discuss it. I am not infallible. But staying here is better, it preserves blue. I will stay here as long as necessary but do not tell the others.

No, I won't. So how do we fix this? I know you have a plan.

You need to construct this bridge link from the gold on board the Hela, he replied on the view screen and also posted a diagram of the link. It was a set of golden cables that would tie in the large bus bars from the *Hela* databank to his recharging receptacle behind the glass chamber. It would be easy, she thought, as the databanks, the ship's core memory, were located beside his chamber. Close by and under his guard, she thought.

We'll need to have the cables custom made; we don't have gold cables that size here on the Hela, she typed.

I need the gold to cope with the transfer of energy units I will create. It was easy getting here – I used blue – but getting back, I won't be able to control the energy output.

We'll have that made on Earth. I'll tell the others you want to stay in the data banks for a while longer, but I'll need Robert's and Tom's help, they have to know.

Thank you, my child. Go now.

'Well, is he ready to go back to his wee house?' shouted Robert across the chamber to Niamh, who had just stepped away from the computer console.

'No, Robert, he wants to stay a while in the databanks,' she lied to them all, and hoped Theia would not sense her subterfuge. She didn't need to worry. Theia, overwrought with the displacement of The Eight's consciousness, completely missed the easy lie. The Eight's secret was safe for the time being. Niamh immediately started to look for a suitable cable manufacturer. They needed someone small who wouldn't ask too many questions and was close to their base of operation. *Another job for Tom*, she mused.

MILFORD SOUND 10TH APRIL 2026

They spent a cold and damp night in the shuttle, sheltering from the bad weather that enveloped them. The following morning, shrouded in cloud, rain and the occasional flurry of snow, John abseiled down the cliff face to the recess. His expertise was the reason Robert had insisted he lead the expedition. It was John who had organised all the equipment and picked the others in the team. Some were Robert's rig crew and the others had mountaineering experience.

Before the Wave, mountaineering was John's pastime, but this expedition would be nothing like a pastime. To gain access to the base portal door the thick vegetation, including bushes growing on the cliff, would have to be cleared out. Positioning himself at the recess on the end of his rope, and using a climbing axe, he started to carefully cut away at the cliff's verdant cover. He had to limit what he dislodged down to the valley below, lest the tourists or boats hear him. It was imperative he leave no trace of their endeavours and used the winch to take the debris back up to the top.

It was gruelling work, but eventually he was able to climb up into the recess. Looking carefully around, he found a flat square shaped rock embedded in the cliff face just inside the top of the recess. Prising it out with his climbing axe, he discovered what he was looking for; a security pad and plate, similar to ones on the *Hela* armoury and a power socket.

After running and attaching a power cable from the shuttle to the power socket, John connected Bri to a "man-riding" winch cable with a full body harness. 'You're not going anywhere, even if you fall upside down you won't fall out of the harness,' he said, reassuring Bri. Despite Bri's happy assurances yesterday in the shuttle, John could see how terrified he was as he stood trembling at the top of the mountain.

'I just don't understand why we have to use such primitive methods. You know we have personnel grav platforms and personnel grav suits.'

'Captain, we are not trained in their use and they are untested in this bad weather and high winds. Stop. Don't interrupt. I know you can use them, but you won't see where you're going in this thick mist and the wind will blow you away. The shuttle can't even approach the cliff in these winds, you know that.' John's team didn't know where to look during this argument and stood back out of earshot. 'Look, Bri, we discussed this before. In this weather it's our only way to get into the base. Believe it or not, but humans also do this for fun,' he said softly as he put his hand on the young purebreed's shoulder. 'You can do this.'

Bri gritted his teeth as he tried hard to conquer his fear. 'All right, John. Let's go, show me where the fun is in this,' he said as he walked to the edge of the cliff.

John abseiled down first as his crew lowered Bri on the winch. At the recess, completely shrouded from view in mist and rain, he adopted a firm bridge stance spread-legged across the recess with each foot on steps he had earlier cleared in the rock. When Bri arrived on the winch John grabbed him and manoeuvred him into the recess. When the old purebreeds left, they locked the base, protecting it from unwanted intrusion. The system to open it, similar to that on the *Hela* armoury, could only be activated by an Aknar. That was why Bri dangled one hundred metres down a cliff face in the rain, snow and cold biting wind on a winch cable.

'John, I can't reach the pad,' he said, stretching both hands upwards into the recess.

'If we hoist you up on the winch, it will pull you out of the recess. Bri, you have to trust me now. I'm going to lift you up myself.'

'Get on with it,' Bri said, shivering with the cold. He was wet and miserable. The rain running down the space between his long neck and waterproof jacket was trickling down his back. The scarf they gave him to wrap around his neck didn't work and it was now sodden with cold water. His hands and feet were nearly numb with the cold. *This is horrible*, he thought, and then realised John had spent half a day working down here on the end of a rope cleaning out the recess. *How did he do that?* he wondered.

John managed to climb under Bri. Putting his head between his legs and sitting him on his shoulders, he climbed up with the young purebreed. Feeling John tremble below him, Bri placed his hand on the plate and entered the codes into the pad. Nothing happened.

'It didn't work.'

'Try it again, rub your hands together first to warm them,' John said, as his legs continued to tremble with the effort. He didn't know how much longer he could hold Bri.

Rubbing his hands together until he felt the feeling return, he placed one hand on the plate, entering the code into the pad with the other. The blood circulating back through his hands was just what the plate needed to decode his Aknar DNA. As the door mechanism activated, an exhausted John felt the trembling in his legs increase.

The door dramatically opened inwards with a loud clang and grinding motion and a burst of dust as the air trapped in the pressurised seals escaped. The dust cloud and the release of pressurised air knocked them both off their perilous position, falling out of the recess onto the main face of the cliff. Bri ended upside down, hanging on the winch cable screaming in Anan.

'You're fine,' John said, not understanding a word he was saying but imagining what it meant. He grabbed Bri and turned him right side up. 'Well done, you did it.'

'Was that supposed to be the fun part?'

'Well yes. Humans do pay money for a similar experience.'

'I don't believe that, John — look now — the weather, it's clearing.'

As they hung on the cliff face they watched as the clouds billowed and slowly thinned. The grey swirling mass lifted, opening up a breath-taking view into their majestic mountain world. Suddenly, they could see the cliff stretch seven hundred metres below them to the floor of the beautiful hanging valley where the large river disappeared in a cloud of spray over another cliff to the waters of Milford Sound, over one thousand metres below them.

'Wow. That makes up for the cold and misery,' Bri said, enthralled by the beautiful scenery opening up in front of them.

For a moment, John feasted his eyes on the views of the fiord and mountains. Then he quickly turned back to face the recess in the cliff face. 'Let's go,' he said pulling at Bri's harness, 'we need to get the base open for the shuttle before we miss this weather window.'

Looking into the open door of the base, John instructed the winch operator to lower Bri as he helped him climb up into the recess. Once inside the small base door, they were able to walk up steps cut into the rock and into the main chamber beyond. Taking off their ropes, cables and harnesses, they both walked into the chamber, dimly lit from the light flowing in through the open doorway. Stopping just inside the entrance of the re-supply base, they looked into the deep cavern beyond. Through the gloom they could see a control room at the back of the main chamber.

'Thank you, John, no one has stood here for thousands of years. We couldn't have got here without your help.'

'You did it as well, Bri,' he said, looking at the young purebreed. His delight was obvious as his eyes darted from one area to another, not knowing where to start. 'You need to start it up, Captain — you have the codes?'

'Yes, John, I do,' he said as he quickly made his way to a control console located to the side of the entrance and entered the start-up codes retrieved from the *Hela* database. Very soon, he had the chamber lights on and the console powered up.

'OK, John, now we see if the door works, call the Pilot and let him know what I am doing,' he said as he activated the main base shuttle access door. For a moment nothing happened, and then they heard the welcome sound of machinery starting up and after a loud groan and a sudden bang, the base shuttle access door slowly started to move.

Forty minutes after John and Bri left the mountain top, the Pilot skilfully flew the shuttle into the chamber. When the shuttle landed he leaped out, followed by Siba, and slapped Bri on the back.

'Well done, Captain. John, thank you. We are back, the first shuttle to come back here in over three thousand years,' he said, with uncharacteristic excitement in his voice.

Siba looked at Bri and smiled, 'well done, Bri, I didn't think you could do it.'

'What do you mean—?'

'Enough,' John said, now anxious they complete their mission, 'we should find and load the blue into the shuttle. Pilot, you, Siba and Bri will fly it back to the *Hela* while we stay here until you return.' His crew were already unloading the equipment they used at the top of the mountain and a portable generator and battery bank to restore the base power from the shuttle. They would leave these here and, in the future, if the batteries died, they could remotely activate the generator to open the shuttle door.

'You're right, John, we need to hurry if I am to depart before nightfall,' the Pilot replied.

Bri found the blue energy in a store room off the main chamber. They had a treasure trove of blue for The Eight, forty energy tanks in total. He would be pleased it was intact. The shuttle could only take half the store to the *Hela*, but it would be enough, they could return later for the rest and to fully explore the base. He watched John and his team load the final tanks onto the shuttle. Their dedication to the project never ceased to astound him. Their work was excellent and they never intruded on the purebreeds' world. Bri noticed they set up tents just inside the base access door for the night they would spend there.

'John, there is a small accommodation block behind the main chamber, you can stay there,' he said.

'We prefer to stay here. The other areas of the base are unexplored. Robert specifically said we should not enter any areas you have not cleared yourself. And, well, we respect your family's property, for this is what it is,' he replied.

'You are welcome here, without you we would never have got back. You are not the servants, you are our partners.'

'Thank you. But we will be more comfortable here in our tents. We have a chemical toilet, cooking gear and food, really, we prefer it this way,' he said, smiling at the young purebreed's concern.

'John, how do you do it? You are always so calm. You know just what to do and when to do it. I'm supposed to be the captain but well-'

'Bri, how old are you in human terms?'

'Probably twenty of your years.'

'Bri, I am nearly double your equivalent age. Very rarely would we give such rank to one so young, maybe in wartime, but not now. Command comes with experience. You need to stop and think more. Think about what you're doing before you do it.'

'All right. I'll try that. I will see you tomorrow,' he said, as he reached out and shook John's hand. 'I am to navigate back to the *Hela*.' He was elated by the success of their mission, the work on the cliff face and his newfound friendship with the older human. Bouncing into the cockpit and planting his blue diamond into the navigation console, he had no problem forming a clear projection, impressing both Siba and the Pilot. By midnight they were back on the *Hela* with the precious cargo of blue.

'How did he do?' asked Mack.

'He did well,' said the Pilot as he sat across from Mack on the *Hela* bridge. 'The work with the human on the cliff was not easy. He surprised me, and he was able to easily navigate back to the Hela. You should be proud of him.'

AUSTRALIA

CHAPTER THIRTEEN

AUSTRALIAN DESERT 13TH APRIL 2026

The shuttle landed on the red sand directly over the *Hela*'s home base in a valley between the parallel sand dunes that this Australian desert was famous for. The base's location, below the harsh barren land, guaranteed it had remained undiscovered since the departure of the *Hela* over three thousand years ago. Fortuitously for the purebreeds, the base location was never designated as a national park, which simplified the granting of a development licence by the Australian Government.

Stepping out of the shuttle, Robert, Tom, Alan and the Pilot looked around at the bleak red sandy landscape. The only amiable attribute of the place was the autumn temperature, a comfortable twenty-five degrees.

'Bleak, isn't it?' Alan said.

'It will be worse in the summer,' Robert warned, knowing the temperature could rise to thirty-five or forty degrees. He realised the size of the task that lay before them. They were to turn this place into a construction site with accommodation for over two thousand people and open the refit base for the *Hela*; all before the end of July, fifteen weeks away. Alan had built on the rumours of a new mining operation in the Australian desert; it would be their cover story. The base construction work would be similar to that of starting a new mine with an accommodation block, or camp as it was called, warehouses, workshops and an airstrip.

'Not much chance of someone breaking in,' Tom said. The location, four hundred kilometres from Alice Springs, with no roads in the area, eased his task.

'Thank you, Robert, we are back,' the Pilot said, happy to be the first Anan in over three thousand years to set foot on their second Earth base. 'Pity we can't enter it.'

'Aye, it is. I can't understand how it was secured; only responding to direct commands from the *Hela* computers.'

'It's quite common, Robert. It's a good method of accessing the base from the ship while it is still in flight.'

'Well, I don't like it. I would prefer to get in now and make sure everything is working. I had that argument with Mack.'

'Short of breaking down the entrance door with explosives, there is no other way in,' the Pilot said.

Tom grinned and looked at them both. 'I could arrange that.'

'Aye, well, if the system doesn't work you might have to,' Robert said, nodding at Tom's suggestion.

They walked about, took some pictures and when they all realised there was not much else to do, got back on the shuttle for the return flight to Sydney.

It would be a busy fifteen weeks, Robert thought, on the flight back. Alan and Kath were well advanced in the hiring of the two thousand five hundred colonists. It was a phased program, and to maintain the secrecy of the Project, the hiring would continue over the *Hela* refit period on Earth. An Australian contractor was needed for the construction and support works at the *Hela* base. Remembering the Leslie family ties in Australia from previous generations, Robert contacted his distant relations, McKinnon and Sons, a family construction business based in Sydney. They were ideal for the job and surprised and delighted when he called them. They were to meet today back in Sydney in the warehouse and yard. One of the properties Alan had procured from Tom was the project's "Sydney Operations" base in an industrial complex on the outskirts of the city.

'Robert, good to see you again, it's been thirteen years. Yeah, last time was in Murrayfield. We beat you then and took the cup back,' said Matt, Roberts's cousin, referring to the last rugby match the family attended together in Scotland in 2013.

'Aye, Matt, dinnae remind me, it was a good match though. I remember it was close, fifteen, twenty-one,' he said, pumping Matt's hand and smiling at him and his three sons.

'Robert, if we negotiate a price today I don't think we'll see the difference between fifteen and twenty-one as being very close,' Matt said, smiling at his distant cousin, then his demeanour changed to a serious and sad tone. 'Look, Robert, we're really sorry for what happened, we tried to get in touch and well, we thought you were gone. Much later we heard you survived, but we couldn't find you. I'm sorry; I believe you lost your family.'

'Aye, that I did, with many others, but thanks, thanks,' Robert said quietly and gave each of them a big bear hug. 'Come on inside, we've a lot to catch up on. I'll introduce you to these guys. I see you've noticed the Pilot is a bit different,' continued Robert, who had purposely brought the Pilot with them.

The McKinnons needed to know everything. If negotiations were successful today they would be the base managers and principle contractors for Anan Corporation's Australian operation. It would be a contract worth millions, and hinge on the McKinnons' ability to guard their secret. Although distant relatives, the Leslie and McKinnon families had re-connected in 1996 at a Scotland versus Australia rugby match in Murrayfield. Robert was twelve, and since then the families had made a point of trying to keep in contact. Robert trusted them and they had the experience to do the job.

'Yeah, Robert, we can do that. Although it's bigger, it's what we've done in the past on the mining sites, and new start-up mines,' Matt said confidently, after they had spent the afternoon poring over pictures of the area and the draft plans of the overground base and support structures. After the initial shock of understanding what Robert was actually project managing and meeting the alien pilot, he and his sons were hooked.

'Now, family aside, business is business. I have four unnegotiable deliverables: quality, safety, security and time. I demand excellence. Cost is not an issue. Whatever you need you get. When you sign the contract, Alan will transfer an initial one hundred million dollars to your company account for start-up costs and as a goodwill bond. Alan will work closely with you on purchasing and provide you with any support you need, he has a team in place for that. Tom will provide the security and will place one of his teams to work with you. You're going to find security a big issue. One day this will all come out. It is going to be hard to keep a lid on it, particularly as the manning levels increase,' Robert said, with deep conviction in his voice.

'Robert, we'll do our best and won't let you down,' Matt said, as he stretched out his hand to shake Robert's in agreement on the deal. 'And, Pilot, how do you like Oz?' Matt asked, lightening the mood of the conversation. He and his sons had been captivated by him through the discussions.

As usual the Pilot was dressed in a shabby flight suit; he lounged in a chair with his feet up sipping beer and smoking, occasionally giving his expert advice. Over time, Robert had gained more of an understanding of his knowledge and suspected the mysterious Pilot was more than just a mere shuttle pilot.

'Well I like this,' the Pilot replied, shaking the bottle of beer, 'but I haven't seen much of this vast continent to give a fair answer.'

'And are all purebreeds like you?' Matt asked.

'Definitely not,' Tom said, smiling at Matt's question.

'That was not very nice of you, Tom. You Earthlings just don't understand me. You know, Matt, they sent me to France on a job, and I don't think this is an unreasonable request, but I wanted to score with a hot French woman. So instead of taking me clubbing they gave me a few bottles of cheap wine and left me in my shuttle on a low-loader at the side of the road. Not very hospitable, was it?' the Pilot said, sticking his nose in the air as he puffed on his cigarette. Matt and his sons were speechless as Robert, Tom and Alan burst out laughing.

It was another project milestone. Contracts were signed, money transferred and the works to open the *Hela*'s Australian base commenced. Matt was true to his word and the family, delighted with the opportunity Robert had given them, threw their heart and soul into the project.

The unrelenting data mining finally gave Chang his first break. His hackers found the records of Tom's security company in Sydney and the address of his first office, now transferred to Anan Corporation and occupied by one of Alan's procurement and hiring teams. Tom, unaware that Chang knew of his existence, completely missed the discovery of their Sydney office.

'Well done,' Chang said to his Australian control agent, after he delivered pictures of the Anan Corp small Sydney office. 'Do not do anything, watch from afar. Use locals as much as you can. Find out what they are doing, and do not get discovered. If you must compromise getting the information, so be it, we play the patience game.'

Over the next two weeks, they watched and surreptitiously followed the coming and goings at the Anan Corp small offices. Finally, and after all Tom's efforts to compartmentalise the different operations and locations, they successfully followed one of the office staff to the project's Sydney operations base. Breaking protocol, the man stopped at the office to collect documents he had forgotten for a meeting he was attending in the operations base. It was the mistakes Chang loved. They now had another location to watch, and it provided the jackpot, as Chang mulled over a picture of Thomas Parker. *I have found you at last*, he thought, delighted to have the upper hand.

The location of the operations base in the old industrial park made surveillance difficult. Chang's directive, that they not be discovered, hampered his operatives in this quiet area. However, with imagination, long lens cameras and the use of overflights and a satellite, they finally built up a puzzling profile of the base activities. The comings and goings were erratic; some people arrived in the evening and didn't leave until the following morning. Yet there did not appear to be accommodation in the industrial unit, or was there? Chang couldn't figure this out. Tom commuted back and forth to a hotel where he stayed with some others in the group. So why were others staying overnight in the base? Was there a night shift, if so, what did they do? Goods arrived but were not dispatched anywhere.

The more they watched, the more intrigued Chang became. He did not know they were watching the commuting and delivery of people and equipment for the cloaked *Hela* shuttles. It was the second supply base, and working to support the Christchurch base. They could also provide transport for Alan and Kath and some of their team back and forth between Christchurch and Sydney. These movements increased their exposure and aggravated Tom, who realised it was only a matter of time before Chang discovered them.

Rhea and Alex were working long hours together in med-bay. It was painstaking work, and she realised how different this research-based work was to what she was trained to do. She found he was an inspiration to her. His methods were slow and methodical. They had developed a blood sample database from all the purebreed crew and the humans on the *Hela*. He was particularly fixated with Niamh's blood sample and had asked Niamh for another. When Rhea learned that Niamh was coming by med-bay for another sample she objected vociferously. The sight of her in her slim T-shirt sitting in front of him and chatting loudly and cheerfully to him made her blood boil. She couldn't understand the feeling, but it just made her mad. Alex found her reaction most unprofessional and told her so.

'There's nothing going on here, she's with the security man, Tom, he's on Earth. I need another sample of her blood, that's all,' he said, in a voice she had not heard him use before. He sounded angry with her and he actually was.

Alex couldn't understand her. He had spent over five weeks working and living with her. They had not taken one day off. They worked together, went for meals together and always he stayed with her. He never mixed with the other humans on the *Hela*, even when the new crews came on board. When the Scotsman, Robert, the project manager had invited him to eat with them, he politely declined. He even heard two of the women, security they were, whispering about him. 'I reckon he's doing her,' said one. 'That's really weird, she isn't a looker, is she? And would you look at the mark on her neck?' said the other. It was hurtful to him. Rhea was quite attractive and the mark was healing up. True, it would remain there, but it did not detract from her striking appearance, he thought.

'So why must it be her blood?' she asked. She couldn't understand why his angry reply had hurt her so much and felt tears well up in her eyes.

'Because I believe she has the purest form of the gene splice that was introduced. If you look here —' he said, until he looked across at her and stopped. She was crying. He melted as he looked at her porcelain white skin and into her deep green tear-filled eyes. 'Rhea, I'm so sorry,' he said. He was now speechless with concern.

'I don't understand this either,' she said, now smiling at him and wiping the tears away.

'So show me why you need a fresh sample from the girl with the red hair.'

Delighted to be able to get back to the science and ignore any emotion, Alex quickly explained his theory. Niamh was considered the most intelligent of her species. Her DNA showed some marked differences to that of the other humans. He believed it was a purer form and not diluted by cross-breeding with the other humanoid species. And then he dropped a real bombshell. For the first time he showed Rhea his own DNA. It was similar to Niamh's with the same markings.

'You kept that quiet,' Rhea said, 'I'm sorry I doubted you. Alex, you're amongst the most intelligent of your species—'

'Rhea, I'm sorry I was angry with you. I didn't want to tell you this until I was sure,' he said, and for the first time he touched her gently on her shoulder as he smiled at her.

Feeling his hand on her she looked back into his brown eyes, and, watching him as he flicked his dark hair back from across his forehead, Rhea began to understand the emotion she was feeling.

SYDNEY 4TH MAY 2026

An excited Niamh, looking out of the shuttle at her first close-up view of Earth in over five weeks, was looking forward to this visit. She felt guilt as well, for the visit was to inspect equipment under construction in a factory in Sydney for the Overlord's transfer back to his energy mass. He had spent four weeks in the *Hela* databanks and, much to her surprise, he was enjoying it. He said he felt no pressure to conserve his blue and no guilt in its use. He believed his energy mass, stabilised by a small part of his consciousness, could last forever.

In addition to the gold transfer cables he asked for, she commissioned the build of the most advanced memory banks available on Earth for him. When she confided in him what she had done, he was ecstatic. When it was finished, he would be able to transfer back and forth from the new memory banks and also store his older memories, reducing his energy needs. The device would be portable too, enabling him to move about freely.

She was to inspect it today at the factory Tom had found for them. He would meet her and accompany her on her short visit on Earth. She had pleaded with him to let her stay overnight with him but he refused. She even presented a prescription written out by Alex for three days' shore leave on Earth. He was concerned by her pale complexion and how tired she looked when he took her blood sample in med-bay.

But Tom would not relent; he was paranoid that she would be kidnapped. He consigned her to the safety of the *Hela*, and she now felt it was her prison. Any other woman would suspect him of cheating but she knew he was incapable of that.

The shuttle landed inside the vast warehouse in their operations base. Fitted with a large hangar door, the warehouse allowed the shuttle's easy access and the loading and unloading was done away from the prying eyes of overflights or satellites. Niamh jumped out and ran straight into Tom's arms. As soon as she embraced him she felt something in his jacket. It frightened her, not the welcome she'd hoped for, she thought sadly. As he embraced her he felt her stiffen with fear and he knew what had caused that.

'I'm sorry, Niamh, but things are getting serious,' he whispered in her ear.

'Did you have to wear it now?' she whispered back, as a gun in his jacket pressed into her.

'I never take it off,' he said, as he kissed her passionately. He hadn't realised how much he had missed her.

Ignoring the intrusion of the gun she responded, holding him tight to her. As the feelings and events of the previous five weeks built up in her stomach into a painful knot, she slowly started to cry. It began in a slow whimper, as she clutched him, and built up into an uncontrollable outpouring of her emotions. How she missed him, the feeling of loneliness, the work pressure and the responsibility that if she failed they were all doomed. She let it all flow out as he held her tight.

'I'm sorry,' she said, trembling in his arms.

'It's OK,' he said softly, as he led her into his small office and some privacy from the eyes of the project personnel around them.

They sat entwined together on his office desk enjoying each other's company. As she relaxed into his closeness, she started to feel his deep fears for her safety. Its intensity frightened her. Surprised at the emotion she could feel from him, she pulled back from their embrace. She realised, enhanced by her blue diamond, her mental abilities were growing. It was something Theia said would happen, but she hadn't expected it to come so soon.

'Is it that bad?' she said.

'Yes, I'm sorry to say Maurice is dead. Chang got him, left his trademark, a bullet in the head.' He didn't mention the missing fingernails.

'That's awful,' she said as she looked into his eyes. 'The poor man. He didn't deserve that.'

'Niamh, there's more. They got your name from him. Demard intercepted an encrypted data transfer from Lyon to Beijing with a picture of your reactor project badge. Chang knows who you are, he's looking for you and I know his agents are here. I'm sorry, Niamh, but you're in real danger.'

She looked at him; *he's as crestfallen and emotional as me*, she thought. She didn't need to delve into his thoughts or feelings with her newfound abilities. It was all in his face and eyes.

'Well, look on the bright side,' she said, as she started to compose herself. 'I'm famous. Sure, in February nobody knew I existed! Yeah, I'll make the cover of the newspapers yet.'

'I sincerely hope not. Come on, time to go visit the factory,' he said, leading her to a large sinister-looking SUV with darkened windows that was parked inside the warehouse between two others.

'Could you not have got an armoured personnel carrier for me?' she asked when she saw her entourage assembled ready to go.

'I did try, but we couldn't get the Australian PM to agree to that,' he replied, thinking she was serious.

'Jeez, Tom, I was joking. You're impossible. But I missed you, I did,' she said and smiled at him.

As they drove out of the warehouse, Niamh couldn't resist having the window down. She missed the sun and the fresh air.

'Can you put the window up, please?' he asked, as they drove out the gate of their base.

'You spoilsport, I was enjoying the breeze.'

'Well, the tinted windows don't work when they're down.'

'You're a horrible man, you really are, and I don't suppose you'll let me stay tonight?' she asked as she put the window up.

'We talked about that, and you know the answer.'

'I knew it! You have some floozy stashed away here. What's she like? I bet she can't fix a fusion reactor, can she?'

And so their conversation playfully continued as Tom drove out to the factory. Both happy to be together, she berated him for protecting her and he simply took it, loving every minute of listening to her lilting Cork accent.

Chang's agents watched as the three SUVs entered the complex early in the morning. *This is different, looks like someone important is leaving*, thought control. As the vehicles sped out the gate, the multi-frame cameras held by his four agents recorded every second that the vehicles were in view. Control noticed one of the windows was open and hoped they had something useful for Chang.

'You have done well,' Chang said, grinning with delight as he looked at the photo of Niamh sitting in the front of the SUV. Her face was just in view but her red hair was unmistakable. In the moments they drove through the gate the open window was enough to reveal her presence in Sydney.

'We have the location they visited. It's a small electronics factory,' control said. 'And then they went back to their complex and she disappeared.'

'Infiltrate the factory. Set up cameras and a warning system. If we miss her at their base, we get the alert from the factory. Plan the hit there. She be back, it's the best place away from Parker's base.'

THE HELA 4TH MAY 2026

'They are getting more powerful,' Theia said, sitting with Niamh on the *Hela* bridge.

'It was a surprise, I could sense them before, emotions and feelings, but now it is much stronger. There is a clarity I did not expect. It surprised me with Tom today, I felt his fear — it was frightening.'

'Your abilities will grow as you learn how to use them. Be careful. You are stronger than most I have trained.'

'I am uneasy using it – I mean, it's not right to delve into people's thoughts…'

'No, Niamh, it is not. But you know I have done that and will do it again. I do not do it easily, only when matters of state or the project need my intervention. Do not use your powers for your own personal needs.'

'Oh, Theia, I couldn't do that.'

'Don't be so naïve. As you become more accustomed to your abilities they will become an extension of you. You will find you feel everything going on around you. That is probably happening now. Yes, I thought so,' she said as Niamh nodded in agreement. 'It will be a matter of time before you start reading people's minds without knowing what you are doing. No, don't shake your head like that. It will take effort to contain your ability.'

'Can all the navigators do this?'

'No, not all. The ability to read minds is not a common trait. But, our feelings are sharper than humans'. To some extent, all purebreeds can sense emotion. Niamh, something you must remember, do not delve where there is darkness. It will hurt you. Do you understand what I am saying?'

'I think so, Tom…'

'Yes. And others like him. Now we train,' said Theia as she turned away from Niamh and cut a deck of cards. 'Focus your mind, what card am I looking at?'

'I, I can't see, Theia, you're blocking me.'

'Of course I am, did you think it would be that easy? Now let's try that the other way, open your mind…'

And so the training continued. When Niamh finally retired she was exhausted from the day in Sydney and the mental gymnastics Theia put her through. As her head hit the pillow, like a knot in her stomach, Tom's fear came back to haunt her.

SYDNEY 6TH MAY 2026

Control had made good progress; he discovered what the factory was making for Anan Corp, concealed cameras in the factory and the surrounding grounds and obtained the plans of it. But best of all, he secreted one of his agents in employment there.

More technology and the most advanced in the world, thought Chang. He wasn't interested in getting the equipment the factory was making for them; it was available on the open market, but Niamh… If they could get her, that would be the prize. That was why he let Tom go about his business – he wanted her and she was the key. A pattern emerged from watching the base; he realised people were travelling. He didn't know where or how but whatever they were on to, it was related to travel by some advanced technology, and the Chinese wanted this more than anything. His superiors, and his other benefactor, were very interested in this operation. The plan was in place, the next time Niamh appeared at the factory they would be ready.

SYDNEY 18TH MAY 2026

Tom watched the sun rise over Sydney from the bedroom of his hotel. Niamh would soon arrive, promising another stressful but welcome day for him. After their short reunion two weeks ago he had realised how much he loved her; she was the most important person in his life, and losing her was not an option. Wondering how they could manage a life together on the project, he re-read his contract with Anan Corp. There was a marriage clause that he had not paid attention to when he first signed, but now he was intrigued by its content. It was a welcome sight, guaranteeing married quarters on the *Hela* and specific rights to time off together. He smiled to himself as he looked at the ring he had purchased that week. He would follow the order Admiral White gave him when they met for the treaty signing. He would ask Niamh to marry him today. When she was finished at the factory, the shuttle would take them to Christchurch, away from Chang and where they could have some quiet time together. She had worked constantly for nearly seven weeks and if she didn't get a break, she would burn out. She knew nothing of his plans but he hoped she would be delighted with the surprise.

Tom knew Chang was watching their operation base. His team had not spotted any of the watchers, but a pattern of flyovers by a small plane and erratic drive-bys emerged, enough to shake Tom to his very core. He made changes in the security detail to protect Niamh today. Instead of arriving at the operations base, he located a secluded landing site behind the factory. She would arrive soon and he would be there to meet her.

'Jeez, Tom, what are you at, having me traipsing through the fields? All we're short of is the cow shite,' she said, as she stepped out of the shuttle into the long grass.

They landed in between some secluded trees in a field directly behind the factory. Tom arranged a short walk through the field and in through a rear gate at the factory. When they arrived, he invented a simple cover story to tell to the factory manager: "their eccentric client just wanted a walk in the fields to clear her head".

'Is it a roll in the hay you're after?' she said as they embraced. As she looked at him, she focused on his emotions. They were all over the place, up and down, happy and concerned. He was planning something, she was sure of it. 'Thomas Parker, what are you up to?'

'Getting you in and out of here safely, that's the priority. Chang is watching our base, that's why you landed here,' he said in his serious tone. He was afraid she had rumbled his plans for later.

'Yep, I should have known better, you horrible man. In, out, and back to the *Hela*,' she said, looking back at him with sad eyes. It took all his concentration to mask his emotions, but he did.

'How much have you to do?' he asked returning to business.

'Check their progress and quality. I will be in the clean room today, looking at the memory banks assembly. The cables are finished; we can take them back to the *Hela*. You coming into the clean room? You'll have to change and leave the gun,' she said.

'We'll see before you go in,' he said. He hadn't thought of that and it nagged at him.

'Chang, Chang, we have her, she's in the factory,' shouted control across to Chang. They were sitting in an office they rented in the industrial estate across from the factory; he was glued to the camera monitor. 'Look, she is inside already. How did she get there? We saw Tom and his team arrive in the car park but she wasn't with them, I'm sure.'

'Never mind how, go get her,' Chang shouted.

Within minutes, control alerted his team that the job was on. He got her schedule from his agent working in the factory and an easy and simple plan for the job. It depended on precise timing between the agent inside and control's team outside.

Thirty minutes later an innocuous looking delivery van with the livery of one of the local freight companies drove in through the factory gate. It easily passed security, and continued around to the back of the factory, parking beside an emergency escape door.

In a small room where the employees working in the factory clean room environment changed, Niamh and Tom, placing all their personal possessions including the gun in lockers, were both finished dressing in the white one-piece suits. Niamh was used to this but Tom, leaving his team outside the changing room, found the garb strange and constraining. There were two others in the room with them, one was to accompany them on their visit and the other was already in the changing room when they entered, cleaning the floors. Tom watched him at his work and, satisfied there was no cause for suspicion, turned to Niamh.

As soon as Tom turned, Chang's agent took a gun out of his small work cart and shot him in the shoulder. Tom never saw it coming, hearing the muffled sound of the three shots - he felt the deep pain and shock - and fell to the floor. The agent pressed a button on a signal device in his pocket and then, grabbing one of the long stainless steel benches, propped it up against the entrance door as a wedge. Seconds later, the emergency exit door blew inwards with a loud bang. Six of Chang's agents flooded into the room and grabbed a surprised and shocked Niamh. They bundled her out through the emergency exit and into the back of the van parked outside. The bench wedged up against the door slowed down Tom's team who, alerted by the loud bang, tried to get in.

Fifteen minutes after it arrived, the delivery van with one extra agent and Niamh exited the factory gates. A terrified Niamh, in the clutches of the dragon, could not forget the image of Tom falling to the floor. But it was his call to her that she read from his mind that troubled her most. *I failed you, my love*, were his last thoughts as he fell to the floor.

·

'Pilot, get the shuttle to the south corner of the factory. You'll see my team there. No, I don't care if you're seen, cover is blown. Clear a flight plan back to the *Hela* and have med-bay ready,' Bill, the security team leader, said over the comms device to the shuttle pilot.

'Alice, is he stabilised?'

'Yes, the bullets missed his heart but his shoulder is a mess. I'll give him morphine.'

'No, no morphine,' whispered a still conscious Tom. 'I can hear her. She is trying to tell me where they're going.'

'OK, Tom, no morphine. You two help Alice get him into the shuttle now,' Bill barked to Gwen and Brian, not understanding a word Tom was saying. 'The rest of you, come with me, we're getting the cables for the Overlord. I heard her tell Tom they're ready.'

The traumatised factory manager gladly handed over the gold cables, wrapped and ready for Niamh to collect, to the Anan Corp security team. He and his staff were relieved to see them leave but troubled by Bill's strict instructions not to call the police.

'Bill, listen to me, I know where they are going. Hold the Pilot here until I have the location,' Tom whispered, as he sat propped up in the shuttle. He had pictures in his mind of road signs and a view of the area she was driving through. He realised she was using her blue diamond and navigation abilities. Directing the shuttle to a country area outside Sydney, they hovered cloaked over the countryside watching the traffic driving back and forth.

'Wait,' Tom said then, after a few minutes, 'they've stopped. I can see the house, it's along this road.' The pilot flew slowly in the direction Tom indicated until he told him to stop. 'There, she's in there,' he said, pointing to a remote old rambling Queenslander surrounded by fields. Parked outside the house were four vans and two cars, a good indication of the number of occupants inside.

'Tom, we need to get you back to the *Hela*, we're not going in now,' Bill said as Tom slowly nodded his head. He knew where she was and that she was still alive; that was enough, he thought, as he slipped into blackness.

Niamh could feel him with her all the way until they got into the house. She could feel him near in the shuttle following her directions, and then he was gone. It scared her. She was alone. Where was he? she thought, as all she connected with was blackness. She feared he was dead, finally succumbing to his wounds, and it was that thought that terrified her most. They bundled her into the house and down into a basement, tying her to a chair.

'Niamh Sullivan, so good to meet you,' he said grinning at her. 'I am Chang Jin, but you probably guessed that. I am so pleased to meet you, you are amazing, so amazing. How do you do it, popping up here and there, and flying across the world without being detected? My boss would love to have you as a guest of the People's Republic of China. Now to business, I want to know everything. Of course you don't want to tell me anything, so I have prepared an interrogation plan. I will ask some questions, and you can, or not, answer them. We will do that for today. Tomorrow, if I am not satisfied with your answers, my colleague, you have not met her yet, will use more persuasive methods.'

Niamh was scared but her intelligence prevailed and she started to analyse her predicament. She needed to stall for time. They knew where she was, and would return to get her. Besides, Chang needed to know who he was dealing with.

'You won't believe me if I tell you,' she said quietly to Chang.

'Try me, and what is that around your neck?' he asked, referring to her blue diamond.

'It's a crystal,' she said, now afraid he would take it from her.

'Remind you of someone?' he asked.

'Yes.'

'You can keep it. Now, who do you work for?' he shouted.

Niamh couldn't believe her luck. When the time was right she would use her pendant. 'I work for Anan Corporation,' she replied.

'Well, we know that, but it's a good start, go on.'

'Mr Chang, I abhor you and all you stand for and you killed Maurice, but what I will tell you is true. You're not going to believe it until you see it for real. So, if I tell you, will you listen to my story?' she asked quietly.

'Go on, I listen, I promise, I listen.'

Niamh told him a story, based on the real events about aliens who came from space with a broken space ship that they were to repair. That's where the parts from the European reactor site went, she explained. She spun the yarn for hours and enchanted Chang with her soft lilting accent. After three hours of stories and questions, Chang stopped her.

'You are a marvellous storyteller. I enjoyed that, I really did. But you know I can't tell my superiors in Beijing that it is aliens who you are working for and not to worry, they mean no harm. No, it wouldn't go down very well. But I believe there is something strange here. I must validate your story. As an engineer, you understand validation,' he said smiling at her. 'My colleague will work with you on the validation of your story tomorrow. You will be treated well tonight, we will provide you with food and a place to sleep and a toilet.' Then bowing his head at her, he left.

For the first time in his life Chang was at a loss and to some extent frightened. He didn't understand what was going on, but her story, although not completely true, was plausible. He recalled the conversation he had with Charl about the strange events in the room in Christchurch. Chang retrieved a sat phone from his bag and walked out of the building. As he walked in the garden he placed the call.

'Something big and different is happening-' he said before the other interrupted.

'Yes, I am sure of it. A change is coming, are you ready?' He waited for the reply.

'No. Why not? You trick me. I chart my own way now. But know this, some day you will come running back to me.' As he turned the phone off he looked at his hands, they were shaking with rage. He walked back to the house and sat on the veranda. Closing his eyes, he thought about the treacherous benefactor he had just called. As the fog of his anger slowly cleared, he smiled to himself. *Who knows*, he thought, *this could be a good thing.*

THE HELA 18TH MAY 2026

The bridge of the *Hela* was a hive of activity. Everybody wanted to do something to help while Tom was in med-bay under the care of Alex and Rhea.

'Niamh was their target,' John said, now the Deputy Security Manager, to Robert and Alan who were in Sydney. 'All our Australian security teams are making their way to protect you.'

'How's Tom?' Robert asked.

'Bullets missed the heart, so Alex is confident he will recover quickly,' John replied. 'You guys stay put for the night. We have surveillance on the house, and they won't get her out of the country.'

'What about getting her back?'

'Not to be discussed like this, Robert, over a comms link. I will talk to you tomorrow,' John replied, as he cut the link with Robert and Alan.

'We will get her back tomorrow,' Mack said. 'Bri, take John and his team to the armoury, introduce them to our weapons, it is time they learned how to use them. Empress, see if you can link with Niamh. I will talk to the Australian PM. I don't want this to get into the public domain. We will handle it.' Her kidnapping was a blow and, coupled with the loss of the Overlord to the *Hela* databank, it had a huge impact on the project personnel, both human and purebreed. The rumour mill had started in earnest, whipping up all sorts of stories of doom and gloom, and stoking their vulnerable fears that the Project was doomed to failure.

RESPITE

CHAPTER FOURTEEN

OUTSKIRTS OF SYDNEY 19TH MAY 2026

'Enjoying your breakfast?' Chang asked Niamh who, surprising herself, tucked into a big breakfast of greasy bacon, eggs and toast. He was true to his word and she had spent a comfortable night locked in a room with a bed and toilet.

'It's lovely,' she mumbled as she chewed her food. 'I hope it tastes as good on the way up.' She had no illusions about what was to come and was resigned to her fate. She suspected by noon she would be screaming for mercy, covered in her own vomit, waste and blood.

'Ha, ha, you are so funny. No, I don't think it will taste so good when you vomit it back today. Now to business,' he said, wiping the crumbs from his mouth and looking intently at Niamh.

She detected an air of fear from him, which was unexpected and out of character. She would not dare look into his mind for fear of the shock his darkness would give her. Theia warned her about this, and she restrained herself when so close to him. But his emotions were out there for her to see clearly, and they surprised her – yes, he was afraid.

'I respect you, you are very intelligent. We heard whispers about your abilities. Don't look so surprised, it is hard to keep such a secret. I suspect they will rescue you soon. We won't be able to get you out of Australia, I am sure. I'm no fool. I may not have believed your story, but I know when something big is brewing. So when you are rescued, tell your masters we will not give up. Everything we learn is another layer of the onion we peel, and eventually we will have the core,' he said, in a quiet and chilling voice.

'So, Chang, I'm just another layer of the onion to you? Is that all there is to this?'

'No, Niamh Sullivan, there is more. This is the precursor to a global war.'

'Chang, no, you and your masters don't have to do this. Please work with us, please, our clients and us; we are not monsters, there is so much to learn. You have no idea what's at stake,' she said, pleading with him now. She sensed he had turned a corner and wanted to drag him back from the brink.

'It is too late; my masters are frothing at the mouth.'

'Chang, you don't know what you're dealing with, please, please listen to me. You can have the technology, not all of it but enough to make a big difference, if you follow a peaceful path. Work with us, not against us,' she said, looking into his eyes, and then surprising Chang she reached out and gently grasped his hand. 'Chang, please don't do this, and I'm not pleading for my life or for you to spare me pain today. I'm talking of war, you must stop it. If you must, kill me today. It won't stop the inevitable change that is coming.' She was surprised to see tears in his eyes, and as they slowly seeped down his face he clasped her hand and gently kissed it.

'You are an extraordinary woman. The rumours about you are right. Unfortunately, business is business, I have a reputation to uphold and my masters are hungry. I go now; my colleague will be in shortly. I have given her strict instructions on how to treat you. It won't be pleasant but will serve my purpose and cause least long term damage to you. Goodbye, Niamh Sullivan,' he said in a sad tone, which conveyed his belief that they would never see each other again. She was the key, he thought. He had her and she would unlock the door. There were cameras all over this place and outside as well. Whatever happened here today would be recorded and sent back to his masters in Beijing. They would finally see who they were dealing with. Leaving Niamh inside, Chang left the building and climbed into a small helicopter waiting outside. Hearing the engine and rotors start up, Niamh realised what was happening. *It's a trap, he planned this all the time; he wants Tom and the shuttle as well*, she thought, as she focused her mind and tried to contact them.

BEIJING 19TH MAY 2026

'We have the pictures, Chang, what do you expect to see?' asked Chang's boss on a comms link from Beijing. He was with a small group of China's top military command watching Chang's live camera feeds from the house in Australia, displayed on a large screen overlooking a secret military control room.

'I don't know, we watch and wait,' he said, aware that his reputation depended on this. He believed Niamh. They were dealing with something beyond their comprehension and this was the only way to get his masters to believe what was to come. It took all responsibility for the future decisions from him. They could not blame him for their failed choices.

The torture was boring; she was using crude water torture, forcing Niamh to ingest and vomit it, then wrapping her head in a wet cloth to simulate drowning. They realised it would be a patience game, and some brought work with them to occupy the long time they believed it would take.

'Who do you work for?' she screamed at Niamh, as Niamh gagged and spluttered. She was restrained, sitting in the chair in her underwear covered with vomit, her own waste and blood. The constant excruciating pain she suffered from the beatings was hard to bear but it was the drowning feeling that terrified her the most. She did not know how long she could bear this. She felt the cold, the pain from her wounds, humiliated and personally degraded. Niamh just wanted the bitch inflicting this horrible nightmare on her to stop. She told her everything she told Chang, over and over. Unknown to Niamh, she endured over three hours of this constant barrage. She was surprised that she was still allowed to keep her pendant. She could feel Theia with her, and tried hard to tell her to back off. *It's a trap, Theia, they are watching*, she kept thinking over and over. But Theia couldn't bear it. She could feel the pain and suffering, the near death experiences as Niamh gagged from the water forced down her throat, and was then revived again, as they pumped the water from her lungs and the pain as they continued to hit her across the face.

I'm getting nowhere, thought Niamh's assailant, a young up and coming agent in Chang's organisation who wanted to impress the group she knew were watching. *There is one thing a woman is fearful of,* she thought, *no children.* Contrary to Chang's instructions she started to beat Niamh in her lower abdomen, targeting her womb.

'No,' screamed Theia, sitting on the bridge of the *Hela* with her blue diamond inserted into the navigation console. She had linked with Niamh and could see and feel everything. Enough, she thought, the potential loss of Niamh's ability to bear children could not happen. *Relax, Niamh,* she said, as she projected her mind out through Niamh's blue diamond.

It happened so fast most of those watching in Beijing missed it. Those that did see it stood up in amazement. A thin blue light flashed out from the crystal hanging around Niamh's neck and hit the young Chinese woman between the eyes. As she slumped to the floor her two male assistants grabbed her and warily withdrew. Their look of abject fear said it all as they left Niamh slumped in the chair.

'So that's what it does,' Chang said, watching in a secure location well away from the house.

'What just happened?' asked his boss, who had missed the event and was now watching it on a replay.

'Again, I don't know, but I wondered what that crystal was. Now I see; it is a weapon of some sort. Why did she not use it before?' Thinking about his own question, he suspected she wanted to guard its secret. 'Wait and see what happens next,' he continued, now excited with the prospect of more to come.

Suddenly, on one of the external camera views of the sky above the house, a group of seven masked warriors, covered in strange grey one-piece suits, mysteriously appeared out of thin air. Six were in a formation that would circle the house when they landed, with the seventh below the main group and off to the side of the formation.

It was Tom, leading the rescue team who had just left the cloaked shuttle hovering above the house. The team were wearing personal grav suits that protected them and provided the wearer with the ability to fly short distances.

Bri had delighted in instructing them in their use in the cavernous *Hela* main cargo hold before they departed that morning. Despite Bri's protest, a partially recovered Tom insisted on leading the mission. If it failed, they could not risk the loss of Bri. A live alien would be paraded on the world stage by the Chinese. It would be a propaganda coup. Up until now, all they had seen were humans, and it would stay that way, he insisted.

The six of the seven landed around the house, and to the horror of those watching in Beijing, just broke through the walls, leaving gaping holes where they entered. To make matters worse, the grey-suited warriors were impervious to the barrage of automatic fire directed at them by Chang's twenty guards. As the warriors encountered opposition, they pointed a slim stick, like a truncheon, at their assailants. The Beijing watchers could see it vibrate and send a pulse that knocked their own men down. But it was the carnage their own men created with the incessant discharge of their automatic weapons that shocked the watchers the most. The bullets ricocheted off the grey-suited warriors, some into Chang's men, killing or wounding them. Unlike Chang, who had foreseen defeat and chosen those most expendable, his masters had not expected to see such a graphic demise of their well-armed force by so few.

Mack warned them about the ricochet problem. It would not affect the team in protective grav suits but a stray bullet could penetrate the basement and hit Niamh. It was their biggest concern. It was up to Tom, flying below the main team, to penetrate the basement and get to her first. Knowing her exact location was a bonus. Programming the suit with the basement coordinates, he was the first in, flying straight in through a small window. It was an ungraceful entrance as he crashed through it, smashing out the wooden wall it was mounted in. He landed hard on the basement floor. Unable to control the new technology and the grav effects from the suit, he bounced back up, hitting the ceiling, and then down again hard onto the floor where he rolled along until he came to a stop metres in front of Niamh.

The impact hurt his recovering wounds, disrupting the Anan healing properties Alex had applied in the med-bay before Tom left that morning. Pumped up with adrenaline, and oblivious to the pain in his shoulder, he ran to her. To protect her from the barrage of bullets to come, he quickly threw a large grey cover, made of the same compound as the personal grav suits over her.

'I'm in, she is secured,' he told his team over their comms system, as they came crashing in above.

The house above exploded with gunfire. The sound of bullets bouncing off the rescue team's grav suits and the screaming of Chang's injured and dying men filtered down to the basement. Tom lifted Niamh, still secured to the chair and covered in the protective grav-blanket, up in his arms. As his team above defeated Chang's men, he carried her through the debris and stray bullets now penetrating the basement. With difficulty he hovered in the grav suit. Breaking through more of the wooden wall to make room for the increased bulk of Niamh, he flew out the way he came in. The Pilot waited precariously above the basement entrance with the shuttle door turned towards him. Carrying Niamh, Tom flew back to the safety of the ship. He crashed into the seats in an ungainly fashion, as the Pilot quickly turned the shuttle away from the fray below and gained height back to safety.

'Niamh, Niamh, it's me, Tom,' he said, as he removed the grav cover and gently cut her out of the chair, throwing it out the shuttle door, and finally wrapping her gently in a clean warm blanket.

'Are we both dead?' she asked in a weak groggy voice.

'We're very much alive,' he said as he cradled her in his arms.

'Where are we and where we going?' she asked, slowly coming around and responding to his warm embrace.

'We're in the shuttle. We'll go to the *Hela* first to have you fixed up. Then, if you'll have me, to Christchurch to see about getting married,' he replied as he held her tightly.

'Jeez, Tom, could you not have picked a more romantic moment to pop the question? I mean, I stink, I'm covered in blood, my own mess and nearly naked. But yes, yes,' she said, happily hugging him as his crew arrived noisily into the shuttle, some crashing ungracefully into the seats and walls around them. Elated with their victory and pumped up by the use of the new technology, they shouted greetings and gave Niamh a warm welcome back.

'All back, boss, and I blew them the goodbye kiss you asked for,' Bill said, their team leader, and the last one in. 'Good to see you, Niamh, you gave us a scare. Wow, you smell. It's like you had a rough night out.'

'Bill, don't be such an asshole. She was just kidnapped,' shouted Alice. 'And just because you smell like that after a night out, don't expect we all do. You OK, Niamh?' She stooped down beside Niamh to attend to her wounds.

'Yes, thanks, lads.' Looking at them, she found it hard to understand why these six and Tom, still recovering from his wounds, had risked their lives for her.

'Where's that blood coming from?' asked Alice, noticing she was now kneeling in front of Niamh in a small pool of blood. 'Tom, is that yours?' she asked as she noticed a grey-looking Tom starting to slump over.

'Help here, men, get that grav suit off him, quickly,' she shouted loudly at the others beside her.

They grabbed Tom, quickly removing his grav suit. The open wound on his shoulder revealed the source of the blood, and it was all over the inside of his suit. As Bill prepared a large field dressing Alice applied pressure to the wound to stem the blood flow. Ignoring Niamh, they quickly applied the dressing and laid Tom out on the floor, with one of the team holding his torso from behind, elevating his head and shoulders.

'Here, Bill, start giving him that fluid Alex gave us, yes, the purebreed plasma from Anan,' she said, passing an intravenous drip to Bill.

'Is he all right?' asked Niamh, looking down at the unconscious Tom, now showing a grey-white pallor from loss of blood. She could feel all the emotions of the crew around her. It changed from happy elation to a deadly fear in seconds. The emotion, the joy of her reunion with Tom, the pain and the suffering she had endured that morning, and now the prospect of losing him again was too much for Niamh to bear. Her mind shut it all out, as she passed out, and slumped in her chair.

'Ah shit, what next?' Alice said, moving quickly to attend to Niamh.

'Having a bad day at the office, dear?' Bill said, as he reached out and put a gentle hand on Alice's shoulder, now stooped beside him holding Niamh. 'You've done good, Alice, we'll be back on the *Hela* soon.' They were hopeful words. Looking at the pool of blood on the floor of the shuttle, Bill knew what a grave condition Tom was in.

Chang was delighted with the spectacle watched by the Chinese military command and his boss in their Beijing control room. It shocked them all, and left no doubt as to the capabilities of their opponents. He couldn't have planned it better; the ball was now clearly in his masters' court. He had delivered with style, they would never have believed him if he had tried to verbally report this. He pitied them. Niamh Sullivan was right; they were up against a formidable foe. There was no profit in fighting them; they should work with them and see what it would bring. But he knew his masters, old men in grey drab suits that matched their single minded ideology for world dominance. They would bungle along, thinking their nuclear weapons were the answer to all. The war would come, and he feared they would lose. He needed to plan for that.

'Are there any left alive?' Chang's boss asked.

'There are five out of the twenty we had. They were the first to get stunned. The rest, including those in the basement, were killed by our own crossfire and ricochet bullets.'

'Are you saying they didn't kill any of our people, only stunned them?'

'Yes, even my assistant. The energy flash stunned her, but she made it up the stairs and was shot by our own fire.'

'What is your assessment of this, Chang?'

'They are a force with new technology, they are human, there is no doubt of that, but where the technology is coming from… I need more information to answer that. You heard the interrogation yourself. They are not working for the Australian government. It's a private firm called Anan Corporation,' he replied, refusing to mention any reference to aliens. It was up to his masters to draw that conclusion on their own, he thought.

The soldiers' movements left no doubt they were human. But it was the gesture of the last to leave, "the kiss" Tom carefully briefed Bill to deliver, which left no doubt in the minds of those watching in Beijing that the soldiers were human. The last they saw of these grey-clad warriors was a masked Bill sticking one middle finger up to a camera, and in case they were in any doubt of the meaning of the gesture, mouthing the words "up yours".

That evening, the news wires ran a story about a gang war that resulted in the shooting of fifteen people. Anan Corp paid the factory handsomely for the inconvenience and the Australian PM called the manager to personally thank him for his discretion. The dragon licked its wounds as Chang wondered what his masters would do next. With the flight of his "benefactor", he contemplated his own precarious position, and resolved to do everything to secure that first.

✦

CHRISTCHURCH 22ND MAY 2026

Kath, sitting beside a sleeping Niamh, found it hard to come to terms with the events of the previous week. It hurt her to think what had happened, and the pain and suffering this woman Kath hired had endured. She tried to blame Tom, but as she looked across to the other bed where he lay, she couldn't. He had done all he possibly could to protect her and nearly made the ultimate sacrifice of his own life to get her back. The diamond he gave her while in med-bay on the *Hela* to cement their engagement sparkled on her finger, and Kath wondered whether they would ever get to enjoy a life together.

Alex arranged their treatment and recuperation in this newly constructed private hospital in Christchurch.

'I am not a god,' he said angrily when they returned Tom, at death's door, to med-bay, 'there are limits, even to Anan technology.'

But it was Rhea who managed to save Tom. She amazed Alex with her surgical skills and the way she stabilised Tom's body, skilfully using all the Anan medical technology and the special plasma they had taken with them from Anan. It served as blood replacement, giving the body time to heal itself after a massive trauma wound. It was what kept him alive on the shuttle journey back to the *Hela*.

Before they both left the *Hela* for this badly needed rest and recovery, Niamh managed to gather enough strength to supervise the fitting of the cables and the transfer of the Overlord back to his energy mass. With the supply of blue, his powers were restored and he could protect the *Hela* from attack. It was the reassurance they all needed to quell the rumour mill and to dispel the stories of doom and gloom.

There was a soft knock on the door; Kath looked surprised as one of the security team entered the room with a large bouquet of flowers. The beautiful display contained orchids and peony roses, mixed with red and white carnations. There was no doubt as to its source, with the motif of a golden dragon embossed on the red paper the flowers were wrapped in.

Tom and Niamh, both sleeping, woke at the sound of the knock on their door. Kath could hear the sharp intake of breath as Niamh spotted the dragon motif.

'They are safe, boss, we scanned them, and there is this,' said their guard, holding up a smartphone. 'You know who it's from, boss.'

'Give it here,' Tom said, looking across at Kath who was now holding Niamh's hand. Looking at the phone he called the only number in its contact list.

'Hello,' came back Chang's unmistakable voice.

'Chang, you found us.'

'Ah, Thomas Parker, I trust you are recovering. Good, I did not mean for my agent to mortally wound you so. Happily, he left this life at the country house, dispatched by one of his fellow agents. How is Niamh? I want to talk to her please, then we talk business. Yes?'

'He wants to talk to you,' Tom said, looking concerned at Niamh as he held his hand over the phone.

'Give it here,' she said. 'Well, ya monster, didn't think I'd be talking to you so soon. How did you find us?'

'Easy, I am Chang, resourceful. But that is not why I called, you got the flowers?'

'Yes, they are beautiful, really beautiful, totally out of character, and there's no bomb in them, I'm told.'

'No bomb, only apologies for what I put you through and for the attack on your abdomen, not sanctioned by me. Happily, the bitch is gone with the other incompetent one. Now let me talk business to Parker please.'

'Chang, for a change, I'm speechless. Here's Tom,' she said, handing the phone over to Tom.

'Go ahead, Chang, I'm listening.'

'I found you easily, and others will too. You're not imaginative enough. I am disappointed in you, Parker. You put that lovely woman in danger again. You know I have a reputation to uphold. If my masters find out about this they skin me alive, literally. You have to up your game, Parker.'

He sounds angry with me, thought a mystified Tom. As he looked at a smiling Niamh, he realised there was a change in Chang's tactics. The implications were enormous. 'I'm sorry, Chang, you are right, I don't deserve her,' he said, tentatively feeling Chang out for an opportunity.

'Don't patronise me. Listen and listen close. Your beau told me you work for a powerful entity and I believe that. I also believe my masters follow a failed ideology. If what your beau told me is true, that dogma could lead to the ruin and destruction of the Chinese nation, something I not stand for.

They will not change despite what I, with your help, have shown them. They do not see what is coming.'

'What do you propose?'

'An alliance. I provide you with information when I can. Parker, you have to up your subterfuge game. Did you see the recent photos of the Russian, disgusting, I know who shot the bear for him, over seventy and he still tries to play the hero! We divert attention to him, He is too old and vain to realise what is happening, and the entourage that fawns on him are no better.'

Tom realised what Chang's game would be. He was referring to the chairman of the newly-formed Great Northern Union, who was recently pictured with blood on his hand as he held the head of a dead bear against his chest with one hand and a rifle with the other. 'What do you need from us?' he asked, intrigued by Chang's proposal and guessing what was coming.

'You send me pictures of you in empty warehouse in Sydney and Christchurch. Send pictures of old abandoned gold mines in the desert. Finally, I don't know how you pulled that job in France, but can you do something similar for the Great Northern Union, close to the Chinese border?'

'Yes, Chang, we can. We can create the illusion of a secret base working to develop weapons systems from a newly discovered technology. One of our alien friends is very good at cyber war, he put together the French job,' Tom said, realising it was the first time he had talked so frankly about the purebreeds to Chang.

'Good, feed me that, I will give you the details as to how I "discover it" and a time scale. I can hold them off as long as possible, but they will eventually become suspicious and there are others who will suspect me. You know, I have bite marks on my ankles from the young hounds chomping at my feet for advancement, it is getting tiresome.'

'So what do you get in return?'

'Niamh mentioned the entity, I am surprised I am still alive, but all I ask is that it spares me when my masters move on your organisation. Is that too much?'

'The Eight, he is called The Eight and he did want to turn you to dust, but Niamh convinced him it was a bad idea. Hold on,' he said to Chang, covering the phone as he turned to Niamh. 'Chang will help us. All he wants is that the Overlord spares him if the Chinese hit us again. Can you talk to him about sparing Chang, will he listen to you?'

'I'll do that, and he will listen, he already spared his life once.'

'Niamh will talk to him, Chang, no guarantees, but I believe he will spare you,' replied Tom, realising Chang's strategy could leave him as the head of the People's Republic of China. It was a momentous play by the spy master, he would either be skinned alive by his masters or left sitting pretty on top of one of the largest powerful nations on Earth. 'So will we see a new dynasty, Chang Jin the First perhaps?'

'Parker, you do me an injustice. I am only doing this for the good of my country.' He paused for his words to sink in, and then continued, 'thank Niamh for me. That is all I can ask and hope for. I go now and will be in touch, keep this phone on and I will arrange other contact details,' and then the line went dead.

Tom looked at Kath and Niamh. 'I think we may have bought the eight months we need before our departure for the new world.'

They spend the next twenty minutes going over the gist of their conversations with Chang. It was a turning point in the fortunes of the Project and an astounding development. However, a cynical Tom reminded Kath and Niamh that Chang was looking after Chang; if he succeeded he could end up as the new Emperor of China.

'Don't be so negative, Tom. You always look for the worst possible outcome,' said Niamh as she lay in her bed with Kath lounging beside her.

'Yes, Tom, you do. And it's what we pay him for, Niamh. He is right, Mr Chang is a monster, he is working on his own survival,' Kath said as she looked across at a pale Tom.

Niamh would be out of the hospital tomorrow and Tom in another week. Rhea had specified the treatment and the time it would take for the purebreed plasma to stabilise him and for his own body to heal. Tom felt the effects of the effort of the conversation with Chang. He was relieved. For the first time in the Project they had gained some respite, some valuable time and the safety to move forward. He relaxed back into the bed. Letting his eyes close he drifted off to sleep, listing to the quiet voices of Kath and Niamh happily planning the wedding.

MED-BAY HELA 28TH MAY 2026

'Alex, don't beat yourself up about it, you have worked wonders,' Rhea said, looking at him. He was now thinner than when she had first met him. His dark hair had grown and his skin was going pale from lack of sunlight. He refused to go back to Earth. If it hadn't been for the intervention of the bossy Earthling with the strange accent she believed Alex would now be incapacitated by lack of exercise. Robert had a small exercise bike delivered to the med-bay and insisted the Doc, as he called Alex, use it every day. The Anan computer tech, Demard, who was now their patient, installed a monitoring device on the machine. If Alex didn't complete his daily routine Demard refused to participate in the treatment program. They developed an interdependent relationship as both had a vested interest in the wellbeing of the other.

'I can't manufacture a cure here on the *Hela*,' he said. He was nearly in tears with the frustration. So near, yet so far. They had identified the genes and compounds needed for the cure and developed an initial first stage treatment. Alex was reluctant to try it on the Anans. It needed to be proven first in a laboratory, he insisted. Theia quickly overruled that, and asked for a volunteer as a test subject. Much to Theia's surprise and delight, all the sick purebreeds volunteered.

And so she had chosen Demard. Initial tests on Demard were positive. The sores were starting to heal and Alex was confident they had at least arrested the progress of the disease. Demard was delighted – if it went wrong, he had nothing to lose. The disease was more advanced in him than in the other purebreeds, he suspected, without this treatment he would die within two of Earth's orbits.

'It takes months and sometimes years to develop and grow a cure on Earth with our technology,' Alex said. 'We are so limited with what we can do here on the *Hela*.'

'Look at the positive, look at what you can do,' she said, now displaying the practical attitude she had assimilated from him. 'With the advanced research equipment you brought up from Earth, you can manufacture the first stage treatment that inhibits the growth of the disease here on the *Hela*. The formula you developed for the cure may be manufactured on Anan. I know that may be some time away but, Alex, that's amazing, truly amazing, you have given us hope, don't you see that?' she said, looking into his brown eyes as they stood together in med-bay. She noticed the sparkle he had when he first arrived was dimming. He was losing his vibrant and infectious energy.

'I'm burnt out,' he said. 'And you are wrong in what I did,' he said, now holding her by her arms and looking straight into her green eyes. 'It was us, you must always remember that, we did this as a team, I would not have achieved anything without you,' he said. Not knowing why, he gently put his arms around her and drew her in to him. She was slightly taller than he and he was able to rest his head on her shoulder. She was surprised and could feel him trembling. She understood what was coming next and placed her hand gently on his head, drawing him closer to her. And then it came, driven by the pressure, the pent-up emotion and the fatigue, Alex started to cry. The work developing a cure, the trauma of the *Hela* accidents and trying to treat Tom's bloody and near fatal wounds had taken their toll on him. As she held him tight, his crying slowly abated to a soft sob.

'I'm sorry, I'm so sorry,' he said in a halting voice as she sat him down gently at his desk, wiping the tears from his eyes.

'It's OK, it's OK, you are after all only human,' she said, trying to cheer him up. 'Purebreeds don't cry like that.'

'Yes you do, we're both made from the same building blocks, remember?' he said, looking at her with an intensity that she had not seen for some time. 'There's a way to finish this here on the *Hela*,' he said as the realisation of what he missed suddenly came to him, it was what he had just said and the use of the purebreed plasma on Tom that triggered the idea.

'Yes, there is and I was wondering when you would come to that conclusion,' she said as her voice dropped coyly.

'You knew?'

'Yes, I believed it would be possible, I was not sure you were ready for that. I mean —'

'Yes, Rhea, I see, it's more than science now. There's much more involved.'

'Think about it, Alex, please do. If it works we will prove the cure here on the *Hela*. We will save two to three years in development time waiting to get back to Anan and can immediately save the crew that are sick.'

'Rhea, Rhea, there's more to it than that. There are moral issues and there will be two lives at risk.'

'I am prepared for that. Risking two for the good of millions is worth it to me. Stop, don't say any more about it, Alex. Just think about it please,' she finished.

THEIA'S APARTMENT HELA EVENING OF 28TH MAY 2026

'Thank you for coming, Doctor,' Theia said. 'Please sit here please,' she said to the Anan doctor who was kneeling before her in her private apartment. She rarely received anyone here and reserved the rooms as her own space.

'No it is not appropriate, Empress,' she said with her head bowed.

'If you value your life, you will sit with me and enjoy a glass of this red fermented grape juice from Earth. We should celebrate the return of our Overlord to his energy mass,' she said, smiling at Rhea as she cautiously sat down beside her Empress. Theia was overjoyed at the change in the doctor. Everything about her had changed for the better, her attitude, her outlook and her work ethic. Her work in saving Tom's life surprised them all. There were limits to their technology and she had pushed it to its boundaries not giving up on Tom. She had gained the deep respect of the humans for that. Looking at her now, Theia realised the doctor's body had also bloomed. 'What happened to your body, Rhea?'

'I participate in the human exercise regime as an experiment in purebreed wellbeing and, well, I am pleasantly surprised at the results. I also changed my diet.' It was true she looked amazing; her figure had filled out in all the right places and her tight ship garb now accentuated her elegant female figure.

'I see, and yes you do look good, I'm envious, well done,' Theia said smiling at her, 'so, please now tell me how things are going.'

Theia did not expect the outpouring of information that came from the doctor. It was like an invisible dam opening. She realised Rhea needed another female purebreed just to talk to and, as it turned out, so did she. They sat together, talked and sipped the red wine for over three hours. It was cathartic for the both of them as they enjoyed each other's company for the first time.

'Rhea, will you grow his seed?' she asked as their conversation drew to an end. It was the solution to the cure that Rhea and Alex had come to. A purebreed human crossbreed would have DNA that would bear the cure for the Anan sickness. The DNA could be easily grown to provide that permanent elusive cure. It was one of the healing methods designed by the old geneticist many years ago.

'Gladly, Empress, I will bear his children, not one but many, they will be the best mix of our two species and I pledge my future family's allegiance to the House of Aknar for without you, I would be nothing,' she said, bowing her head in reverence to her Empress.

Theia got up and went to a small compartment in the wall. Opening it, she retrieved a golden pendant with a jewel encrusted crest. It was the Seal of The House of Aknar, an honour she had not yet given to any of her subjects.

'You will wear this, please, whatever happens in the future, what you have done and achieved so far deserves this,' she said placing it around Rhea's neck.

'Empress, I, I can't, please, it's too much.'

'Is it not good enough for you?' asked Theia, now joking with her. They both burst out laughing as the effects of the alcohol were flowing through their bodies.

The following morning Rhea was late up and suffering from a headache. The light also hurt her eyes. When she finally made it to the med-bay, one quick smell of her breath revealed the cause of her ailment to a surprised Alex.

'You have a hangover, here take these, it's paracetamol and vitamin C, drink plenty of water and go back to bed. No, I won't have you working here today, go on, off with you,' he said quite abruptly as she took the tablets and meekly left. Women, regardless of their species, he just didn't understand them, he thought. Where did she get drunk like that? He was mystified.

DECEPTION

CHAPTER FIFTEEN

HELA 29TH MAY 2026

The Eight, shimmering with excitement, hovered around his new energy mass and data storage device. His erratic movement troubled Niamh's six technicians who were putting the finishing touches to the device. They rarely worked in his private chamber and were in awe of working so close to one of the most powerful entities in the universe.

'Don't worry, lads, he doesn't bite. And would you stop hovering over them? You're making them nervous,' she said, scolding The Eight.

'I did not think it would look like that, I am pleased with its visual appearance. Who designed it?' he asked.

'We all did. I had the initial concept and everybody here had input to the design. The lads worked on the chariot, as we call it, in their spare time in the workshop. They wove spare gold cables and had the silver panels with the blue pearls made in Christchurch. We wanted to make it elegant and beautiful without taking away from your powerful and formidable appearance.'

'Well, you achieved that. My kind thought of this before, but none wanted to consign themselves to machines, it was believed to be demeaning and unattractive. "A jump too far", they said. With diminishing supplies of blue, those who don't adapt will fade away. I like it. Can we test it?'

'Will you have patience? Let them finish,' she said, shooing him away from it.

An hour later he was happily "seated" majestically in his new glistening chariot. The oval-shaped chariot contained the new memory banks made in Sydney; they were mounted below his glass energy mass container and blue energy tanks. A silver-like spoon, at the front of the chariot served as his "throne". The whole affair was mounted on a small grav platform and he could move anywhere without using his blue energy. He could store and access his old memories in the databanks, reducing his power needs, and, as he did before, he could hibernate in his glass container. The chariot was adorned with the woven golden cables and the silver panels mounted with the blue pearls. The effect gave the chariot an appearance of a floating throne, shining with gold and shimmering with his blue light. Niamh and her team got it right. He looked formidable, elegant, beautiful and above all powerful when seated in his chariot.

'Thank you, it is beautiful and should reduce my blue usage by half. You made this in your "spare time", is that right?' The Eight asked Niamh's technicians.

'Yes,' they quietly murmured, overawed that he had spoken to them.

'Niamh, give Theia their names. You will be rewarded for this. Thank you, you may go now. Niamh, you stay,' he said abruptly to them. The six technicians, not used to The Eight's dismissals, looked uncertainly at Niamh.

'Lads, yes, take up your tools, ye can go now, and thanks,' she said gently to her team as they busied themselves cleaning up and leaving his chamber. She knew what he wanted to talk about next.

'My child, sit and talk to me, how are you?' he asked in a soft voice.

'I'm fine, thanks.'

'And Tom, he gets out of hospital today, how is he?'

'He's fine, I'll see him tonight. We'll stay in Christchurch over the long weekend,' she said, referring to the Queen's Birthday, a public holiday and welcome break they were all looking forward to. 'You know I am marrying him, I should have told you before, but, well it happened so fast,' she said. She felt guilty, like sitting in front of her father and not telling him about such an important change in her life. He easily read her thoughts.

'Don't feel guilty for not telling me. I understand your limitations more than you. I am pleased for you both. I sense your yearning for him. Thomas Parker is a good man, despite his dark side. It is a good and powerful match. You will have many gifted children.'

'Jeez, you're embarrassing me now, we're only getting married. We haven't even discussed kids. Give us a chance,' she said, as she felt her face going red.

'Now, I believe it is customary to give a gift for these occasions. What would you like?'

His question surprised her. What do you ask an Overlord for? she wondered, and then it hit her; 'I want my own spaceship,' she said quickly.

'Impossible, you can't have a spaceship, where would you get blue for it? They are reserved for us and you couldn't afford to run one.'

'No, I think you misunderstood. I want to buy the old ones, like the *Hela,* and fix them up. I just want your permission to buy them myself, that's all. I need your permission for me to own and hold the technology,' she said getting more uncomfortable with this. She could feel the heat in her face as she continued to blush. She hated asking for anything for herself.

'Yes, I see, I see what you want. I thought you were asking for a new intergalactic ship. That is a brilliant idea; of course you shall have that. Yes and more. I will arrange it with Theia. You and Thomas Parker deserve that. I am so proud of you,' he said as his energy mass pulsed with clear blue light. 'I see what you want to do. You will repair them on Earth, yes, the old grav ships, there are thousands of them, tell me what you hope to do.'

Niamh spent the next two hours quietly chatting with The Eight about her plans and her hopes for the future; she also explained what Chang and Tom were to do together and he agreed to spare Chang if the plan worked out. Finally she helped him settle into his new chariot and made sure it was adjusted to suit him. 'The after sales service,' she called it.

'Go now, my child, you will be late for your date!' he said abruptly and she laughed at his humour. Enjoying the time she had spent with him, she left to prepare for her journey to Christchurch.

CHRISTCHURCH 30TH MAY 2026

Tom woke to the sounds coming from the adjacent room. It was room service delivering their late breakfast. She was wrapped around him asleep and breathing deeply. He lay there quietly admiring her beauty and luxuriating in the feeling of her warm naked body beside him. Continuing their incessant enjoyment of each other throughout the night, they finally fell into a deep sleep in the early hours of the morning. Disturbed by the noise in the adjacent room, her eyes opened and she looked into his and smiled.

'Is that breakfast? I'm starving,' she said and kissed him on the lips.

He went out to get the breakfast trolley and when he returned she was propped up in bed with her red hair falling across her shoulders and naked breasts.

'Niamh, you are beautiful, and I do love you,' he said softly.

'You're not so bad yourself,' she said, admiring his naked body as he opened up the leaves of the trolley beside the bed.

They both devoured the breakfast. They were happy to be together, the first time they could enjoy this quiet time and their own company. Niamh noticed a difference in him, she could see the tension was gone from his face and for the first time he radiated a deep feeling of happiness. She needed to know and decided to broach the subject.

'Operation Deception, how's it going?' she asked as she sipped her tea.

'It's early days yet, only a week, but John and Demard have started with Chang. He's done all he said he would so far. You know me, I'm the pessimist, but I think this cyber war might actually work. It will give us some time, that's for sure.'

Chang did everything he said he would, providing contact details, hard and soft drop boxes and internet sites and email addresses. John and Demard put a team together in Christchurch; the same team that had worked on the French purchase. Pictures of Tom in empty warehouses and an abandoned mine in Australia were fabricated and delivered to Chang. With Chang's input they chose the site in South Eastern Siberia for the fictitious base, and were forming a plan to reveal Anan Corp as a Great Northern Union shell company.

Tom was pleased with the progress, considering it was only a week since he had talked with Chang. They had stopped running, and now had the time to develop a solid defence strategy. 'There's something else we need to do — and I'm not taking no for an answer. You need to learn how to handle a gun.'

She looked at him and paused as she thought about this new challenge. He hadn't mentioned it before. 'You know I don't like guns.'

'I know, but get over it. You need to be able to protect yourself.'

'Jeez, Tom that was harsh. But I suppose you're right. Yeah, I do need to learn that. When do we start?' she said slowly as she thought more about it.

'We start today. I have a place arranged and Alice will start you off. Is that OK with you? Good,' he said, as she nodded in agreement. 'About Chang, did you talk to The Eight?'

'Yes, he agreed to spare Chang's life if the plan works, and we're getting a wedding present from him,' she said smiling.

'What's he giving us?' asked Tom, looking at Niamh in surprise at this unexpected news.

'Permission to buy and hold their tech. We can buy our own ships,' she said, grinning broadly and holding her arms up over her head in delight as she sat back in the chair.

'Niamh, that's a game changer for us. Well done,' he said, as he got up and threw his arms around her. Lifting her up from the chair he carried her back to the bed.

HELA BASE AUSTRALIAN DESERT 8TH JUNE 2026

Looking out from the shuttle cockpit Theia was surprised at the progress. Prompted by Robert, who insisted she come, it was her first visit to the *Hela* Base in the Australian desert. Robert wanted Theia to see what they were doing before she arrived here on the *Hela*. As the shuttle hovered over the base they could see a large airplane landing at their newly constructed airbase.

'We have one cargo plane landing every six hours, we need to move over one hundred thousand tons of freight for the load-out before we depart for the New World. It's a massive undertaking,' he said, pointing out the base layout to her. 'Over there, the camp is nearly finished. There is the warehouse and storage area and the *Hela* landing site is directly below us. They are working to uncover the three docking posts.'

'Are those the living quarters?' she said, pointing to square container-shaped objects.

'Yes, Theia, they are the pods, they have started coming from Germany,' he said, referring to the modular accommodation. The pods would provide living accommodation in the *Hela* and then would be unloaded on the New World to form the colonists' first settlement. 'They are pre-fabricated with all our human habitation needs. They're like a small apartment, Theia, with fitted kitchens and bathrooms.'

'Robert, we never realised the scale of what was required, normally we do this with our own ships and resources,' she said, as the shuttle landed.

'Did you by chance underestimate the logistical challenge?'

'Yes, Robert, we definitely did. You and the McKinnons have worked wonders.'

'No, Theia, not really. We just pushed a road in through the desert, constructed an airstrip, and laid out the site and camp — all in two months. Come meet Matt,' he said, smiling as he led her over to Matt's office.

Matt drove them all around the site. She inspected everything and was particularly interested in the uncovering of the *Hela* docking posts, where she would land the great ship. Finally, after two hours of touring, they arrived back at the shuttle.

'Matt, you have done well, thank you, I am pleased,' she said, smiling at him. She had delved into his soul and saw a simple hardworking honourable man. She was delighted they had him.

'We do the best we can,' Matt replied, with a broad grin. He was delighted his first alien client was pleased with the work. Shaking hands with Robert, he was relieved to see a big grin on his face as well.

'I look forward to seeing you again when we land,' Theia replied, as she climbed back into the shuttle.

WINERY NORTH OF CHRISTCHURCH 20TH JUNE 2026

As the cold light of dawn spilled over the beautiful setting, the staff of the winery busied themselves preparing for another visit by Kath's unusual visitors. Leaving their footprints in the frost encrusted grass on this clear winter day, they hurried in and out of the big marquee, fussing with its set up. Surprised that the visit would be for a mid-winter wedding, the owner, Kath's friend, pushed the boat out to make this a beautiful day for the bride despite Niamh's insistence on a simple and small ceremony.

By noon the guests were arriving. They invited most of their own Project personnel, the extended family they worked with and the purebreeds from the *Hela* crew. By two o'clock Niamh, escorted in by Robert, was standing beside Tom in the garden, warmed by the bright winter sun, in front of the marriage celebrant taking their vows. She wore a simple white wedding dress, her blue diamond, the blue pearl earrings and carried a white bouquet.

She looked stunning. He was dressed in a grey formal suit. Janet, Niamh's first true friend in Christchurch, was her bridesmaid. John, a long term friend and colleague of Tom was the best man.

The guests, including the New Zealand PM with Kath by his side, congratulated the happy couple. The purebreeds were surprised at the beauty and pageantry of such an event.

'We don't have such a formal event for taking a life partner,' said Bri to John after the ceremony.

'And how is that done?' he asked.

'Generally, it's arranged, but the couples can refuse. Then we sign a contract.'

'Is there someone lined up for you, Bri? A beautiful alien princess…'

'John, really, I am still too young for that.'

'Yet, you are still expected to captain a ship.'

'That's quite different. It is part of my training and there was no one else available. Do you understand why we are called purebreeds?'

'No. I always wondered where that came from,' he said.

'We have served the Overlords for eons. We are the original intelligent population they first touched and we have not interbred with any other species. Those of our species that do are cast out from our society. There are Anans who are not purebreeds. We are now a population of less than a billion. Sadly, from our own inbreeding, our DNA is breaking down over time.'

John turned to look at the young captain. 'No Bri, I didn't know that.'

'I am the last of the Aknar line. Heir to the throne — or a crown prince — as you say on Earth. Finding "a beautiful alien princess" for me, as you ask, will not happen. I've probably said too much. It's the drink you gave me.'

'Not at all, young man,' John replied, trying to mask his surprise, as he clapped Bri on the shoulder. 'Come on, we start the best part of the ceremony now, the food and the drink. You're sitting with Bill and Alice's crew, they'll show you how to drink,' he said as he led Bri into the marquee.

Niamh enjoyed her wedding day, she was surprised at the emotion it generated in them both and she could sense the happy feelings of their guests as well. But it was what Theia delivered to them after the speeches that made their day.

'It is the Charter for the Sullivan-Parker family to own and to develop Anan technology and includes your right to buy trading and extraction ships and the right to modify those ships. You are the first Earthlings to be admitted to an exclusive universal group. The Charter extends to your descendants – and there is more. The Eight will fund the purchase of the first two ships,' she announced, as she presented the golden embossed charter to them in front of their guests who stood and applauded in earnest.

As they sat down, Mack leaned over and whispered to Janet, Kath and Harold, 'you know this is big, it is the first new dynasty admitted to our intergalactic club in nearly a thousand years. It will cause, as you say here, a storm of excrement back in the Energy Exchange. You are seeing history being made.'

Niamh and Tom spent the following Sunday and Monday in a small cottage Janet rented for them in the Banks Peninsula south of Christchurch. On Monday Tom took her walking out in the beautiful landscape of the extinct volcano that formed the peninsula. Niamh, having being cooped up on the *Hela* for so long, realised how much she missed fresh air and the countryside. As they sat enjoying the views Niamh's phone rang.

'Hi, sorry to disturb you love birds. You having a good time?' Janet asked.

'Yeah, it was great until you rang,' Niamh replied, looking at Tom who was shaking his head.

'We're having a planning meeting. The Oz base is near ready for the *Hela* and we think all your repairs are done. I've looked at your reports and I see you have started on refit work. Yes?'

'Yes, I'm ahead, I've started work we planned in Oz.'

'Robert wants to bring the landing three weeks forward to the ninth. He wants to be sure you and Tom are OK with that.'

'They want to move the landing date to the ninth, you ready for that, Tom?' Niamh asked.

'We're all ready to go in Oz, the team's in place already,' he said as he nodded to her.

'Janet, yes, we're both ready.'

'Good. Robert, yes they are both ready. It's done — we go on the ninth of July. See you soon, have fun,' she said as the line went dead.

'So, husband, we're landing the *Hela* in two and a half weeks.'

'Don't look so worried, it will work, you've checked and checked,' he said trying to reassure her.

'What if it doesn't?'

'You mustn't think that, Niamh, believe in yourself, it'll work,' he said confidently as he hugged her close to him. They sat arm in arm together enjoying the wild countryside and the scenery around them as she contemplated the huge responsibility she had taken on. Her abilities would soon be tested.

HELA MED-BAY 30TH JUNE 2026

After their meeting in Theia's apartment she and the Anan doctor became firm friends. Rather than giving orders as she did in the past, Theia was now able to offer guiding advice and options. Her words of wisdom were to take it all one step at a time, to review and secure what they had achieved so far before moving on to another major step. Rhea and Alex did just that. They spent four weeks packing samples for future transportation to Anan, manufacturing batches of the first stage treatment, or FST as it was now known, for the crew. They were able to manufacture enough for three years' use for those affected on the *Hela*. They reviewed and diligently recorded all their notes and formula and crucially, they backed up their data. Alex insisted on two separate or duplicate samples, and that the back-up samples were secured in a safe alternate location. They even established two safe separate storage locations for the FST on the *Hela*.

Over that time they agreed Rhea would bear his child. It took Alex some time to accept the moral issues and the responsibilities of bringing a child into the world that was intended to provide a cure for a sickness. He kept these demons to himself. How they would impregnate Rhea had bewildered Alex from the outset. It was a subject he just could not broach with her and he decided a clinical solution would be best and perhaps less demanding of her.

The clinical tools he ordered for the task arrived late the previous evening on the shuttle. In the morning, he arrived early into the med-bay to prepare them, laying them out carefully on the bench and rehearsing how he would explain their use to Rhea. As soon as she entered the med-bay she noticed how awkward Alex was looking.

'What's up, Alex?' she asked.

'I thought we might discuss how we may progress to the next stage today,' he said looking at her hopefully. He did not expect what was to come.

When Rhea saw the crude and primitive tools he set out, and that they included a syringe, she exploded. Grabbing them one at a time she started screaming at him and throwing them. Alex cowered down behind the bench as she threw everything within reach at him. He was quickly covered in medical equipment and broken glass. Finally Rhea grabbed a chair and was just lifting it above her head when she felt a gentle hand on her shoulder.

'I don't think that's a good idea, lassie,' she heard in a soft voice from behind her. It was in that strange accent she had heard the bossy human use. 'You might damage some of the delicate equipment behind him and we won't be able to repair it for you,' he said gently taking the chair out of her hands. 'Aye, you're quite strong now, lassie,' he said placing the chair back on the floor. He had heard the commotion while seated in his office above the med-bay. *It's a good job I got here when I did*, Robert thought.

'Having a lovers' tiff are you, Doc?' he asked Alex who was slowly getting up from behind the bench. He looked comical covered in glass and medical tools. Rhea just stood there, looking dejected now with her head hanging forward over her long neck.

'Doc, you might want to sort this out, flowers, or chocolates or something like that for your lady. Don't leave her in a huff now,' Robert said. 'I'll leave you to it,' he said as he hastily left.

Alex looked at her, he was ashamed of himself. He had devoted most of his life to his work and had no experience with women before. He just didn't realise what had happened between them. Robert's comment opened his eyes. It was his use of the words "lovers' tiff" and "your lady" that did it. Everyone else on the ship could see it but him.

'I'm sorry, I really am,' he said, looking at her for forgiveness.

'Alex, sorry is just not good enough. I can't believe you think so little of me as to do it that way. Am I so alien and repulsive to you?' she said as she stormed out of med-bay.

It took Theia the whole day to try to calm her friend and having no experience with human relationships she finally took her to see Janet. After downing two bottles of wine on her own, Theia and Janet put a very drunk Rhea to bed.

'We're really not that different,' Janet said to Theia as they both parted company for the night.

The following morning the lovers' tiff was the scuttlebutt of the ship and very noticeable in the galley. Rhea, with a major hangover, sat with the girls and after some awkward movements Alex finally sat with the men. It was the first time they did not sit together since his arrival on the *Hela*.

HELA 2ND JULY 2026 ROBERT'S OFFICE

It was Robert who saved the day. After a brief prompting by Theia he came up with a solution to their problem. It was not contrived but born out of necessity.

'Doc, you and your lady will need to secure everything in med-bay and go back to Earth while we land this beast,' Robert said to Alex, who he had asked to come to his office. 'We have safe storage arranged for your samples and medicines in our Australian *Hela* base as well. And before you ask, it's all at the temperature you specified in laboratory grade refrigerators and freezers in a clean facility, as you agreed with Niamh. So no excuses, you knew this was coming,' Robert finished in his no-nonsense voice. It was crisp and resounded with authority.

'Yes, I did. It's all packed up ready. It will take about twelve hours to secure med-bay,' Alex said quietly. 'But you will have to make arrangements for Rhea —' he said as his voice trailed off with misery.

Robert looked at him. *If I had a dollar for every one of these dejected men who sat in front of me with their problems I'd be rich now*, he thought. It was a cycle of life and obviously didn't change when aliens were involved. He just needed to reassure the doc.

'Doc,' he started gently, 'Rhea is a fine woman. You are lucky to have her and between the two of you, you have both worked miracles.' It was true; Demard's improvement and Tom's survival was testament to that. 'Did you ever give up working on that cure? No you didn't! So why give up on Rhea? I don't know what your tiff was about but you need to get over it. No buts please. We've arranged accommodation in Queenstown for non-essential personnel during the landing. I believe it's beautiful there. Tom has a protection detail there so you will have nothing to worry about. No, I'm not going to tell her, you are,' Robert said finishing off this one-sided discussion in his no-nonsense voice and smiling at Alex.

QUEENSTOWN

CHAPTER SIXTEEN

It took longer than twelve hours to secure med-bay and dispatch the samples and medicines including the batches of FST to the clean store in their Australian *Hela* base. Alex and Rhea worked together through two straight days without taking any rest. They finally arrived late in the evening at the luxury complex Anan Corp rented on the last shuttle of the day. It was Rhea's first time on Earth but she was so tired she couldn't absorb all the different sights sounds and smells and just wanted to get to a bed.

'Where are you sleeping, and why did we get one room?' she asked him abruptly, as they entered the room they were shown to by their security detail. She noticed it had one enormous bed. She couldn't believe the size of it, well, it would do for her.

'I asked for one room,' he lied, knowing Robert arranged it. It was the best room in the complex.

'Look, what's that?' she said, pointing to a couch. Then, taking down a spare duvet from the open wardrobe, she threw it at him; 'there that's yours,' she said pointing again to the couch. 'I'll take the bed. Where do I wash? Oh in here, look at the size of this,' she said as she closed the bathroom door. Lounging in the deep bath she tried not to laugh as she remembered his face, it was the picture of disappointment. Janet told her to make him suffer. She also warned Rhea he may not like women, it was not unusual and if that was the case she should not continue to chastise him. How will I know? she asked Janet, and when the answer was whispered in her ear they both collapsed in fits of laughter.

QUEENSTOWN 5TH JULY 2026

Rhea was wakened by the soft light now spilling into the room. After her luxurious bath, the night before, she ate some fruit and went to bed. As she lay down she heard him in the bathroom. It was the last thing she remembered, she was asleep when her head touched the pillow. She was curious now to get her first sight of Earth in the early morning light. Getting up, she walked quietly to the window, not wanting to wake him. She gasped with surprise at the beauty that greeted her. She was looking out over a lake. She could see a snow-covered mountain rise majestically above the mist-covered lake. It appeared that the mountain was floating above the lake as the light mist swirled below it. The different colours were spectacular. The calm lake acted like a mirror, reflecting the beauty of the snow-covered mountain above. She had never seen anything like it before.

Unknown to her a wide awake Alex was watching her supple naked body moving across the room. She looked amazing in the soft dawn light. He was mesmerized by her porcelain white skin, her shapely female body and her firm breasts. *She looks like a beautiful marble statue*, he thought.

'Alex, Alex,' she cried out, 'look at this. Come quick, look at this view — I've never seen anything so beautiful.'

'Well,' he said sitting up on the couch and looking at her, 'I haven't seen anything so beautiful either,' he managed in a soft and strained voice.

'You can't see from there,' she replied, turning to look at him.

'Yes I can — and you're beautiful, Rhea, you really are…' he said as he stood up and walked naked toward her.

'Mmm, you're not so bad yourself,' she said smiling coyly at him. She had never seen his naked body before now. His dark hair, washed and clean, hung to his shoulders, his lean fair-skinned body and his muscles were toned by the exercise regime. She was relieved to see he had shaved off the beard he had grown in space and his attractive face was fully revealed. To her delight his erect member advertised his sexuality and his feelings for her. *Janet was right*, she thought, his male member betrayed everything he was feeling. They gently touched, exploring their bodies and the deep feelings they felt before collapsing on the big bed, enveloped in their passion for each other.

✖

TSS EARNSLAW 7TH JULY 2026

Dressed in a blue, down-filled jacket, padded ski pants, a bright multi-coloured merino wool hat with scarf and mittens, Rhea was cold. She was standing in the saloon on the top deck of the TSS Earnslaw. Alex explained to her that it was an old steamship and was one of the main tourist attractions in Queenstown. 'It is known as the Lady of the Lake,' he said to her, trying to explain that being addressed as "Lady" or "My Lady", as the humans were now calling her, was an honour.

'So I'm like a boat. Is that what they are saying about me?' she asked him sharply, trying to maintain a serious face. As usual he got into a hopeless muddle in trying to explain himself. Early on in their developing relationship she realised he was socially inept at understanding or dealing with female feelings. Janet explained this was quite usual in human males, and that she could use it to her advantage. She was now doing this at every opportunity and totally loving it! She wondered when he would realise she was "winding him up", as Janet called it.

Rhea had enjoyed every minute of the previous two days and two nights they had spent together in their room. When they were not making love, they lounged around doing nothing but enjoying the luxurious facilities available to them: the deep bath, the large bed, the couch and the food that was delivered when they called for it. It was pampering she had never experienced before. She knew that rest time was badly needed by both of them. Her time on the *Hela* spanned nearly ten months as she had not availed herself of the short shore leave offered on Earth until now. His time on the *Hela* was over three months, which was a long time for a human. That time in space and their punishing work schedule had exhausted them both. Arriving in Queenstown, the rest and relaxation was vital to her wellbeing and would complement the demanding exercise and diet regime she adopted on the *Hela*.

At an early stage of their research, unknown to Alex, she realised a purebreed and human crossbreed child could hold the key to a cure. Her biological clock was an unknown variable that would work against this. It was tied to the Anan planetary orbit and limited to one mating cycle per orbit. Rhea did not know what effect being in space or on another planet would have on her fertility. To aggravate the matter, fertility rates in Anan females was reducing. She knew she would have to be in peak physical condition to give her any chance of conceiving in this distant galaxy. Deep within her was a burning desire to bear Alex's children.

She could see he was enthralled with the workings of the boat's engine and was now trying to explain to her how it worked, pointing to the large diagrams of the engine covering the walls above it. They were standing together at the edge of an opening in the centre of the ship's saloon where the passengers could look down into the engine room. She had no interest in it but simply loved his closeness and warmth. As the ship moved out onto the lake, the engine room emitted loud banging, and hissing sounds mixed with an occasional ringing noise. She noticed the other human males, like excited children, were pointing out the same things as he to their female companions. But most of all what stirred the deep emotion within her was the sight of the families with their children in their arms looking down into this spectacle exuding its unique cacophony of sounds. She had never seen so many children together; it was unseen in Anan where birth rates had fallen to an all-time low. The children were mesmerised by it and it was obvious their parents were enthralled by their child's delight. It brought tears to her eyes as she hoped one day to be in that privileged situation. There was a term in English she had learnt and now she understood the meaning of the word, it was "blessed". Would she ever be blessed with his children? she wondered as tears streamed down her face.

'Rhea, are you all right, darling, you're freezing?' Alex asked, quite concerned at the sudden appearance of her tears that were now intruding on the magical spectacle of the antique engine unfolding before them. He held her tight to him and slowly with his closeness and warmth her deep emotional clamour abated.

'Yes, Yes, Alex, I am. Really I am. Can I have a hot drink please?' she asked, and dutifully he led her aft to seats with two rolled up blankets. Sitting her down, he gently wrapped her in the blankets and went off to get hot drinks.

From this position in the aft section, Rhea could look back towards Queenstown as the ship steamed out onto Lake Wakatipu. She was enjoying this, the view, the colours and the unique sounds were now touching all her senses. She started to pay attention to the detail of what she could see; the town and its dock where they had just left from, she could make out the area where the complex they were staying at, the snow-covered mountains and the thing he called a cable car or gondola which took people up the mountain. He intended to take her on that as well. It was now obvious to her that human males were fixated with machines. Suddenly she noticed something flying up from the end of the lake into the sky. It was silver and from what she could see, shaped like a large cross. *What is that?* she wondered.

'Alex,' she asked him excitedly as he approached with two hot chocolate drinks, 'what's that — look there in the sky, what is it?'

'Shhh,' he said to her, as he placed the drinks on the table. He could see their protection detail, seated quite close by, looking at them concerned with the question and loudness of her voice. 'Please, Rhea, not so loud, people will hear you.'

She was about to say something quite rude to him when she heard a young girl, seated near them say, 'Mummy, Mummy, does the funny lady not know it's an airplane? Is there something wrong with her?' Fortunately the parents were engaged in their own conversation and easily placated the child who was still staring at Rhea with suspicion.

'Sorry,' she said, smiling awkwardly at Alex.

'She knows there's something different about you, Rhea. And yes, she's right. It's an airplane — we use them to transport people through the sky.'

'How does that work, Alex? You're supposed to be a primitive species, you don't have grav?'

'The planes are powered by fossil fuel engines,' he said. 'Jet engines on that one.'

'I'm missing something, Alex. The engine in this boat its sheer size, the engine in the car that brought us to the dock and now the airplane. There are differences that I don't understand. You need to explain all that,' she said. Her face was screwed up with the effort to understand.

'OK, first off this is a steam ship. Its maiden voyage was in 1912. That's one hundred and fourteen years ago,' he started to explain as she sipped her hot chocolate. 'The steam engine, what powers this ship, was the first type of propulsion engine humans developed. Then we developed the internal combustion engine, the engine that powers the cars,' he said and she noticed he was now reading from his communication device. 'First powered flight was in late 1903, and then developed into what we have today. The airplane you saw. That's how I got to Christchurch from where I was working last in Switzerland.'

'Alex, what you're saying, is that in just over one hundred of your planet's orbits, humans have developed from this method of transport, the steam ship, to flight. No, that's not possible,' she said, surprised. 'Alex, you know I'm just over one hundred of your years.'

'Yes, I do. And, my lovely Anan beauty, we did just that and went to the Moon as well. Not bad for a primitive species. You weren't complaining about my primitive techniques over the past two days,' he said with a wicked smile.

'You're bold,' she exclaimed, hitting him playfully on the shoulder. 'Show me around this ship,' she now demanded. Her voice took on a different tone as Rhea the scientist started to analyse what she was now seeing.

The following day, much to his surprise, she demanded he take her on the gondola. To the delight of their protection detail, they took the cable car up to an extension of the town in the mountains above it. Rhea spent the day sampling all the attractions, the technology and the food on offer in the restaurant. Alex noticed she was lost in thought at every new experience. Finally, as they eat in the restaurant overlooking the town below, she processed what she saw. She had seen all the history, on the ship, in the town and now at this resort. Not part of the purebreed Earth survey team, when they arrived first, she now understood for herself, the human technological advances that took place over the past one hundred years.

It was unprecedented; no other species had achieved that advancement in so short a time span. Looking down at the town, as she ate in this lofty restaurant, she realised one hundred and sixty-six years ago it wasn't even here. Yes, she had heard the crew talk about it, but she was not interested in it then. Now, in the context of the genetic experiments she and Alex had looked at in the past, it had far-reaching consequences. She knew what the gap in the video meant, what the old geneticist used and the secret that was missing from the database. It scared her and she realised she shouldn't even think about it. It was more than anything she was expecting. Looking at Alex, she realised he contained that essence as well and hoped it was now growing in her, regardless of what happened she would never tell him.

'Alex, you know I love you,' she said quietly to him.

'Yes, yes, I gathered you do. I mean I do too, I…'

'Yes,' she said, looking at him. She was frowning now while trying not to laugh; he was really hopeless at this.

'I ah, I love you t-too,' he managed to stammer out as he felt his face blushing with embarrassment.

⧓

SOUTH-EAST SIBERIA AND SHANGHAI 8TH JULY 2026

Charl Jacobs couldn't believe his luck. He was surprised when Chang contacted him in Hong Kong for this job. After the disaster in Christchurch, he believed Chang was finished with him. It was a poor end to their good working relationship. Charl never forgave the mysterious ruthless Englishman, who bested him and his team. Chang wondered if Charl would still take the money if he realised it was Thomas Parker they were both working with now. *Of course he would*, thought Chang, *business is business*!

'You have made progress,' Chang said to Charl over the secure video link.

'Yes, we have rented an old derelict factory and set up the satellite communication system. I have two technicians working on the data system and we have four others working in the base, you know, storing and dispatching the containers, the logistics.'

The job was in a godforsaken bleak part of the world. There was nothing for miles and they would be here for another six months. The money Chang offered was the best he had ever paid. Charl and his team were delighted with the job. He was to provide the illusion of the secret base in South Eastern Siberia. Shipments of empty containers would come and go and be part of the plan to reveal Anan Corp as a Great Northern Union shell company. Charl installed the data servers that now contained the bogus identities and email accounts of the "scientists and managers" working to develop the secret technology. Unknown to Charl, who believed Chang's cyber war team were the source of the data, Demard had access to his server, and loaded up all the fake data needed for the cyber war illusion.

'Have you made progress linking with my data team?' Chang asked.

'Yes, we are impressed with the quality of what your guys have sent. If anyone hacks our servers they will see a secret factory and research base with a staff of over one hundred and fifty. We have bogus camera feeds as well, showing the working factory and research stations. I believe your team get the feeds from other semiconductor factories. We have company registration documents linking this facility to Anan Corp and also emails from Anan Corp "managers" to the Defence Department of the Great Northern Union. There is a cash trail of real money transfers, the proverbial bribes, as well,' Charl said; he had enjoyed transferring the large bribes, skimming to his own account.

'Good, I have news for you. We now have an agent in the Northern Union Defence Department. He will assist with channelling the documents or emails to their servers. I'll send on his contact details.' The agent was first discovered in videos Tom had stolen from Charl's employer's hard drives in Hong Kong. When Chang showed the official the salacious videos, taken during a visit to Paris, he meekly capitulated. 'He is the assistant secretary to the Defence Minister. Don't mess this one up, Charl. It is hard to get a contact like that.'

'Chang, you know me better than that.'

'Yes, Charl, I do. You failed me once, don't let it happen again,' he said as he cut the video link. He looked at his watch, time to go — he couldn't be late for this next important meeting.

Chang stepped out of the car. He stood and looked around at this large and inaccessible construction site, on the outskirts of the city. As he took in the landscape of the empty buildings, the machinery and the cranes, he shook his head. The meeting was scheduled on the partially completed sixth floor of this now derelict building. Slowly, still looking and watching, he made his way over to a construction hoist. At five in the morning the place was deserted. As he entered the hoist cage, the gates squeaked and clattered. Pressing the button for the sixth floor, he noticed the small yellow chalk mark on the panel. *They are here*, he thought, as the old machinery started up, lurching the cage noisily up the side of the building.

On the sixth floor, he stepped out and walked across the bare concrete slab to a group of four men. Deliberately placing himself with three behind, Chang looked across at his boss. 'Good to see you, we have not met in such a long time. We should meet more often. Did you get the photos?' he said, bowing his head in respect.

'Good to see you too, Chang, yes, it's a long time since we met. But you are always so busy. Or you make out that you are. I got the pictures, and I'm not convinced,' he said as he threw them down on an empty crate. 'Our satellite photos show much more activity than the ones you sent.'

Chang smiled to himself. 'You doubt my information?' he asked his boss. *The young fool*, he thought, *promoted by nepotism into a job that I should have. He is so stupid, does he not think I know what he is up to?*

'Yes, Chang. I do. You have more experience in these matters than I. But still — I do not see it. There is no way our allies could be embroiled in this.'

'Have you ever thought the photos from your satellite are compromised?'

'Not possible. How could you suggest something so ridiculous?'

Chang kneeled down in front of his boss and slowly, deliberately looking at all around him, took out a gun. Holding it by the barrel, he laid it down in front of his boss. Looking up at the young man, Chang's cold eyes bore into him, as he squirmed with unease; 'you are right to doubt me. Always question everything. But if you suspect me of treachery, shoot me now, here with my own gun.'

He did not expect this, it was too easy, he thought as he looked down at Chang. 'No, Chang, it is nothing like that…'

'You must understand, all I do is for the people of China, I serve them. I have worked hard all my life for my people. Do you understand that?'

He is going to plead for his life, he thought, as he nodded to his three men standing behind Chang. 'Yes, you —'

In the blink of an eye Chang was up, with his gun in one hand and a long knife in the other. Like a coiled spring, he leaped into the air, and as he turned, the knife sliced through his boss's throat, severing one of his carotid arteries. As the bright red blood spurted out, in mid-flight, Chang twisted away from his boss, and dropped down behind the crate — his agility surprising the other three. Before they could compose themselves, he opened fire, shooting one in the head. As the bullet exploded, blood and brains burst out in a red cloud behind the dead man.

Suddenly, on ropes, two more rappelled down through an opening from the floor above, landing silently behind the ill-fated boss's last two men. They didn't stand a chance, as they were cut down with a hail of automatic gunfire.

Standing up from behind the crate, he dusted down his suit. As he looked at the cuff of the right hand, which had held the knife, he clucked in disapproval, his disappointment was obvious. One of his men handed him a cloth. Wiping off the small spots of blood, he looked around at the four dead bodies and the pool of blood seeping from his boss's throat. 'You played that close.'

'Master, we never doubted you were in danger, too early and we spoil your fun. We know we cannot win. We are always too early or too late. But you were slow this time, you got blood on your jacket. It is that European food, it goes straight to the waist.'

'Ha, ha, ha,' he laughed as he looked at his two loyal companions. 'He was so stupid, did he not realise he gave the game away? A meeting in a place like this, and in Shanghai, what was he thinking? Our leaders are such fools.'

'We must hurry, master, there is a large concrete pour starting soon in the next building, ideal for the clean-up.'

After such a crucial kill, he needed to gauge their feelings. He held up his hand to stop them both; 'wait, regardless of where I go, will you follow me?' It was not every day they got to see him slit the boss's throat.

'Of course, Chang, always,' they said.

'Even if I were to work for an alien, would you doubt me?'

'Ha, ha, ha,' they both held their sides as they laughed. 'Master, that is why we love working for you, after such carnage, you always crack such funny jokes. We go get the clean-up bags. Goodbye.'

Chang shook his head and smiled as they left. Pausing to think, he dialled a number on his sat phone. 'Parker, it lands tomorrow, yes?'

'Yes, Chang. The landing is scheduled between the satellite overflights.'

'My boss did not believe me. I had to take drastic action — never mind what,' he said as Tom tried to interrupt. 'I have wanted to do it for some time and now, well, it was so enjoyable. To business, I will send you a data packet and an I.P. address of a computer in Beijing. Get your alien friend to imbed the data on that machine. Make sure it is not easy to find. It will help our illusion.'

'A money trail —'

'Shut up, Parker, and listen. Yes, a money trail would be helpful. Link it to Anan Corp's Siberian operation. When our leaders, discoverer his "treachery" they will come running to me. Then I introduce more data from Siberia. But, remember this, Parker, make sure your ship is not seen. If they get a clear picture of it with the satellite, the game is up — you are on your own.'

'Chang, you are always so helpful. Rest assured they won't see us.'

'Good luck with the landing. My regards to your wife, she will be busy tomorrow.'

'Yes, Chang, she will,' he said cutting the link.

Chang looked at the sat phone, there was one number showing a miss-call. He had deliberately let it ring out. Now was the time, he thought, as he hit re-dial. 'So, you come crawling back for information,' he said to his treacherous benefactor.

'Chang, there is no need for that. Relationships ebb and flow with the tide. You, of all people, know that.'

'What do you want?'

'What is going on with the Great Northern Union? I have business interests there. I hear rumours.'

'They are true. Sell up and run.'

'No.'

'Yes, and remember in the future who gave you that advice.'

'Have you any more?'

'Stay in touch, as the tide changes, there is more to come,' he said, ending the call. He smiled to himself as he thought of the message the Moscow Exchange would get when the sell orders hit. As he walked away, he thought how it would further his illusion of rising acrimony between Beijing and Moscow.

CHAPTER SEVENTEEN

HELA 9TH JULY 2026

At four o'clock in the morning, The *Hela* bridge, was bustling with activity. Robert's crew spent the night working their way through the ship to ensure everything was secure. They had spent the previous week tying down all movable equipment and transporting all non-essential personnel to their bases on Earth. Matt, now well established as the *Hela* base manager, had uncovered the three large landing posts. All the new buildings, equipment and support structures were ready. Robert was still concerned that they could not test or access the Anan base, but Mack and Theia assured him it was not a problem. If the docking posts didn't work, they had the option to "go around," for a second landing onto a freshly cleared site. It would cause delays but would prevent a disaster. Niamh had plotted the "go around", course as a fall back plan.

'Mack, all secured,' Robert said, 'We've been over this beast from stem to stern a number of times and we're ready to go.'

'All right, Robert, take your crews in on the shuttles with the non-essential purebreds. I'll see you on the ground. Demard, where are we on the Chinese satellite pass?'

'On schedule, General. We will have landed well before it gets over the desert.'

'Niamh, Captain, you both ready?' Mack asked as the two continued with their preparations at the engineering console.

'Yes, General, we are,' Bri said, as Niamh nodded in agreement. 'We go after the last shuttle departs. We have enough energy from the grav engines without the fusion reactor to power the control systems.'

'My friend,' Mack said, quietly to the Pilot who was standing to one side on the bridge, 'it all rests with you and your tractor,' referring to the most powerful shuttle they had. 'If you can't stop us, get out, you know the drill. What about the other five, will they be able to do their part?'

'Arie,' he said, using Mack's first name, 'I will do my best, as for the other shuttle pilots, we have trained for this over the past three weeks. I know they are inexperienced, but they know what to do and will not let you down.'

'Thank you. I'll have a drink with you on the ground to celebrate our return to our *Hela* base.'

'I'll hold you to that, Arie. I'll let you know when the last shuttle is clear,' he said as he left the bridge.

Niamh finished her final system checks. This was up to her, the whole landing sequence and flight plan was hers. All the temporary repairs to the *Hela* structure and the equipment were from her ideas. From the structural repairs of the leak to the grav engine controls, it was all her work. The *Hela* was designed for a one hundred and seventy-five thousand tonne pay load flying up into and down from planetary orbit. The ship would be landing empty and Niamh believed it could easily cope with the stress of entering Earth's atmosphere. She had plotted the Anan classic corkscrew flight plan to lose height and prevent over-speed. She remembered the demonstration to Tom and Robert with the pellet of grav fuel. The fuel properties counteracted the effects of gravity.

Theoretically, the *Hela* could float down slowly to Earth, but it would burn huge amounts of the grav fuel. Her job was to minimise fuel consumption and minimise the flight time, without compromising the structural integrity of the ship. It was a fine balance and the corkscrew flight plan did just this. It allowed the ship to lose or gain height in a controlled descent or take-off. That strategy, when used with the grav shields, minimised the landing and take-off times — without building up disastrous temperatures or structural stress that would cause the *Hela* to burn or break up. From her navigation console she would have to ensure they stayed on the course line. Theia and the Captain would fly the *Hela* together. All three had their blue diamonds inserted into their control stations. Normally it only took one to pilot the ship and one to navigate, but today with an old and broken ship and limited controls, they would need all their skills to get it to perform the landing manoeuvres.

Behind them, seated in his gleaming chariot, The Eight watched quietly as the purebreeds and humans prepared for this challenge in their Project. He had calculated how much blue energy he would need to rescue them if it all went wrong. Despite their best efforts, he did not have enough. They were on their own in this venture and if it failed the hopes of their three species would die here today. He hadn't told them that depressing news.

'Last shuttle is away and clear, Empress, it's all yours,' Mack said, handing over control to Theia.

Forty minutes later the *Hela* had braved the buffeting and shaking of entry and flight into Earth's atmosphere. Niamh's flight plan brought them down over Antarctica and gave them plenty of time for their final route to the *Hela* base in the Australian desert. The route carefully aligned the *Hela* with the north-south orientation of the sand dunes and valleys at their base.

'Niamh, start venting the helium filled compartments with air,' Theia said. 'Demard, initiate the digital handshake with the base and open communications with the Pilot and Robert. Let me know if the docking posts don't activate,' she said, looking at Niamh's navigation projection. Thirty minutes from their scheduled docking as they crossed the coast of Southern Australia, she needed to lose speed and quickly. 'Niamh, we need more reverse grav. Can you get another twenty per cent?' she asked.

'No, most I can give you is eighteen — otherwise we lose height too quickly,' Niamh replied looking at the engine temperatures readouts; *not good*, she thought. 'The engines are nearly done, Theia. We won't have enough in them for a "go around". We have to land, we're committed now,' she said with a strained voice.

'Niamh, we bring in the tractor early,' Mack said. 'Yes, I know we have to lose the cloak, but the area is empty. The Chinese satellite overpass isn't due yet, we have to risk it. Pilot, we will need you five kilometres early, get into position with your shuttles and the tractor,' he said over the comms system.

The people at the *Hela* base were limited to the purebreeds, colonists and the specialists who would work on the ship. Mack invited the Australian and New Zealand Prime Ministers and a small contingent from their governments and armed forces. All other non-essential personnel were flown out to Alice Springs for the day and all freight flights suspended.

Twenty minutes later at one thousand metres above the desert floor the *Hela* burst out of its cloak. Those left at the base were treated to a breath-taking spectacle of the golden shimmering cylinder-shaped *Hela* glistening in the sun five kilometres away. Its eight hundred metre long hull and its one hundred metre beam and height gave it the appearance of a floating golden monster, earning it the name that Robert always referred to it as, "the Beast". The ground crew could see the six shuttles working themselves into position. The *Hela* was perfectly aligned along the desert valley to dock with the three enormous posts that had risen up one hundred metres above the desert floor. With the large docking rings at the top, they looked like huge shining mushrooms. They could see one shuttle, three times the size of the others, position itself in front of the *Hela*. The five other shuttles positioned themselves two at each side with one at the rear. From the ground they appeared as aerial tugs guiding the vast bulk of the *Hela* into position over its three large docking posts.

'Arie, you are coming in too fast,' the Pilot said as his tractor strained to slow the *Hela*. It was pushing into the nose of the *Hela* with its grav engines at full power to slow the great ship down. He could hear the hum of his engine strain under the load but its temperature stayed just below the critical level. He had Niamh service all the shuttle engines before the landing and it would prove decisive today. He watched as the other shuttles kept the ship straight. If they couldn't hold it straight as he tried to slow it from the front, the inertia would induce it to slew sideways with disastrous consequence.

'I know that! The automatic docking assist isn't working. We missed the three thousand year refit. Can you slow us down? Our grav engines are maxed out, keeping us up,' he replied, trying to appear calm and in control. The jokes were deliberate; he couldn't let Theia, Bri or Niamh worry for an instant. He had to keep their spirits and concentration up.   Theia   had linked their minds and the trio's skills were taxed to their limits to control the ship. He had felt the shudders and heard the moans and groans coming from the depths of the *Hela* as they came in on the final approach. He had felt such protestations from a great ship once before. It didn't end well and he hoped never to feel or hear them again. The deafening silence from The Eight added to the foreboding feeling of doom. Mack knew he did not have enough blue energy to help them. What little he had, he was conserving to save himself if they crashed, he thought.

'Yes, we can, we can, you are slowing,' the Pilot said.

The *Hela* lumbered on for another four and a half kilometres with the shuttles guiding it and the Pilot's tractor slowing it down. Finally, two hundred metres from the posts it stopped. It was an awesome sight shining above those watching from the ground, and its grav engines humming with the energy they needed to keep it floating above the desert.

'Arie, my shuttles will manoeuvre you over the docking posts. Empress, maintain your height,' the Pilot said. Within minutes his shuttles pushed the *Hela* over its three docking posts. 'Empress, you are ready to dock, you should engage the locking rings.'

They felt the shaking and heard the deep metallic sounds of the base docking posts engaging with the *Hela's* three large round docking rings. They were the docking ports that supplied services and some access to the *Hela* from the base.

'Reduce your engine output by thirty per cent, Niamh,' Theia said. 'We will test these posts, and see if they hold.'

As Niamh slowly reduced the power, a deep moan and a shudder came up from the decks below.

'Stop, stop…'

'I've stopped, Theia, we're back up to minimal float power, the middle post is not holding. We'll break in half if we try to use it.'

'How long can we float here?' Mack asked standing up and coming across to the engineering console.

Niamh scanned her readouts, reconfiguring the cooling she looked up at Mack, 'the engine temperature is near the maximum. I've boosted the cooling. Maybe an hour at the most…'

'Robert,' Mack called over the comms, 'you need to get into that base. See what is happening with the centre post. It's not holding.'

'Will do, Mack.' Robert looked across at Blair, 'I knew it,' he muttered as he shook his head from side to side.

'That's not going to help, Robert. Pull yourself together. We need to get in there. If that beast falls out of the sky we're standing under it.'

'Aye, you're right, Blair. Grab the crew and two of Niamh's mechie's.'

Five minutes later, Robert and the crew, armed with torches and tools made their way down a darkened stairway into the docking posts' machine room.

'There's no lights on,' Blair said.

Robert looked around. 'No power, it couldn't be as simple as that,' he said as they approached a door at the bottom of the stairs.

One of the mechanics tried to open it. 'It's locked.'

'No for long,' Robert said, as he and Blair attacked the door with two sledge hammers. Within minutes, they had it off the hinges and thrown to the side. As they entered the room, Robert shone his torch at the machinery within.

The Eight's voice flashed in his brain; 'get out, Robert, now get out.'

He turned and, grabbing the others, ran from the room as a dark shape unfolded from the machinery and started to follow them.

'Get the humans back, it is grey matter,' The Eight suddenly said. 'Where it came from I do not know. General, you have the tool to deal with it in the armoury.'

'Yes, we do, Bri, go, you know what to do. Hurry now. We don't have much time left.'

The Eight turned his chariot to face Niamh; 'there is a last resort, in the engine room. If Bri fails, you need to use it. Do you know how?'

'Yes, Overlord, I do,' she said as she followed Bri out of the bridge. She ran down to the engine room. The heat was unbearable and in the depths of it, she found what she was looking for. The interlock bypass, the system that protected the huge grav drives, mounted between them both, deep down in the heart of the *Hela's* main engine room.

As Bri made his way to the armoury, he took out his small flask, held it to his lips and emptied its contents.

'What was that stuff?' Blair asked as they made it to the top of the stairs, panting.

'Are we all here?' Robert said, looking around and counting the team members. 'Aye, Mack, we're out,' he said over his comms. 'What was that?'

'It's grey matter.'

'Where did that come from?'

'We don't know, Robert. It can be generated when blue decays. It probably stirred when we first activated the base. It latches on to things and well it…'

'Don't tell me anymore. I remember, when we cleaned the hybrid drive, you talked about such things. The tools, we need them.'

'Bri will be with you, he has them. Robert, we don't have much time, the engines are near done and the Chinese satellite will be over soon.'

Five minutes later Bri flew out of a port on the side of the *Hela* on a small grav platform. Making his way down into the base, he landed beside Robert's team now joined by Tom and John.

'I need one to help me,' he said looking around at the humans.

'That'll be me,' John said, stepping up on the grav platform to help Bri unload the tools.

'Are you sure you are up for this, old man?'

'No need to be cheeky, Captain, just show me how that thing works.'

'John, the energy, it can contaminate your body. Are you sure…'

'Let's get on with it. No, Tom,' he said as Tom stepped up on the platform, 'you're not going. If this goes south, you'll be needed more than me.'

Niamh looked at her watch, they had fifteen minutes left. The sweat rolled down her face, and her clothes under her ship garb were sodden with it. Resigned now to her fate, she entered the command codes into the console. The engine room was filled with a strange ringing sound, and a purple flashing light. She looked at the console and, watching the readouts as they came alive, listened to the change in pitch of the cooling pumps as the safety interlocks were removed. She moved out through the engine room adjusting the cooling flow and balancing the engines for maximum output. The heat was unbearable. Finally she sat back on the dirty floor beside the console and contacted Mack.

'It's all on manual.'

'How long?'

'It's not an exact science any more, but I guess they'll hold together for another half an hour. After that…'

'The Overlord wants you back on the bridge.'

'I can't leave, he knows that.'

With the tools mounted on their back and carrying matter depleteors, John and Bri made their way down the bottom of the stairs.

'It's there, John, to your right,' he shouted, as a grey cloud uncurled from the bilge in the stairwell.

'I have it – watch, it's curling back around you,' John shouted back, as Bri swung around with his depleteor.

Attracted to the warm energy generated by their presence, the grey matter swirled around them. Bri focused his mind and firing his depleteor, he drew the energy into the containment tool on his back. The Anan tool, designed to capture and neutralise, quenched its force.

Finding a weakness in the human, the energy swirled around John. He screamed. Twisting and turning – refusing to give in – he fired his depleteor. Slowly through the deep pain the energy generated as it infiltrated his body, he managed to defuse some of the grey matter. As he slumped to the floor, Bri rushed to him, neutralising the last of the grey swirling mass with the Anan tools. Exhausted, he sat on the steps, his head slumped down, as he looked at John, unconscious on the floor in front of him.

'Robert,' he called over his comms, 'we have it. I need help, it's John. General, try the posts again.' As he heard Robert and his team approach down the stairs, Bri listened to the welcome sound of the machinery starting up.

Niamh realised they had minutes left — it would be all over soon. She could hear the cooling pumps scream as the stress of the temperature and pressure pushed against the casings. The old machinery strained under the load of keeping the great beast in the air. How strange it was, she thought, that technology, regardless of who made it, always had limits. Relaxing on the floor, she inhaled the pungent smell of the burning grav as she remembered the short time she had with Tom. The crackle of her comms broke her idle daydream.

'Reduce engines by thirty per cent,' came back Theia's welcome voice.

After five minutes with the weight of the *Hela* distributed over the three posts, Theia instructed Niamh to slowly reduce the engine output again. She linked with the base computer and took control of the posts. They slowly retracted and lowered the *Hela* to two metres above the desert floor. Finally they heard the welcome loud metallic sounds as the posts locks engaged deep inside the underground base.

'Turn your engines to idle, Niamh,' Theia said. 'We've landed. We've landed on Earth, well done, Bri, Niamh, General, Pilot, well done,' she said over their comms system. She couldn't believe they had actually done it and felt the emotion build up inside her. Exhausted from the effort, she slouched down in the chair by her control station.

'You have done well, Empress, General. You have put together a good team. When the Pilot as you call him is ready, let me know and I will transfer to my island base,' The Eight said, referring to Milford Sound. He left the bridge, returning to his quarters on his chariot.

Mack hurried to meet Robert at the main cargo hatch which was opened from the bridge. They had minutes to secure the *Hela* before the Chinese satellite flew over the base. When he arrived in the main cargo hold, Niamh's electricians were already connecting the base power cables into the *Hela*, allowing her to shut down the engines. He met Robert and Matt who were waiting for him in a jeep below the vast cargo hatch ramp.

'Robert, Matt, are you ready with it?' he asked as he hurried up to the jeep.

'Aye, Mack, it's already on the move, come on.'

They quickly drove to the bow of the *Hela* to watch a lumbering giant building slowly moving over the *Hela* to swallow it up. It was a giant hangar constructed in three pieces by a clever mix of metal sheeting, bracing, scaffolding and tarpaulins. Its purpose was to hide the *Hela* from the satellite overflights. It was supported on each side on hundreds of large wheels, and they watched as Matt's crew slowly towed the three sections into position over the eight hundred metre long *Hela* with twelve large tractors. The whole operation took twenty nail-biting minutes as Matt, Robert and Mack fussed about watching and directing. By the time the satellite approached the "gold mine" the long building was back at its original position. However, this time the *Hela* lay cleverly concealed beneath, unseen by those watching above.

'How's John?' Robert asked Tom, as they sat with Niamh, Bri and Janet at a table outside the camp galley that evening. They were enjoying some quiet time sipping beer as Theia, Mack and Kath entertained the visiting government dignitaries in Janet's large office. To celebrate this Project milestone, Robert arranged a celebration meal and provided free beer for all. Around them they could hear the happy chatter of their project staff.

'He's in the new sick bay. He'll be fine, thanks to Bri's quick work with that stuff.'

'You did well, Captain. I have to say, I was totally at a loss when it appeared.'

Bri smiled at the humans, he was not used to such attention. 'Get used to it, Robert. There are stranger things in space. I am trained to deal with them, you are not.'

'Bri, Robert is right, you saved the day,' Tom said as he handed the young captain another beer. 'You've earned the respect of my crew for saving John, we will always be grateful for that.' He paused and then smiled as he turned to look at his new wife, 'and you, Mrs Parker, what were you so worried about?'

'Jeez, Tom, would ya give it a rest, we came in too fast, and that mouldy energy stopped the post from working.'

'Not what I heard,' Robert said.

'No, I heard that the engines just didn't have it in them to deliver the reverse thrust, and if it wasn't for a certain red-haired person, wouldn't have got the *Hela* this far,' Janet said, with her arm wrapped around Niamh.

Taking the bottle of beer from his lips, Robert looked across at her. 'Aye, Niamh, our mysterious Pilot was amazed, said if you hadn't worked on that ship in space, it would be scattered over the desert floor in bits.'

'Ah go on, lads, would ye shut up,' she said as her face reddened. 'But seriously, the work starts now. It's a full refit and you, Robert, you slave driver — you want to leave in six months. Do you understand what we have to do, it's not possible and to make it harder you constructed that monstrosity over it?'

'Not my idea,' Robert said looking at Tom who smiled and waved his hand at Niamh.

'Was that yours, Tom, what were you thinking, how am I supposed to get at the engines?' she scolded. 'You're on the couch tonight,' she said as they all burst out laughing.

PROJECT REPORT TWO. EARTH DATE; 10TH JULY 2026. TO THE ONE.

My Lord,

I have resolved my blue energy deficiencies and re-charged my energy mass. We have reclaimed both our assets and landed on Earth. A successful landing and another Project milestone achieved. I reside now in my island base during the refit of the ship at its main base. We have all the equipment and supplies needed and I am confident the humans in our employ have the skills to complete the refit on time. My next report will follow our departure from Earth. I will confirm this within half an orbit of Anan.

Dedicated to your Service

The Eight

And still I hear nothing from him, he thought, after sending the report.

HELA BASE AUSTRALIAN DESERT 27TH JULY 2026

'How was Queenstown?' Theia asked. They were seated in the Portacabin that served as Theia's office and living quarters.

'Empress, it is truly amazing, you should go there,' Rhea replied.

'Would you have found it so amazing on your own?' she asked as she leaned forward and touched Rhea on the shoulder. She immediately sensed the presence of another.

'No, Empress, it is truly beautiful and its inhabitants are warm and welcoming but you are right, I would not. I dare say on my own I would have found it cold and lonely. It was his company that made the trip so wonderful for me.'

'Rhea, I sense it, congratulations. Your transformation has amazed me. You truly deserve this.'

'Thank you, Empress. It would not have happened without your intervention in my life. I owe you so much. We believe it will be a ten month pregnancy, slightly longer than humans and shorter than purebreeds. The baby should be born near the end of our journey to the New World.'

'And how do you feel about that?'

'Ecstatic, really ecstatic, look at my skin, it glows,' she said as she lifted her arms and turned her hands over and over. 'I have never felt so alive.'

'You know you are both not really needed full time here.'

'What should we do?'

'I want you and Alex to set up a treatment program for the sick purebreeds. You only need to see them every two weeks, right?'

'Yes, that's right.'

'The rest of the time you spend in one of our complexes in New Zealand. You will be safe there. It will give you time for your baby to develop, and for you to grow your strength for the arduous journey we face.'

'We could go back to Queenstown.'

'Yes, that would be convenient; it is near our home base in the South Island. We have returned to it now, The Eight stays there during the refit period. We have a regular shuttle service set up, the one you came on today, it runs between here and Christchurch with stops at Milford and Queenstown. The humans call it the bus.'

'Queenstown it is,' Rhea said, happy with the arrangements and spent another while chatting happily with her friend.

HELA BASE AUSTRALIAN DESERT 30TH JULY 2026

After the near fatal landing, Robert spent a hectic three weeks pushing the crews and organising the shifts for the start of the *Hela* refit. With Janet, Niamh and Matt he reorganised the base management, giving him the time, as project manager, for some forward planning.

'I need time to get into the base and explore it and I want to go to Milford Sound,' he explained to his team. 'And above all, I want to see how we can improve on the load-out of that beast.'

Taking time to look over the pods coming from Germany, he was surprised to see little was done to prepare them for the load-out into the *Hela*. 'So why don't we assemble them into modules, like apartment blocks and load them with a grav carrier?' he asked the supervisor in charge of them.

'We didn't think of that,' he replied, 'I don't know the loads the grav carriers can handle.'

'Talk to Niamh, she'll give you the loads, we have to remember, what goes into the belly of that beast we have to take out at the other end,' he said. Based on his ideas, the pods were assembled into accommodation blocks on the site. During the short load-out period, the grav carriers would fly them right into the *Hela* cargo bay. On the New World they would come out like that as well. It would save them days of work at the load-out and when they unloaded on the New World.

Robert was delighted with the new technology that came with the *Hela*. The big grav carriers superseded the need for cranes. The smaller grav platforms provide access and lifting platforms for carrying people, machinery and materials. The use of the grav technology revolutionised the fit-out and construction work. Using the purebreed crew he started a training program for the colonists in its use. Those who did not have a specific fit-out skill were utilised as grav drivers, and pretty soon they were indispensable.

After working with the pods, Robert moved on to explore the *Hela* base. When they arrived, the purebreeds completed a quick survey of it with

Niamh, confirming the parts she needed were there and that there was no more grey matter. Her technicians rigged up temporary lights, but went no further in its exploration. The base intrigued him, he was mindful of any more hidden dangers or secrets it may hold. As no one had delved deep into its interior, he used the same methods and crew they previously used for the *Hela* survey.

The base was on two levels, constructed with a system of air vents, and although it was stale, they found breathable atmosphere throughout. The upper level was filled with the *Hela* spare parts and a small derelict accommodation block. It was on the lower level where he made a welcomed discovery — an extensive collection of grav driven machinery. The purebreeds had left behind the construction and blue energy extraction equipment they used on Earth in the past. If the machinery still worked, or could be repaired, it would be invaluable to them.   .

'Oh yes, look at this, look at this,' he said with delight. He was like a child with new toys and immediately called Niamh down to join them. 'See how many grav platforms and grav carriers there are, we need as many of those as we can get.'

When Niamh arrived she immediately climbed on top of one of the grav carriers to get a look at what was there. She gazed out over the dimly lit alien machinery; 'wow — look at this. If it works, it will save time converting the Earth equipment,' she said referring to the drilling and quarrying machinery they planned to buy and convert to grav power.

They spend hours climbing in and out of the machinery and inspecting a whole range of tools they also discovered.

'It looks like about half of it was hardly used and it's covered with some sort of protective film as well, like plastic,' she said running her hands over the alien covering. 'We've a good chance to get this stuff going. Robert, you could use those grav platforms and carriers now. I'll have my guys look at them.'

'That lot over there must be the blue extraction equipment,' he said. 'You know if you can get them going it'll save us months when we get to the New World. Demard showed me a video of how they extract blue. I was going to use our own drilling and quarrying equipment, but those four machines, they do the whole process in one go from the surface,' he said as they moved closer to one of the giant strange-shaped machines.

It looked like a cross between a massive excavator and a drilling machine and was mounted on a huge grav platform. There were four blue energy tanks and a control cabin mounted on the deck of the platform. They could see it was hardly used before and stored with the strange protective film wrapped all over it.

'Robert, this one looks nearly new, if you get that up to the workshop, I'll get a team working on it,' Niamh said, inspecting another machine.

'Aye, lads,' he said to his crew of six, 'you're going to be running this when we get to the New World. Get with Niamh's guys, they'll get it going. You all need to know how it operates. I'm telling you now, when we get to the New World, I want that machine out first and you guys off drilling. No excuses. Don't tell us when we get there you forgot the fuel or the drill bit was left on Earth, or there's a hose burst. No excuses. It's last into the *Hela* and first out. And look, that piece behind it, that looks like an accommodation platform. Aye, it is,' he said, looking at the large accommodation block mounted on another grav platform. It was where the purebreeds and their human crew lived during their time out extracting blue on Earth. 'Blair, you're the crew leader, clean that up and get it fixed up. You'll be living in it. I'll get Tom to mount a gun on it to protect you from any animals. Don't turn your nose up at it, Shona, we've lived in worse.'

'No, Robert, I was just expecting a bit more, I mean we'll find it hard to live in that on the New World,' she said, looking at the strange accommodation.

'No, it'll only be for when you're out extracting blue. You and Blair have a large pod together,' he said, visibly exasperated by her reply as he removed his hard hat and wrung his hands through his hair.

'What's a pod?' she asked.

'Jeez, Robert, you're a hard task master. I'm going to get you a whip. Did you not tell them where we'd be living? Lads, the pods, it's our accommodation when we travel out on the *Hela* and then on the New World. You can see them on the edge of the site,' Niamh said as she slapped Robert on his arm. 'Robert, we'll have to put an info pack together for the colonists, we can't have them wondering where they're going to live. That's terrible, you have to do better.'

'Aye, you're right, Niamh,' he said, nodding his head. 'I'll show you all a pod tomorrow. Blair, mind what I said, when we get there, your crew is first out and off drilling and extracting blue. And if ye mess it up, I have it on good authority, there are plenty of hungry monsters to feed ye to,' he said, smiling at them as they laughed at his threat.

As he continued his exploration of the base he found a large locked door at the back of the lower chamber with a strange seal he had not seen before. It was fitted with a similar locking arrangement as the *Hela* armoury. Calling Mack to tell him, Robert was surprised to see him arrive with the Pilot, a short time later.

'Robert, this is a treasure trove, really we are lucky with this equipment. I didn't expect it to be here and in such good condition. I guess the dry desert air and the preservative they applied did the job,' he said as he walked off inspecting the equipment.

Robert left him to it and as he watched, the Pilot called him over to the locked door.

'Robert this belongs to my family. They were as you say a "rum lot", so it's probably full of drugs and maybe some weapons. I'll need a hand to open the door,' he said as he activated the lock. Robert helped him push open the big door and entering the chamber, they were both surprised at its cavernous size.

'What is all that?' Robert asked. The chamber was filled with strange containers and at the back a compartment that looked like a safe. He looked at the Pilot and un-characteristically, he was crying. 'Pilot, are you OK?' he asked.

'Yes, I am, they are containers of grav fuel for the engines and helium three for the fusion reactor. My family were energy traders. Call Mack please, and leave us,' asked the Pilot.

Mack joined the Pilot as he opened the large safe at the back of the chamber. They were both surprised at its contents. Hesitating, the Pilot slowly opened some of the boxes sitting on the shelves above the large pile of gold bullion. They were filled with precious stones and clear uncut diamonds. As his bony hands shook, the Pilot took out a large uncut diamond of about four hundred carats from one of the boxes. It was a giant of a stone.

'Arie, please take this. No, I insist, take it before we inventory what is here in fuel and precious stones and metal,' said the Pilot in a faltering voice.

'Zaval, my friend, this is not necessary, you have done enough,' Mack said trying to hand back the big stone, embarrassed at his friend's dilemma.

'No, I had heard this was here, but did not believe it, nor did I think there was so much. I will pay my family's debt to the Overlord. And that stone should more than repay the kindness and help the Aknars have given to me and my family.'

'Before you are so hasty, look at what else is here,' Mack said as he looked deeper into the locker. 'What's in that box?' he said. Pulling out a long silver box hidden at the back, they started to open it.

'By The One,' whispered the Pilot as he stepped back from the open box in shock.

'Zaval, you cannot give that away. It is your family's birthright.'

'No, Arie, I cannot keep it. They are steeped in so much blood.'

'The clear uncut diamond you gave me, is that not steeped in the same blood? Do we burn all the grav and helium three here? Is that not steeped in blood as well? Zaval, when will you stop?' he said, shaking his hands at his friend in anger. 'You cannot live with the sins of your ancestors. This was not tainted with blood. It was and still is your birthright.'

'I cannot, Arie.'

'Zaval, you can — and it is not yours to refuse. Look at them, such a deep colour. Those blue diamonds were mined in this quadrant of the galaxy, long before blood was spilled. They were never used. All of this hoard, it was put away long before the demons. This one,' he said, lifting out the largest blue diamond from the silver box, 'I will have it mounted and you will give it to Siba. She is an excellent navigator and deserves her own crystal. The rest of your family deserve one as well. You cannot deny them, Zaval. I will not hear of it.'

As he glanced in through the large open door Robert was surprised to see Mack and the Pilot, with fresh tears streaming down his face, embracing. As they withdrew from their manly embrace, Mack happily clapped the Pilot on the back. Strange, thought Robert, more mystery surrounding their eccentric Pilot.

DISCOVERY

CHAPTER EIGHTEEN

'Boss, can I come in?' he said to Tom, seated in his office in the *Hela* base camp.

'Brian, yes, come in, what's up?' Tom replied, wondering why this shy young Welsh soldier wanted to see him.

'Boss, it's a bit delicate, but you know we've been bringing in the new hires thick and fast?'

'Yes, I do,' he said, sitting up at his desk, all ears now.

'Well I'm seeing this Kiwi girl, she's gorgeous, a real stunner.'

'Yes, Brian, go on, I've got the picture.'

'Boss, I know there's going to be trouble but you need to see this,' he said, handing over a small tablet computer to Tom.

'Come round here, show me what I'm looking at,' Tom said, moving over to give Brian room beside him.

'It's here, it's a new social site called Crowdchat. It's like a blog — really popular with the young twenties scene.'

They had no open internet cover on the site so there should be no live content on this tablet, thought Tom. 'Well that leaves me out,' he said, as he wondered what was coming next.

Brian opened a folder on the tablet. 'Kora, that's her name, showed it to me today. She saved all her content before she came here.'

'Ah shit,' Tom shouted as he looked at the content scrolling across the small screen. 'Where did that come from?'

'Sorry, boss, it's why she applied for the job. Most of her friends think it's a hoax. Look, see the comments. But it's growing. Kora and six of her mates are colonists and here on the base. When they don't get in touch with their friends at home, they'll cotton on pretty quick it's not a hoax,' the young soldier said. He paused as he looked at Tom, and then continued with more bad news. 'Boss, there are others here as well who will be in the same boat. The secret's nearly out.'

'I have the best computer technician in the galaxy with a team of agents in Christchurch. I have a Chinese spymaster with a team of agents in Siberia — all running defensive cyber war illusions to cover our tracks. We have the biggest shed in the world covering the *Hela* — from satellite overflights. And now you show me we're beat by a social media site on your girlfriend's fifty dollar tablet,' Tom said, his face pale and haggard. 'You did well coming here. No, don't look like that. You did well. Can you get Kora please? Bring her over to Janet's office, and tell her she's not in any trouble,' he said. Looking across to Janet's office, he could see her talking to Bri.

'It's not me,' Bri lied, looking at the pictures — he knew when they were taken.

'And what other Anan was drinking in that pub in Christchurch?' Tom asked, shaking with anger as he looked at Bri.

'Now, Tom, it's not the only picture,' Janet said. She was right. The blog was titled "aliens are here", and featured all sorts of wild pictures and way out theories. But there was one popular thread that was gaining traction. It featured Project Anan with pictures of the *Hela* base, some of the purebreeds and a grav carrier in flight. All were taken from the outer fence of the base, by their airport, most likely by visiting contractors or the flight crew of the planes. But it was the ones of Bri that were the most vivid, capturing him sitting in a darkened corner of a bar drinking a pint of beer. Most worrying were the comments, all about the jobs on offer with the aliens.

'Boss, this is Kora,' Brian said standing just inside the doorway of Janet's office behind his beautiful girlfriend.

'Kora, thanks for coming, No, don't look so worried. How many of the colonists do you think are on the social site?' Tom asked.

'About a hundred, I think.'

'And what happens when they don't reply?'

'They get noticed, it's called "go dark" and you can see the post their friends leave, look,' she said as she took the tablet from Bri and refreshed the screen. They were all mortified to see the words of the posts, "another one gobbled by aliens".

'That's not fair — we don't eat humans,' Bri said.

'Bri, you really need to take this seriously. This puts us on the cusp of a global war, something we've worked hard to prevent,' Tom said in a low and frightening voice. 'I can see where those pictures were taken. Look,' he said lifting up the tablet. 'There's the bar's name on the wall behind you. What were you thinking, Bri?' He knew Bri visited Christchurch regularly on "the bus" to help Kath with the new colonist interviews. The office was close to the Central Business District. It was obvious that Bri had surreptitiously slipped out for a lunchtime drink. From the pictures, it was more than once and he was easily identifiable, despite his attempts to disguise his alien appearance with human clothes.

'Tom, I'm sorry… I really am. What do we do now?' he asked. He had not fully understood how serious these social media revelations were. As his hands began to shake and a tear ran down the side of his white face, they all could see how upset the young Anan captain was.

'We manage it,' Tom said, as the colour returned to his face. 'We knew this day would come. Thanks to Kora and Brian we have probably about four to five days to stop it before it goes viral. I'll let Mack and Theia know, Janet, you call Kath. Tell her to brief Harold. Brian, you and Kora call Demard in Christchurch, explain what's going on with the blog. I'll call John and all our team leaders for a staff meeting in one hour and, Brian, I want you there as well.'

SYDNEY 12TH NOVEMBER 2026

'Thomas Parker, we finally meet,' Chang said as Tom entered the small dingy office Chang rented in an industrial park outside Sydney.

'Chang, I never thought I'd say this, but it's good to finally meet. You have done all you said you would.' It was true – Operation Deception had sown the seeds of disharmony between the Chinese and the Great Northern Union. The Chinese believed Anan Corp was a Great Northern Union company, developing new and secret technology. The disappearance of Chang's boss, the discovery of the money trail and the data on his computer, compounded the illusion. Chang was the flavour of the month in Beijing and given free rein to do as he pleased.

'Of course I did. I am a man of my word. How is your lovely wife? And the shooting lessons you said you were giving her — how she doing with that?' he said, stretching out his hand to Tom.

'She's good, Chang. I've to thank you for the guns you sent her. She loves them, and the lessons are going great,' he said as he grasped and shook the hand of the man who once was his enemy.

'They are the best in the world. I had them made special for our female agents, so well balanced. To business, you want to discuss "chat to the crowd", the social site.'

'It's called Crowdchat. Chang, you really need to get with it and up your game,' Tom said, returning Chang's previous teasing of him. 'I'm afraid after all our hard work, it could have exposed us. I have our alien computer tech working with the colonists involved. He will cover their tracks, cleaning some of the content. We will also show some as a hoax. He can neutralise the immediate threat, but it's a wake-up call, Chang.'

'A blog, we are beaten by a blog. I will have them banned in China.'

'You might be a bit early giving such dictates, you're not Emperor yet,' Tom said, still teasing Chang. 'Look, I'll show you,' he said taking out a tablet computer with a copy of Kora's files. As Tom showed him the files, Chang clucked, emitting disapproving noises and gasps of displeasure.

'Not what I expected, Parker. I am disappointed. Yes, you can clean it now, but damage is done. They will pick that up in Beijing, if it's not yet analysed it soon will be.'

'I agree, Chang. I am disappointed, but it is what it is. The Project is so big – it's just a matter of time – soon the main stream news media will pick it up. We have to deal with that before we see it on television. No — stop clucking, Chang,' he said holding up his hand to silence his old adversary. 'We both knew this day would come. You did a good job with Operation Deception. Our Overlord has acknowledged that. He will honour his agreement with you.'

'Thank the Overlord,' Chang said as he bowed his head and sighed. He looked back up, 'you are right, Parker. We did know this day would come. Tell me what you do.'

Tom looked at the Chinese spymaster, he had agonised at how much he should tell him before they met, but now he knew, he must be honest and warn Chang of what was to come. 'There is a meeting planned shortly between our close allies. It will ratify our decision to announce the arrival of the aliens at the United Nations in Geneva. You need to have your people safe before we make that announcement. We can also offer you safety or asylum — whatever you want, Chang.'

'Thank you, but it would be traitorous of me to avail myself of that. You know I have loyal followers, I must look after them. They are important to me and support me. If there is a void left after all this is settled, I may be able to fill that gap. They are counting on that. Thank you for warning me, Parker. I enjoy working with you — but still you must up your game — imagine to be beaten by a blog. Oh, the shame of that. In my country that never happen. No, never,' he said smiling at Tom.

The two old enemies laughed at Chang's joke. Before Tom left they continued with some small talk and reflections of old jobs where they both previously crossed swords. They both realised if each could weather the storm that rapidly approached, their new friendship could be the start of an important alliance for the future.

MILFORD SOUND 23RD NOVEMBER 2026

The main chamber of the Milford Sound base resounded with the clamour of activity as the blue-suited Project Anan personnel hurried about their work. At the side of the chamber, behind some simple clear screens, an important meeting had just started. The visiting dignitaries attending the venue found the arrangements strange. Instead of the usual meeting table, they were sitting around a large oval console. It was supported on boxes and serviced by cables laid through temporary ramps to the main control room.

The place looked more like a mobile military base with generators running quietly in the background and the temporary paraphernalia needed for habitation arranged throughout the vast chamber. Most distracting to the guests, was the activities of the blue-suited personnel in the control room. They could see Robert and Niamh, busily directing six other technicians and hear the occasional sound of buzzing alarms, emitting from inside of the control room. But when he floated into the chamber on his gleaming chariot and entered their meeting area, it was The Eight who surprised them the most.

'Welcome to my island base,' he said, pausing for them to adjust to his presence. It was the first time he had met any people from the governments of Earth. 'George, Harold, Admiral White — thank you for coming. I must apologise for the background noise, but as you are aware, events overtake us. Thomas Parker, perhaps you can start with a brief update on where we are.'

Tom started the meeting with a brief summary of how much was known about their Project and critically, how the social media blog had nearly exposed them. It was he who called this meeting today, and had arranged for George, the Australian PM and Harold, the New Zealand PM and Admiral White to attend with Theia, Mack and Kath. He was delighted when Theia confirmed the Overlord would host it here at his base.

'Finally, we terminated Operation Deception. Chang Jin has disappeared. The Chinese discovered the blog before we cleaned it out. With their intelligence counterparts in the Great Northern Union, they are actively reviewing the information we fed them from Deception. They now know it was us. We see large fleet movements again in our direction,' Tom said finishing his brief.

'Katherine, I believe you have the first strand of our strategy,' The Eight said.

'Yes,' she said, looking across at The Eight and wondering how she had arrived in such a bizarre situation. 'Now it is a rumour. We need to take control of that rumour, make it ours, deliver it to the people and prove we are not a threat. It's out there already, so we go public and announce it at the United Nations in Geneva. There is no advantage in trying to disprove it. We have the full complement of colonists, two thousand five hundred. I allowed for a change of mind rate of five per cent. If that happens, we may have about a hundred disgruntled people returning from the *Hela* base with their own negative stories. There's no going back. We must front up now and announce it to the world. We can't keep the lid on it anymore.'

'Yes, I agree with that,' The Eight said. 'How do we go about it? George, Harold, do you agree? Speak up, I am not a monster,' he said in a gentle tone.

'Overlord, yes I agree, but you know my concerns and I believe we speak about that later,' George said.

'Yes, we do. Harold, speak up.'

'I agree with an announcement, Overlord. I have made tentative inquiries as to a suitable date. We can't just blurt it out. We need the right venue. There is a general assembly meeting planned for the ninth of December. Once they know what it's about, I hope they'll clear the floor for us. New Zealand will sponsor the announcement. If they don't, we will plan for that as well. Empress, General, although you are the logical choice to announce your presence here, I and Admiral Cyril think that would be a bad idea. We cannot guarantee your security. I believe Kath is —.'

'Harold, how could you suggest that? Could you not have told me this morning? Really, you expect too much,' she said, visibly surprised and annoyed at his suggestion and oblivious to the smiles the others were making at her blunt statement.

'I knew you wouldn't like to do it, but you are the most qualified. A communications and human resources expert — and you were the Anans' first contact. That is so important, Kath,' Harold said looking at her.

'He is right, Katherine. You have served our cause. Our Project would not have advanced to this stage without you. I ask you please, to personally represent me, The Eight, at this council. Before you do this, I will work with you on your speech and presentation.'

Kath was overwhelmed by his words. They resounded in her mind; "please personally represent me" he had asked. 'Of course, Overlord, I would be honoured,' she replied, still in shock at what she was yet to do. Theia, sitting beside her, squeezed her hand and smiled at her in encouragement. She was delighted the Overlord had honoured Kath in this way.

'Security next, Overlord, I'll get Niamh and Bri,' Tom said as he left the table.

He returned shortly with Niamh, and Bri, who looked somewhat uncomfortable. Earlier, Niamh could feel strange fearful emotions emanating from Bri. She noticed as they got closer to the Overlord, his fear increased. Unknown to Niamh, Bri had confessed his now infamous indiscretions to the Overlord, who already knew all about them. Also unknown to Niamh, when Tom learned of his fate, he pleaded for Bri's life.

'We are mortal, Overlord, and we make mistakes. He is young and impetuous. You know the young don't always follow the rules and believe they are invincible. Spare him, please —we need him — and if you do this, it will kill all trust the colonists have in you. They will simply say "you killed him for going out for a beer". They will not see your bigger picture,' Tom said bluntly to The Eight.

'I will spare him. But there are consequences,' he said. He also suspected there was something else but didn't delve, it was Aknar business, not his. The Eight spared Bri, but left him under no illusions. The Overlord was displeased with him and he now had a debt to pay. Theia and Mack were ashamed of this black mark, a blot on the House of Aknar.

The Eight's displeasure and his debt bore heavily on Bri, who hoped his feelings would not impair his navigation abilities today. He and Niamh put their blue diamonds into ports on the console. Harold, George and Admiral White sat back in surprise when a three dimensional coloured projection flickered and jumped up in front of them.

'Ladies and gentlemen, what you see is the Pacific Theatre and the Far East,' he said as he pointed to the map generated from his and Niamh's navigation abilities. 'The red dots indicate the Chinese and Great Northern Union vessels, the blue dots are your combined forces, Admiral. The green dots are commercial vessels — and these dots, the grey ones, are deep nuclear powered submarines. I believe they are American, am I right in that assumption?' Bri asked Admiral White.

'Yes, I believe you are. It would be typical of their new tactic, watch from afar. The Europeans are noticeable by their absence,' Admiral White said.

'No, they have no vessels in the southern hemisphere or the far east. Thank you, Admiral. What you see is a real time plot of the vessels as they move. I have monitored the movements of the Chinese and Great Northern Union vessels. Since Mr Parker shut down Deception, they have re-deployed their forces. They are making steady advances towards this area and the Australian continent. We have plotted their projected route, you can see them here,' he said, pointing to a new overlay that Niamh projected over the table. 'Their destinations are obvious. They are coming, Overlord,' he said, bowing his head to him as he finished.

'Captain, hold that display for a moment. George, Harold, Admiral, what I say now is not negotiable. You will not engage in war. I forbid it. Leave the others to me. Is that clear?' The Eight said.

'Yes, Overlord, you make that quite clear,' replied George, sitting back in his chair in shock at what was just said. 'If you would permit, we would prefer to shadow their fleet.'

'You may until I start. Before I start, I will advise you with enough time to withdraw your forces. I may have difficulty differentiating who is who. I am not infallible. It is better to get your vessels at a safe distance. Niamh, how is the recovery of blue going?' he asked, abruptly changing the subject.

'On track and the inventory will be above the theoretical estimates,' she replied, referring to their recovery of the residue blue energy — the slops — from the large storage tanks deep down in the mountain. She looked at Tom he smiled and nodded, they were not needed any more. She and Bri both removed their blue diamonds from the console and left the meeting.

'Thank you, ladies and gentlemen, you are welcome to stay. I go now,' the Overlord said as he turned in his chariot and left the meeting, returning to a small part of the accommodation block he had reclaimed as his own.

The group continued with informal discussions on the inevitable conflict while enjoying some welcome refreshments. Suddenly, a loud bang that shook the mountain and the base within abruptly disturbed their chat. The shock dislodged clouds of dust and small particles of rock from the walls and the ceiling of the cavern, knocking the console off the boxes it was perched on and spilling their refreshments onto the dusty floor. But it was the scene from the control room that shocked George, Harold and Kath the most. Robert, Niamh and their staff were jumping up and down and shouting with joy as they clapped each other on the back. Robert, noticing their surprise and look of horror, quickly approached.

'You got it moving,' Mack said, smiling at Robert.

'Yes, Mack we did. Apologies, ladies and gentlemen, we were working on the *Hela* docking post inside the base. It was reluctant to move and its docking ring, on top of the mountain was planted with the deposits of time. We lifted the protective cap rock this morning and just got the post moving.

'Mack, we're finished as well with the blue recovery. We've two of the base's large shipping tanks full of blue and ready to refuel the *Hela*,' he said grinning from ear to ear. He was delighted. Today was a good day for the Project and had followed on from their success in the Australian desert. Niamh had nearly finished with the refit. They had three weeks of work remaining to commission the ship and finish the accommodation upgrade. 'We're getting nearer to that test fight, Mack,' Robert said, still smiling.

TEMPORARY BUILDING UNITED NATIONS GENEVA 9TH DECEMBER 2026

Nothing went as Harold planned, the changed dynamics of the Security Council, favouring a Chinese and Great Northern Union block, denied the New Zealand delegation the access they previously asked for.

'We notified you two weeks ago, we wished to discuss – today – matters of grave importance to the human race. Secretary General, you indicated we would be given the time,' Harold said forcefully as he glowered at the man.

'It was an indication only, not a commitment. The Security Council has blocked your speaking time,' the Secretary General replied.

'Very well — I suspected this. We arranged an alternative venue. I will announce it to the press outside. I will also inform them – as the United Nations is now run by a cabal of dictators – you refused us speaking time. The rest of the world will be interested in our announcement. Thank you. Have a good day, Secretary General,' he said as he got up from his seat and motioned for his delegation to follow him. He was right not to bring Theia and Mack — it was turning into a debacle.

'Are they waiting?' Harold asked Kath as they hurried out.

'Yes, I sent the texts as soon as I saw how the meeting was going,' she replied.

As soon as they exited the building they were faced with a barrage of media. It was a frenzy as they all jockeyed for position to interview Harold. To add to the turmoil, the Secretary General and his entourage were quickly following Harold's delegation, trying to disrupt the media interview on the steps of the building. But Harold wouldn't falter and made his announcement. With Kath's careful priming, the media were drooling at the prospect of a scoop. They rushed to the large function rooms of the nearby hotel she rented to gain their seats, for what they believed was to be the revelation of the millennia. Over the previous week, Kath had carefully fed the rumour of aliens on Earth. She had gently linked it to an important announcement that would be made in Geneva. The hungry pack assembled from all over the world looking for any morsel thrown their way.

⏳

'My name is Katherine Phillips,' she started as she looked out into the sea of faces in the packed function room. They represented the world's media and some foreign dignitaries who had abandoned the United Nations conference. She had booked this venue as a backup and as a post announcement briefing centre. Arranging the television cameras and ensuring the live television and internet feed be provided by the venue to all media outlets on request, Kath was now live and global. 'I am going to tell you a story you will not believe, I did not believe them when they arrived in February at my Christchurch office on my fiftieth birthday.'

She easily recounted her story. The Eight prepared her and gave her the holographic projector and a message he recorded for the people of Earth. He had included video from the past and explained the link between human intelligence, the Overlords and the purebreeds, emphasising the link between the three species. Finally, on the encouragement of The Eight, Kath displayed the only picture of their first contact. The world was treated to the spectacle of a picture of Theia Aknar, Empress of the Planet Anan, General Arie Machai of her Protective Guard positioned on each side of Kath, with Janet beside Mack and Alan. It was the picture taken in the kitchen of Kath's house in Christchurch with Kath's fiftieth balloons and streamers in the background. That day, the picture gained iconic status, fuelling the headlines, "Aliens crash birthday bash", and the news story that followed.

"Katherine Phillips a human resource consultant from Christchurch in New Zealand got more than she bargained for when aliens arrived at her office on the morning of her 50th birthday. After spending a day with her at the office they returned home with her to her surprise birthday party. Katherine advised the world today -"

The story was out on the news wire as the conference centre erupted with a confused mix of applause, shouts and the expected screams of protestation and of course, the constant questions. But there was more to come. As Harold tried to calm the baying crowd the final proof was moved up from the basement below.

He travelled from the Australian *Hela* base on a New Zealand military plane. Parts of the transfer were made with him secreted in a large box marked as the "Diplomatic Bag". "Personal items belonging to the ambassador", was the explanation given to any airport officials who asked about its size. The journey was uncomfortable. He was accompanied by a protection detail from the New Zealand military and Anan Corp led by John. He felt miserable and cramped throughout. Tom refused to allow his transport by shuttle; it was too risky. Bri had time on this thirty-eight hour journey in a primitive Earth airplane to contemplate what he had done. During the flight, he sat beside John. He could never understand why John always tried to look out for him, until Alice explained it at the wedding. John's only son was killed in the Wave. In Earth terms, he would be Bri's age now. Sitting beside the older man, his head hung down over his long neck as he felt he had let his friend down.

When they arrived in Geneva, they took him to a small basement hotel room. John stayed with him as he changed into his captain's uniform. The screaming, shouting and thumping of people stamping their feet on the ground above scared him. To aggravate Bri's forlorn feelings of hopelessness and dejection, he missed his flask. He couldn't take his special drink on this journey. The pain it caused slowly gnawed at the pit of his stomach, pushing Bri further into a down ward spiral of despair.

'Please, I would like to introduce you to someone else,' Harold said to the audience as the noise finally abated. 'I would appreciate if you would treat him with respect and dignity; may I introduce you to the Captain of the *Hela*.'

John whipped off a dark cloak covering Bri as he stepped up onto the podium beside Harold. He stood there looking at them. It frightened him to the core, the shouting, the flashing lights from the photography equipment and the emotion that was in the room. It was overwhelming, a mix of fear, hatred, love and elation. The emotion froze him to the spot. He could hear Harold beside him.

'Captain, Captain are you OK?' he said but Bri couldn't reply, he just stared at the crowd of baying humans. It was the worst moment of his life, until Kath rescued him. Standing beside the young frightened captain, she held his hand and nodded in encouragement. Bri, unable to hear what Kath was saying, eventually started to speak.

'My name is Brizo Sema, Captain of the *Hela* and an Aknar from the Planet Anan,' he said in a halting quiet voice. 'I am here as living proof that this is not a hoax,' he continued, first in Anan and then in English. Looking at the crowd as they sat in silence, he realised he had paid half his debt to the Overlord. It was horrible and humiliating; ignoring the deep pain in his stomach he continued, as he delivered another simple message of friendship, carefully scripted in Anan and English.

As soon as he finished his speech, John covered Bri with the cloak and they smuggled him back to the vehicle waiting in the basement car park below. The convoy, escorted by the Swiss police, sped out of the hotel with Bri safely contained in a large bullet proof jeep. But Bri, now on the verge of a breakdown, was inconsolable, crying and moaning and asking for his flask, he scared Kath. Realising something very bad was happening, Kath called Queenstown.

'I don't know what's happening to him. I told him we are going to a clinic for some medical tests and he exploded. He is having a breakdown, Alex, Rhea you have to help, he can't go through with the tests, he keeps crying that they will find his "bawrak", I think he called it,' Kath said over the phone to them.

As soon as Kath said the words "bawrak" Rhea screamed in anguish. She surprised Alex with the fear in her voice. There was a short pause, as Kath heard Rhea and Alex discuss something in Anan. Finally Alex's soft and calm voice came on the line.

'Kath, this is important, give the phone to Bri,' he said. 'Bri, Bri, it's Alex, listen to me, you must calm down, there will be no invasive or urine tests. Do you understand?'

'Yes, Alex, I do, thank you,' Bri said, still shaking. 'What will they do to me?'

'You will have something called a magnetic resonance imaging scan of your torso. It will show the positions of your organs in the upper body and the differences between purebreed and humans. You will also have a DNA swab taken from your mouth and something called an ECG which will record the electrical activity of your heart. It will show your different heartbeat profile. That is all. You must go through with this, The Eight asked for it. You have nothing to fear. I personally know the staff at the clinic — they will look after you — now give the phone back to Kath,' he asked.

'He has calmed down. Alex, what did you tell him?' she asked.

'Kath, he is sick. I will advise the clinic as soon as we hang up. But Kath, Rhea will relieve Bri of his command —'

'What? How can she do that — and why?' Kath asked, shocked at what she was hearing.

'As the *Ilela* medical officer, I'm afraid it's her duty. She is on the other phone to Mack. I need to talk to John,' he said.

'John, you have Alice with you, right?' Alex asked, referring to the security team's amazing medic and soldier who treated Tom and Niamh during the rescue.

'Yes, Alex. Alice is with us.'

'John, Bri must not be left alone, Alice must accompany him everywhere and I mean everywhere, no locked doors. He is relieved of his captain's command and orders will come through shortly for you to transfer him to Queenstown to our care after departing Geneva.'

'I see, and am I to be told why?'

'Yes John and you can tell Alice, but no one else. Bri is addicted to a powerful brain enhancing narcotic. It is called "bawrak". Its loose translation to English means "lightening". It enhances the brainwave projection and navigation capabilities the Anans have. Over time the Anans are losing this ability. It is not uncommon for the older navigators to be addicted to this stuff. It also amplifies the senses and physical abilities. I'm sorry, John,' he said, knowing John had invested much time in schooling the young man.

'That's OK, Alex. Can you do anything to help him get through the next few hours and the long plane journey?' John asked, focusing on Bri's care.

'Yes, I will provide the clinic with instructions. I need to go now, you must be nearly there. Goodbye, John and good luck,' he said as he hung up.

Alex turned and looked at a crestfallen Rhea who had just delivered the devastating news to Mack. Before he could console her he rang his contact at the clinic. He knew them from his work in Switzerland. They were the best. They would provide verified documentation from the limited tests Alex prescribed, that Bri was not from Earth. The three tests would not expose his addiction. He advised them that Captain Sema was feeling the effects of the stress away from his people and Overlord. It was understandable, they agreed. He relayed what they should do to help him through the examination and then prepare him for the long trip to Queenstown. Finally, after terminating the call he turned to Rhea, who collapsed into his arms crying.

'Oh, Alex,' she cried, 'It's not Bri's fault. It's the pressure they put on them to perform. To have to tell Mack that his nephew is a —' but she just could not finish the sentence as she clung to Alex for his emotional support.

As Bri and entourage entered the medical centre they were welcomed by the courteous Swiss staff that assembled to greet their unexpected and bizarre client. The director would not normally entertain such a request. But coming from the eminent Doctor Alex Barber, who she personally knew, and with the large fee offered by his employer, she cleared the centre for the day and swore her staff to secrecy.

They prepared everything as Alex requested, even the late but not unexpected request for refreshments. Of course with Swiss precision, it was already planned and before the examination Bri and entourage were spoiled with hot drinks and fresh pastries. It was Alex's first simple request for Bri, a sweet double expresso. The sugar and caffeine gave Bri the energy and kick to get him through the simple procedures. He realised Alex was right; the medical staff were charming and polite. The friendly and respectful emotions they gave off put him at ease. When it was finished, they were brought to the centre's canteen for a light meal in preparation for the long flight back. Finally, Alex's travel prescription, a strong sedative, was administered to Bri by the centre's director, who also provided Alice with top up medication and instructions on its use.

Bri left the medical centre realising he had paid his debt to the Overlord. Within an hour they were back on the plane. As it took off, John looked down at a comatose Bri swaddled in blankets secure on the floor of the plane. *What next for him?* he wondered. The sedative whisked the fallen Aknar Prince into oblivion, releasing him from the troubling thoughts of the second scandal he had unleashed on the proud House of Aknar.

Kath returned to their hotel headquarters to help Harold appease the media, the UN delegates and other government leaders hungry for information. The following day, she hosted a press conference that included the director of the medical centre, three other independent doctors and Alex, who participated by video link. The director announced "that the anatomy, DNA and heart rate of Captain Brizo Sema indicates he is not of this Earth". The other three doctors, who verified the examination results, agreed with her findings and dismissed the accusations of a hoax.

Alex delivered the final proof that dispelled all notions of a fraud by the video link from his office in Queenstown. It was a detailed presentation and contained information from his doctoral thesis on sources of DNA. He explained he noticed some common traits across different and diverse populations. He believed they may share common ancestry dating back some seventy thousand years. Alex's thesis, published years before the Anans arrived, proved the Overlord's story.

'Humans are related to the Anans. Our DNA is similar and we are from the same family of bipeds. There is no doubt of that,' Alex said. 'The Anans are more evolved than us. Anthropologists predict we will evolve into what the Anans are now. We will be taller, with longer necks and lose all our hair,' he said. His final statement that ended the presentation caused the most consternation. 'Our ancestors are back, they have returned,' he said.

It was all downhill from there. The voracity of the human reaction surprised The Eight. The humans in Project Anan and Harold and George were not. They expected the turmoil that followed the announcement. Theological discussions, coupled with violent riots and civil unrest, erupted in all corners of the globe. It was an unthinkable dilemma and fractured the popular evolutionary and religious theories of the origin of man. The United Nation assembly delegates were enraged when they discovered the Security Council refused the New Zealand delegation speaking time, to reveal this earth shattering disclosure. Harold's accusation that the United Nations was run by a cabal of dictators went global, heaping embarrassment and shame on a once proud and important organisation.

The Chinese and the Great Northern Union demanded they get access to the new alien technology. Harold's simple reply was "go ask The Eight", and maintained truthfully, Australia and New Zealand did not have access to alien technology. Niamh's design for the fusion reactor she had given to the Australians, was Earth-based and only contained Earth technology.

Finally, the desire for informed debate within the United Nations forum sponsored by moderate countries prevailed. The assembly debated the crisis but reached no conclusive resolution. Over the next two weeks they could not agree on anything and even rejected The Eight's request for nuclear disarmament. It was as Harold and George had feared, the foundations for global war were laid.

CHAPTER NINETEEN

HELA BRIDGE AUSTRALIAN BASE 10TH DECEMBER 2026

'Where's the captain?' Niamh asked the Anan crew as they started to file into the newly fitted *Hela* Bridge.

'We don't know,' they replied, as they looked anywhere but at her.

Niamh knew they were lying. 'Let's get to work,' she said, 'my technicians will help you get your systems back on line.' She and her team had been working since five that morning preparing for the *Hela*'s test flight. They were scheduled to take off in four hours; after the Chinese satellite overflight was past. The flight plan would be across to Milford Sound, dock at the Milford base and take on the blue they recovered from the base's large shipping tanks. The slops, Robert carefully pumped from the bottoms of each of the sixteen large shipping tanks and the surrounding pipework. The Overlord would transfer back to the *Hela* by shuttle during the blue transfer.

After the transfer, Niamh planned a test flight into orbit, and then out into the solar system to test run the hybrid drive. She needed Bri for this flight. For the first time Niamh was angry with the captain. They couldn't delay the take-off. It was more work for Niamh to do, she thought, and she couldn't run the ship in deep space without Bri.

'Niamh, lassie, we need to talk,' she heard Robert say quietly. Looking up, she was surprised to see Robert and Tom.

'Tom, how did the announcement go? What's up?' she asked suddenly as she felt their fear. When he dispatched Bri to Geneva, Tom couldn't tell Niamh. They both threw themselves into their work and had not seen each other for two days. He stayed in the security centre and monitored the Geneva announcement. Niamh stayed on the *Hela* for those two days, grabbing some sleep in an empty cabin. Now she felt sick from their fearful emotions and silently followed them to the empty captain's ready room, beside the bridge.

'Bri was relieved of his captain's position,' Robert said.

'When, how, why?' shouted Niamh, distraught at the news.

'It was Rhea, about four days ago when Bri was in Geneva.'

'Bri, in Geneva, and did you not think I should know that, Tom?' she said, glowering at him through squinted eyes. He had never seen her so angry, and squirmed under her gaze.

'No, Niamh, he couldn't tell you. I was told an hour ago, and there's more I'm afraid,' Robert said as he explained the whole mess. She sat beside Tom, who held her tight on the small couch as she listened.

'How long until the satellite is passed?' Niamh asked Tom.

'We have three hours.'

'I'll fly the *Hela* to Milford. We get the Overlord and the blue. We scrub the long hybrid drive test flight. I'll take us around the Moon to test the grav engines. But we have to get the blue. It delays everything. We can't start the *Hela* load-out until we get the blue. We can't dock fully loaded in Milford. It will be impossible to manoeuvre the ship fully laden in that tight area. If it goes wrong, we could crash and kill everybody – no – that's not happening. We have to go today. And if what you tell me is right, we could be in the middle of a war next week. We need the Overlord and the blue. We have to leave in three hours,' she said.

'Are you sure you can fly it, it's the test flight, Niamh, are you sure about this?' Tom asked. He could feel his pulse quicken as he contemplated what she was taking on. It was huge, something they had not planned for.

'Course I can. If Theia is unable to navigate or fly, I'll get the Pilot to help. I don't know who he is, but he can fly this thing as well. The docking assist is fully operational. The ship will dock and undock automatically — the engine control systems are automated. We checked the controls with the engines off and everything works,' she said.

'What about the Aknar codes, do you need those?' he asked.

'No, all codes except the *Hela* Armoury are changed. I — we, Tom — have access to both bases. I mean the "Sullivan Parker Charter" has. It gives us access on orders of The Eight. Demard re-programmed them with my DNA profile and I have the codes.'

'Theia's out of the picture for the time being, she's distraught at the news about Bri,' Robert said. 'Mack's available, he will authorise anything you ask. He more or less came up with the same scenario you just suggested, Niamh,' he said as they left the captain's ready room for the bridge.

'Listen to me now,' she said, addressing the purebreed bridge crew and her own technicians, 'we're taking off for Milford base in three hours. Demard, start the countdown,' she said to the computer technician already sitting at the communications console. 'Robert, get Matt organised, I want that shed off as soon as the satellite is past and all ground equipment clear. I need half an hour to warm the engines. My guys; get the fusion reactor started and online, then disconnect the shore power and services. I want to be on ship's power in an hour. Bridge crew, start your systems up now. Yes, now. You've spent the last week commissioning them — they should be all ready to go. What are ye all looking at, come on — get moving — or I'll have my husband throw you in the brig,' she shouted, 'and will someone get me the Pilot, we'll need him soon.'

Robert smiled at Tom as they watched the stunned bridge crew spring into action. Niamh's own technicians tried not to laugh; they were well used to the lash of her tongue.

'Mrs Parker, I will get the Pilot, but can I talk to you first?' Siba, one of the shuttle pilots, asked. On hearing the news about Bri, she had come to the bridge hoping for such an opportunity.

'Yes, course you can, come in here,' Niamh said, wondering what she wanted as she led the young Anan girl back to the captain's ready room.

'Mrs Parker, I can help with the navigation. I have some abilities and helped on the long journey from Anan. If you are happy with my work on the way to the New Colony, perhaps you might consider employing me for your own Charter,' she said quietly with her head bowed.

Niamh was dumbstruck by her words. She sensed a genuine feeling of respect and honour from the young shuttle pilot that surprised her.

'Do you have a blue diamond?' was all she could think to ask.

'I did not have one on the journey out, but I have one now,' she said proudly revealing a big deep coloured blue diamond, very different to Niamh's.

Niamh looked at the pendant as the girl turned it over and over. 'What do they call you?' she asked.

'I am Siba, I usually pilot shuttle two. I have a family name, and soon we will have it back,' she said, her smile showing how much she looked forward to this.

Niamh looked at her, yes, she thought, she remembered something John had said about his first trip to Milford. Siba had navigated instead of Bri. 'Siba, we would be glad to have you, but first I need the Pilot.'

'I will get him,' she said, smiling at Niamh as she left.

Niamh was mystified by the Anan girl's words "soon we will have our names back". It was one for Tom to decipher. The young navigator's offer was something Niamh never imagined they would or could get. She knew their future venture would fail if they could not get such people.

She had hoped there were other humans with the ability and planned to look over the results of the questionnaires the colonists completed before they were considered for employment. The results would contain an indication of the predominance of the gene enhancement, introduced by the geneticist some seventy thousand years ago. It was that gene that gave Niamh the ability to navigate. She knew others must have it. Theia had told her "there were no others with Niamh's intelligence". But now, after meeting Siba, Theia's words took on a whole new meaning. Looking out across the bridge from the captain's ready room, she caught Tom's eye. Realising something was up, he quickly approached.

'Tom, I have a job for you,' she said quietly. 'I don't think our clients are entirely honest with us.'

'And was that such a surprise to you,' he asked trying not to laugh at her honest naivety. 'Tell me,' he said, as he sat beside her on the captain's desk looking out at the bridge — and she did. The new dynasty, a formidable couple together, had arrived.

Niamh pulled it off. With Mack and the Pilot's help they took off from the Australian base and easily flew across to New Zealand, successfully docking with the one docking post of the Milford Sound base. The automatic docking system made it easy. They couldn't have docked at Milford without it. It calculated and distributed the control signals to the engines and slowly manoeuvred the great ship into position. With one post at the Milford base and the large ship affected by the wind, the automated system kept the *Hela* at height and in position while they loaded the blue to the hybrid holding tanks. The recondition grav engines, freshly stoked with fuel from the Pilot's family hoard, worked a dream. She was delighted with the performance of the engines with this new clean grav fuel.

After all her hard work and the trauma of losing Bri, it was the sight of The Eight returning to the *Hela* bridge on his shining chariot that brought tears to her eyes.

'My child,' he whispered, 'you have done well. You bring me a new ship. What happened to the old rust bucket?'

'Overlord, welcome back to the *Hela*, still the same *Hela*, but we fixed her up a bit,' she said, wiping the tears from her eyes.

It was a glorious sunny day over the beautiful Milford Sound. The tourists couldn't believe their luck as they watched the *Hela* floating in above the mountains high above the Sound. It glistened with a golden hue in the sunshine, and they watched as it approached one of the mountains. There were sounds of amazement as a long shining post with a silver coloured ring on top extended from the mountain and slowly docked with the great ship. It was an amazing sight and the pictures of the return of the reconditioned *Hela* to its Milford base flashed around the globe. The headlines said it all; *"Great Hela Returns To Milford Sound After Three Thousand Year Absence"*, Alex's final words of his briefing gained traction with a new headline *"Our Ancestors Are Back"*, printed above the picture of the *Hela*.

The *Hela* lay uncloaked for an hour at Milford Sound as Niamh and her new assistant, Siba, monitored the skies around them on their navigation projection.

'There look — finally — they have scrambled their stealth fighters,' she said, pointing to a group of planes taking off from an aircraft carrier in the Pacific.

'Their intentions are obvious,' The Eight said as he studied the navigation projection 'when you are ready, depart. I have seen enough. If you need my help with your test flight, call me,' he said as he left the bridge for his chambers.

Once the loading was complete the tourists were treated to the sight of the great ship slowly floating away from the post. As the post retreated into the mountain, the *Hela* gently rose until it disappeared into the southern sky. With the help of Mack, Niamh, the Pilot and Siba took the *Hela* out on a short test flight into space and around the Moon. It was a hectic flight showing up minor faults in the newly fitted control systems. With Mack and Robert's help she tested everything including her crew. They shut down the engines and fusion reactor in space between the Moon and Earth and retired to the captain's ready room. Robert had the foresight to bring the old Pilot in with them.

'We don't want to make it too easy for them,' he said as the four of them, Mack, Robert, Niamh and the Pilot, sat looking out at the pandemonium on the bridge. The purebreed crew and the human technicians were screaming and shouting at each other in the dim emergency lighting. Any requests for help from the four in the ready room were answered with a curt 'don't ask us, we're all dead. Figure it out yourselves. You now have one hour before the ship crashes into the Moon.' Finally, Demard jumped up from the communications station and took charge, giving the vital orders to the human technicians and the purebreed bridge crew. Within an hour, the ship was underway again with full power, a navigation display and a classic corkscrew course plotted for the descent to the *Hela* base in Australia.

'A very good test, Robert. It surprised me, very clever. Niamh, I have a test for you. Please land the *Hela* with your crew. I and the Pilot will remain here,' Mack said, smiling at Niamh and Robert as they got up to leave the ready room.

'A smart request, Arie,' the Pilot said when Niamh and Robert were gone.

'Robert was right, Zaval, you make it too easy for them.'

'Arie, I am sorry, really sorry. How is he?' the Pilot asked, referring to Bri.

'He is recovering in Queenstown, and will stay with Rhea and Alex until we depart. He had not been using the drug for a long time. Rhea told me he started after we arrived here. She believes it was the pressure he was under as captain. And that makes sense, as it amplifies all of his abilities, not just the navigation. He was achieving so much. I didn't understand how he could do it. Now I know. I'm devastated. He is like a son to me.'

The two old friends continued their conversation as Niamh and her crew brought the *Hela* in to land at the Australian base. Thirty-six hours after their departure and following the punishing test fight, it was an exhausted but happy crew who safely landed the big ship. The *Hela* and her crew were ready, another important Project milestone achieved.

SINO GREAT NORTHERN UNION BORDER 18TH DECEMBER 2026

In a secluded house close to their borders, the two leaders looked at each other across the table. Their meeting, a closely guarded secret, would define the fate of their two nations.

'We cannot allow another to gain a foothold on our planet. History shows advanced technology always conquers the inferior. Their technology is beyond ours and when they gain in strength, they will dominate us,' the Leader of the Great Northern Union said.

'My spies have tried to get their hands on it, but failed. The Australians gave us the plans for a working fusion reactor that the Irish engineer developed. Yes, we have it. I will give it to you. But it is all earth-based technology and requires helium three. You know we mine that on the Moon. We know their advanced technology is based on an energy we do not have, something called "grav". It counteracts the effects of gravity and "blue energy", which I believe is running out. We will get nothing from them,' the Chinese leader said.

'What about the ultimatum?' the other asked, referring to The Eight's demand for unilateral nuclear disarmament delivered at the UN on his behalf by Harold, two days after the dramatic announcement of their arrival on Earth.

'What about it? We ignore it. Who is going to make us do that? No, I say we attack the two bases. Wipe out the alien infestation. If they are as strong as they say they are, there would be hundreds of ships invading by now. There is only one. I have that on good authority from my spies. One of Chang's men came back to us. When he found out there was only one ship he got cold feet and begged for forgiveness.'

'One ship, so the story delivered at the UN is true.'

'Yes, they are weak; there is a limit to their power. Besides, I am getting tired of all this procrastination. We need more land for our expanding population. Australia has that. It is a good excuse to finally move and seize the Far East and the Australian continent. We will take Japan as well. Our troops are ready, and the fleet has advanced with no opposition from the Combined Forces. Will you support me?' he asked.

'What's in it for us? We gain nothing supporting you,' the leader of the Great Northern Union replied.

'You can have Europe or the Middle East.'

'I already have what I want of Europe; I took that after the Wave when we re-established our Great Republic. The Middle East, no thank you, we have access to as much cheap oil as we want, you take it if you want,' he said, pausing to reflect on what was said. 'Regardless of that, I will support you. I agree. We must wipe out the alien infestation. Unilateral nuclear disarmament is not an option for us. It is too convenient for the aliens. They ask us to disarm the one weapon we have that could defeat them. My intelligence people believe it is all part of a larger invasion strategy. Threaten us now, get us to disarm and then the rest come to conquer our world. Do they think we are so inferior as not to see through such a ruse? Yes. I will support you,' he said, believing he would extract some favours in the future as payment for this unconditional support.

AUSTRALIAN BASE 20TH DECEMBER 2026

The busy workforce and colonists were one week into this final part of Project Anan; the loading of one hundred and fourteen thousand tonnes of cargo into the belly of the *Hela*. Over the preceding months the equipment and containers were carefully prepared by Matt and his ground crew for "the load-out". It was the culmination of months of careful planning by the colony logistics team. They divided the *Hela* into coloured zones and ensured the equipment was colour coded to match the predefined areas in the large cargo holds before loading. Niamh calculated the weight distribution. The equipment's correct dispersal was critical to the *Hela*'s ability to carry such a large payload. The equipment and the pods had to go into the *Hela* in the order specified in the plan. Everything would come out on the New World in reverse of the Earth loading sequence.

Robert planned that the effort they put in on Earth would make it easy to unload on the New World. However, during this critical loading phase, they were as Robert had said, "sitting here with our pants down". The *Hela*, sitting on the ground with its doors open, no camouflage and surrounded by the busy workforces flying the equipment into its belly, made for an easy target. Tom insisted they prepared for the possibility of an attack. With Robert and Niamh's help, he devised a plan for the *Hela* to make a quick departure to space. It was a critical part of the load-out plan and was integrated with the shift system Matt had organised. The work continued through the night, only stopping at the hottest part of the day, during the hot desert summer sun.

In the early hours of the morning the base attack alarm sounded. On hearing the shrill alarm the grav carrier driver looked down onto the accommodation block of pods he had set on the deck of the main cargo hold. His grav carrier was still connected and he could see the load was partially secured in place to the *Hela* deck; it was the Load Masters decision as to what would happen next.

'Get ready to fly this back out. We'll have the shipping stays off in ten,' the Load Master said over the comms system, referring to the steel and cable shipping braces the team were busily fitting.

Ten minutes later, Robert ran up the pedestrian access ramp into the *Hela* and watched as the grav carrier gracefully flew the large accommodation block out.

'I'll have this area secured and the ramp up in fifteen,' the Load Master said to Robert.

'Good, and when you're done get your crew into the underground Anan base. I'm afraid this is not a drill, it's real — they're coming.'

WAR

CHAPTER TWENTY

AUSTRALIAN BASE 20TH DECEMBER 2026

One hour after the alarm was raised the *Hela* slowly lifted off its three docking posts. Following a preprogrammed route, it steadily made progress flying in the classic corkscrew manoeuvre towards low Earth orbit over Australia.

'How far out are they?' Mack asked, referring to the squadron of twelve Chinese stealth bombers whose launch triggered the alarm. Detecting them was a problem, but the two measures he put in place to spot any attack worked. Admiral White's fleet, shadowing the Chinese carrier, reported the launch and Siba spotted it on her navigation projection. Spread between the six with navigation abilities, Theia set up a twenty-four-hour watch. The *Hela* had twenty-four-hour protective surveillance from the navigation projections and they could track everything in real time.

'Estimated time at Milford is forty minutes, and at our *Hela* base in one hour,' Siba said.

'General, inform Admiral White to get his forces out of the area. Is the armoury on line?' The Eight asked.

'Yes, Overlord, the armoury is primed and Parker has sent the order to the Admiral. We are ready for you.'

'General, eliminate the twelve planes. Their intentions and flight plan are clear. I have looked at their orders — they are intent on destroying both bases. Are the colonists safe?'

'Yes, Overlord, they are all sheltering in the underground base with our ground staff,' Robert replied.

'Good. Niamh, how is the ship performing with the load?'

'As expected, Overlord. We have fifty thousand tonnes of equipment on board. It's not as evenly distributed as I would want. But she can handle it. We'll be in a stable orbit in three minutes. All systems working and we are fully cloaked.'

'Overlord, six drones away,' Mack said. The *Hela* had two thousand five hundred drones. To test its efficiency, he had cycled the mechanical system and the launch doors many times. But he had never actually launched a drone. He was relieved to see them gracefully fly away from the *Hela* on the bridge view screen. With the coordinates from the main *Hela* navigation projection, the armoury crew would deliver their fatal blow.

'Parker, what do you see?' The Eight asked Tom, who manned the communications station with Demard.

'We have a lot of chatter coming from a bunker below the Chinese military headquarters in Beijing and from a bunker in Moscow. There is communication between both governments and we can decode it. There it is, scrolling down the side of the bridge view screen.' The screen showed split images of space around the *Hela*, the drones target and the scrolling feed from the encrypted data between the Chinese and Great Northern Union. It was clearly a pre-planned attack to annihilate the alien presence on Earth. But something more sinister started to emerge, their plans to invade Australia and the Far Eastern countries.

'Overlord, they plan to invade —'

'Yes, Thomas, I see what they are up to. This is such a waste of my blue,' he said in an angry voice they had not heard before.

The Eight left the navigation console they were all gathered around and moved in his chariot to the rear of the bridge. They watched, as he grew in size and colour, extracting the blue in the tanks on his chariot. He looked frightening, floating away from his chariot and back to the navigation console. He was larger, much larger and now shimmering a deep blue. His bulky energy mass took up one side of the navigation console and stretched to the ceiling of the bridge. For the first time since meeting him, Niamh was scared. He looked foreboding and angry, and the energy he exuded shimmered with this. It flashed erratically with the occasional crackle and spark.

'Empress, translate this please again for me,' he ordered Theia, who again took him through each of the vessels, their position and importantly, what government they represented.

'Robert, please stand beside me. You will be my point of contact. You will know what to do and when. Niamh, are we in a stable orbit?'

'Yes, Overlord.'

'Good, keep the *Hela* in this position. Empress, maintain that navigation projection, I will need it. Parker, monitor your intelligence sources. Keep Robert informed of changes. Mack, use your drones as you see fit. If we are threatened you know what to do. My people, do not fear me, I will not hurt you. Stay at your stations. I need your help with what I plan. It will conserve my energy and solve our problem,' he said in a very deep and strong voice, and then, with his chosen mortal crew around him, he started.

As The Eight started his war, Mack watched the six drones approach the twelve stealth bombers. The drones caught them over the Pacific before the formation split to attack the Milford and Australia bases. Each drone contained four grav missiles. Five kilometres from the bombers the drones opened like large airborne flowers releasing their deadly cargo. The twenty-four missiles shot out of the drones, flying straight for their assigned targets.

The stealth bombers crew never knew what hit them. There was no warning as two grav missiles imbedded themselves into each of the twelve bombers. The missiles opened up releasing pure grav into the interior of each plane. Each grav droplet repelled itself from the next and from the gravity exerted on the plane by the Earth. The effect was spectacular as the planes simultaneously disintegrated in mid-flight.

The Eight had pre-planned his actions, calculating how much energy he would use to battle with the Chinese forces. Normally, it would be one quick burst from space and wipe out the population. But now that blue was in short supply, such actions were inefficient and wasteful. He would use more time and less energy and employ the Chinese to defeat themselves. It was a simple solution. It would reduce the projected twenty-five per cent of the energy reserves he would have to expend, to extinguish the whole population to only one per cent. He was quite pleased with this modern approach. It would remove their destructive capability, decisively defeat their warmonger leaders and preserve his precious energy. If it worked, he would save twenty-four per cent of his energy and spare an innocent population. Yes, he agonised, the planet could not support them all, but it was a problem the people of Earth and the planet should face themselves.

His energy mass erupted with blue flashing light as he projected his energy waves down to the Chinese Pacific fleet. He entered the minds of the admirals, captains and officers with his powerful consciousness, scrambling their thought patterns. They lost their orders and the all-important codes. To hasten the process, he reprogrammed their brains with fear of each other. The Eight moved from ship to ship sowing fear and mayhem amongst the top commanders. The ships started firing at each other – but the vessels with nuclear capability were unable to launch – as their commanders could not access the all-important launch codes. Where he found these offensive weapons, he spent more of his energy burning their detonation systems.

As he embarked on his mission of destruction the *Hela* bridge erupted with the power of his energy. Like blue lightening it flashed out through the ship as he projected it down to Earth. He radiated fear and death. Except for Mack, it was something the mortals around him had not expected. Mack had experienced this before, and hoped he would never see it again. It shocked them to their core as they felt his anger and the fear and death he unleashed. As he asked of them, they all diligently stayed at their stations through the conflagration he unleashed below.

Decimating the Pacific fleet, he felt something within his deepest energy, something he had never expected. They were dying in their thousands. Killing each other, and as their life force left their bodies he felt it. At first it was like a tiny pulse, like a sting, but as the death rate increased, so too did the intensity of the feeling. He could feel their pain, see into their souls and the lives and loves that they had enjoyed. It was something he had never experienced before. Pushing on, he tried to ignore it, but finally it affected his energy mass, changing some of the colours from deep blue to greys and purples.

Robert noticed it first. Seeing the change in colour, he stuck his arm into The Eight's energy mass and reached out to him. 'Overlord, what is wrong, why does your colour fade like that?'

'I did not realise how hard it would be to personally kill so many and there is something else I feel.'

'You feel — Overlord, have you not done this before?'

'No, Robert, never like this, it is always from afar. There is something else – do you ever wonder why I call Niamh "my child"? What that means?'

'I suppose I have, but first you must stop, come back to the Hela.'

Looking around at the devastation in the Chinese Pacific fleet, he watched the burning and drowning bodies and the sinking ships. As he listened to the screams of the dying he turned away and let his energy relax back to the *Hela*. 'I am back, now I will show you – look,' he said as he retrieved an image of the old geneticist walking into his chamber.

Robert watched with interest, he was carrying a smaller version of the tool they used to reclaim blue and what Bri had used in the fight with the grey matter. Walking up to The Eight, he placed the tool into the energy mass, filling the small receptacle with The Eight's blue. 'I never noticed what he did. I was so busy searching for blue in this solar system. He used that blue for his gene splice. I only realise it years later, after I transferred the records from the old ship to the *Hela*. You are all from my essence. That is why.'

'And now killings humans is affecting you?'

'Yes, in such large numbers, I did not realise that would happen.'

'Do you not fight with your own kind, the other Overlords?'

'No, Robert – such a strange question – we never physically fight between ourselves. What's your point?'

'Overlord, I do not know everything about your kind, but the day will come when you will fight them. You need to be ready for that. If a few million humans with your essence are stopping you fight, you are finished. Overlord, if you do not prevail today it is all over. We need you. Everything we have done so far is for you. If you stop now, millions more will die. Our friends will lose their lands and be ruled by evil dictators — you know that!'

'You are right, Robert, but I see I must rest, it will take longer than I anticipated.'

'We will hold them off, Overlord.'

As The Eight rested back on the *Hela*, it was Tom who picked up the first sign of a fight back from Earth. 'They're up to something,' he shouted out loud, 'I don't know what, but the chatter between Beijing and Moscow is up — it's so fast we can't decipher it. The Chinese are opening the doors of their missile silos. They're going to launch multiple missiles.'

Robert looked at The Eight's energy mass and said, 'we'll have to manage it Tom. His colour is still not back to blue. We need to give him more time — he's only had a few hours.'

'Empress, plot their trajectories. I will launch our drones. We should be able to stop them,' Mack said. 'As soon as you have the targets, let me know.'

As they waited, Tom and Demard tried to decipher the chatter and hack into the launch sequences.

'I won't have enough time,' Demard said, as he hunched down over the comms console. 'I have the targets, from their chatter. It's Sydney, Milford Sound, the Hela base and…'

'It's us,' screamed the Empress. 'They have six missiles headed for us – look at the trajectory,' she said as their flight plans appeared on her navigation projection. 'How did they get our location?'

'They must have triangulated our first launch of the drones and his energy bursts,' Mack said as he stood up and looked closely at the projection. 'They are smarter than I thought. Niamh, we need maximum power to the grav shields. Extend the bubble out as far as you can. But wait until I have launched my drones. Empress, as soon as you have the strike coordinates, send them to the armoury.'

'Mack, how long will he need to recover?' Tom asked, looking across at The Eight's energy mass.

'As long as he needs, Tom, we will hold them off. My drones will do the job.'

'I hope you're right, Mack,' he said as they watched the missile trajectories starting to plot on the three dimensional projection in front of them.

Five minutes later Mack launched twenty drones, 'Niamh, maximum power to the grav bubble and extend it out as far as you can. All of you sit down and buckle up.'

They sat in silence as they watched the real time plot of their drones and the missiles. The first missile the drones destroyed was the one for Sydney.

Tom broke the silence as a message scrolled across his screen, 'incoming from Admiral White "thanks for that, good luck with the rest".'

'Mack, there goes the Milford missile,' Tom said as they watched another flash on the projection.

'How many are left?'

'Two headed for the base in Australia, and six for us. Any time now,' he said as the trajectories converged on the navigation projection.

They all watched — there was nothing else they could do. Mack had committed it all to his drones, the fate of the *Hela* and the Australian base rested on the three-thousand–year-old weapons. The flashes on the projection announced the contact of the drones with the missiles. They watched as Theia, Niamh and Siba concentrated to re-draw the post impact outcome. What normally took an instant took nail-biting seconds as they grappled with peering through the debris created by the drones. After a painful minute the projection flickered and one missile flew out of the debris cloud continuing upwards towards the *Hela*.

'Niamh — full power to the engines — straight up to an outer orbit.'

'Mack, I…'

'Yes, I know, do your best. We can't launch again. We'd have to drop the grav bubble. Demard, can you direct a comms pulse at that thing? Either fry its circuits, or get it to detonate early.'

'In progress General — pulse away.'

Theia jumped up, grabbing Niamh's, Siba's and her crystals, pulling them from the navigation console. As the projection died they looked at her in surprise, but their looks were cut short as the shockwave from the nuclear blast tore into the *Hela*. Like a small boat in a storm, the blast's impact sent the eight hundred metre long ship careering — end over end —through space. Theia was tossed across the console and grabbed by Robert.

'Can you do anything?' he shouted across at Niamh. 'The cargo, it'll break out and tear the ship in two.'

'Jeez, Robert, what do ya think I'm doing? I'm trying. We're lucky, the grav bubble absorbed most of the energy,' she shouted at him over the noise of the shaking and groaning now coming from the ship. She thought she would never hear that again. 'I need to stabilise the turning first,' she shouted as they all held on to their seats.

After five agonising minutes of firing grav pulses from the engines, they felt the spin slow and stop as she stabilised the great ship.

'Well done, Niamh, can you get us back to a stable orbit?' Mack asked.

'I need navigation again. Is it safe to do that with the radiation outside?'

'Yes, Mrs Parker, it is. I can do that,' Siba said as she replaced her crystal back into the console.

Twenty minutes later they were back in a higher orbit over Australia. Theia, with a large gash on her head bandaged up, was back in her seat. She watched as Robert wiped her blood off the console.

'Thank you, Robert, I would be in a much worse state if you had not grabbed me.'

'Theia, if you hadn't pulled those crystals, I guess the blast would have fried you and our two navigators' brains.'

'Yes, something like that, Robert. Do we know — is there any damage to the ship?'

'Not from what we can see on the cameras in the cargo bay. She looks good,' he said. 'Mack, Tom, what's the plan now?'

'I fight on,' The Eight said, as he started to flash with blue light. 'There will be no mercy now.'

'Aye, well there's nothing like a nuclear blast to focus the mind, Overlord.'

'Hold that thought, Robert. What intelligence do you have, Thomas?'

'More chatter, Overlord. We can decipher some of it now. The Northern Union is trying to launch missiles. The Chinese are asking, why they didn't launch earlier? Overlord, I think they have a problem with the launch codes.'

'Robert, I will need your help. Find their leaders and disable their threat.'

'How do I do that?'

'It's simple, Robert — as you did before — place your hand into my energy mass. Then find their minds and destroy them with your own thoughts. You will see as you find them. But remember to use my energy sparingly. I will take care of the others. Empress, we will need a full navigation projection of our enemy's forces. The one you provided before.'

'Robert,' Tom said, realising what Robert was to do, 'look for these two,' he said as the pictures of two tall Russians appeared on the view screen. 'They are Russia's "young Turks", and spoiling for change. They will help you. And mention my name,' he said, smiling at his friend who was now glowing blue with his right arm imbedded in The Eight's energy mass.

Robert closed his eyes and opened his mind, filling it with the images from Theia's navigation projection. The more he concentrated on the projection, the more he could see. Focusing on Moscow, he found himself looking at a group of men assembled in a control bunker below the Kremlin. The more he concentrated the closer he got, until he was standing beside them listening to them shouting at each other. To add to the surprises from this new surreal experience, Robert realised he could understand every word they said, although it was all in Russian.

'You should stop this madness, President. Launching missiles, now you take us back to the old Cold War days,' said one young man dressed in a navy uniform. One of the "young Turks" from Tom's picture, realised Robert.

'You are weak, we need to wipe the aliens from the face of the Earth,' said the old president. Robert recognised him from infamous television pictures and the most recent, cradling the head of a bear. 'You will launch the missiles or I will shoot you here.'

Robert concentrated to project his image into the room so the group could see him. To the surprise of all in this deep secure bunker, a blue shimmering apparition of a tall man dressed in a kilt appeared.

'I represent The Eight and I really think that is a bad idea,' was all Robert could think of saying.

Shocked at this intrusion, the old president took out a gun and started to shoot at Robert's apparition. The bullets passed through Robert, killing two of the president's generals who were standing behind him. Concentrating, and with the help of The Eight's energy, Robert reached out into the president's mind. The man didn't know what hit him as the brave Scotsman's thoughts infiltrated his own mind. Screaming, and in an attempt to kill Robert, he turned the gun on himself, blowing his brains across the missile launch console.

'Who's next?' Robert asked looking at the rest of those in the room. There were two other foolish generals who started shooting at him and quickly, they followed the ill-fated path of their president. 'Anyone else?' asked Robert as he looked around again at the shocked faces of those remaining in the room.

'Who are you?' asked the young man dressed in the navy uniform.

'I'm Robert Leslie; I represent the Overlord, The Eight.'

'What does he want?'

'Stop trying to fire your nukes. Are you all mad, in this day and age? Firing nukes. You need to disarm them. Remember, that's what he asked for.'

'We are not mad, but he was and the clique that followed him,' said the young man pointing at the dead president. 'We wanted none of it. We will follow your Overlord's request,'

'How do I know you will be true to your word?' Robert asked.

'Will this help?' said the young man as he took out his gun and shot two others. 'They were his supporters. The six of us here represent the new guard, army, navy and the air force. We will disarm. You have my word,' said the young man.

'Admiral, we can re-programme the code sequence to block all launches of our missiles,' said one of the others. Robert recognised him from Tom's picture.

'OK, do it,' Robert said as he watched the two sit down at a large computer console. Opening two separate cases, they retrieved two keys which they inserted into locks on the console. After five minutes of work the young admiral turned to Robert.

'It is done. We can't launch any missiles and all the detonation codes for our bombs are scrambled. We will need time to ensure they are removed from service but we will sign anything your Overlord wants. Believe me when I say this,' said the young admiral, saluting Robert.

'I will relay your promise to the Overlord. Thomas Parker also vouches for you, Admiral.'

'We thought he was dead. Give him my regards. Tell him we are finally in control. He will know how to contact us, we should meet.'

'What about the Chinese, they are not finished yet?' asked the other.

'Our Overlord is taking care of that as we speak. He's pretty pissed off with them as well,' Robert said as he allowed his image to fade back to the Hela.

A NEW EPOCH

CHAPTER TWENTY ONE

L ike a great blue spectre he returned to Earth, picking up his onslaught where he finished at the edge of the Pacific Ocean. Moving across the Far East, he decimated every Chinese vessel he came across. It was war on a scale not seen since the major conflicts of the twentieth century. But it was only between the Chinese vessels and aircraft. The Chinese who were not touched by The Eight's power believed the war was a coup d'état and quickly joined the fray. The internal conflict he started quickly heralded the demise of this nation's powerful military machine.

With his powers restored he was now prepared for this aggressive action. Robert's questions had provoked a thought, deep down in his energy mass. While he rested on the *Hela* he searched back in time looking through his old memories. He was wrong — Overlords had fought between themselves — eons ago. The winning faction had developed an algorithm to channel their energy. It was not only about energy quantity but magnifying its impact. He employed that algorithm now as he worked his way across the South China Sea. The ability of the new algorithm to shield him from the mayhem he created pleased him. As he moved on towards mainland China, his energy mass crackled and pulsed a deep blue, surprising the mortal crew on the *Hela* bridge.

When The Eight finally made it into the Chinese leaders' bunker he was enraged by their hatred and scheming. Their greed for his technology, their desire to wipe the aliens from Earth and the land grab they planned. But most of all, their targeting of him with their nuclear weapons, had pushed him to deeds he did not realise he was capable of. It was too much for him. As he entered their minds they screamed at the hate and fear he instilled in them. It was a slow painful death as their hearts finally burst from the adrenalin overdose their bodies generated by their fright. Within minutes of his arrival it was over, the Chinese government and military commanders were dead. Satisfied with what he achieved, The Eight slowly let his energy relax into his mass back on the *Hela*.

Opening his eyes, Robert found his consciousness returned to his body on the *Hela*. Withdrawing his arm from The Eight, he was surprised to see it was blue and all the hair was gone. 'Will that heal, Overlord?' he asked.

'No, Robert. It is my reward for your help. You will have gifted children. Get over your loss. Your mortal life is short, enjoy it.'

'Aye, well there's no answer to that, Overlord,' he said, totally bemused by the Overlord's statement after such a horrendous event.

'You did well and you hardly used any of my precious energy.'

'You did ask me to be frugal, I was mindful of that.'

'Parker, you have news?'

'Overlord, you have kindled a civil war between the Chinese military. Their vessels in the Pacific theatre are all ablaze. They have lost all their aircraft carriers and their remaining submarines are busy hunting each other. We see three quarters of their submarine fleet is sunk or ablaze on the surface. The air force is disabled. From our assessment it will take some days for this to die down. They all believe a coup d'état and the fight for supremacy amongst those left standing has started. Robert appears to have quelled our northern enemies. Robert, how did that go?'

'Aye, I met your mates, Tom, fine bunch of lads they are too. Shot their bosses dead to prove a point. The Admiral sends his regards and I've to tell you they are finally in control. He said you will know how to contact them. I gather they want to meet over tea and biscuits. Wear a bulletproof vest if you do take up their polite invitation,' he said, as Tom smiled at his dry humour. 'Overlord, I believe them, they will disarm and have already changed their launch and detonation codes.'

'Good. I am tired, but there is another I must visit. Hold your positions please,' The Eight said as his energy mass started to glow and crackle again.

The President of America looked at his security council assembled around him in this newly constructed command bunker below the Cheyenne mountains. Anticipating global change, they had assembled here four days ago and were now monitoring some alarming developments. He appeared quickly, his blue shimmering mass surprising all in this small command bunker.

'I am The Eight, Overlord of this galaxy, who is in charge, who do I talk to?' he said in his friendly but authoritative voice.

'We will pray to cast out this beast of Satan that has demonised our world. How dare you violate our presence, our sovereignty and our humble beliefs? Be gone — be gone now — and forever,' shouted the President, shaking a bible at the apparition of the Overlord.

It took the Overlord completely by surprise. He was exhausted. Despite the new algorithm, the use of time to conserve his precious blue had taken its toll on him. He was experiencing a rare feeling, fatigue. He could not remember his age but he was old, even for an Overlord. Looking at this tall strange man shouting nonsense and shaking a black book at him, the old and tired Overlord finally gave in, and using more energy that he allowed for, turned the President of America into dust.

'Now I am weary. Who is in charge?' roared the Overlord. His deep booming voice shook the room and the occupants within. No one spoke, and after a long silence one tall man in a green military uniform stepped up in front of The Eight and saluted him.

'Overlord, I am General Marsh, the Chairman of the Joint Chiefs of Staff, our military command. Admiral White mentioned you might drop by, you are welcome here, sir. How may we help you?'

'General, you are not in charge, I am the Vice President, I am in charge here,' said another man now standing.

To the Overlord's surprise a woman in uniform standing beside Marsh took out a gun and marched up to the Vice President and the man he was sitting beside.

'Vice President, Secretary of Defence, you are both under arrest for spreading a fundamental terrorist agenda and endangering the safety of our population. Soldiers,' she shouted at six guards standing to the side of the room, 'please remove these two fundamentalist whack jobs from our presence. Apologies for interrupting you, General — just cleaning house for you — sir.'

'Thank you, Gloria,' Marsh said, smiling at the woman as he watched the two men being marched out by the soldiers. 'Overlord, we should have done that a long time ago. I am in charge, I have the backing of all here and we are happy to work with you,' he said in a quiet voice filled with sincerity.

'General, I am tired of this. First I want nuclear disarmament, and then I want you to work with Admiral White. You must engage with the others. Your world is facing an apocalyptic end and you all still fight for supremacy and land. The Earth cannot sustain eight billion people, you are facing so many problems and you all do nothing. I do not believe you can stop it, it may be too late but you must try.

'My ship will shortly leave this planet with the first colonists for a New World. Before I leave I want to be sure those people that helped me are safe. I will be back; this was a small demonstration of my power. If I return and find my friends' safety compromised I will wipe humanity off the face of this planet,' The Eight said, and he meant it, regardless of how much energy it took. If George or Harold's nations were harmed The Eight would respond.

'Overlord, you have nothing to fear from us. We will work with Admiral White.'

'Thank you,' the Overlord said; *there is hope*, he thought, as his energy relaxed back to his energy mass on the *Hela*.

Following The Eight's battle, they stayed in orbit for two days until Tom verified it was safe for them to land and continue with the load-out. Admiral White, George and Harold were astounded by the power of The Eight. He was true to his word and protected his friends. The story of the demise of the American President sent shockwaves throughout diplomatic circles. It was the legend that cemented The Eight's power on Earth. The old and tired Overlord had no idea the man he turned to dust used to be considered the most powerful man on Earth.

Very quickly, the smaller countries with nuclear weapons lined up to disarm. George and Admiral White found themselves as the point persons for Earth's military, co-ordinating disarmament and co-operation. The UN assembly was in uproar after The Eight's intervention, and finally, they invited Harold to attend as the Overlord's representative. But there was no word from China. The country descended into a vicious civil war. 'It may take months,' said Tom. He had received a simple message from Chang. "Parker, give my thanks to the Overlord. I play the patience game. Time will tell. My regards to your wife".

Three days after they departed the Overlord spoke to Niamh for the first time since his battle. He had spent all the time alone in his chamber. 'Are you all right, my child?' he asked Niamh quietly.

'You scared me.'

'I know, and there may be more of that to come. I am not sure what we will face on my return to Anan. Gather your crew. You may land now.' he said quietly to her as he pulsed with a clear blue light.

As her crew guided the great ship into land she looked around at the bridge. *What a mess he made*, she thought, as she looked at the scorch marks on the ceiling and walls where The Eight's energy bolts had flashed through the ship.

'What are you looking at?' Tom asked beside her on the bridge.

'The mess he made look, more bloody work for me to fix,' she said, pointing out the scorch marks.

'I love you, Niamh,' he said trying not to laugh.

AUSTRALIA BASE 23RD DECEMBER 2026

'Aye, here they come,' said Robert referring to the colonists as they started to file out onto a large open area in front of the camp. It would be the last of his now famous early morning briefs, delivered before a change or after a Project milestone.

'Ladies and gentlemen, good morning,' he said, now standing with Niamh, Tom and Matt at a podium constructed on top of the camp canteen.

'Good morning, Robert,' was the reply from the large crowd eagerly looking up at their boss.

After the usual ribald comments and shouts he started his brief, a synopsis of the war and their success. Finally, he announced the one thing they all wanted to hear; the departure date. They would leave Earth on the fourth of January. On the twenty-sixth of December, the colonists would start a staged move into the *Hela*. There was a buzz of excitement as they realised they would shortly get their boarding sequence and pod number. He reminded them of the "change of mind clause in the contracts". If anyone wanted out, now was the time. He was greeted with cheers after announcing the holiday arrangements and the "barbies" Matt planned over Christmas and Hogmanay. It would be the last time they celebrated these holidays on Earth and he knew it would be an emotional time for many.

'Finally, some of you have never met him, but the Overlord wants to talk to you. If you all turn around, please,' he said, as the surprised colonists turned around to see The Eight. He was floating in his chariot just above them. He looked formidable in the early morning desert light as the gold, silver and the blue pearls glistened and reflected his deep blue light, still glowing and flashing from the war he had just won.

'My people, thank you for committing to my Project. Considering the dangers we faced, you have achieved all I expected of you and more. Shortly we will begin our journey to a New World. None of you have travelled in space before. It will not be easy and you must not underestimate the perils of such a long journey. You will be the first humans to travel across intergalactic space to a New World, travelling faster than light in a bubble protected by the ship's gravity. That is an achievement you should all be proud of.

'I am not infallible, and I cannot predict the future, but from what I see so far, together, we can shape our destiny for the better. As a species, you have achieved more than I ever thought possible. This Project is a seminal event in the change of order within the galaxies. You were probably not aware of that, but you should know, before we depart, what your involvement in it means to me. Again thank you. Robert, please continue,' he said as he turned his chariot away from the crowd and returned to the *Hela*.

'Thank you, Overlord. Now I'm done. Have a good holiday; you've been great so far. The four of us here are proud of you all. Next time we talk will be in space,' Robert said trying not to get emotional.

'Jeez, Robert, I hope you're not going to cry now,' Niamh said as they listened to the applause and shouts from the colonists. They were excited, the waiting and planning was nearly over, the expectation and hope was bubbling at the top, and all they could talk of was the lift-off and the journey.

The return of the *Hela* from space after the Overlord defeated Earth's military might was a watershed moment for the colonists. They had heard stories of his power. Some were sceptical. After all, he did not arrive in style. Many asked, "If he is so powerful, why did he arrive on a clapped-out three-thousand-year-old ship?" But to actually witness what he was capable of, that was a game changer. His scorch marks on the bridge surprised the technicians who worked on the refit. Demard captured the events on the cameras. The video footage — of The Eight's Energy Mass in full fury — was closely guarded. But slowly, some of the human technicians got to see it, and it added to the legend of The Eight's power.

There was no change of minds. The colonists were all committed to building a new life on the New World in his service. His short appearance and speech, in the half light of the early desert morning scaled their commitment to him. But it was his mysterious words "seminal event in the change of order within the galaxies" that caused the most hubbub. Those words charged the colonists' youthful exuberance with excitement and the expectation of future wonders.

CHRISTCHURCH 24TH DECEMBER 2026

'I looked over the finances, you have worked wonders, Alan,' Mack said as they sat in Alan's office.

'We had your help,' he replied, referring to the black box still working in the basement. 'When do you want to remove it?'

'Keep it going, but at a slower pace. Eventually, you will have made so much from the system, it will become redundant. You have already done those calculations?'

'Yes, Mack, I have. We will become the most powerful corporation on Earth.'

'It is the Overlord's planet, he just wants to ensure he can control it,' Mack said, looking across at Alan, 'Do you have a problem with that?'

'No, Mack, I don't. I realised this would happen when we first installed it.'

'Good. We need the resources, Alan. You got Niamh's shopping list?'

'Yes, I did. The size surprised me. I knew she and Tom would probably return with about two ships, but this, it's enough equipment to refit a fleet.'

'It is not all from her. The Overlord had a hand in it and approved it all. It is based on Earth technology and can be manufactured here. You will need to start up new manufacturing plants for this. It will not be easy but I believe you can do it. Use Matt to help and don't be afraid to approach Harold and George. The Prime Ministers deserve to know what we want and their two countries should profit from it. They will arrange any business introductions you may need.'

'I can do that. You said there's more,' he said, looking at Mack intently.

'Yes, there is,' Mack said, handing a small data drive to Alan. 'This is Anan technology; it can be manufactured on Earth. It cannot be used without grav, which is also locked in our base on Earth.' He paused as Alan realised the implications of what Mack had just given him. 'The Overlord has approved this. It is weapons specifications, just the casings and the drive chambers. Don't worry, Earth does not have the tools or the knowhow to load the grav. Niamh and her team will do that when they return.

'Only use Australian or New Zealand manufacturers. I am told there are small factories who can build want we want here and in Australia. Don't look so worried, my friend,' Mack said, smiling at Alan's crestfallen look. 'It's Christmas, it's supposed to be a holiday here.'

'Mack, you're impossible. I will need the military to help with this.'

'Use Admiral White if you need some military expertise. He will help with security and finding the right people for you. People you can trust. I will have Tom call him before we go. Will that help?'

'Yes, it will. Thank you. With Cyril's help, we can make that work. Are you joining us tomorrow? Kath's doing a barbeque.'

'Yes, thank you, I'd like that,' Mack replied, looking across at Alan whose relaxed manner said it all. *We can trust him*, he thought. *Once we leave, he will make it all happen*. 'Alan, I do not know when, or what we will return with, but I am sure you will be ready when we do.'

'Yes, we will, and I look forward to that day, Mack.'

✦

HELA BASE AUSTRALIAN DESERT 1ST JANUARY 2027

New Year 2027 heralded the arrival of a new epoch for mankind. The New Year celebrations around the globe reflected this era change, with the celebrations at the *Hela* base taking centre stage. Lavish fireworks erupted over the base shattering the dark desert sky with a wondrous display of colour and noise. The night was enjoyed by all the colonists; those who left for Christmas, returning to "party central" for the celebrations. Mack extended invitations to the Project's friends and associates in Australian and New Zealand and begrudgingly, included a contingent from Earth's media.

'It is times like this that I would appreciate Chang's help to stop all the unwanted attention,' he said to Tom.

'What else did you expect, Mack? It is the story of the millennium. We do have freedom of the press.'

'It's not quite like that on Anan. We have a different system.'

'Oh, now you tell us, after sucking us into your alien web,' Tom said, grinning at Mack as he wondered what diverse political, legal and economic systems they would encounter in their new endeavours. 'Talking of Chang, I have made contact with him.'

'How is he?'

'He is surviving the civil war and quietly building his support. More and more are following him. He has the backing of the big industrialists — one was a "benefactor of his" before the war. They are hungry for a return to China's manufacturing supremacy and see Chang's alliance with us as a way to that. But he still has much to do. It will be a year at least before he sees any outcome. The war is taking its toll on the country and the population. The supporters of the old order won't capitulate easily.'

'I hope he prevails, we may need his help in the future,' said Mack thoughtfully. His mysterious statement was no surprise to Tom.

'Time will tell, Mack. Now, can we finalise the security measures and the media access up to the take-off?'

'Yes, we should.'

With all the visitors and media on the base, security was becoming a large headache. They had agreed limited media access to the colonists' accommodation in the *Hela* cargo bay. Mack believed showing how well it was designed would enhance the future off-world employment drives, showing the aliens were not monsters — as some on Earth still believed.

HELA BASE AUSTRALIAN DESERT 2ND JANUARY 2027

From midnight on the second of January the holidays ended and the countdown commenced. The preparations for the take-off moved up a gear with security around the *Hela* expanded to include strict exclusion zones. By the end of the following day the colonists were all on board, settling into their new home, a home that would transport them on a one-way trip, far away from their home planet.

For Anan Corp, media relations were now a key part of the Project's success on Earth. There could be no "negativity or scandal" — as Kath explained the importance of public relations to Mack. It was a clear message they portrayed, a safe take-off with humans and purebreeds working together.

QUEENSTOWN 4TH JANUARY 2027

It was the sound of the television in the next room that woke him. He lay there and stretched out his arm, but there was no one there. *Where was she?* he thought, as he looked across the empty bed. He pulled her pillow closer so he could smell her sweet fragrance. He missed her — and the strength of the feeling surprised him. Then the alcohol-fuelled churning started in his gut, he jumped up and ran to the toilet.

Five minutes later, after empting his stomach and bowel, he stumbled into the hostel living room.

'G'day, Bri. How ya feeling, mate?' asked the young man lounging on the couch watching television.

'Like excrement. What are you watching?'

'It's the launch. Not too far from my home in Oz. Alice Springs, you should know it — nearest town to your base.'

Again, Bri felt his stomach churn. 'What launch?'

'Your ship, mate. It's leaving today. Guess your stay —'

'Your communication device – phone, give it to me,' screamed Bri as he ran to the table scrabbling frantically through the mess. 'Where is it?'

'Here, ya alien pisshead, but you can't call Oz, it's only a cheap burner,' he said, throwing a small phone to Bri. 'Don't use all my credit either.'

Bri closed his eyes and recalled the Christchurch number. It rang twice; to his relief, someone answered, 'Anan Corp helpline. State your identity please.'

'Brizo Sema, I am in trouble.'

'Brizo, are you OK? We've been looking for you. Tell me where you are?' the woman said. Three of them had been sitting by this phone line for the past four days. He had gone missing on New Year's Eve, escaping from the complex where he was staying with Alex and Rhea. Since then, despite them looking, there was no sign of him.

'Queenstown. In a place outside Queenstown.'

'Give me the address. We'll have you picked up. There's a shuttle waiting at the airport.'

'I don't know it.'

'Is there anyone there who does?'

'Hold on,' he said, and passed the phone back to his human friend. He had met them on the wharf in Queenstown while watching the fireworks and stayed with them since then. It was the girl who had attracted him.

When he'd finished giving directions, the young Australian hung up the phone. 'Police will be here in a few minutes to pick you up. What about your sheila, the girl?'

'Where is she?'

'Went out to get some food, mate — for breakfast. You taking her with you?'

'No, that is not possible,' he said.

A blue light flashing through the window and the sound of squealing tyres announced the arrival of his lift. He grabbed paper and pen and scribbled a note. 'Here give her this,' Bri said taking his blue pendant off and putting it on the table on top of the note.

'She'll be pissed, mate. She's a stunner. That means beautiful,' he said carefully mouthing the word. 'Human women do not come much better than that — you know. You understand that, mate.'

'Yes,' he said, as he ran down to the police car outside.

Walking up the road, the girl turned the corner to see the car pull away from the hostel. As it sped past her she glimpsed Bri sitting in the back. She ran the rest of the way back to the hostel.

'Where'd Bri go?'

The young man turned and looked at the beautiful girl standing in the doorway. He was dreading this. Rubbing his stubble, he turned away from her forlorn gaze. *She knew*, he thought. 'Space, he's going home. You just missed him. He left you that,' he said pointing to the pendant and letter.

Dropping the fruit and bread on the table, she picked up the pendant. 'That's it,' she said as she stuffed the letter in her pocket. 'One cheap crystal, that's all he left. Men — alien and human – you're all the bloody same,' and she stomped out of the room.

He lounged back in the chair and as he returned to watch the launch, he could hear the crashes as she noisily packed her bag and cursed in the room next door. *What an arsehole of an alien*, he thought.

LIFT-OFF 4TH JANUARY 2027

She was fully laden with one hundred and twenty thousand tonnes of equipment, machinery and life supporting food, water and oxygen for the colonists and the *Hela* crew. Everything was weighed before loading and they found there was always more to take. The ship could carry a maximum of one hundred and seventy-five thousand tonnes, so Niamh was happy the extra weight, above their planned load, did not exceed the safety margin.

The goodbyes on Earth were emotional. Robert, having recently found his only surviving relatives, bade a tearful goodbye to the McKinnon family. During their final hours on Earth; Kath, Harold, Alan and George were allowed on board to see them off. Kath found it hard to believe they were actually going, ten and a half months after her fateful meeting of Theia and Mack in Christchurch — and Janet was going with them. It was Mack who had requested she go. Her work as the planner was invaluable and she had also doubled up as his personal assistant. He found he would miss her and — she wanted to go as well.

The Earth stood still for the dramatic lift-off while the pictures of the *Hela*, with the first human colonists departing Earth, were watched around the globe. With the grav dampers on maximum and the grav engines on full power the golden coloured *Hela*, shining in the desert sun, slowly lifted off its three docking posts. After completing a one hundred and eighty degree turn over its base in the desert, it took over an hour on a slow wide corkscrew flight path for the *Hela* to clear Earth's gravity into orbit. She shook and groaned, but with the modifications and changes Niamh made, the reconditioned ship easily made it. The crew and colonists erupted into loud cheers when it was happily announced over the comms system they were in Earth orbit.

As the last shuttle up from Earth docked, Mack looked across at Theia; 'we are all on board, Empress, the full complement of colonists and our own purebreeds.'

She turned slightly to him and nodded in understanding. Without Bri to captain the ship, Theia had taken command, and with the help of the Pilot, Niamh and the purebreed bridge crew, started their long journey to the New World.

PROJECT REPORT THREE. EARTH DATE: 4TH JANUARY 2027. TO THE ONE

My Lord,

We have departed Earth. The *Hela*'s refit was successful and the ship's systems are fully operational. We have the two thousand five hundred human colonists on board and functional equipment for the extraction of blue energy when we arrive.

I am concerned that you have not acknowledged my two previous reports. I suspect you conserve your energy. My next report will follow our departure from the New World. You will hear from me within an orbit of Anan.

Dedicated to your service.

The Eight

That is enough information, thought The Eight. *Why has he not contacted me? I should have heard something by now*, he thought. He was worried he was too late to save his Lord and friend.

CHAPTER TWENTY TWO

THE HELA 5TH JANUARY 2027

Robert sat back from the table and looked around at the large canteen. He watched as the colonists started to file out, getting ready for their first Project brief in space. Sitting with Mack, Tom and Janet he would give them all time to assemble. 'Janet, food's great, you did a good job getting those chefs.'

'Yes, Robert. They were a real find.' She stood up from the table, 'there's Alfonso. I need to talk to him about the meal plans. I'll be back before you start.'

They watched as she walked over to a tall handsome man, dressed in whites with a towel slung across his shoulder. His jet black hair was tucked up into his tall chef's hat. As soon as he saw Janet he beamed. Opening his arms and placing them on her shoulders, he drew her to him, kissing her on both cheeks.

Mack's head snapped back in surprise as he watched. The chef then kissed her hand and led her back to a small office in the kitchen. 'Why is that man so familiar with her, and where is he from?'

Robert tried not to laugh as he replied, 'Aye, Mack, he's from Italy. Very continental. We say on Earth "he's all over her like a hot rash". Reckon you have competition there. Yes you do,' he said as he kicked Tom's leg. Tom turned away from the two, as he tried to hold in his laughter. 'Reckon you should make a move soon, Mack. She'll no be available for long. She's a fine woman. Aye, a fine woman —'

'Robert, that's enough of that, really. We take things much slower on Anan.' Mack looked around at the canteen, now nearly empty. He watched as some of the catering staff set a table for six over to one side. 'The catering staff — are they all full time?' he said, quickly changing the subject.

'No, Mack, most have dual skills. That girl over there, she's a botanist and the guy beside her is a geologist. If they don't have specific ship duties, everyone must take a turn working for the catering crew and looking after the accommodation. There are no passengers.'

'And the training regime, Robert, have you organised that?'

'You'll hear that at the brief. It's quite detailed. Here she is,' he said as Janet bounced across the canteen with a big smile on her face.

'He's such a gentleman, a lovely man. He's worked wonders with the kitchens and the accommodation. Robert, you did right giving him and Serge a free hand in the design.'

'We were lucky to get them both. Is he happy with the supplies? I know he —'

'They both had a hissy fit when you refused so much fresh produce. It was a compromise — with the preserved, the dried and the frozen stuff.'

'Janet, we hadn't enough room and it would spoil.'

'Don't try to convince me, I know. You were right. Some of the colonists had romantic notions of hydroponics and gardens in space. We'd better go,' she said as the sound of a slow handclap wafted in from the courtyard outside.

The accommodation blocks were assembled, from the pods, in six separate quadrangles in the large *Hela* cargo bay. The ground floor of each block contained a canteen, communal lounge and entertainment areas. The open squares were set out for the humans to exercise in. Each pod contained its own toilet and a small kitchen. But for the journey, eating would be confined to the canteens. All the services were connected, providing the humans with water, power and waste. Robert and Niamh designed the transportation concept around a set of simple values — maintain a healthy population travelling in safety and comfort.

The colonists had assembled around three of the large squares. Robert's brief would be delivered to them all on view screens. Stepping into a grav platform with Mack, they floated up above one square.

'Good morning, all,' he started.

'Good morning, Robert,' they all shouted back.

'Can you all hear and see me?' he asked, 'yes' he heard with the usual ribald comments. 'Welcome to the *Hela*. We're finally underway and making good time through our solar system. We should be passing Uranus shortly.'

'Mind ya don't get stuck up it, ya daft Jock,' one in the crowd shouted loudly. They all laughed.

Robert grinned, he had expected that. 'Actually, I think it's Neptune.'

'Oh shit. We're lost in space already,' shouted back the reply.

'All right, to business, I'm going to go over your daily schedules, what you will all be doing on the journey. It'll be four months and we need to keep you all occupied and healthy. There's …'

He continued to detail the self-defence training, the sports activities and exercise programs they would all be involved in. The strict regimes were designed to help the humans survive the deep space flight. They were told Bri, now suffering from the Anan sickness, was relieved of his duties. He would be available to train the colonists in Anan technology. It was Tom's idea and perfect work for the young Aknar Prince. After his escapade in Queenstown, Alex recommended active and physical work. His days would be busy and, unknown to the colonists, help him recover from his addictions. He would also train the defence teams to use the grav suits and in operating the Anan military tech.

As Robert continued with his brief, Niamh and her crew walked out of the central corridor and made their way into the canteen. As soon as Serge saw her he rushed over. 'I have a place set for you, sit here, please.'

'No, Serge, we don't have time, we just want some —'

'Junk food, you insult me. We have it all ready for you, sit,' he ordered, as he took out the chair at the head of the table for her.

'All right, come on, lads, ye haven't eaten since yesterday,' she said to her crew as they wearily sat down.

'You didn't eat here. Where you ate yesterday?' he asked.

'In the Anan canteen — beside the bridge.'

'With the aliens? All they serve there is raw mice.'

'Serge, they eat cooked food like we do. You watch too much TV,' she said as she watched two others come out from the kitchen with trays of food.

'It is shit they serve there.'

'Maybe. Talking of shit, how are the drains coping with the full load?'

'Impeccable. But time will tell. So far we are coping, no bad smells either. Now eat. And here is your husband. I have much to say to him. Sir, you are a monster. Allowing your wife to go so long without food. She works too hard. If my husband treat me like that, I slit his throat,' he said, as he drew his finger across his throat and walked off.

'How long have you been at it?' Tom asked as he looked at the pile of food on the table Serge and Alfonso had put out.

'We haven't stopped since we took off. Oh, this food – it's amazing — taste the omelette,' she said as she sat back and handed Tom a spoonful.

'No thanks Niamh, I had some earlier. Napoleon said "an army marches on its stomach". Those two guys are brilliant. We'll easily march across intergalactic space. Now, tell me, what's up?' he said as he watched her comms unit buzz on the table beside her.

She looked at the screen and put it back down, unanswered. 'It's the hybrid drive. I can't figure how to get it to work with the grav engines. We have to start it, bring it up to speed and then synchronise them. I can't figure out how to do it. I wanted to do that on the test flight. But…'

'Can the Pilot or The Eight help?'

'No, the Pilot hasn't run one before. And The Eight, he gave me as much info as he can get from his memories. But those drives are so scarce, there's not much info on them,' she said as she continued to eat.

As he waited until they finished, he looked at her. He had never seen her so weary before, and her crew were no better. They all had dark circles under their eyes and white faces. Just over a day out from Earth, and the chief engineer and her crew were exhausted.

'You need some sleep, all of you,' he said as they finished their food. 'No, don't argue Niamh. Look at your crew — they are beat. Come on, we're going back to our pod. You guys,' he said to her crew, 'get some rest. I'll square it with the bridge.'

As soon as she lay down, she was asleep. As she lay there on the bed, he took her comms unit. Walking out of the pod onto the balcony, he called the bridge. 'Who's in command?' he asked.

'We are on autopilot,' Siba said, 'If I have any problems, I am to call the Empress.'

He felt a shiver run through his body. Siba, shuttle pilot two, was effectively in command, as the great ship sped through space with over two and a half thousands souls on board. 'Thanks, Siba,' was all he could say.

She woke up at eleven at night, after nearly fourteen hours of sleep. She sat up in bed and looked across at Tom, still dressed, lying beside her.

He opened his eyes and blinked the sleep from them. 'How are you?' he asked.

'Good, I've solved it.'

'What?'

'Jeez, the problem — you horrible man. I know what's wrong,' she said, grinning at him. 'I need my tablet. I left it in the hybrid engine room.'

'Come on, you go to the canteen and get some food. I'll get your tablet,' he said, getting up from the bed.

'You're a gent, Tom. Thanks. It's on the control console in the gallery,' she said as she jumped up and started to dress.

As he walked down the long central corridor towards the aft section of the ship, he passed the spot where Blair was nearly killed. She had shown it to him during the refit. They had come so far since then, he thought. As he walked on, he stopped and listened. It was music — where was that coming from? It got louder as he continued down the corridor until he arrived at an open door. As he walked into the compartment, loud dance music assaulted his ears. As his eyes adjusted to the gloom and the flashing light, he realised he was looking at a large group of bodies pulsating in rhythm to the music.

'Boss, what's wrong, can't sleep?' shouted Bill, one of his team leaders.

'Bill, what the hell's this?'

'What's it look like boss? It's a night club.'

'Who — I mean how...'

'Alice runs it, with that guy over there, he's one of Robert's team,' he said as he pointed to the bar.

As Tom looked over, Alice smiled and waved. She was busy pouring drinks beside a large man Tom recognised as their Load Master. 'Did you -'

'Get permission. Yes, boss. We were going to get that tomorrow, opening night tonight. We're closing in ten, last drinks at twenty-three thirty. Can I get you one?'

'No, no thanks.'

'Boss, this'll be great for intel. We've already hoovered up some gear. I'll bring it to your office in the morning. Nothing hard — only weed.'

'Very good, Bill, well I'll see you then,' he said, shaking his head as he left. Not what he expected, but he should have known. The first question his crew asked when they walked on board was, "where's the bar?"

He continued down the long corridor to the aft engine room. She had shown him it before. But now, as he looked down on the vast compartment with its alien engine, it took on an eerie silence. Finding her tablet, he turned and left, walking back down the central corridor. As he passed the night club, he followed the last of the noisy revellers, slowly trolling their way to their pods. At the canteen he realised it was over one kilometre there and back, and she had been trudging up and down to that engine room since they left Earth.

'You found it. Thanks, what took you so long?'

'Niamh, it's a one kilometre round trip – and I stopped at the night club. Did you know anything about that?'

'Yeah, course I did. Did you not know?'

'No, how did you know?

'Power, they need power. Some of my guys wired it up. I gave them the breaker slots. Some spy master you are. Don't even know what your own lads are up to. Chang was right, Thomas Parker, you have to up your game,' she said as he sat down and handed her the tablet. She tried not to laugh at his look of dejection.

'OK, to work. I'll get my lads up. We need to rewire the controls,' she said as she looked at the schematics on her tablet screen. 'I checked with the bridge, we'll be just out past the solar system in about twelve hours. I'll run it then.'

It took Niamh and her team over fourteen hours to re-configure the hybrid controls. The drive was so badly installed, they had to re-wire the signal modulator and strengthen the supports to the blue pulse regulator. It was work they only discovered when they tried to run the machine. Once they finished, she called the bridge.

'Theia, I'm ready to run the hybrid. I need you to slow the grav drives by half. Call me back when you're ready.' She turned from the control console and looked out from the edge of the command gallery down to the vast engine room. It was so big her crew called it "the cathedral". She loved looking at this alien machine, its size, shape and mysterious origins always mesmerised her. All her trawling through the records never revealed who had built it. Despite the botched retrofit, the drive itself was an engineering marvel and she believed, was the future for intergalactic travel.

Mounted in a huge pit, the great drive towered above the blue energy feed manifolds way below. The main rotor, a spherical polyhedron, sparkled as it floated inside the lattice shaped containment chamber — from which the two pulse cylinders vented — and disappeared out through the aft section of the ship. Turning away from the gallery, Niamh looked at her crew and said, 'start that thing up, lads - just put it on idle.'

Ten minutes later Theia called. 'We're ready here, Theia. You at half, fine, here we go. OK, bring that drive on, watch the control sequence,' she said as they watched a screen showing the output of the two grav engines and the hybrid. As they increased power to the hybrid, the two curves converged. She closed the synchronisation feed, balancing the three engines. The drive whined as the rotor accelerated inside the containment field, then flickered in a deep blue glow and flashed with bolts of white light. Surprised, they all jumped back from the gallery edge. With the strange light that filled the vast "cathedral" and the blurred movement of the rotor, it looked like the hybrid was moving into another dimension.

Her heart thumped in her chest. 'Ah shit, lads, I hope we got this right,' she said, as her hand hovered over the emergency stop. Slowly, still flickering in blue light, the drive stabilised and the noise reduced to a low hum. As it loaded up, they could feel a change in the ship as the grav dampers compensated for the speed increase. She took her hand away from the emergency stop when her comms unit buzzed. 'It's running, Theia. You're doing how much? Wow, that's great. As you increase the power to the grav engines, this one will follow. But, Theia, we'll need to monitor this all the time. Yes, I'll arrange that,' she said as she looked across at the drive. The rotor had disappeared into a ball of white light while the rest of the alien machine was bathed in the strange blurred blue light.

'Jeez, lads, that's awesome. It's increased the speed by half. I wonder where we could get more like it.'

MED-BAY 18TH JANUARY 2027

'We really don't have to do this, Rhea,' Alex said.

'Alex, we agreed on this months ago.'

'I know, I know. But looking at you now, well you're both so vulnerable,' he said. 'I don't want anything to go wrong.' He didn't. She was near six months pregnant and with her bump advanced she looked very vulnerable to him. He was amazed at the changes in her body. She was concerned he would find her bloated and unattractive but he found it the total opposite. He thought that she was blooming, and the energy and beauty she projected overwhelmed him.

'It won't, Alex. We have sterilised and checked the equipment. It's really safe. You have to learn to trust our Anan medical equipment. Do you think I would suggest it if it wasn't?' Rhea said with real conviction in her voice.

They were two weeks out in space after leaving Earth. Under her orders as the chief medical officer, med-bay was sealed during the ship's refit on Earth. She refused a request from Niamh to include the med-bay equipment within the ship maintenance program. She and Alex initiated the med-bay maintenance protocols when he first arrived on the *Hela*.

When they returned to the *Hela* before the take-off they removed Rhea's unbroken seal. They deep-cleaned med-bay and initiated the maintenance protocols that included the sterilisation of all equipment. She was right, he thought, looking at the calibration labels he insisted they put on their equipment once the inspection routines were completed. He was being overprotective of her and yes, he didn't understand every working part of this Anan equipment. It was the same in the laboratories he worked in on Earth; he didn't understand every working part of that machinery either. *So, why the feeling of unease?* he thought. *My head says one thing and my heart another.*

'OK, but we take it one step at a time, any indication of undue stress to you or the baby, we stop,' he said to Rhea with an authority in his voice she had not heard before. She liked that. He was now so protective of her, she thought he would wrap her up in cotton wool all day. He was impossible when the *Hela* took off, insisting she lie down and have blankets and pillows to protect her. 'From what?' she asked, totally embarrassed by his assiduous attention. 'If the grav dampers don't work, we'll all be squashed flat,' she cheerfully reminded him.

Now both attentive to the task in hand, she explained to him for the umpteen time how the machine worked, and how it would take a fluid sample of the baby. Although invasive, the process would not harm their foetus.

It was far easier than he ever thought. Rhea lay on the treatment table with her mid-section exposed. He manipulated the machine over her and it simply followed the preprogrammed process Rhea had installed. The procedure was automatic and all he had to do was monitor her and their baby. Within minutes it was all over and there were no ill effects apparent to her or the foetus.

'There, you see, we are both fine. You know, Alex, I often wonder where the baby really is,' she teased him as he helped her up from the treatment table, not missing an opportunity to kiss and embrace her.

'Be patient with me,' he said. 'This is all new to me and well -'

'Yes, Alex, I know,' she said gently, returning his kiss and holding him tight.

They were both now amazed at how far they had come in the search for a cure to the Anan sickness. It was what brought them together in the first place and to this moment where their own child could generate a cure for the sick purebreeds on the *Hela*. The first sample of their baby's DNA. It was the first human and purebreed offspring, and they were in awe of its potential. They would need more samples and more research, but the way ahead was slowly opening up to them.

BRIDGE READY ROOM 20TH JANUARY 2027

'I'm not complaining, but for the first time I'm having difficulty with the work,' said Niamh. 'Managing the hybrid drive is more than we realised, I have to keep it balanced with the main grav engines. Remember, it was a retrofit and doesn't have an automatic balancing system. We're travelling nearly fully laden and the grav dampers need constant attention. If we let the gravity bubble falter for an instant at this speed, well, you all know what happens. There'll be two thousand five hundred and thirty-two lumps of paste splattered between the walls of this squashed ship,' she said, referring to the fate of the human and purebreed crew. 'It's a different trip than the one you made out to Earth, Theia.'

Niamh had called this meeting with Theia, Robert and Tom in the captain's ready room. Three days after leaving Earth and clearing the solar system into open space she started the hybrid drive for the first time. Now she had far too much work, she was exhausted, running and navigating the *Hela* at full speed for two weeks. She missed Bri's help. Niamh needed time to herself for her own personal wellbeing, or she wouldn't survive the journey. She was afraid if she made a mistake they would all die.

She's right, thought Theia. *It's a faster and heavier ship and we travel through an uncharted section of space. Unlike the trip out from Anan, navigation is more complicated. We need continuous long range plotting and monitoring of space. The Overlord is concerned our secret may be compromised, and that others have learned of the New World. If they find us, we are ruined. It would be a complex journey. We need a strong crew to manage this voyage and the next one immediately after it*, thought Theia, who was also suffering from exhaustion.

'You're right, Niamh, I am also exhausted. If we get it wrong at this stage we fail after so much work. Bri cannot take his command,' she said. 'We use the Pilot and his shuttle pilots. The Pilot will provide consultancy with course plotting and management of the hybrid drive and the ship. He will be my second in command. Yes, he is well able to do this. His three shuttle pilots will serve as navigators as they did in the past. This releases you from navigation, Niamh. It gives you time to train our five Anan engineering crew to operate the hybrid drive.'

'That will help, Theia, but we need more help with navigation,' Niamh replied, hoping Theia would finally respond to Tom's previous probing.

'Yes. Tom, I have the files you requested,' she said, referring to the results of the initial computer questionnaire the colonists took. 'It was one per cent — twenty five colonists have navigation abilities. We will train five to assist on the bridge. Here are the files, you may choose. They may use the Aknar blue diamonds while they are on the bridge.'

'Thank you, Theia. That will help,' Niamh said, as she and Tom quickly looked at the files. They pulled out five and handed them to Robert for approval.

'Aye, Theia, these five will be our trainee navigators,' he said as he handed the files back to Theia.

MED-BAY 6TH MARCH 2027

The DNA sample of their creation was truly beautiful. It was a pure sample and the test equipment showed it contained a mix of both of them. During this euphoric time Alex and Rhea found it hard to concentrate on their work and took more time to simply enjoy their creation and their feelings for each other.

Seven weeks after recovering the first DNA sample from the foetus, they were ready to take the second sample. They used the entire first sample for tests and research and intended to use the second sample, which was to be twice the size of the first, to grow the Anan cure. Their preparation was not as meticulous as the first, but Alex still fussed about med-bay ensuring she was comfortable and the machinery was programmed properly.

'Alex, really, you are making me nervous with your continual flapping,' she said. 'Can we get on with it please?'

The extended sampling process took slightly longer than first. As with the first, immediately after, there were no ill effects apparent to her or the foetus.

'There you see. That went well,' she said, proud of what they had accomplished.

'Yes, yes it did,' Alex replied, analysing the sample which was as pure as the first.

A day after they took the second sample Rhea felt there was something wrong with her baby. She couldn't understand what it was, but realised something had changed. When they went to bed that night, Alex noticed a change in her. She was preoccupied with her own thoughts and seemed to be in a world of her own.

'Rhea, are you all right?' he asked.

'Yes, Alex, yes, I'm just tired,' she lied. She did not want to try to explain this strange feeling to him. However in the early hours of the following morning she awoke screaming and convulsed with pain coming from her abdomen.

'Alex, Alex,' she screamed, 'make it stop make it stop. Oh, what have I done? Alex, please, please, make it stop,' she continually cried as he helped her to med-bay.

Within minutes he had her lying down on the treatment table and immediately noticed some strange movements in her abdomen. He was petrified for her, but his professionalism guided his treatment of her pain with morphine. As it coursed through her body, it relieved her pain, calming her convulsions and distress. Much to Alex's relief, the strange movement in her abdomen diminished. He needed her calm and sedated to perform a thorough examination of her and the baby. *I need to find out what's happened*, was the thought continually going through his mind. As he went to work, he blocked out all his emotional feelings.

'Rhea, I'm here, my love. It's OK, it's OK,' he repeated over and over to reassure her as he worked to get the diagnostic equipment in place.

Nothing prepared him for what he was looking at on the screen of the Anan diagnostic machine. Their beautiful fair purebreed human baby with its tiny limbs, fingers and toes was replaced by a dark-shaped monster with small claws at the end of its limbs. He could see it still developing, as parts of the head were fair-skinned and the transformation had not yet reached the face. For the time being, the morphine dulled its growth and movement. It had given Alex some time to prepare for what he would do next. Above all else he knew, to save her, he would have to cut it out. Driven by his love for her, he set about preparing the tools and equipment to do just that.

Sitting at his desk sipping a cup of coffee, Robert looked at the reports from yesterday's activities. It was his daily ritual and he looked forward to this early morning quiet period. *Good*, he thought, *the training is going well and the colonists bonding as a team. Two month out and just half way*, he happily thought. The change to the bridge team worked wonders.

The mysterious Pilot proved his worth with a wealth of experience to give to the young crew. The hybrid drive would knock two months off the journey as well. It was all too good to be true, thought Robert, when suddenly a loud intrusive noise shattered his thoughts. Realising it was the biological contamination alarm from med-bay; he quickly ran from his office and was the first to arrive at the locked med-bay door.

Robert was shocked and repulsed by the horrific scene that greeted him. He could see through the glass walls of the treatment room. Rhea was lying restrained on the treatment table covered with blood. Robert could see that her abdomen was cut open and there was a dark shaped object appearing half in and half out of her. As Robert watched in horror, Alex grappled with it as he tried to extract it from her. The thing turned and something like a head and a small mouth opened, biting Alex's hand. Then its claws withdrew from Rhea's stomach and started slashing at Alex, who finally let it go. The thing withdrew back into her stomach. Hearing a scream behind him, Robert turned from the macabre scene and looked at Theia who, hearing the alarm, had rushed to med-bay.

'Rhea, Rhea,' she screamed, pushing at Robert to get to the door of med-bay. But, with the bulk of his body, Robert faithfully guarded it. He watched, as Alex approached the door.

'Let him out, let him out,' Theia screamed.

Alex pointed to a light flashing ominously over a lever mechanism on one side of the door. Although the instructions were in Anan, Robert understood what he was to do. The configuration of the levers left no doubt as to its intention. As he reached to activate the mechanism, Theia screamed behind him, pounding her fists into his back.

'No, no, no,' she screamed frantically trying to reach another set of controls that opened the door. However, Robert's bulk stopped her.

Alex, pointing at the mechanism, nodded his head. He knew this was the only course of action. He had failed his wife and child; he was not going to fail the *Hela* and allow that evil being out to gestate among the crew. He had observed its growth rate even under the influence of the morphine, it was phenomenal. When it had sensed his presence trying to remove it from Rhea, it had grown barbs and latched on to her.

'Now, do it now,' Alex shouted at Robert who couldn't hear him through the thick glass, but he could read his lips, and fully understood what he must do.

Robert pulled the protective cover off the small box-shaped compartment that housed the control lever for the decontamination process. As he started to pull the lever down he felt Theia's thoughts in his mind screaming at him to stop. She was too late; he had already started to move the lever down. Robert's desire to protect his crew was far greater than her mental abilities. *Anything that threatens the ship or crew must be dealt with*, his mind screamed back, as he continued to pull the lever starting the fatal process.

It first released an orange-coloured gas inside med-bay. Before he choked on the gas Alex smiled at him and Robert could see him mouthing the words, "thank you," as he fell and died on the floor. The orange gas quickly filled med-bay, killing Rhea and the monster inside her. A silver-coloured gas followed. It contained nanites that were programmed to feed on the now dead contaminates. They devoured all tissue, bone and liquids. Nothing was left except the expended nanites. The decontamination process was over within minutes and the alarms finally stopped.

Robert, still standing protectively in front of the med-bay door, slowly turned to face Theia who was now slumped on the ground crying. Others had arrived to investigate the alarm and Robert could see Mack approaching. His normal white face was darkened and wrinkled with the worry of what he might find.

'Nobody is to touch anything. I want this area secured immediately,' he said to Tom who just arrived.

'Empress, are you all right?' he asked Theia as he knelt down beside her, gently taking her hand.

'No, no, my friend Rhea, her baby and Alex they are gone, gone, Robert why did you do that, why, why?' she cried, as Mack lifted her up and carried her away to her quarters.

As news of the disastrous event travelled quickly through the ship, it devastated the crew morale and threatened the working relationship build up between the Anan clients and their human crews. The scuttlebutt quickly embellished the story with reports of the humans killing Rhea, the exalted Anan doctor bearer of the Seal of the House of Aknar and source of their cure. The colonists wouldn't believe this and soon acrimony between both species developed.

When the alarms in med-bay first activated, The Eight, immediately sensing the danger, watched the enfolding drama. He could access the med-bay systems, read the data storage registers and knew before anyone else what caused the event. He was angry, very angry and the realisation that his mission may have been compromised by Theia's "personal project" as he called it, deeply disturbed him. Before matters deteriorated further, he called them to his chamber. But first, he needed to talk to Robert who was now standing before him.

As always, thought Robert, whenever things went wrong, you were summoned to explain it to the boss. Today it involved loss of life and that, thought Robert, was his own ultimate failure.

'Robert, do you know what you have done?' asked The Eight in a quiet voice.

'My duty, Overlord. It is my duty to protect the *Hela*, I perceived a threat and followed Alex's final instructions to neutralise it. I make no apologies nor do I take any pride in killing those unfortunate souls,' he said.

'I am sorry to tell you, one day you may again meet the foul species that you saw in med-bay this morning. If you are ever faced by an onslaught of their vicious hordes you will realise how right you were to follow Alex's directions, hard as it was for you to do so.

'You and Alex have saved the crew of this vessel from a fate worse than death. Believe that, and never doubt your judgement. Once again I am in your debt,' said the Overlord, and unknown to Robert gently probed his thoughts and feelings. Robert was filled with remorse for the loss of Rhea, Alex and their child, fear that his actions would compromise the trust built up between purebreed and humans, and fear of where the contamination came from. *He is a giant among mortals and never ceases to amaze me*, thought The Eight. 'Show the others in.'

Robert opened the door and the others filed in. As their eyes met, he could see and feel the hatred for him still in Theia's eyes and mind. Theia, Mack, Robert, Tom and Niamh stood before The Eight in silence. They were all still in shock from the events that morning.

'Let there be no doubt I am disappointed that this event has happened and intruded on the safety of this Project,' the Overlord said. 'The loss of Rhea, Alex and their child bears heavily on me and the entire population of this small vessel. A consequence of this is the divisions that are forming between purebreed and human. I cannot countenance that. I alone know what happened, before and during this sad event and what vital actions were needed to contain it. But it is not enough for me to give you that information. If we are to move on and learn from it, you must investigate it and draw your own conclusions. Is that clear?' he asked.

'Yes,' they all said quietly.

'General, you will lead the team. It will comprise of Niamh, a human doctor from the colonists and the computer technician. Two purebreeds and two humans with all the skills to decipher this event, you have forty-eight hours. You may go now. Empress, please remain.'

'Empress, you disappointed me,' the Eight said, after the others had left. 'You never approached me about your personal project. Knowing I must surely know what you were doing, you still failed to talk to me about it. Why?' he said, with so much anger in his voice, it cut through Theia's heart and mind. She fell to the floor on her knees before him.

'Forgive me, Overlord, I did not want to add to your burden with this, I believed I could do it on my own.'

'You lie, you lie,' he roared at her, 'when you found out about the link between human and purebreeds and what the old geneticist used, you tried to hide that from me. Stop your whimpering, Empress, it does not become you,' he said loudly as she shook and moaned with fear. 'I am not the monster you think I am. If you were truthful, I could have advanced your project without the risk you allowed your dear friend Rhea and her lover, Alex, to take. Their blood is on your hands,' he finished in a soft voice. 'Once we have set up the colony, I will arrange your return to Anan. You can manufacture your cure there as planned. I will not deny you that. As a condition of its delivery, you will reform the population of Anan. You will do with them what you did with this crew. You will expunge the corruption, the laziness, the graft and the belief that they are a superior race from your subjects. That is the price for their cure I will have,' he roared again, 'if they are to continue as a civilisation in our galaxy, they will change. Is that clear?'

'Thank you. Thank you, Overlord,' she said. She was genuinely elated at his offer and he could see that in her. It was more than she could ever have hoped for.

'Once we get to the New World, you will not involve yourself in my Project. The General will be my representative. Go now,' he said ending her audience with him. It was a monumental change in the Project management and recognition by the Overlord of the General's capabilities.

Within twenty-four hours the Overlord's chosen team had reviewed the harrowing video and data from med-bay. Niamh and Demard found the initial fault that led to the contamination of the foetus.

'Can you retrieve the latest maintenance data and heat mapping for the equipment?' Niamh asked Demard. All machinery, whether from Earth or Anan needed maintenance, medical equipment required specialist maintenance and those records should always be available.

'Yes, we can still access the med-bay logs,' he replied, as he opened the records. The first line that appeared on the screen in front of them stated "do not use this machine until independent validation routine complete". It did not bode well for the team.

Niamh and Demard checked what was done. They noticed that both doctors cleaned and sterilised the machine. But the full sterilisation and validation program was incomplete. It appeared that Rhea and Alex did not know how to run the full sequence, and thought, what they did was enough. From the databank, Demard recovered the temperature mapping profile from their last sterilisation.

'Look there, the sterilisation process did not reach all parts of the machine,' Niamh said in a quivering voice. 'Any contaminated matter in that part of the machine would be slowly flushed down to the patient during sampling.' She paused to look at the data and fully digest the impact of what they had discovered. Once she understood it, she explained to Mack and the team, the workings of the complex sampling system, and how the contamination finally made its way through the machine and into the baby.

'So,' Mack said, 'that is why there were no ill effects after the first sample was taken seven weeks ago.'

'Yes, Mack, and unfortunately that lucky encounter lulled them into a false sense of security. The second sample was larger than the first and over a longer period, more chance for the contamination to get into the foetus,' she said. 'Before we came on board, what was this machine last used for?'

'Let's see,' Demard said looking through the database. 'Look, someone had a Ceirim in here before we took over the ship at the Energy Exchange.'

'What's a Ceirim?' asked the colonists' doctor.

'Here, look at a picture of one. They dwell on one of The Sixth's planets,' said Demard, calling up a picture on screen of a black biped with long arms. Its epidermis was formed by long thin spikes. There were vicious claws on its hands and feet and its jaws were packed with thin sharp teeth. Its name did not fully do justice to its frightening form.

'That is truly horrific,' said Niamh, turning away from the screen. She noticed the doctor was now holding his head in his hands trying not to cry. 'Can you tell how long ago and by whom?' she asked Demard.

'Yes,' Demard said, 'records show a geneticist, look, here is his name, was conducting routine tests on a group of the Ceirim, it was about one hundred of your years ago, while the *Hela* was in its dock. See, here are the test results. Some of their DNA stayed in the machine. That was the contaminated matter that entered the foetus.'

'The DNA of the Ceirim is very voracious. It will take over a host and transform the body quite quickly. I heard The One asked The Sixth to terminate them. As we see, that never happened… ' Mack said.

'We're lucky the contamination was contained to this one rarely used machine. But the whole of med-bay is in question. I cannot guarantee its integrity, the machinery is too old and no one will use it after the event yesterday,' Niamh said.

'We can eject it from the ship. It is designed that way,' Mack said. 'Doctor, will you allow us to use your field hospital in the cargo bay if needed?'

'Yes, and I will set up a small sick bay for you in one of the offices before we take it off at the colony.'

'What about all the work they did here to heal the Anan sickness?' Mack asked. 'Is that all contaminated? Have we lost the treatment they manufactured for the crew and the samples prepared and stored to be sent to Anan for the final cure?'

'I looked through Alex's notes, he used equipment from Earth for that work,' the doctor said.

Demard turned from the screen. 'General, we found he used Anan technology for the research work. He used Earth equipment for the samples and the medicine he made and kept in storage. Only the research samples touched Anan technology — and these are sealed in med-bay.' Turning back to the screen he retrieved some more data. 'He kept detailed records in the database – look.' They looked at the records of all the samples and medicines and how and where they came from. From what they could see, none in storage touched any of the Anan machines.

'Doctor, to verify this, can you work with my computer technician?' Mack asked. 'I know it may take some time but, considering the consequences, for the samples and the medicine, we must be sure. Yes, Demard, I know you take it as well,' he said as Demard nodded his head vigorously in agreement.

Mack's investigation team finished delivering their findings to The Eight. Seated to the side of him Theia, Mack, Tom and Robert listened attentively in silence.

'I appreciate your diligent work in such a short time,' The Eight said quietly. 'Sadly, you come to the same conclusions as I. It was a tragedy not of your making,' he said, looking around at all in his chamber. No one noticed that Theia squirmed under his gaze.

'What do I do about this?' he asked as he started to hover around the chamber. 'If I was consulted I would have prohibited those experiments. That I was not consulted on such an important matter disheartened me. I am your Overlord. I am grumpy, I know that, but you must consult me. I cannot see everything all the time. If we are to survive the challenges ahead you need my help. Remember that,' he said in a loud and powerful voice, leaving no doubt as to his expectations from them in the future.

'Robert's prompt actions saved purebreed and human life on this ship. I am again in his debt. You may all go,' he said, as usual finishing the meeting abruptly.

The full details of the event, how it happened and Robert's actions were communicated to the purebreed and human crew. As the news quickly spread, it killed off the acrimony that developed between them. The Anans were all too familiar with the reputation of the Ceirim. The knowledge that one gestated on board the *Hela* horrified them.

Med-bay was ejected, and as it passed the ship in space the Overlord destroyed it and all remnants of the horrific events that took place within. On board the *Hela*, the burden of emptying Rhea and Alex's quarters remained. The unhappy task was assigned to Tom and two of his staff, experts in evidence collection and storage. Despite their experience in such tasks, they found it harrowing to go through the two doctors' personal effects. The Seal of the House of Aknar was returned to Theia. Two unopened oval-shaped kit bags they found were left until last. The battle-hardened group were uneasy and the task was left to Tom.

The first bag he opened contained the child's toys ranging from a rattle to a rugby ball. But it was the second bag that caused the most distress. As he pulled the zipper back and removed the contents he felt the tears well up in his eyes. The two men, who accompanied him, looked on silently. The bag contained clothes of different sizes from a new-born to a four-year-old. They were in different colours and designs but it was the logo that each one had on the chest that caused the most upset. Around a silver fern on a black background were the words, "Made in New Zealand". On the four blue one-piece new-born suits, embossed in a circle that contained the silver fern, were the words, "I was made with Love in Queenstown, New Zealand".

That night as they lay in bed together, Tom told Niamh what he found. She was, to his surprise, quite dispassionate.

'I did offer to maintain and validate all her equipment in Australia and she refused that,' she said quietly, holding him tight. 'Machinery is like a woman, you have to look after it, maintain it and treat it with respect. Otherwise, it will completely screw you over. Remember that, Thomas Parker.'

The doctor and Demard did not find any evidence of contamination in Alex's medicine or samples. They quickly realised that his work was amazing and found he left clear and concise instructions, directions and formulae for all his discoveries. The extent of his genius was finally realised. They had the First Stage Treatment medicine to treat the initial symptoms, the medicine that arrested the disease in the crew. They also had the critical purebreed and human DNA samples and a formula for a cure that could be synthesised on Anan, all stored in carefully maintained refrigeration units in the cargo bay.

CHAPTER TWENTY THREE

NEW WORLD, DAY 1 MONTH 1 YEAR 1.

One month out from their arrival, they were close enough to start scanning and mapping the planet. When Robert ordered they change their clocks, the colonists realised the journey was nearly over. 'We need to adopt a new shift system based on daylight hours, of the time zone our settlement will be in,' he told them. It was an exciting time, and reinvigorated the colonists after the loss of Alex and Rhea.

As expected, their new home resembled Earth during its prehistoric eras. It was mainly covered with lush dense forest, where large animals, similar in size to Earth prehistoric mammals and dinosaurs, roamed. The ecosystem was predictable, with an established food chain of herbivores and carnivores. As Tom expected, their early scans confirmed his fears — the biggest problem would be from large airborne carnivores.

Mack picked the settlement location for its proximity to the richest blue energy deposits on the planet. The "low hanging fruit", as Robert described the shallow deposits of blue in the rock of the mountains behind their chosen home. The location provided a natural landing site for the *Hela*, on a large sandy flat along a river estuary, and beside a beach on the shores of one of the planet's oceans. It was surrounded by hills broken by a valley leading back into the high mountain interior. The hills and the mountains would provide security from the roaming land-based carnivores. With the construction of a heavy duty force field, Tom planned to make use of the natural amphitheatre the hills created, to secure their settlement. The sandy estuary was well away from the thick forest boundary and a natural choice for their home.

NEW WORLD, DAY 28 MONTH1 YEAR 1.

'Are you looking forward to this, Tom?' Mack asked, as he inspected their first landing party in the shuttle bay.

'Mack, you have no idea how excited we are,' he said, smiling at his boss. His four teams were busy loading the shuttles with the arms and equipment they would need to secure a beach head on the planet.

'It will be hard and dangerous, Tom. There are so many species, we have not yet listed them all.'

'Mack, that's what makes this so interesting — first humans on another planet. Alice, John, Bill,' he shouted to his team leaders, 'you all know the plan, I'll be first down on shuttle one with the Pilot. Before you land, shuttles two three and four, wait for my signal — departure in five,' he shouted as he jumped into the shuttle.

Forty minutes later, they were down hovering over the landing site.

'That'll do, right there, Pilot,' Tom said pointing to a flat sandy area.

The shuttle touched down. Tom, toting his favourite C8 carbine and dressed in a black Anan combat suit, jumped out. His boots imprinted the sandy soil, marking the historic moment of the first human to land on a distant planet. Mankind had arrived. There were no words of wisdom or pre-scripted speech. As he warily looked around at the landing site, he noticed how similar it was to Earth. The early morning sun, shining through the blue cloudless sky, was warming the land. *At least the weather is kind*, he thought, as he looked over at the forest edge and then at the river where the large animals were watering. They were watching the strange biped with interest. As he looked through his binoculars he could see that some had stood up while others had stopped drinking, raising their heads with curiosity. But it was the mouths of a smaller pack, which said it all — they were wide open and salivating while their teeth glistened in the sun.

'Right, you lot, all out,' he shouted, 'Brian, Gwen, you two take point, shoot anything that approaches. I don't want to be breakfast. The way that lot are looking at us, we might well be. The rest, let's get this shit out of the shuttle.' Hitting the button of his comms unit, 'shuttles two, three and four, you're clear to land,' he said, jumping back into shuttle one to help unload their cargo.

The great flying beasts had developed unchallenged from their humble beginnings as lizards. Their bodies averaged ten metres in length, and defying aerodynamics, had a wingspan of near thirty metres. Their giant curved beaks, filled with razor teeth and long sharp talons, ensured their supremacy at the top of the planet's food chain.

'Here they come,' Tom said, as they sheltered under a protective grav field, the four bubbles anchored into the ground provided.

They had landed two hours ago and unloaded the shuttles, while the sentries easily chased the land-based animals back into the forest. After four hungry beasts rushed the humans, their quick death and the sound of gunfire and small explosives, dispatched the others into a frenzied stampede. They were working on the perimeter force field, when a call from the *Hela* announced the imminent arrival of this flock. The large carnivores' curiosity was aroused by the noise and smell of this new biped. With the departure of their land-based competitors, a fresh feed was too hard to resist.

As the terrifying flock flew down, Tom looked up from his bubble. 'Hold your fire,' he said. As his four teams dug in under their Anan shelters, he had ordered the shuttles back to space for more well-needed supplies. 'Fire,' he shouted as the huge birds dove down on them.

They opened fire with the grav stun cannons. But the shots bounced off the birds' leathery skin. To the surprise of the humans, they kept coming, swooping down on top of the grav bubbles, landing on and around them. The flock of beasts jostled for position, as they tried to peck their way through the force fields with their long-toothed beaks.

'Weapons fire, use our guns. Let them have it,' Tom shouted, as the birds pecked and clawed at the bubbles. Without his prompting, his teams had already abandoned the Anan weapons and were busily shooting at the flock with their guns. The sound of the gunfire had more of an effect than the bullets, which bounced off the hard leathery skin.

'Hit them in the eyes or the soft tissue under their beaks,' John screamed over the sound of the flapping, the crowing and the gunfire. He had the first successful kill, as a bird fell away, twitching in the throes of death.

As they hopped across the ground flapping and pecking, the furious attack raised up the dust and sand, enveloping the fray in a thick dirty cloud.

'We need heavier weapons, boss,' Brian shouted, as the bullets kept bouncing off the leathery hides.

Reaching back into the weapons locker, Tom lifted out a grenade launcher and fitted it to his carbine. Peering through the dust cloud, he targeted a bird circling above their bubble and fired. The grenade sped straight to its mark and exploded on impact, knocking the great beast out of the air. It hit two others as it fell to ground, metres from their own bubble.

'That's done it, boss. Look, the others are lifting off,' he said, as they watched the flock, frightened by the noise of the explosion, retreat. As they hovered noisily over the grav bubbles, it was clear to the humans their appetite was not quelled.

'Fit your grenade launchers,' Tom shouted to his team and across the comms to the other three. 'Take them out, as many as you can get.'

The four teams fired a barrage of grenades, killing five of the flying beasts. But again, it was the noise of the explosions that achieved the most. The flock withdrew to the air, circling the human encampment below.

'Are they gone? We don't have many grenades left.'

Tom looked up at the flock above. 'No such luck, Gwen. They won't leave with all that fresh meat on the ground — and us as well.' Thinking on her comment, he realised they couldn't last here forever.

He was right, they returned, swooping down to continue their onslaught. Some of the flock attacked the carcasses, while the rest rushed the humans. They crowed and squawked as they clawed at the grav bubbles. One of the birds managed to push his head through the gun slot of Alice's team's bubble.

'Holy shit,' she screamed at her team of six, 'get down, get down.' The beast's head twisted and snapped as the humans tried in vain to push it back out of their bubble. Three tried to hack at it with their knives while the others beat at it with the butts of their guns. With her side-arm clenched in both hands, Alice dropped down to the ground and rolled under the beast's head. Ignoring the others, the bird tried to force itself down to reach her. Inches from her face, its beak snapped open and close, as it tried to grab her with the razor sharp teeth. As she smelt its rancid breath and felt saliva drip on her cheeks, she squeezed the trigger, discharging six bullets upwards, into the soft underbelly of its jaw. It died instantly when the bullets imbedded in its brain. The head slouched down onto Alice as its brains and blood spilled out, covering her in a yellow mess.

Before Alice was up, the hungry beasts outside, hacked and tore at their dead cohort. The intensity of the onslaught pitched the grav bubble out from its mounting in the ground. As the birds' blood spurted out, more of the flock joined the fray, trying to get a morsel of food - the force of their furious hunt pushed the bubble across the flat sandy ground.

Trapped in his own bubble Tom looked on. 'There must be at least ten of them.'

'Shit, boss, they'll tear her bubble apart,' Brian said.

Suddenly as they were strafed from above, the birds erupted, their bodies exploding under the onslaught of fifty-calibre multipurpose projectiles. Tom looked up to see two of his men strapped into the doorway of shuttle two, hammering away with the large weapon, at the birds below. As he looked at the shuttle he could see two huge beasts circling above.

'Siba,' he shouted over his comms unit, 'get out of there now.' She couldn't hear him, the weapons fire drowning out all other sound in her shuttle. As his men kept hammering away at the birds, Tom pointed his grenade launcher at the beast above and fired. The shot missed, and as he took aim again, one of the large beasts swooped down and struck the shuttle, trying to claw at the two exposed men.

As it tried to hack at the careering shuttle the gunners, fighting for their lives, managed to strafe one of the bird's wings. Erupting in blood and gristle, the huge bird swirled down to fall amongst its now faltering flock. The sound of the exploding fifty-calibre gunfire and the sight of their fallen leader frightened them off. Abandoning a free feed from their fallen cohorts, the fearsome monsters took flight, heading back to their mountain lair, the sound of their crowing and squawking fading as they disappeared into the distance.

Standing outside his bubble, Tom watched the damaged shuttle as it struggled to level out. However, with smoke coming from its grav ports, it spun downwards out of control. Shaking his head, he watched as it disappeared over one of the small hillocks. He called the *Hela*. 'Mack we have trouble, shuttle two is down, you probably heard. I copy that, we'll hold here.' He turned to Alice, John and Bill who had left their shelters to join him. 'He has the Pilot and our back up team on their way.'

'Base one to shuttle two, base one to shuttle two, are you receiving me over,' he called on the comms. There was no reply — he repeated the message over and over. Frowning, he shook his head as he looked at his team leaders. The four stood in silence, listening for any sign of hope. Then they heard it, a crackle on the comms and the welcome sound of Siba's haltering voice, 'Mr Parker, we are alive. One of your men is hurt, and the shuttle is disabled. We have crashed in a rocky valley beyond the hills. I will send you the coordinates.'

'Stay in the shuttle, help is coming. The Pilot will be with you shortly.'

There was a pause and some more crackle and then the sound of Siba's voice, this time with more confidence in it; 'thank you, Mr Parker, I have sent him our coordinates.'

'What about our own casualties?' Tom asked.

'We're lucky,' John said. 'One broken arm, some minor cuts and bruises, a dislocated shoulder and one covered in some hazardous alien yellow mess,' he said as Alice stood back and laughed. 'Those Anan grav bubbles did their job, boss. From what I counted there are sixteen carcases — must have been near fifty live ones in that flock.'

Tom smiled for the first time, 'you guys did —'

'Tom, look over there,' Alice said, pointing to the edge of the woods.

'What are they?'

'Looks like a cross between a cat and a bear,' she said. 'One has a cub on her back, must be the mum.'

'Boss, they want the meat from the birds' carcases,' Bill said. 'Look at them, they're starving — must be well down the food chain. I'll carve it up and give 'em some. Our Italian cooks want fresh meat as well,' he said, and quickly stripped off some meaty steaks with his long sharp knife.

'Bill, what are you doing with that?' Tom asked, as Bill walked over to the edge of the woods with the meat dripping with the bird's yellow blood.

'Watch, boss,' he said as he threw it to the largest of the beasts. 'Well I'll be …' he said as the beast took the meat, pulled it into smaller chunks and handed it to his mate, standing beside him. Putting her cub down, she started to feed it, softening the chunks in her mouth. Bill gestured to the larger one to come over to the carcase. As he timidly approached, they could see he was definitely the male. His large head looked like a lion's, but his fur was matted and pockmarked with sores.

'Watch yourself, Bill,' Tom said as he quietly un-holstered his side-arm.

Bill pointed to the meat, and the beast, not taking his eyes off Bill, gathered it up. Walking backwards on his hind legs, he retreated to the edge of the forest with his prize. The humans watched as the three strange mammals sat there and gorged themselves.

'There's more, boss. Look,' Bill said as he pointed up into the trees. 'They live in the trees. There's six more climbing down.'

He looked at the beasts, Alice was right. They were like a cross between a large cat and a bear and covered with green and brown stripes. *Natural camouflage for them in the forest*, thought Tom. 'Give them some food as well. We don't need it all.'

'Boss, look who's back. That's the poxy lot who rushed us when we first arrived,' she said, referring to a fresh group that had noisily returned to the edge of the forest. 'They're not as friendly as our catbears.'

'Our new friends don't like them either,' Bill said, as the male started to growl and retreat.

Tom watched with interest, as the catbears started to climb up the trees, growling and gesturing to the humans to follow. In a flash, it suddenly came to him — these were the most intelligent species on the planet. Like the humanoid hunters and gathers that The Eight first touched on earth. He had said there was no advanced intelligence on this planet. This was as good as it got without his intervention. Waving at the male they had fed, he deliberately walked towards the group that had just returned, large two legged-beasts that resembled Earth's dinosaurs. *Biped liz*ards, thought Tom, as the long-toothed animals hissed and spat. They were about four metres tall with long jaws and sharp teeth. As they rushed Tom, he shouldered his gun and sprayed them with bullets. Three fell onto the forest floor as the herd behind stopped their charge, turned, and disappeared back into the undergrowth.

Tom looked around at the catbear, who was visibly disturbed by the gunfire — he was shaking in the tree. Walking over to a lizard carcass, he cut a hide of meat and returning to the catbear, threw it up to him. 'If these things are friendly, we need to keep them on our side,' he said as the catbear dropped down from the tree with his steak of fresh meat. He looked at Tom, and offered a clenched paw to him. Tom gingerly lifted up his fist and gently punched the male's paw. The catbear stood up on its hind legs, raised his furry head and roared. He then sat back down, stretched out like a large dog in front of Tom and started to chew on his steak.

'Boss, we've made a new friend,' Alice said as she scratched the catbear behind his long ears.

'Right, that's enough of this, here's the rescue squad,' he said, as shuttle one flew over them into the valley beyond. 'We need to secure the perimeter and plan an attack on those birds. John, let's get the grav forts set up on top of those hillocks. We can use that grav platform.'

✦

As the sun set on their first day on the New World, they sat around a fire outside a grav fort on the beach of their landing site. Tom could see the lights from the grav forts they had set up on the three hillocks and the flashing lights from the temporary force field. He looked across at Siba and his two men — one had a bandage around his head and his arm in a sling.

'You guys, and Siba, you did well, that was some risk you took.'

'Thanks, boss, but it was Siba's idea. She came up with the idea of mounting the fifty in the shuttle.'

'How's the arm?'

'I'll live, boss. I've had worse.'

'Yes, you have. We need to finish those birds off tomorrow. Pilot, can we open up both sides of your shuttle?'

'A bit unconventional, Tom, but yes, I can do that.'

'Good, we'll mount the fifty in the doorway and have the lads with grenade launchers on the other side. We'll get the nests. Blow them to kingdom come.'

'A bit drastic, Tom.'

'Alice, The Eight has said "their time has come" and to "annihilate them". It's his planet. Look at the catbears, scrawny and starving. In the food chain they hardly get a look in. He said it would balance that up. We should be able to "mutually co-exist in a symbiotic relationship". Don't laugh – those were his words not mine,' he said, trying not to laugh himself. *What the Eight said was right. Those catbears are beautiful beasts, with looking after, their health will improve and*, he thought, *they are sentient beings, there's no doubt of that.*

✦

Their second day dawned with the sound of the animals calling from the forest. As he sat going over the plan with his team and the Pilot, the mix of roars and shrieks reminded Tom of his days in Earth's jungles. 'We've already lost one shuttle. We can't afford to lose another.'

'Make sure you are all strapped in. I will not let the birds near us. Siba will navigate, we will see them coming. It will be as you humans say, "a bumpy ride".

The Pilot was right, as they circled the nests he had to swerve and dodge to escape the airborne carnivores' onslaught.

'The big one, it is coming down, from behind the mountain, you will see him on the port side,' Siba shouted to the crew in the back.

'That's the other flock leader. Now, take it out — multiple grenades,' Tom said as the Pilot angled the shuttle for a clear shot.

They got three rocket-powered grenades away, two missed their mark, but one exploded on the wing of the great bird. 'It's hit — it's hit. Pilot, go around again, we'll finish him off with the fifty,' Tom shouted.

As he flew down the valley, a flock of about twenty chased them. Suddenly, the Pilot turned the shuttle and the machine gun opened up, strafing the flock with explosive rounds. He then completed the turn and flew back straight through the dying flock. The huge monster was perched on a rock, licking the wounds on his wing. When he saw the approaching shuttle, squawking, he took flight, straight up the cliff and over the mountain top. The remaining beasts flew after him, leaving their young in the nests or sitting out on the cliffs.

'Get the nests — grenades into them all. Leave nothing,' Tom shouted.

It took another hour to clear out the nests from the valleys around and destroy any eggs or young left behind.

'How many got away?' Tom asked the Pilot.

'About fifteen and the flock leader.'

'They're not the only flock of those things on the planet. We'll have our work cut out for us.'

They spent another two hours inspecting all the valleys running back from their settlement. There were four more strays that were quickly dispatched by the lethal fifty-calibre gun.

'OK, Pilot, we're done — back to base,' Tom said.

HELA LANDING, DAY 3 MONTH 2 YEAR 1

The four large grav-dozers flew down from the open cargo door of the *Hela* to the landing site below. It took the bridge crew all their skill to keep the fully laden *Hela* floating two hundred metres above the beach as it waited for the grav-dozers to carve out a huge landing plinth in the estuary sand. It was an emotional touchdown and when Theia gave the final order to shut down the engines, the crew and colonists erupted in cheers and tears.

Following Robert and Tom's disembarking plan, the impatient colonists quickly filed out of the *Hela* onto the flat plain of the river estuary to see their new home and planet. Within two hours the exuberance of the arrival subsided, the hard work of unloading the *Hela* and building a secure settlement started in earnest.

We're finally here, thought Robert as he watched the *Hela* unloading sequence unfold on the plain below.

'Well done, Robert, you made it,' The Eight said, as he floated in his chariot beside Roberts's grav platform.

'Not without your help, Overlord,' he replied as he smiled, happy The Eight had accompanied him to this hill overlooking the landing site. 'There they go, look, Overlord —our first blue energy extraction rigs. Blair and Shona's rigs, we fixed up one and it went so well, we fixed up another.' They watched the two strange looking rigs fly out of the *Hela* followed by their support platform. All three landed on a flat sandy beach beside the ship.

'Are you happy now?' Blair asked over Robert's comms system.

'Aye. Are they all ready?'

'No, we left the drill bits on Earth. Of course they are,' Blair replied, sounding annoyed. 'Is that you up there with the boss?' he asked, waving at Robert and the Overlord.

Robert waved back. 'Aye, it is. Good luck to you and Shona.' They watched as two other strange looking craft floated over beside the two rigs. They were Tom and Niamh's creation.

The arguments for weight and space started the previous March in Christchurch. Tom was adamant; they needed the best military equipment available for his security force. He started the arguments with tanks and gunboats, and when Niamh showed him grav, it opened up a whole new range of "toys" as she called them. Their creation was a mixture of a special operations boat and an armoured personnel carrier. The "craft" were built and fitted out by an Australian defence company. They were surprised by the unusual design but delighted with the price Alan offered for a quick delivery.

When the destination of their creations leaked out, the small company couldn't do enough to help. They sent engineers to the *Hela* base to help with the final fit-out and installation of grav drives. Tom was delighted with the forty craft in three different sizes. They would prove their worth securing this area, their settlement and their new home. The two largest of his craft would accompany Blair and Shona, providing protection for their extraction crew and their rigs from the large animals that roamed the New World.

As they watched the rigs guarded by Tom's craft disappear into the mountains, another grav platform approached from the landing site below.

'Mack, Janet,' shouted Robert as they quickly approached, 'you here as well for the view?'

'No, Robert. Overlord, you wished to see us,' Mack said, as he parked beside them.

'Janet, General, you have both worked hard to get us here. You, Janet, as our project planner and you, General, as the Protector and – I will use an Earth term – the "de facto" leader of the Colonists. General, you will stay here as my representative. Your expertise will be needed. Janet, you will continue as the planner on this New World. If all goes well, we will return to Earth for the second colony. You may return then, if you wish.'

'Thank you, Overlord,' they both said. 'Overlord,' Mack continued, 'I am very happy to stay here, but I would like to have accompanied you to —'

'Yes, General, I know. Do not fear, I will prevail, and it is more reason for you to stay.'

'I understand. We will leave you both – again, thank you, Overlord,' Mack said. As he turned his grav platform away and flew back to the *Hela*, he wondered about his new life on this planet. He turned and smiled at Janet, 'you see, Janet Cooper, I told you once, "you will turn out to be our main administrator and planner." I was right.'

'Yes, Mack, you were,' she said, as she held on tight to him as he flew their grav platform back to the *Hela*. She looked up at him and wondered — would she ever go back to Earth?

The Eight turned his chariot to face Robert. 'Robert, I need to tell you an important secret. You must know this — it is part of your burden of responsibility.'

'Aye, go on, out with it. I did not think all this technology and a brand new planet would fall into our lap for a few barrels of blue energy,' the canny Scotsman replied. He had always wondered when all would be revealed.

'Robert, there is no need for sarcasm. We did tell you some of the truth. But now I will tell you more. I first came here as a young entity with my friend, partner, brother, call it what you like, but my friend was as close to me as our kind may have family. We were young, travelling through the universe gorging on blue and mapping out future deposits. We did not need ships. We travelled through space with our energy mass. At that time we were about the size of the *Hela* —'

'Overlord, are you telling me your energy mass was the size of the *Hela*? That's a humongous amount of power,' Robert said, so surprised, he interrupted The Eight.

'Yes, Robert, it was. We could easily fold space and travel through it. Anyway to continue, we came upon this solar system. We were surprised at the amount of blue it contained. Not just on this planet, but contained on all of them and in the adjacent solar systems. This quadrant of the galaxy is rich with blue. We made a pact. We would not touch it. We would hide it from the others. As you say "put it away for a rainy day". Well the rainy day came not so long ago. My friend is now The One —'

'I gather he's the boss of your kind.'

'Yes, Robert, he is, and I fear he is deposed or overwhelmed by others. The Empress told you that "there is a problem with the supply of blue energy that threatens the existence of the Overlords and her own civilization", that is correct. But she did not tell you what the problem is. It is an energy grab sponsored by an Overlord called The Sixth and two others. They formed a rebel troika and control the small supply of blue we have in the Anan galaxy. They intend to starve out The One and the rest of our kind,' The Eight said, pausing from his narrative.

'What nature or temperament may we expect this troika to have?' Robert asked. *I am concerned*, he thought. *Perhaps this venture was not such a saving grace after all.*

'I am considered to be the soft and easy one. And you are right to be concerned.'

'Really,' Robert said, thinking about the hundred million Chinese casualties in their ongoing civil war and the American President who ended up in a dustpan.

'Don't forget the Russian President and his two generals you killed as well,' The Eight said, with humour now in his voice. Robert laughed at his joke.

'If you're the soft and easy one, I don't want to meet the others.'

'No, Robert, they will use you, and then snuff you out. You know when your two crews fill the *Hela* tanks with blue, I leave for Anan.'

'Yes.'

'I am afraid all is not well. I sent messages to The One and he has not answered. I am to send one from here when I leave, but I will not do that. I will not risk its interception. I take the Empress back to Anan. Mack does not know I lost contact with The One and you must not tell him. There are others affected as well, you must not tell them either. That is so important, Robert. I do not want to think of the consequences if I am too late.'

'When or how will I know?'

'I will be back within one orbit of this planet, six to eight of your Earth months. This planet, Anan and Earth are similar. They are what we call in the "biped belt", planets where your species exist. If I do not come back, we are lost, you must fear the worst. Your species can flourish here on your New World. Find a new place to live, away from here, secluded and secret. Hide the rigs and the blue extraction equipment. Make a home deep in the forest. It will be your only hope of survival if The Sixth finds this planet.'

'What about our homes, the pods? How do I manage that?' asked, Robert shocked at what he had just heard.

'Sink them, Robert, drop them in the ocean with the grav carriers and sink them. I am sorry to burden you with this but I cannot leave you all in dire peril with no hope of saving yourselves. Now you must know why I returned to Earth. I told you some of it during our war. Seventy thousand years ago, on my first visit to Earth, an old Anan geneticist made changes to humans we did not approve. He made those changes to provide a cure for the ailment you know of as the Anan Sickness. You know, he used blue from my own energy mass, taking it without me noticing, I was young and naive. You are all offspring from my essence. I knew humans would be so adaptable and intelligent they could survive the transplant and start a new colony regardless of the obstacles. You can survive, Robert, if you plan wisely, I am sure of that.'

Robert immersed himself in the work during their busy first month on the New World. The extraction of blue and the simultaneous unloading of the *Hela* went like clockwork. The planning they did on Earth paid dividends. Within three weeks the pods were unloaded and their first temporary settlement established. Blair and Shona returned every six days with their tanks full of blue, resting their crews for a day and then going straight back out. It took four weeks to fully load the blue energy tanks on the *Hela*. The colonists, Mack, Janet, Theia, Niamh and Tom all were ecstatic at how well everything worked; all except Robert, who deep down felt the burden of what The Eight had told him.

The Eight watched on as his colonists of humans surpassed all his expectations. If he succeeded, the humans were a new force to be reckoned with and would change the old stale and crumbling order in the Anan galaxy.

EPILOGUE

Niamh and Tom spent their last night together in the pod they called home. They couldn't get enough of each other and made love with the passion and intensity of two people condemned to die or be pulled apart forever. She couldn't bear to let go of him. The journey to Anan and back could be six months or more. The unknown perils of his own work on the New World and her trip to Anan could result in the untimely demise of either.

Lying beside him in the early hours of the morning, she gently caressed the scars of the near fatal wound on his shoulder. She nearly lost him once, and found it too much to bear. 'I don't want to leave you,' she cried, burying her face in his chest.

'Niamh, Niamh, stop. I have to stay and you have to go. Now think, did you enjoy our time together in our home, every day and night together?' he asked.

'Of course I did,' she replied wondering why he would ask such a question.

'Think, why you enjoy it so much, and discount the obvious answers.'

'I really don't know where you're going with this.'

'Think about it, we live and love here in our pod, happy and safe,' he said, 'who gives us the safety to do that?'

'You do.'

'No, my team do, they do. We fought for this settlement from the flying monsters and animals outside. We drove them back and my team provides the security for everyone to live here safely, unseen to the colonists. Look outside,' he said.

Through the window, they watch their neighbour, the young Welsh soldier Brian with his New Zealand wife Kora, on the terrace of their pod. He kissed her and then gently touched the bump on her stomach. They sat down to eat breakfast with the fresh bread he collected on his way back from his night shift guard duty. One of Tom's round the clock detail that guarded the settlement and colonists.

'He is from the night shift. While we sleep he and his team are looking out for us. It would be the same if we were back on Earth. I would be away for four to six months at a time on jobs. That's what I did to make life safe for the people at home, so they can sleep safely at night. I have to stay and fulfil my responsibilities, to keep the colonists safe. You have to go and navigate the *Hela* and look after its engineering systems, for the safety of the crew. There are others depending on us. I will miss you, I really will,' he said holding her tightly.

'I hate it but I know you're right,' she said, relaxing into his tight embrace. Shortly after she kissed him and quietly left their pod making her way down to the *Hela*, sitting majestically below beside the beach.

Looking at her other love, sitting quietly beside the beach, she felt a deep pride within. She had fixed it. It was now packed with the culmination of Project Anan, blue energy and Alex and Rhea's samples for the Anan cure and their First Stage Treatment; blue for the Overlords and a cure for the purebreeds, a successful outcome for The Eight. Also stored in the belly of the *Hela* were four forty-foot containers. The shipment was consigned to "Haret the Trader" on the authority of the Sullivan Parker Charter. They contained samples of Earth's finest fashions and produce from Janet Cooper and Partners Ltd.

Quelling her emotions, her mind churning with thoughts of grav, fusion, hybrid drives and navigation plots through the curve of space, she entered the great ship.

Although she and her purebreed team had checked and re-checked everything, she busied herself at her engineering console. She needed to reassure herself all was ready before their imminent departure.

'Mrs Parker, is everything ready in engineering?' asked the Pilot from the captain's station.

'Yes, Captain,' Niamh replied, 'engines are freshly stoked with grav. The fusion reactor is on line and the hybrid drive is primed with blue. You have full power available to the armoury and the cloak. We're ready,' she said as she moved to the navigation console and placed her blue diamond into it.

'All clear on the dock, Captain, we are clear to leave,' Demard said at comms.

'All crew, all crew, this is your captain, secure yourself for departure. I repeat, secure for departure,' the Pilot announced over the *Hela* comms system. 'Grav engines on line at ten percent,' he said to the bridge crew. Checking his console readouts and looking at the bridge view screen, the Pilot watched as the ship slowly floated up from the New World beach or "space dock" as they called it now. 'Navigation please,' he asked Niamh.

'Navigation is up with the corkscrew fight plan to the outer atmosphere plotted,' Niamh replied, as she concentrated on her plot of the route which was now projected in front of the crew. 'Flight plan coordinates are now at your console, Captain.'

As the ship reached one thousand metres above the space dock, the Pilot gently increased power to the grav engines and brought the *Hela* slowly around to follow Niamh's flight plan to the outer atmosphere. It was a tense forty minutes as the bridge crew, under the Pilot's command and Niamh's navigation, flew the ship out of the gravitation pull of the New World into orbit at four hundred kilometres above the planet in its thermosphere.

'We're in orbit, Captain,' Niamh said as she adjusted her navigation readout to show outer space and their curved plan to Anan. It was the first time she realised they were all communicating in Anan. She had not noticed her subconscious switch to their language when she first stepped on the bridge.

'Overlord,' the Pilot said turning to The Eight, 'we are ready. Ship is cloaked, the armoury is powered up and ready for your command. All engines including the hybrid drive are operational and ready for your orders.'

'Well done, Captain, Mrs Parker. Captain, take us home please,' The Eight said to the mysterious Pilot, as the crew erupted with loud cheers. Finally after so much time they would return to Anan.

'Siba, take us clear of this solar system before we balance the grav engines with the hybrid drive. Mrs Parker, let's look at your planned route through the space-curve. I'm sure we can cut some time off the journey and get you back to your husband sooner,' he said, smiling at Niamh.

They both pored over her navigation projection discussing the possible route changes as Siba piloted the great ship clear of the New World's solar system on their journey back to Anan.

Two weeks following the departure of the *Hela,* Robert sat alone at his desk brooding over the maps of the New World. Looking for a safe haven — a bolt hole for his colonists — had become an obsessive habit late into the evening. Hearing the door behind him open, he turned around to face Tom.

'Robert, I don't know the dark secret the Overlord left with you, and I don't want to know. It's killing you. Everybody can see it.'

'Is it that obvious?'

'It is. Lighten up. Whatever happens in the Anan galaxy — you can't change the outcome. And you forget — my wife's with him.'

'Aye, you're right there. I'm sorry Tom, I forgot that.'

'Come on, let's go have a drink. Alice and your Load Master re-opened the night club they had on the *Hela.*'

'What, who gave them permission?'

'Opening night tonight, Robert — they're applying for it tomorrow.'

Robert got up from his desk, scooping up the maps, he opened a drawer and flung them in. Grinning at Tom, he slapped him on the back, 'Aye. We'd better go check that out. They might be serving home brew or some other bootleg alcoholic drink.'

As he walked with Tom to the club he noticed the noisy colonists, all dressed up, hurrying down to the settlement. Their happy chatter and laughter added to their excitement. Suddenly he realised what was going on. 'We closed out Project Anan today. Mack signed off on the contract. Bonuses are paid!'

'You missed it, Robert, the significance of the event.'

'I did, Tom,' he said as he stopped and looked around at the town square, for that is what it was now — a town. They had finished reconfiguring the pods and added some small buildings constructed from wood from the forest. It was their new town centre, a mixture of the modern pods and hand-crafted wood buildings, styled on the old earth pioneering days. The colonists thronged into the square, shouting and laughing and calling at Robert.

He looked on in pride and reflected on what they had achieved, his arm glowing blue.

'Robert, that's so weird, your arm, it's shining.'

'Aye, it's pride, Tom. You're right, look what we achieved — The Eight's away with the first cargo. We transported two thousand five hundred souls safely across space — and established the first human colony on a distant planet.' *An immense challenge*, he thought, *but a success*. They would have more challenges, more battles and insurmountable problems — but that would be in the future. Against all the odds, they had done it, Project Anan was a success.

Looking over, he saw Mack and Janet sitting on a bench together. Mack raised his glass and nodded to Robert, 'well done,' he shouted across the noisy crowd.

Tom looked up at his friend. 'You did it Robert — you led us here. They've all chosen a name for our first town and founding colony. Right, lads,' he shouted to his men standing holding two ropes.

The crowd fell silent as they watched a huge banner unfurled above their town centre. As Robert read the words, he felt his pulse race and tears well up in his eyes. Reading them over and over, he realised, he would never forget this day.

"Fort Leslie. New World. Earth Colony 1".

THE END

AUTHORS NOTE

Thank you for reading Project Anan.

I hope you enjoyed reading it. If you liked the book I would appreciate a short review on Amazon.com. Reviews make a huge difference to a new author.

For more information on how I wrote Project Anan and for news and updates on Book 2 of the Energy Exchange series check out my website;

www.lionellazarus.com

If you have any questions, feedback or want to be included on news for the launch of book 2 drop me a line at;

lionel@lionellazarus.com

You can also find me at;

www.facebook.com/pages/Lionel-Lazarus/939683776076271

ACKNOWLEDGEMENTS

Starting out as a new author is a frightening experience. For me it was like a career change with so many "what ifs" and self-doubt. Without the encouragement of family and friends I would never have got this far.

To Carol and your family, for "putting up with me". Without your support this would never have happened. To my daughter in Christchurch, New Zealand, without you, there would be no story! To my son, you kept me focused on the storyline and the Sci-Fi. Brendan, your encouragement over drinks in the pub was inspirational. Without that, I would have lost the plot in the mists of self-doubt. To my sister and brother-in law at www.the-consultancy.com/ for advertising and help in the marketing. To my beta readers for reading the first draft. What a chore that must have been! Thank you all for your help.

So where did I start? An idea for a book is not enough. I realised I would need much more. Searching the information for indi-authors on the internet led me to The Creative Penn www.thecreativepenn.com/ the website of Joanna Penn. Joanna's site provided the road map of how I should progress my project. One of Joanna's mantras is to get a professional editor and cover designer. Thank you Joanna, your website led me to two places.

The Scarlett Rugers Book Design Agency. www.booksat.scarlettrugers.com/

Thank you Scarlett, for a remarkable cover, book format and website design. The professional help you provided was invaluable.

BubbleCow Book Editing and Proofreading Writers. www.bubblecow.com/

Thank you Gary and the two editors at Bubble Cow. The editing and proofreading lifted the book to another level. What I learned during that process, from you and your editors, will prove invaluable in the future.

Finally, a big thanks to all the people in New Zealand who I met. You were awesome!

My thanks to the staff at "Visualising Future Christchurch at Re:START" for your invaluable help. For an inspirational trip of a lifetime, thank you to the people at Real Journeys www.realjourneys.co.nz/ and the staff at i-SITE New Zealand.

ABOUT THE AUTHOR

With no academic background Lionel Lazarus picked up his writing skills while working as a Toolpusher on the North Sea Rigs. Following a long career working off-shore, Lionel returned to work on-shore in the Health and Safety profession. He recently retired to work full time on his writing. When not writing, Lionel loves to travel and to walk in the mountains. He lives in Dublin, Ireland.

Printed in Great Britain
by Amazon